A Young Man's Guide to Late Capitalism

# A Young Man's Guide to
# LATE CAPITALISM

*Peter Mountford*

A MARINER ORIGINAL • MARINER BOOKS
HOUGHTON MIFFLIN HARCOURT
BOSTON   NEW YORK
2011

For information about permission to reproduce selections from this book, write to Permissions, Houghton Mifflin Harcourt Publishing Company, 215 Park Avenue South, New York, New York 10003.

www.hmhbooks.com

*Library of Congress Cataloging-in-Publication Data*
Mountford, Peter, date.
A young man's guide to late capitalism / Peter Mountford.
p. cm.
"A Mariner book."
ISBN 978-0-547-47335-2
1. Young men—Fiction. 2. Capitalism—Fiction. 3. Bolivia—Fiction. I. Title.
PS3613.O865Y68 2011
813'.6 — dc22
2010025564

Book design by Greta D. Sibley

Printed in the United States of America

DOC 10 9 8 7 6 5 4 3 2 1

This is a work of fiction. Any references to historical events, to real people, living or dead, or to real locales are either the product of the author's imagination or are used fictitiously for verisimilitude. While some of the information about the election of Evo Morales is true, Morales's role and the roles of his staff in the events of this book are entirely fabricated. Various aspects of the city of La Paz, likewise, have been altered. Other names, characters, places, and incidents either are the product of the author's imagination or are used fictitiously.

*For Jennifer*

A Young Man's Guide to Late Capitalism

# Article IV Report

## *Friday, November 25, 2005*

IT BEGAN WITH a single reedy voice calling out an incomprehensible refrain, some nasally phrase that would repeat all morning. Gabriel opened his eyes. The day's first light glowed pale at the edge of the curtains. He'd requested an eighth-floor room hoping to avoid this. He closed his eyes again, optimistically. Another voice—this one burpy, froggish—joined in; this phrase was shorter. What could they be selling at that hour? A third voice entered and they were a chorus singing some garbled tune, a puzzle of phrases intoned with the distinctive eagerness of street vendors across the world. Car horns added a percussive layer. A policeman blew a whistle, hoping to introduce order, but all he added was a shrill note. Still, the sound didn't truly find its center until the buses and *micros* joined in, shoving their way down the narrow roads. Gabriel knew that the noise had reached its peak register then: a din that would blast for sixteen hours. A symphony forever tuning up before its concert—it brayed him awake, brayed him to sleep. It was pure dissonance, but as he lay there he found that the anticipation of future harmony was palpable.

Gabriel walked through to the bathroom, flipped on the light, and observed himself, hair askew, eyes puffy with sleep. Puberty had hit him young, at ten, but full-blown manhood seemed to be still in the offing. In college, he'd tried to grow an I-don't-care-about-all-that-shit beard, but he'd ended up looking weird, and the truth — that he cared a lot — became obvious because he wouldn't stop talking about the beard, so he had to give up and shave it off. Five years later, he was just as willowy, but he'd cut away the profusion of black hair and was shaving regularly.

He brushed his teeth with bottled water and showered, making sure not to let any of the water into his mouth. Typhoid, amoebas, hepatitis, and dozens of other dangerous microbes swam in those pipes. The tap water even smelled different: chalky, it seemed. The water was so hard it swept the soap off his skin before he could lather up.

Back in his bedroom with a teeny white towel wrapped around his waist, he slid open the curtains to see the crisp alpine light streaming down on the chaos below.

The protests usually ended by lunchtime. If there was a march, it finished in Plaza Murillo, in front of the presidential palace. It had been this way since he arrived. The police stashed anti-riot gear in a dozen ministerial buildings on or near the plaza. Tear gas drifted through La Paz's narrow streets like morning mist. When the gas seeped into Gabriel's room at Hotel Gloria, it felt like a cloud of cayenne had been blown into his face. The first time this happened, he found that it took hours to dissipate, so when it happened again today, he abandoned his room. He took his laptop and went across the street to the Lookout, the top-floor restaurant at Hotel Presidente, where he could write in peace while his room aired out.

No sooner had he sat down at the bar of the Lookout and opened his laptop than the bartender, Severo, told him that he'd already made enough pisco sours to get all the journalists in La Paz drunk. Gabriel smiled obligingly. It was ten in the morning and a few journalists were already gathering in the booths, drinking pisco sours. This was the end of the so-called Bolivian Gas War, and the fact that the war had been little more than a protracted series of protests did nothing to diminish the atmosphere of doomsday hedonism among the foreign press. Severo had latched on to Gabriel, who was set apart from the others by his youth, his ambiguous ethnicity, his fluency in Spanish, and, perhaps, the fact that he was Fiona's boy toy.

He and Fiona had first met a week before, when they both arrived on that day's American Airlines flight from Miami. They had stood next to each other in line at the taxi stand, misty breath vanishing in gusts. She introduced herself and suggested that they share a taxi if he was headed downtown as well. They sat in the back seat of a cramped yellow car, which zipped down the winding road to La Paz, its engine emitting an ominous burning odor the whole way.

Later that day, Fiona had gone behind the bar at the Lookout to show Severo how to make the best pisco sour in the world. "It's all about the quantity of egg white and the ratio of ice to liquid," she explained, delivering a tray of the cocktails to the table of journalists who were all there to cover the presidential race. "I slipped a Rohypnol into yours," she said to Gabriel and winked, and maybe it was just his first two pisco sours, but for a second he had felt as though he could fall in love with someone like her.

Fiona's pisco sours were such a hit with the journalists that apparently Severo was now making them by the bucketful before his shift.

Gabriel wrote for fifteen minutes at the bar before Severo said, "Where is your girl?"

"Fiona?" How generous of him to call Fiona a *girl*. Generous too, if in a different way, to imply that she was Gabriel's. "I'm going to meet her soon."

Severo nodded. "Is she a good journalist?"

Gabriel said that she was great. He said that she seemed to get interviews with whomever she wanted. Then he qualified this by explaining that she worked for the *Wall Street Journal*.

"Your newspaper is not so big?"

Gabriel held up a pinkie finger to indicate the size, and Severo laughed. "Actually," Gabriel said, "I don't even have a newspaper. I am freelance." He didn't know the Spanish word for *freelance* so he just said it in English.

Severo nodded, his eyebrows scrunched, and Gabriel could see that he didn't understand. It didn't matter to Severo. He just wanted to know whether he should be impressed. He just needed to know how to react. Gabriel said, "Not that many people read what I write, but the ones who do are big international investors."

Severo seemed to appreciate that. "What do you say about us?"

Gabriel shrugged. "I try to be honest."

"Don't you think that things will get better?" Severo said. "I do."

Gabriel grimaced. "I hope so."

And Severo, who had seemed so blasé a few minutes before, so carefree, stared at Gabriel, a plastic jar of pisco sour in his hand, and said, "Please don't write anything bad about us." It was the most heartfelt thing Gabriel had heard all week.

"I won't," Gabriel assured him. He made plenty of eye contact, to indicate his sincerity.

But as it happened, he was mid-draft in a brief stating that the Bolivian government's reluctance to publish their latest Article IV report only reinforced his doubts about their future.

The Article IV report was a candid—and therefore highly classified—analysis of a country's economy and problems, including a critical assessment of its policies, written by the International Monetary Fund. Gabriel had been trying to get his hands on a copy since he'd arrived. Most countries published their Article IV reports, even if these documents gave grim appraisals of the future. They published the reports ostensibly in the interest of full disclosure but really to assure investors they had nothing to hide. So the fact that Bolivia was so reluctant to publish its latest A-IV indicated, Gabriel wrote, "that this is probably among the most dour A-IVs in the country's history."

To ensure that the report would not be leaked, the Bolivian authorities had asked that the IMF print only a handful of specially numbered copies and carefully restrict who saw them. Within Bolivia, President

Rodríguez had a copy, as did the head of the central bank, the finance minister, and the vice president. President Rodríguez's unpopularity was such that he was no longer even talking to the press, so Gabriel didn't bother trying to contact him about the A-IV. The others wouldn't return his calls. A fifth copy of the report was in the hands of the IMF's resident representative, Grayson McMillan, who had agreed to meet Gabriel that afternoon. The snag was that Grayson didn't have the authority to give out the report. There was only one other copy that Gabriel knew of, and that was Fiona's. She had admitted she had it the other night, in a rare postcoital moment of tenderness. "The vice president gave it to me," she'd said.

"Did he really?"

"Yes, he really did. But I can't quote from it."

"Oh, that's too bad."

Gabriel didn't bother asking her if she'd let him see it. She was the only journalist with a copy and she'd be crazy to endanger her exclusivity by showing it to anyone, whether or not she was sleeping with him.

What Fiona did not know, and had no way of knowing, was that despite what he'd been telling everyone, Gabriel was not actually a freelance writer. He was not a journalist at all, in fact. Not anymore. For the last month, Gabriel had been working as a political analyst for the Calloway Group, a hedge fund.

Once he'd finished the first five pages of his report, Gabriel went to an empty side of the restaurant, got out his cell phone, read the finance minister's number, and took a deep breath. He attempted to assemble his ideas. He had not yet grown accustomed to interviewing these genuinely powerful people. For the past four years, when he'd been writing for the online financial paper *Investors Business International*, he'd felt like a hack. Now, at the Calloway Group, it was worse: he was expected to weasel sensitive information from these people. And the stakes were dizzyingly high. There could be tens of millions of dollars on the line. His boss, Priya, would not tell him exactly how much or where it was going.

In theory, his job at Calloway wasn't so unlike his job at *Investors*

*Business International*, except that what he wrote now wouldn't be published. Quite the reverse; what he wrote now was confidential. The less their competitors knew, the better. Gabriel's cover, such as it was, was that he was a freelance writer hoping to do a long piece on the Bolivian election for a magazine — it was precisely the kind of assignment he'd have been given by *IBI* a few months before.

He took another deep breath, looked out the window. La Paz was a long and narrow city. It filled a craggy ravine on the eastern outskirts of the altiplano, or high plain: thirteen thousand feet high in this case. The steep faces of the canyon around the city were covered with slums. The slums were colored red by the cheap bricks of mountain mud the inhabitants used to build their shacks. Even farther up, toward the ridge, the hills were studded with clusters of shantytowns, home to only the most intrepid of the city's poor. The terrain was unforgiving, desolate, rocky; it looked primitive. It looked Afghani; it looked like al-Qaeda territory.

Gabriel dialed the number, pressed Send. The phone rang once. A brief silence. It rang a second time. Someone answered. *"¿Aló?"* the voice said. A man's voice.

"Hello, I am a friend of Fiona Musgrave," Gabriel said in Spanish. He spoke too fast, intending to make it clear he was fluent, because sometimes he had a slight hint of a gringo's accent. "I was hoping to talk to you about the Article IV report."

"Fiona gave you this number?" the man responded.

"She did."

"You're a journalist?"

"I'm a freelance writer," he said, leaving the word *freelance* in English again. He added a pause. "I need to speak off the record."

"What kind of journalist wants to speak off the record?"

This was the problem. Presenting himself as a freelance writer did not, it turned out, engender much enthusiasm with interviewees. Gabriel wanted to believe that if he told people for whom he really worked, they'd be impressed. He wanted to think that they'd give him the same star treatment they gave Fiona. But he couldn't risk it getting out that the Calloway Group was interested in Bolivia. He was lucky to have the job—more than lucky, in fact—and they wouldn't need much of an excuse to fire him. He hadn't even told his mother about the job. Still, he needed to entice the minister to speak somehow, so he went forward with innuendo. "Have you heard of the Calloway Group?" He said *the Calloway Group* in English, in an American accent.

"The hedge fund?" The finance minister was still in Spanish. "You work for them?"

Gabriel didn't answer the question. This was the plan, to imply that he worked for them but stop short of stating the fact directly. It was important that the minister know that the stakes for Bolivia were real; until now, few hedge funds had ventured near countries as backward and unstable as Bolivia. But it was also important that the minister see that the Calloway Group wanted to be discreet about their interest. "I'm just asking to take a look at the Article Four report," he said. "It'd be completely off the record. It's all just deep background for a long piece I'm researching."

The minister let out a weary sigh. "Does Fiona know whom you work for?"

"Fiona knows that I am a consultant." Gabriel paused again, in case the insinuation wasn't clear. "If you have another opinion, that's your business." Gabriel wondered if this was going well. It was hard to tell.

"Why would I share a classified document with a hedge fund that has a reputation for vampirism?"

"Excuse me?" Gabriel said. "I think you've misunderstood me."

"I was with Morgan Stanley in 2001, and I remember Calloway. They'd nudge a price until it triggered a short spike. They'd milk the spike on the upside, and back down again on the fall to equilibrium. They were like feral animals during the Argentina crisis: went from a hundred percent long to a hundred percent short in seconds on a rumor that they themselves probably started. They may have done well, but we all found the strategy sleazy. There was no vision, no philosophy, except to play as fast and dirty as possible."

"If they were interested in Bolivian industry, it'd be a very different thing," Gabriel said.

"Right. They'd be looking at multinationals with significant exposure to Bolivian commodities, gas, I suppose, in the face of this unusual election?"

Gabriel hesitated. The purpose of his cover was now clear to him. Based solely on his hint that he worked for Calloway, the minister had triangulated a very accurate reading of Calloway's investment strategy in Bolivia. With a tiny intimation, Gabriel had exposed everything Priya had wanted to keep under wraps. "I'm not going to speculate on what they would do here."

"Right, right." The minister cleared his throat. "I'm surprised they sent you. Are you sure you didn't go to the wrong country? Brazil is a little to the right."

"You don't want to show me the Article Four, I take it."

"You are at the bottom of the list of people I would show that report to." His voice was hoarse. He sounded wrecked. He sounded exhausted.

Eager to backpedal, Gabriel said, "I'm just a writer looking for material."

"And I'm Ronald McDonald. But you don't need to worry. I won't tell anyone."

Gabriel felt a great relief hearing that.

The minister said, "I don't want to repel you people any more than I want to throw the door open to you. It's hard for me to imagine, but I do hope that people like your boss will eventually see the wealth available here to foreign investors. It is a very rich country if you are prepared to commit for the long term." His voice had been lifting there at the end, and he caught himself, shut it down. He sighed. He must have known he was talking to the wrong person.

"I understand," Gabriel said. He didn't know what to say.

"Anything else?" the minister said.

"No. Thank you for your time," he said. Gabriel could hear that the minister was in traffic. Riding in a limousine through the squalor, probably. It had to be hard.

"Fine. Don't call this number again." The minister hung up.

Fiona answered the door in her white terry-cloth bathrobe, BlackBerry at her ear. She winked hello and slammed the door behind him. Gabriel sat down on the sofa, kicked his feet up on the coffee table. Fiona shimmied out of the robe and flung it onto the bed. She peeked around the curtain at the city. "I know," she said into the phone, "that's what I was saying, but we can always pad it if we're still short." Fiona had been the South America correspondent for the *Journal* since Gabriel was a freshman at Claremont High. And she was proud, he supposed, of her body—rightfully so.

He took his laptop out of its bag and checked his e-mail. Nothing. It was Friday, and he was supposed to turn in his report tomorrow. When she finished her conversation, Fiona chucked her BlackBerry onto the sofa. "Tell me, Gabriel, why are you still wearing clothes?"

"I've been gassed out of my hotel again," he said, not looking up from the screen.

She lit a cigarette and flopped on the sofa beside him. "That's the advantage of a five-star hotel: airtight windows." She smiled. It was a joke. Sort of. Hotel Presidente boasted that it was the highest five-star hotel in the world, and though its elevation wasn't in dispute, the five-star status seemed, to the foreign press who stayed there, a hilarious example of Bolivian pride in the face of meager circumstances.

Hotel Gloria, across the street, had a three-star rating but cost half as much, without much discernible difference in quality. Calloway would have paid for whatever hotel Gabriel wanted, but Hotel Gloria was modest enough to help him maintain his cover. So went his thinking. The décor of both the Gloria and the Presidente must have seemed terribly modern when they were decorated in the 1970s—all pumpkin shag carpets, cucumber walls, clunky chandeliers, and lots of tawny glass. It was a look that would have read hip and ironic in New York, and Gabriel was probably the only foreigner who found its sincerity in Bolivia refreshing. Unlike the others, he believed that the management of the hotels knew perfectly well how outmoded their décor was. It wasn't any funnier than the fact that their roads were falling apart. It just made an easier target.

"What do you have planned for the day?" Fiona asked. Little puffs of smoke staggered out of her mouth as she spoke.

"I'm meeting the IMF's resident representative at three."

"Grayson! I'm meeting him at one." She put her cigarette back in the ashtray. She had ordered scrambled eggs for breakfast, and the plate sat, untouched, on the coffee table. "I'm having lunch with him. You better not scoop me!" She flashed a lupine grin, and he understood that it had been a joke: he could *never* scoop her. Not that it mattered, really. "Well, Gabriel," she said, "I've got forty-five minutes before I have to go meet him, so I suggest you undress."

"I was just wondering if you have the vice president's number," he said.

"No luck with the finance minister?"

"No luck with him."

"Well, I can't give out the vice president's number."

He nodded, started typing. She made a little show of checking her watch. "Look," she said, "there are protests in Sopocachi today, and traffic will be awful, so if we're not going to fuck right now, I should get dressed."

He looked up at her, blankly as possible, and, feigning befuddlement, said, "Right, um . . . I just—" He gestured vaguely toward the screen.

She smiled, barely. Stubbed out her cigarette. "Ouch," she said.

"No, no, it's not—" he began, but he didn't finish because she waved him off. It was a funny trick, a special talent of hers, to come across simultaneously as mocking and genuinely hurt.

Gabriel believed that Fiona's caustic streak was a big part of why she was still single; that, and the bizarre nudity. In the six days since they'd shared a taxi from the airport to downtown La Paz, she had been naked at least half the time he saw her. She wrote dispatches naked, ate room service naked, watched television and conducted conference calls naked. She had a hearty appetite for sex and fucked vigorously, as if it were an aerobic routine and he were a piece of equipment in her gym. At climax her volt-blue eyes squinted and her nostrils flared. When she smoked afterward, he could sometimes see her heart flexing in her rib cage. With Fiona, he was often aware that she was a living being, that her body was a strange thing, a sack full of organs and bones and fluids, everything in shades of pink and ivory and aubergine.

She lit a new cigarette, stood up, and went over to her suitcase, which was splayed on the floor. "What should I wear to lunch?" she said. "I've heard Grayson's a dreamboat."

"Buck-naked seems to work pretty well for you," Gabriel said. "Maybe you should show up in the buff?" Then, unable to resist, he added, "It'd simplify the exchange."

She didn't bother answering. She picked up a gray skirt and a pair of vintage oxblood heels, sat on the edge of the bed, and started to dress, her cigarette dangling from the corner of her mouth, smoke rising into her eyes. He put his computer away and stood up.

"You leaving?" she said from the side of her mouth, squinting at him through the smoke. She pulled on the skirt, zipped it at the side. She was not going to wear underwear, apparently.

"Yeah, I'll see you after."

"Do me a favor: bring your libido."

Two months earlier, a young and overly eager fact checker at *Investors Business International* had forwarded the e-mail about the opening at the Calloway Group to Gabriel. Edmund, the fact checker in question, was ambitious in the way that young men often were when they'd just arrived in New York after doing well at a university where doing well was just the thing to do. So Gabriel's first thought was that Edmund was angling to replace him by revealing a tempting route out; it was a cynical theory, though probably true. He read the posting anyway:

TO: gabo_de_boya@yahoo.com
FROM: Edmund_Samuelson@IBI.com
SUBJECT: Fwd: Calloway posting...

Regional Political Analyst (Latin America)

The Calloway Group seeks a full-time contractor as a political analyst for the Latin America region. Responsibilities include making regular trips to Latin America, interviewing corporate and political leaders, writing reports and briefs on a range of financial issues in the region. Areas of investigation include: individual corporate, sector/regional, commodities, macro, forex.

A successful candidate will be eager to spend six months or more per year abroad.

REQUIREMENTS:
- Minimum 3 years' experience as a financial journalist and/or analyst
- Fluency in Spanish
- Experience working in South America with political and business leaders
- Willingness to spend weeks/months at a time abroad
- Degree in economics (with macro, BOP, and quantitative analysis)

COMPENSATION:
- $19,500 / month (6-month renewable contract)
- No min. investment for personal accounts in the Calloway Group's products
- Full health/dental, including international coverage
- Per diem while traveling
- Substantial bonuses (based on performance)

Sitting there on the screen like that, so innocuously, the number seemed to lack proper emphasis: $19,500 a month? Could it be? It seemed absurd that such a thing could be possible. Some quick arithmetic and he saw that it would be $234,000 per year.

It entered his consciousness like something illicit, like the offer of no-strings-attached sex from the attractive girlfriend of an acquaintance: the instinct was to start explaining his interest, how this was the girlfriend of an acquaintance, and not of a close *friend*.

Once he'd processed the notion of the money, he scanned back up to the job description itself and was surprised to find that, on paper at least, he was qualified. So he sent in his résumé and some clippings. He wanted to forget about the position altogether, but he found it hard to shake the impression it'd made. The infatuation was as base as it was predictable. It was irrefutable, a deeply embedded thing. The hunger was in his design.

He didn't expect to hear back, but two days later he got an e-mail from an Oscar Velazquez, requesting that he come in for an interview with Priya Singh, the fund manager.

Calloway was a relatively small hedge fund, with about $1.5 billion pre-leveraged capital. Unlike many small funds, which had lower hurdles to entry, Calloway required each investor to pony up at least $2 million, though most of them had considerably more than that on the line. Until a few years ago, it had been run by a small group of quants and a single fund manager, Priya. Very little of the work took place outside of the office. But an increasing number of competing funds were able to nearly match their returns at lower fees, so Priya began hiring analysts to go out into the world and investigate her murkier leads firsthand. Whether or not she paid any attention at all to what the analysts said, their mere existence helped justify Calloway's fees.

The protesters were still outside the IMF's offices when Gabriel arrived. The leader had a bullhorn, but his words were lost in the fuzzy distortion, and the crowd looked befuddled. Meanwhile, peddlers bent under burdens twice their size hurried up and down the steep road, unconcerned. That high in the Andes, humans evolved huge torsos to accommodate their giant lungs and powerful hearts; they needed to have short and strong limbs, for better circulation while hiking. Their skin was hardened against the sun. A stout man in a tobacco-colored suit cut for 1971, wearing an era-appropriate haircut, sideburns included, stood nearby, watching; he was eating a sandwich, one foot on a young man's shoeshine box. The filthy shoe shiner sat on the pavement bent over the boot in question, his black ski mask pulled over his face. The uniform of *lustrabotas* (Bolivian shoe-shine boys), the ski masks ostensibly hid their identities, since the job was deemed lowly, but also served as a sign of solidarity among the boys.

The IMF's offices were in a tall peach-colored building across from the Alliance Française in Sopocachi. The building was also home to the offices of the World Bank and the Inter-American Development Bank. Needless to say, security was heavy; Gabriel had to leave his passport at the front desk. The guard who escorted him up used a keycard to illuminate the ninth-floor button.

Up there, a female receptionist informed Gabriel that Grayson was still out to lunch. She led the way back to Grayson's office and told Gabriel to wait. There were two leather armchairs and a coffee table. There was nothing very fancy and nothing very cheap; it was intended to suggest honest middle-class values. Gabriel perused bookshelves full of outdated World Bank and IMF reports on assorted aspects of the Bolivian economy. There were no pictures of family or friends. No plants. Gabriel glanced around the papers on the desk and saw nothing clearly identified as the Article IV report. He wasn't going to dig around.

The room's main feature was a large framed reproduction of a de Kooning painting mounted on the wall opposite the window. It came into Gabriel's vision like a giant fireball, all fuchsia and burgundy and canary, but forced flat. It was evidently meant to be taken as an advertisement of Grayson's unique manliness. The only other flair on display was a complementarily reddish world map on an adjacent wall. On closer inspection, Gabriel saw that the countries in the map were shaded by their infant-mortality rates. Africa was brick red; Asia a wacky multihued camouflage; and most of South America a healthy, if variegated, pink—except for Bolivia, which was arterial crimson (seventy to a hundred deaths per one thousand births). The map was doubtlessly intended to convey Grayson's concern for humanity, and provide something to contrast and complement the de Kooning. Grayson could, if outflanked by a journalist, point to the map and talk earnestly about how he put it there to remind himself of the mission's importance. Gabriel was still staring at the map when he heard "Hello!" and turned to shake Grayson's extended hand, noticing, with relief, that Fiona was not with him. She had probably dashed off to another lunch with another VIP.

Gabriel had found that when interviewing a man older and more accomplished than he, it was best to stare into his eyes during the handshake and say, "A pleasure," and nothing else. He did this now. Grayson nodded once in reply and moved swiftly to his chair while motioning for Gabriel to sit. Every gesture was impatient and alert; he whizzed, he zoomed, but the commotion didn't disturb his crisp appearance. He wore a dark suit with a bright yellow pocket square and a matching tie, its double Windsor indecently engorged. His face was aquiline, almost aerodynamic, a human javelin. His hair had that uncanny quality common among politicians of looking dry but remaining set in a perfect part; if there was no gel, Gabriel wondered, what kept it in place?

"Are you adjusting to the altitude? It can be a killer!" Grayson flashed a row of teeth that were as pale and shapely as dominoes. He had a powerful, orangey tan. Gabriel recognized beneath the glossy veneer a blinkered austerity baked into the man; the impression issued, specifically, from the healthy and grim folds in his brow. He had been at it for a while, and had learned to marshal his sympathies carefully.

"The altitude was painful on the first day, but I'm fine now," Gabriel said.

"Well, you're extremely young. Midtwenties?" he asked, but did not wait for a response. "Me, I've been here two years and I still get headaches all the time."

"Are you sure it's the altitude?"

The coif shook when he chuckled. Grayson was Irish, but with all his years in D.C. and the years abroad on mission, his accent was neutral. Like Pierce Brosnan's. Grayson pursed his lips. "And you're with—"

"I'm freelance, actually," Gabriel said. "I used to write for *IBI*."

"That's right! I just had lunch with Fiona; she said that you're a very serious young journalist and I should watch myself with you." The creases at the sides of his eyes folded in another grin. Gabriel detected a hint of alcohol on Grayson's breath and wondered what they were drinking at lunch.

Grayson glanced at his monitor and clicked his mouse. "Excuse me, I'm expecting an e-mail." He clicked the mouse again, squinted at the screen. "Nope! Still not there! So"—he turned back to Gabriel—"what do you want to know?"

"I was wondering if you have a copy of the Article Four report?"

"I practically wrote it."

"Can you show it to me?"

Grayson smiled calmly. "As you probably already know, the only people with the power to disseminate it are the president, vice president, finance minister, and head of the central bank. There might be a couple other copies floating around, but I wouldn't know how to find them."

"Would you be willing to tell me which one of those four men you think I should focus my energies on?"

"To be honest, I don't think any of them will collapse under the pressure of your charm. If you had impressive credentials, maybe. Fiona probably has a copy."

"She does," Gabriel said. Then, switching gears, he asked, "What about this rumor of a revolution? You think Rodríguez will manage to finish his term?"

"It's funny you mention that. Yesterday, I had no idea. But now I can say that there is almost zero chance that Rodríguez will get kicked out."

"What makes you so certain?"

"Again, I can't say, but Fiona can. She didn't tell you?"

Gabriel shook his head.

"Well," Grayson said and took a deep breath. He leaned back and rubbed his eyes. "What else do you want to know?"

"Let's see." Gabriel opened his steno pad and started flipping pages. While surveying Grayson's office, he had noticed that the windows were made of tinted two-inch-thick bulletproof glass, and he wanted to ask why, if the IMF was there to help, its representatives needed bulletproof glass, but that wouldn't have been useful. Instead, he glanced over his questions. None of them looked remotely interesting. As he sat there trying to think of something else to say, he could hear through the thick glass, very faintly, nine stories below, a mob chanting for death to the IMF.

"What about natural gas, will it—" He was about to ask if it would be renationalized, but he knew the answer. It was precisely the kind of question that would be valuable to a journalist, because it elicited concise and information-rich quotes, but it just invited another well-educated guess about what might happen, so in the end it was irrelevant to a hedge fund. If Grayson couldn't provide Gabriel with any real information, any otherwise unavailable information, they had nothing else to discuss. Gabriel had come to find out if Grayson could help him get the A-IV, and he had his answer.

"Will it what?" Grayson said.

"Do you know the vice president?"

Grayson chuckled, glanced at his monitor again; this time he checked the time in the lower right-hand corner. "He's not going to want to talk to you either."

Fiona answered the door in her bathrobe again, her BlackBerry back at her ear. She stepped aside and Gabriel entered. She threw her robe off, as before, and wandered the room. She was talking to the person on the other end about Grayson McMillan, who was, she said, "an impeccably dressed divorcé from Northern Ireland. He's a doll, flirtatious, and witty as hell."

The Grayson gossip continued thusly while Gabriel sat on the sofa, looking over notes and pretending not to eavesdrop. When he glanced up, he could see that there was a little cellulite on her thighs after all, though no more than he would expect on a girl his own age. For a forty-five-year-old lush, she looked remarkably, almost unbelievably, fit. She had an impressive strut too, he thought, and he wondered if her success as a journalist had anything to do with her sexual prowess. There had to be a reason other than talent and hard work; he hoped there was another reason. Fiona certainly brandished her sexuality in a bold way. She wore candy-colored thongs and had a fresh Brazilian wax, but it all registered several shades sadder than sexy. In bed she whimpered.

Eventually, she hung up and flopped across her bed. Gabriel didn't look up from his pad.

"Romeo, O Romeo?" she called.

"Are you doing a bachelor-of-the-year piece on Grayson?"

"*Jealousy!*" she chirped, as if locating a lost earring. She jumped up and bounded over. She tossed herself into the nearby armchair and planted her feet up on the edge of the coffee table. Her eggs were still there, still untouched. If the ashtray had been emptied, it had filled back up. Fiona put her face into a fake frown. "Tell me more, Gaby."

He smiled, put the pad aside. "It's not jealousy."

"Well, lover boy, if you insist on knowing, my boss is a bachelorette as well, and I like to let her know when there's a peacock in the chicken coop."

"Oh. So why aren't you telling her about the young freelance writer?"

She winced a little, as if noticing an unidentified foul odor emanating from the refrigerator. She wasn't going to answer, or he didn't want to wait for her answer, so he said, "And how else was Grayson?"

"Fun, but useless. He's a pro. And you? How did he treat you?"

"Same." He made himself smile. "No, it was bland, really—my fault, though; I had nothing I wanted to ask him. But he had this map on his wall that caught my attention."

"Oh, is *that* what you're writing about, his map?"

"I am," he said and laughed at himself. It was true: he had managed to squeeze a description of the map into his report, despite the fact that there was probably nothing on earth that the hedge fund could care less about.

"By the way," he said, "Grayson mentioned that you have it on good authority that there isn't going to be a revolution."

"He said that?"

He was tempted to ask her why she was telling Grayson her secrets, not sharing them with him, but he didn't want to seem insecure. And having been rebuffed twice already that day, he knew she was his last hope of finding out something valuable. He needed to placate her. He swallowed his pride and went for a flip tone. "He did say that. Why would he say that?"

"I don't know. Because he's a mind reader?" She threw her sinewy legs over his thighs. Her body language was adolescent. The exuberance came off as prepubescent, and her flirtation was often PG-13, but she was doubtlessly aiming for a pornographic conclusion. That seemed to be the nature of the transaction. It was his duty to negotiate this maze of innuendo without embarrassing himself or her, but it was his job—put bluntly—to extract information from her at any cost. So he said, "Now, Ms. Musgrave, I would be sorely disappointed if I found out you were withholding something."

She shrugged, batted her eyelashes. "Can I really tell you?"

Holding on to his composure, he said, "I won't breathe a word."

Her smile lost its innocence in two steps; it departed her eyes first, and then the rest of her face. She was back within her professional station, even with her StairMastered legs slung across his lap. She blinked once, twice, considering it. He recalibrated his own attitude to meet her at this new place. "I guess it doesn't matter," she said, to his immense relief. "The article will be in tomorrow's paper." She pulled her legs off his lap, sat straight up, lit a cigarette. She had a long drag, exhaled a long cone of smoke across the room. "We did a poll."

"The *Journal*? In Bolivia?"

She nodded. "Evo Morales has a fifteen-point lead."

"Evo?" He was stunned.

She winked. "Didn't see that coming, did you?"

He stood. "Jesus. I thought he'd be, if anything, fifteen points behind."

"Likewise."

"Are you sure?"

She had a drag, nodding. "And tomorrow," she said, smoke jetting from her mouth, "once we publish the results, and his angry constituents realize that their man is going to win, they'll stop rioting. So that's why there won't be any revolution. Not now, anyway."

Aware that the election was in mid-December, the inauguration in January, Gabriel—aiming for nonchalance—said, "You going to stick around to see it through?"

"Would you miss me if I went?" she said, and laughed hard, and her laughter disintegrated into a tar-shifting cough. He waited, watching her curl inward, flexing. It was a brutal event and he had a merciless vantage point. Watching it made him feel more compassion for her, if less desire. She was withered within, he knew, damaged right beneath the skin and straight through to her core. Once she'd recovered, she looked at him as if nothing had happened and said, "Let's get a drink."

Severo poured, and Gabriel excused himself, went to the empty side of the restaurant. His report was only half finished and wouldn't be done in time. Fiona's piece would render his findings obsolete anyway. A bitter consolation. Regardless, he needed to tell Priya the results of the poll. When word got out that Evo Morales was going to win the election, stock prices for mining and gas companies with significant operations in Bolivia would take a hit on the fear that Evo would nationalize the industries. If Priya found out about it first, she could start short-selling the vulnerable companies before anyone else and make a profit.

He pushed Call. A long hissing pause, then it rang. She picked up immediately. "Gabriel?"

"Yes."

"And bearing exciting news, I presume."

"Yes. Evo Morales is going to win the election."

A pause. She was typing. Eventually, she stopped typing and said, "What makes you think that?"

He told her the rest. She resumed typing and kept it up as they talked, which made the rhythm of the conversation strange. During the pauses, he just stood there, staring out across the valley, listening to the clacking keys. At the end, she said, "We'll see how this plays. Let's talk tomorrow."

He put the cell phone back in his pocket and went to the bar, where Severo was howling with laughter at something Fiona had said. Gabriel sat down and felt her hand slide up his thigh.

The cocaine belonged to a Canadian journalist named Trent who smoked thick cigars, wore an immaculate Panama hat, and seemed to aspire to be a bland Hunter S. Thompson. He wrangled five male and two female journalists from the Lookout, including Gabriel and Fiona, and they adjourned to Fiona's suite. Gabriel spent the next several hours watching the others snort rocky lines off Fiona's glass coffee table. He talked to whichever wide-eyed enthusiast happened to be sitting in the armchair nearest his spot on the sofa, a list of people that at no point included Fiona herself.

"Straight from the source," Trent had said of the cocaine. "Completely organic too; we're supporting local farmers." This was a joke, of sorts — the joke being that it was a tree-hugging liberal thing to do, snort cocaine in the plush suite of a five-star hotel in the poorest country in South America. Buried shallowly within the joke, Gabriel saw a squirmy urge to make nice with the journalists' tricky white-liberal guilt and the sense that they were only the latest foreign buccaneers to raid that terrain. And if it seemed like hyperbole to consider journalism a kind of plundering, the purity of that distinction was smudged by the constant presence of Bolivian poverty and the equally constant reminders of the journalists' own relative prosperity.

Gabriel did one line of cocaine and then abstained. The burst of enthusiasm did not last. Watching everyone, he noticed a conspicuous lack of feeling among them all — himself too. The intoxication should have been an escape mechanism for the world-weary, but it seemed plainly intended to do the opposite: to generate connections and stimulate feeling.

When someone mentioned that it was four in the morning, Gabriel decided he would not wait around to see if Fiona would kick everyone else out. If she decided to sleep with one of the other men, he would be either angry or not angry, but he would not tell her either way. He drained the last of his stale beer and stood. At the door he bowed, deeply, before shuffling into the hall. Then—booze burning the belly, cocaine numbing the nostrils—he was pitched against the wall of an elevator going down too fast.

A lobby!

He waved goodbye to one guard, walked outside, crossed a narrow street, and said hello to another guard, confident that a joke was in there somewhere, even if he couldn't locate it.

He entered his room still nowhere near sleep. In their week together, Fiona had not been there once. He had spent five nights in her bed. He was, rationally if not otherwise, aware of an enormous sadness about them, together and separate. He sat at the desk and looked out the window to north La Paz, where the city lights sprayed up around the walls of the valley like jaundiced, sagging stars. Behind him, the television played badly dubbed soft-core porn.

On Hotel Gloria stationery, he wrote:

> *The thing about that map on Grayson's wall is that it makes Bolivia look like the sickly enlarged heart of a torso, w/ Chile as her swooping spine, Brazil as her big breasts. And also I predict that the results of F's poll will change things for me.*
>
> *To do:*
> *1. Become indispensible to Priya*
> *2.*

He put the pen down. In tenth-grade biology at Claremont High, he'd learned that the horseshoe crab hadn't changed in five hundred million years. It didn't need to evolve any further. It wasn't glamorous, but it perfectly occupied its small niche. Gabriel could see, even under the dull light of his late-night gaze, that he needed to become similarly useful to Priya—or at least appear so—if he was going to keep his job. He would do well not to shine too much. Better to establish himself as useful in a way not difficult to sustain.

She should have been more impressed by his information yesterday afternoon. Maybe she'd be pleased after the news had played out in the markets. It seemed unlikely.

She would want to know first and foremost whether Evo Morales was serious about his campaign promises. Evo had promised to nationalize the natural gas industry, Bolivia's largest source of revenue. The Bolivian gas industry had been bought up by foreign companies when it was privatized in the eighties and nineties. Those companies had seen a tenfold return on their investments, and when the extent of their profits came to light in 2003, protests—mostly led by Evo—swept across the country. One president was ousted. The chief justice of the supreme court, Eduardo Rodríguez Veltzé, took over—yet another in a long line of pale-skinned men with degrees from Ivy League universities to hold that office. Now, Veltzé would be succeeded by Evo Morales.

Evo proposed to buy the entire natural gas industry back from the foreign companies for a fraction of their real value, then pass the revenue to the poor. He insinuated that he might nationalize or expropriate other foreign-owned businesses. The mathematics for Priya were very straightforward: if a foreign company's Bolivia-based income represented a significant portion of its overall revenue, then Evo's decisions regarding that industry would have a significant impact on the value of the company's stock. Whatever his plans, if she knew them in advance of her competitors, she could make a tidy profit on the companies in question.

Gabriel was no doubt the only analyst for a hedge fund who was actually in Bolivia studying the situation, so Calloway had a unique advantage, assuming Gabriel could deliver usable information. Priya would be the only fund manager positioned to make an informed play on the Bolivian situation. So Gabriel would *not* be called back to New York, not soon anyway. Not until after the election. The election would be in December, the inauguration in January, he reminded himself. He needed to keep track of these things.

He opened the calendar in his cell phone. It was November 26, a Saturday. The election was weeks away. Looking at the dates, he discovered with a little dread that he would probably have to spend Christmas and New Year's in Bolivia. His mother would not be pleased.

And what about Thanksgiving?

If it was already the end of November, what had happened to Thanksgiving? How could he misplace such a conspicuous holiday? It had to be very soon. His poor mind struggled in a dim bog. Then it became clear: Thanksgiving had passed. Thanksgiving had been two days ago.

Now *that* was a worthy joke. He smiled glumly as the dread descended in a twisting motion, like a giant corkscrew burrowing through his torso.

He had spent all twenty-six Thanksgivings of his life so far with his mother, who, although Chilean and ferociously liberal, hosted an elaborate dinner for the holiday. Her party was a celebration out of spite. In the fourth grade, his mother had been called to the principal's office because he had said, on the Wednesday before the holiday, "The English settlers were more bloodthirsty than the Huns." His mother said to the principal, "It's true, isn't it?" And then, aghast, "Do you *disagree?*" That was the end of that conversation.

On every Thanksgiving—which she'd celebrated this same way ever since she'd moved to the United States, in 1978, when Gabriel was little more than a zygote—she would say, in lieu of grace, "This is a conquistador's celebration, but tonight we dine for the conquered, for our exterminated ancestors."

Gabriel was an only child. His mother had fled Chile during Pinochet's regime, in the early seventies. She'd been offered amnesty by the Soviet Union and had gone there to study anthropology at Lomonosov University, in Moscow, where she met a man. The man, also a student, was Russian, handsome. He did not welcome her pregnancy, however, and refused to marry her. Distraught and pregnant in Moscow that winter, she decided to defect to the United States. To Southern California, specifically, the sunniest city in the country. By the time Gabriel was born she had resumed work on her dissertation at UCLA.

Most of his mother's family members were either dead or still in Chile. One cousin lived in Chicago, but he and Gabriel's mother were estranged because he'd given passive support to Pinochet, who had ordered Gabriel's socialist grandfather, his mother's father, murdered in 1973.

So the Thanksgiving guests were nonfamily, mostly colleagues from Pomona College, where his mother was a professor of anthropology. For two decades Gabriel and a handful of other children sat once a year at the kids' table, trying to ignore their impossibly verbose parents volleying abbreviated lectures across the long table in the adjacent dining room. Actual literacy was preceded, in Gabriel's case, by a working knowledge of the *Communist Manifesto*.

That he had not only skipped the party this year but had forgotten even to call would require weeks of amelioration. Aftershocks might be felt for years. He'd be hearing about it, in one form or another, until one of them died. She might have abandoned the Catholicism of her childhood, but the need to absorb and impart whopping doses of guilt would never leave her.

But how had Thanksgiving slipped his mind? What had he done? And why had no one mentioned it? There had been no sign from the other North American journalists that they knew it was Thanksgiving. No one had even ordered a turkey sandwich for dinner. He and Fiona stayed up late, he remembered. Later, they had screwed slowly in the darkness. Afterward, she smoked and he saw the dull orange spot of her cigarette brighten in the darkness when she inhaled. The smoke was caustic. Her clothes were crumpled by the foot of the bed. Her underwear shone white at the crotch of the splayed slacks. Still unable to sleep, they watched bad action movies dubbed in Spanish. They laughed a lot at the movies. She smoked several cigarettes and Gabriel wondered if maybe he could eventually get used to her smoking after all. Outside, the cacophony had settled back into silence. He and Fiona said very little to each other that night that he could remember. Of course, there was very little worth saying.

# 2

# Plaza Murillo

*Saturday, November 26, 2005*

IN THE MORNING, Gabriel read his sloppily scrawled note about Bolivia being the "sickly enlarged heart" of South America, which he took as evidence that he had been a very serious-minded drunk the previous night. He tossed the note and had a long shower, but it didn't help his hangover. His blood was plaster in his veins. A mess of half memories scrimmaged in his aching mind. He ate four aspirins. Measurements of things were off at that altitude, he knew. Water boiled at 80 degrees Celsius, the quantity of oxygen in the air was nearly halved, and doses for painkillers needed to be doubled. He went downstairs and checked his e-mail at the hotel's business center. There was a message from Priya telling him to call.

Fiona had e-mailed her article, along with a note saying that she was going to do a quick interview with Evo Morales at 10:45 before catching the 2:20 to Lima. She wanted to meet Gabriel at 10:30 at the lamppost in Plaza Murillo where Presidente Villarroel had been hanged.

He printed her article and took it with him to the cafeteria above the lobby. At lunchtime, the cafeteria served a delicious vegetarian buffet, popular with local business folk, but the breakfast was foul, and he had the whole place to himself. He ate a bowl of partially frozen watermelon and drank a pint of tepid coca tea, which tasted a little like green tea but felt like a shot of epinephrine jammed straight into his soggy brain.

Fiona's piece had been—presumably because of Bolivia's geopolitical insignificance—packaged as one of the *Journal*'s elliptically titled page-one curiosities, or, in the paper's own jargon, A-heds. The headline, in this case, read "Bolivian Election: Populist Morales Ahead; Indigenous Win; Gassers Lose." Her lede trumpeted the results of the poll: "Morales holds a 15% advantage over Jorge Fernando 'Tuto' Quiroga Ramírez..." Ramírez, she went on to explain, was "a generic Bolivian technocrat and self-described 'corporate yuppie.'" The gist of her story was that this was only the latest in a string of such moments in Latin American history. It was further evidence of a continentwide—perhaps global—sea change: a grass-roots shift to the left. "The era of investor-friendly Latin American leaders might be coming to an end," she wrote. Gabriel was close to the end of the article when he checked his watch and saw that he was supposed to meet her in twenty minutes. He deposited his tray on the conveyor belt and headed back up to his room.

He sat down on the bed and dialed Calloway's office in Weehawken. He keyed through to Priya's extension. She answered on the first ring. "You sleeping late down there, Gabriel?"

"Not exactly. What did you think of the piece in the *Journal*?"

"I thought, 'Gosh, I'm glad I sent Gabriel down to Bolivia, because otherwise I wouldn't know this exciting information already.'"

"I'm meeting the author in fifteen minutes."

"Fine," she said.

"How do you think the markets will react?"

"Barely, with a few exceptions. Paul's on it. So, Gabriel, now I want to know more about Evo Morales. When does he take office?"

"January."

"Well, as soon as possible I want to know which foreign-owned companies he's going to expropriate, if any, and I want to know what he's going to do with them."

"No problem."

"And what will the World Bank and IMF do if he does expropriate foreign property? Will it affect Bolivian aid? And—and this is the most important—if Bolivian aid is cut off, how long before the Bolivians are angry enough to throw out their new leader?"

"That last part will be conjecture."

"I know, Gabriel, but you're not a journalist anymore, you're an analyst. Conjecture is a big part of your job." He heard her begin typing.

He cleared his throat. "This could take a month. You want me in Bolivia for that long?"

She stopped typing. "Yes. In Bolivia, if you fuck up, it won't hurt us. If you succeed, there might be some valuable upside, but that's not the point. The point is that you're flying a shitty worthless Cessna, not one of our gold-plated seven-forty-sevens."

Charm was not among Priya's gifts. She was lean, like Fiona, and she too was ambitious and had a temperament of hammered iron. But the similarities ended there. Priya was from Bombay and had been in charge of emerging-markets equity for the Calloway Group for five years. She had studied at Oxford in the nineties and when she finished there had promptly been launched as a fund manager at Lehman, where her portfolio was the only one to turn a profit during the Asian crisis. A millionaire by twenty-eight, she could supposedly intuit peaks and troughs in the market as well as Warren Buffett could. Every day she spent an hour at the gym with her personal trainer, ate a great many vitamins, and drank two liters of green tea. She didn't touch alcohol or cigarettes. "I would like to outlive my own children," she'd said to a *Financial Times* reporter in an interview in 1997. But as it turned out, the conception, carrying, birthing, and rearing of children were not activities that interested her much.

When he'd sat down with her for his interview at Calloway's office in Weehawken, she'd stared at him and said nothing. He held back too. He had already decided to say as little as possible. Better to lure her out. Oscar Velazquez—Calloway's analyst for the wealthier Latin American countries, and Gabriel's first interviewer—had said she was thirty-seven, which would make her ten years Gabriel's senior, but she looked like a child. Even in her austere gunmetal gray Helmut Lang suit she looked juvenile: the most solemn and ponderous adolescent on the planet, but an adolescent nonetheless.

After a while, when Gabriel said nothing, she'd nodded once and said, "You would be Oscar's counterpart in the poorer countries. We like you because you're like Oscar: you know the places, you know people, you speak Spanish, and you even sort of look like a native." She enumerated his qualities very matter-of-factly, including the part about his ethnicity. "Since I came to Calloway," Priya said, "I have steered clear of what I call the cucarachas, those chronically dysfunctional Latin American countries like Guatemala, Panama, et cetera." She inhaled deeply, noisily, through her nose, exhaled slowly and quietly through her mouth. She said, "Our default position will continue to be zero involvement with them, but we need to pay attention, which is why we're creating this position. We can't afford to miss anything."

"I understand," he said. He waited, but she didn't elaborate. She had the corner office, and the views across the Hudson to lower Manhattan were postcard-ready. She also had two large wide-screen LCD monitors mounted on the wall like art running a colorful array of stats from Bloomberg. But she never took her eyes off Gabriel, so he avoided looking at the views and tried instead to match her gaze. She did not seem a particularly mysterious person. She exhibited above all a surgical focus. So while she could address whatever problem sat directly in front of her, multitasking would be difficult, and this, he realized, was the source of her awkwardness, because conversations require a certain talent for juggling.

Hedge funds had traditionally played the numbers from a safe distance, but they had also found that there were huge surprises occasionally, which was why it was theoretically worth it to Calloway to spend a few million in wages and travel expenses every year to have half a dozen analysts out in the world, keeping an eye on things. He waited for her to continue, but when she didn't say anything, he resuscitated the conversation. "So, I'll research the cucarachas?"

"Yes," she said and picked up her line of thought. "Oscar has his hands full with Brazil, Argentina, and so on, so you'll baby-sit the basket cases. There's not much action there, but that's life. Meanwhile, I stay here and go over the numbers with our quant for Latin America, Paul. You should meet him, but I think he just went down to the pier. He goes there twice a day to do a thousand jumping jacks."

Gabriel nodded. "A thousand jumping jacks?"

"Yes, he's concerned about his heart. It's a sedentary life."

"Right. Better safe than sorry."

"Not really. Paul's an idiot." Her mouth twitched as if she was trying to smile, but her muscles couldn't manage it and instead made the gesture of someone who was famished and anticipating food. Gabriel bit his lower lip and laced his fingers together in his lap. He did not let his gaze wander, despite an overwhelming urge to look away. It had been sarcasm, of course. Paul was not an idiot. A quant's analytical powers were expected to be cripplingly powerful. It was one of the few jobs for which a dash of autism was considered a plus.

Priya—who was, it seemed, something of a quant herself—straightened her back, sucked in her cheeks, twisted her head in one direction, then the other, and relaxed. She looked at Gabriel for a while, and when he didn't speak, she sighed as though already exasperated. "Listen," she said, "we like you because you seem kind of cunning, and, after reading your work, we think you might have a talent for reading people. Why do you want to work for us?"

He did not have an answer ready. To buy time, he broke eye contact and looked across the river at lower Manhattan. They were still scooping out the ground down there, but everyone knew that no more bodies would be found; there was nothing left but a giant ragged hole. Gabriel looked back at her and, for lack of a better position, told the truth. He said, "I want to make a shitload of money for a while."

She nodded, unsurprised. She seemed to want him to say more, so he added, "I'd like to retire at forty."

"If you manage to keep your job, that shouldn't be a problem." She glanced at the Bloomberg screens and he thought she almost smiled.

Then she looked back at him. "So where do you see Mexican interest rates in a year?"

The millionaire thing hadn't interested Gabriel during high school, when his bright yellow Sony Walkman was full of punk rock, and it hadn't meant much to him when he was in college either, where he manned a soft-serve ice cream stand on campus for fifteen hours a week. It didn't really mean much then that he was broke, because everyone was broke. But five years of scraping by in New York City was another thing. Being young and well-educated and destitute in the city had a way of sharpening a person's desires. Demonstrations, overt and implied, of the advantages of having heaps of money were so common that they ceased to register. So the feeling of wanting matured until what had been straightforward professional ambition became tinged by a hint of avarice. Not that Gabriel was, or ever had been, a greedy person; but money, in general—the plain and unassailable acts of acquiring and spending it—had turned out to occupy a more important role in adulthood than he'd expected. The issue finally wasn't that he wanted to be rich, per se, but that he wanted to be done with so much *wanting*. It was a feedback loop, and the only way out was deeper in: he needed to have enough money to be done with the issue of money forever.

And though he wished it weren't so, once certain college buddies started buying giant condos in the Meatpacking District and kicking up their midnight blue Prada sneakers on their burnished leather ottomans, he did feel a many-pronged discontent. The shame did not temper the envy; it just made it queasy. Of course, they were *all* privileged, spectacularly so, on the global level. But this was not a global situation. It was the United States, where he had been born and seemed likely to remain in the bland band of the upper-middle class.

It wasn't lost on him that each one of his young and newly rich friends, all of whom had been dateless for years, was now constantly anchored to the lithe arm of a woman so beautiful that her beauty itself seemed monstrous. Those friends started to look different too. They wore pointy black shoes, sunglasses on cloudy days. At Sunday brunch, they ordered off the menu, made easy banter with the waiters, and were altogether more confident and self-assured than anyone their age had a right to be. It was as if some irksome and never fully identified existential question that still nagged the rest of them had been finally and completely resolved for those few.

So there was, in the end, no question about whether Gabriel would take the job at Calloway. The question literally never presented itself to him. After Gabriel's interview with Priya, Oscar handed him a binder full of legal disclosures and recommended that he go through the paperwork with his lawyer before signing.

Gabriel didn't have a lawyer and didn't want to hire one, couldn't really afford one. Anyway, he didn't want to hear about the fine print. So he signed and initialed the papers while sitting on the PATH train back to New York from Weehawken.

The figure was $27,751.33, after tax. That was his first paycheck. It was for less than a full month of work, but it included a ten-thousand-dollar signing bonus. He had direct deposit, so the funds magically appeared in his checking account one morning. His future suddenly blasted out in front of him, as glorious and wide as the sea. That evening, after changing out of his suit, he went to the liquor store for a bottle of Veuve Clicquot, and as he walked along Manhattan Avenue he felt something akin to vertigo. He was dizzy. It occurred to him that his mother, a prominent professor at Pomona College, made a little more than half as much as he.

On his sofa that night, he drank the champagne from a coffee mug and watched *Dateline*.

Later, flushed and tipsy, he picked up his laptop, logged on to his credit card account, and erased five years of debt. He watched Letterman for a while and then, during a commercial break, opened a brokerage account at E-Trade. He muted Letterman and began researching stocks. He stayed up for hours making notes, the TV flickering silently in front of him, behind his computer screen.

Plaza Murillo was named for Pedro Murillo, a revolutionary who had been hanged there in 1810. Were it not for the presence of the stout indigenous women in their antiquated garb—shawls, petticoats, tunics, and felt bowler hats worn at an incongruous tilt—the city could have been Florence, and Gabriel on his way to a café behind the Duomo. But this was not Italy. There were beggars everywhere, and grubby shoeshine boys zooted on shoe polish. A block from the square, Gabriel cut through an alley full of street vendors. A griller of meats stood beside his shabby old stove, burning homemade charcoal that emitted a noxious effluvia: motor oil and sour beef. As Gabriel entered the plaza, pigeons flapped aloft to get out of his way. The morning was chilly, despite the screaming sunlight. At twelve thousand feet, and a short distance from the equator, La Paz was as close to the sun as any place on the planet. With a full mile less atmosphere to filter it, the light looked young, naked; it felt different too. It prickled. It was as if each individual photon were a teeny arrow, and there were billions of them raining down on him.

The congress was on the far side of the plaza, catty-corner to the presidential palace, known as Palacio Quemado, "burned palace," because it had been torched repeatedly in the last two centuries. In 1947, a mob dragged then-president Gualberto Villarroel outside and hanged him from one of the plaza's lampposts. There was a small commemorative plaque on the post. With 191 coups under its belt since its 1825 independence, Bolivia had averaged more than one revolution a year.

The façades of the buildings on the nongovernmental side of the square were pocked with bullet holes from a gunfight between police and the military in October of 2003, the height of the Bolivian Gas War. Earlier that year, peasants, led by the indigenous Evo Morales, took to the streets in protest of the unequal distribution of gas revenues. Violence flared, dozens of people were shot, and then the president dashed off to an idling Learjet. He vanished before the mob torched the palace for the eighth time. Now, two years later, normalcy had caught a toehold. Dapper old men in fedoras and three-piece suits congregated on the benches lining the square to smoke cigarillos and play chess in the shade of eucalyptus trees.

Fiona was on one of the benches nearest Palacio Quemado, reading over her notes. So far, every time he had seen her she had been either naked or sharply dressed, but now she was just wearing jeans, heels, and a white V-neck sweater (Evo didn't wear suits and wasn't impressed by people who did). She'd tied her hair back in a ponytail.

As he neared, pigeons edged out of his way and Fiona looked up. He sat beside her and she kissed his cheek. He could feel the dot of saliva drying coolly in the wind. He smelled a hint of stale alcohol on her, but there was no other evidence of last night's debauchery. He crossed his legs and put on an air of mock magnanimity. "And how are you this morning?" He patted her knee.

"I feel like slapped ass," she said and rolled her eyes. "I can't party like I used to, and I talk too much."

"Well, you're almost done here."

"Almost! One more interview and I can go," she said and then smiled, awkwardly, as if confounded by secondary meanings. "But I'll be back for the election in a couple weeks," she added. He said nothing, so she continued, "I'm meeting Evo in fifteen minutes."

"Can I tag along?" he joked.

She shook her head. "Sorry, Gabriel. You'll get him, I'm sure." She was just being nice, which wasn't her style. Apparently, her faculties weren't entirely intact. Normally, she led in a brisk dance, but now there was no one leading, and the whole interaction was more awkward and more sincere than those to which Gabriel had become accustomed.

"The thing is," she said, "I'm sure you'll excel at this if you stick with it, Gabriel, but—and I'm only going to say this to you once, I promise—but if there is another job that you can stomach doing, anything at all, you should do it."

"You don't understand my situation, Fiona."

She squinted at him. "I don't want to sound patronizing, because you're clearly made of just the right stuff. Really, you've got the razor edges, the scary ambition. That's all right, but that ambition does wear out eventually, and you're not left with much to show for it."

"No offense, Fiona, but I think it must be easy to say that when you're a features writer at the *Wall Street Journal*. You're set."

"Maybe."

"No. Not maybe. *Definitely*. Look, your ambition might have worn out, but you can coast on the dividends for the rest of your life. Me—if this doesn't work, I don't know what I'm going to do. I honestly don't."

"Fine." In a strangely self-conscious maneuver, one that read as childish, she tucked some of her hair behind her ear and crossed her legs. Then she pursed her lips, and he could see all the thin lines around her mouth that were normally invisible.

"And you must have millions of air miles," he said, just wanting to lighten it up again.

"And those miles will be the most valuable item in my will when I die." A pause. "Bequeathed to whom? I have no idea." She took a cigarette out of her pack, twirled it in her fingers. "Oh, there are perks. What else?" she said. She lit the cigarette. "I'm a connoisseur of luggage." She was recovering her poise.

"Then tell me about luggage," he said.

"Samsonite is okay." Her smoke paused in the wake of one gust and then vanished in another. "It lasts a year or so. Tumi is better, but it's expensive, so I only use it for carry-on. Victorinox is a good option for the bigger pieces. None of it will last you more than two, maybe three years. I could write a dissertation on luggage. But I have no experience with houseplants or pets. I've never had either. I love dogs, but . . .

"And I find that the only people I am comfortable around anymore are people like me. There aren't that many of us, but we're all happy. We'll tell you how happy we are. You've seen us. You were there last night. If you're going to join the club, maybe you and I can date. That would be fun for a while. It might last a year. Probably not." She had a drag and tapped the ash away. Her hair blew into her face and she pulled it back behind her ear again.

She looked at him sympathetically, and he could see then that she was three-dimensional after all. The height and width had been obvious from the first, but the depth (her sorrow, it might be called) had eluded him. Now it was there: naked too, and just as proud.

"I used to adore room service," she continued. "The whole fact of room service. That was what I loved: ordering meals and having them delivered to my room. There was something so fun about that. I could just sit there naked, eating whatever I wanted, watching horrible television, and there was no one to complain about it. I got used to the convenience of an in-house gym, laundry service. I got used to being naked all the time, eating whatever the fuck I wanted. The novelty does expire, though." She had a drag and blew out the smoke immediately. "Maybe you'll disagree?" She shrugged. "But I've never met anyone who disagreed."

Gabriel looked at the cathedral beside the presidential palace. There were pigeons embedded in the façade. Huge tattered vultures groomed themselves in the spires. Gabriel watched as one vulture waddled after a pigeon that got too close. The spry pigeon hopped out of reach and fluttered off to a nearby ledge. The vulture lost interest, returned to its perch.

During Gabriel's interview at Calloway, Priya had spoken about the need for secrecy. "Especially," she said, "with poorer countries, which are usually one- or two-industry economies, the fact that we're interested at all will tip our hand. With a bigger economy, like Brazil, there are hundreds of potentially attractive inroads. But if someone finds out that we're looking at, say, El Salvador, they'll be able to instantly deduce which corporation we're interested in."

"I won't tell anyone unless I think it will be advantageous," he had said to Priya.

But now, though it had little strategic value, he couldn't resist the temptation to set Fiona straight about himself. Maybe once she knew she wouldn't keep talking to him like he was an intern in the press pool. In any case, she was leaving, so it couldn't hurt too much. He took a deep breath and said, "I want to tell you something, and it has to be off the record."

She smiled. "Please don't tell me you have herpes."

"No, that's not it."

"You're Spider-Man!"

"No." He laughed. "But almost—I kind of am leading a double life." He watched, inwardly pleased, as her smile faded. "I'm not really a free-lance journalist." He let it sink in. She looked appropriately shocked and impressed, so he went on. "I'm an analyst for the Calloway Group."

Her expression drooped. She was disappointed that it wasn't some-thing more interesting—a spy, maybe. His swelling pride began to de-flate. "Priya's looking at Bolivia?" she asked.

"Oh—" He stalled. She knew who Priya was. Of course, he should have known better. Fiona was not impressed by boys like him, whether they worked for hedge funds or not. Still, now that he'd started on the path, he had to see it through. "I'm just trying to figure out what's going to happen in Bolivia. We're interested in Evo. So, if you—"

"*That's* why you're here?" She cut him off. For the first time that day, she sounded annoyed with him. "Gabriel, is it possible that they're test-ing you? Is this your first assignment with them?" When he didn't an-swer, she said, "Do you know Oscar Velazquez?"

"He's the other analyst for Latin America." She knew Oscar too. At-tempting to put a floor under his sinking ego, he said, "Same job, differ-ent jurisdictions."

She wasn't having it. "Oscar covers the rich parts and you do the poor?"

Again, he didn't answer.

"How do you know Oscar?" he said.

She shrugged. "Similar circumstances."

His comeuppance complete, Gabriel leaned back, crossed his legs. Neither of them said anything for a while.

He watched a pigeon pecking at an empty box of matches near one of the old men on a bench. The man had an astonishing face, its con-tours chiseled by the sun. It was a face like the countryside itself, bare, brown, ragged with canyons and cliffs—it looked formidable, secre-tive. The old man wore no socks, and his old black wingtips were buffed to a glassy sheen. He wore an elegant double-breasted suit, a pressed shirt, and a burgundy tie. He was alone, a newspaper on the bench beside him. He stared at the dry fountain.

At the center of the fountain, Neptune, in blackened bronze, stood on a raised goblet of sorts, completely naked, trident slung over his shoulder. God of naval armadas and the patron deity of colonists, he'd been put there by the Spanish conquistadors two centuries earlier, when the plaza was home to a well from which locals drew water. Now that the country had forfeited its entire coastline in a series of lost wars against its neighbors, the irony of having such a conspicuous Neptune might have seemed bad for national morale, but this was, after all, the same landlocked country that refused to disband its navy. Indeed, La Paz held a celebration once a year in Plaza Avaroa, named for the general who lost the war with Chile for the Pacific. The loss, which had occurred in the late 1800s, continued to transfix the Bolivian people in much the same way that the lost Confederacy remained—culturally, if not otherwise—a fixation of the U.S. South. The eventual reclamation of Bolivia's coastline was a powerful fantasy, and the futility of the issue was well beyond the believers' comprehension. They couldn't accept that the Bolivian coast would not be reclaimed, ever. Mexico might as well ask for the return of California.

When Gabriel had interviewed the director of one of Bolivia's larger banks two days earlier, the man had said, "The magical thing about Bolivia is that our history does not move in a line like other histories, it does not march; our history stands in one place and observes itself in a mirror, amazed."

Gabriel appreciated this fact about Bolivia, that it was a country that openly preferred to see things as they *should be*, rather than as they were. A long-standing pattern of humiliation brings that out in a nation, just as it does in individuals; an active imagination is most useful to those for whom reality is a great disappointment. In Bolivia, a national bovarysme had taken hold. Fantasy was just as important as reality, the citizens seemed to insist. Gabriel was no stranger to the allure of a well-manicured daydream. He knew that those dreams, if cared for properly, could grow like bonsai: trimmed back constantly until they'd matured in miniature, shrunken lives. Perfection was much easier to achieve at that smaller scale. And if daydreams were just the mind's mechanism for giving space to a perfect vision of life, then maybe daydreams could be read backward to find a person's most fundamental desires. In his own case, Gabriel had for some years entertained fantasies of being a Pulitzer Prize–winning journalist — someone not unlike Fiona. Read backward, it was about the fact that he wanted to be not only rich and famous (banal, if pervasive, features of most daydreams) but also respected for his efforts. And, still generically, he wanted to make the world a better place in his own little way.

That whole daydream ended when he started at Calloway. After years of cultivation, it just stopped. The one that replaced it was peculiar in that it didn't involve him winning any Pulitzers or fame. Instead, he merely dreamed of money. He didn't need gazillions. He just wanted to buy his way out of the question of money itself; $3.5 to 4 million would do it. With that, even the most conservative portfolio could be counted on to generate $200,000 a year in pre-tax revenue.

Neither Gabriel nor Fiona had spoken in a while when a woman in a moth-colored skirt approached, a little boy maybe five or six years old a few steps behind her. "Excuse me," she said to Fiona in heavily accented English, "are you Fiona Musgrave?"

"Yes," Fiona said in Spanish, "are you Lenka?" Fiona's Spanish was nearly as fluent as Gabriel's, but it was marred, badly, by her accent.

The woman nodded. Fiona and Gabriel stood. They each kissed the woman hello and introduced themselves, in Spanish. Then Fiona bent down and asked the boy what his name was, but he just shook his head and ducked behind his mother's legs.

"His name is Ernesto." Lenka had settled into Spanish now as well. Gabriel had noticed that a delicate linguistic dance occurred in first meetings between bilingual people, though he had yet to figure out how they decided on one language or the other. The woman, he gathered, worked for Evo Morales. She was attractive, with a long neck and a cinnamon complexion. On her chin there was a splash of reverse freckles, a spray of paler, vanilla dots fanning up toward her cheek. Her eyes and nose were Asiatic, her cheekbones Amerindian, and she wore her long hair wrenched back in a no-nonsense ponytail. Why had she brought her child? He scanned and saw no ring on her finger.

Gabriel crouched to talk to Ernesto, who eyed him suspiciously from behind his mother's legs. She wore the kind of dull, flesh-colored pantyhose that Gabriel's mother wore often, and which men sometimes pulled over their heads before robbing a bank. "How are you today?"

Ernesto's smile widened, veered mischievous, and he shook his head. He stuck several fingers in his mouth.

"Come here," Gabriel said, beckoning. Ernesto emerged from behind his mother's legs and approached warily.

Up above, the women were talking business, but Gabriel could sense that both were glancing down at him, and at Ernesto too. So he led Ernesto away, back to the bench, where they both sat down.

"Tell me about your school," Gabriel said.

Ernesto was mature enough to grasp the concept of body language, if not its nuances, so he threw up his hands, apropos of nothing whatsoever, and said, "It's nice."

Gabriel asked Ernesto if he had any girlfriends and Ernesto raised one index finger. "Only one?" Gabriel said, as if disappointed.

The boy shrugged, brought up three little fingers, and giggled.

Lenka and Fiona approached, and Lenka smiled at her son, then glanced at Gabriel appreciatively, warmly. *"Muy precioso tu maldito,"* Gabriel said to Lenka, who rolled her eyes and laughed.

"Yeah, he's a little bit of a menace," she conceded, also in Spanish.

Ernesto was shadowboxing now, so Gabriel held up his palms and Ernesto punched them.

"Take it easy," his mother said to him.

"Yeah"—Gabriel withdrew his hands and shook them off as if they were hurting from the tiny fists—"you'll break my hands."

Ernesto growled at him fiercely, adorably, and Gabriel looked back at Lenka. "You work for Evo?"

"I'm his press liaison." She was staring at him now, her face tilted down slightly. "Are you a member of the press?"

"If I were, would we be able to meet sometime?" He stood up.

"Okay, Gabriel," Fiona interrupted in English, "the president-elect is waiting for us. I'll see you when I return in a couple weeks, I hope—assuming you'll still be here."

Presumably she'd returned to English because that was their native language, but it was still awkward, since Lenka was clearly more comfortable with Spanish. That was the point, no doubt, to highlight Gabriel's foreignness to Lenka, and to douse their flirtation.

"I'll still be here," he said to her. Then, turning to Ernesto, he said, *"Un gran placer conocerte. Y tú tambien,"* he added to Lenka, making sure his accent was natural enough to make it apparent that he spoke like a native. He asked Lenka if he could have her card. Maybe they could get lunch someday.

"I would like that," she said and opened her handbag.

While she fished around in her bag, he turned to Fiona, who was frowning in a way he didn't know how to interpret. Could it be jealousy? It was hard to imagine.

"Keep in touch," he said to Fiona, switching to English now himself.

*"Te llamo cuando vuelvo,"* Fiona replied, her cadence stiff with her bad accent.

They kissed each other on the cheek.

He took Lenka's card and told her he'd call tomorrow morning.

"I look forward to it," she said.

They kissed cheeks a second time. He mussed Ernesto's hair. *"¡Nos vemos chico!"* he said and turned and walked briskly into a swarm of pigeons, which batted aloft. The old man on the bench looked up and tugged on the brim of his fedora in greeting as Gabriel passed. He decided to grab a coffee from the café there on the plaza and then head up the hill in search of a chicken salteña. At the far side of the square he glanced back, hoping to see Fiona and Lenka again, but they were already gone.

# 3

# Hedged

*Monday, November 28, 2005*

ON SEPTEMBER 11, 2001, when Priya was new at Calloway, their offices were on the twenty-second floor of the World Financial Center, opposite the World Trade Center; according to Oscar—who was in Argentina at the time but heard about it when he returned—she and Paul were at the office when the first plane hit, and the explosion nearly blew their windows out. Then, while the rest of the building was busy evacuating, she and Paul started setting up hedges against the inevitable crash. Outside, paper drifted down like a ticker-tape parade. Markets in New York were not yet open, but Priya and Paul were able to sell most of their long positions in Brazil and set up some short sales on the FTSE. They preemptively called in various futures. Then, when the second plane hit, she and Paul grabbed their laptops and set off. They headed uptown. Paul's place was closer, in Tribeca, so they went there. By the time the first tower fell, they were back online, reinforcing their defensive positions. All capital from the sale of their substantial LAN Peru stake went directly to futures on Lockheed Martin.

A month later, quarterly statements went out to Calloway's clients, and dozens called to ask if there had been a mistake, because it looked like the portfolio had grown by 4.28 percent in September. No other New York fund had managed to pull off gains that month.

The staff at Calloway was forbidden to discuss the matter in detail. "Tell them the numbers are correct, but do not under any circumstances explain how we achieved them," Priya wrote in a memo, according to Oscar.

During Gabriel's orientation, Oscar said, "I had that memo in my briefcase, and my wife saw it. She was shocked. I tried to explain what Priya was thinking, because I understand it, as I'm sure you do, but it's not the kind of thing I could explain to my wife, you know?"

Gabriel nodded. He did understand. He understood quite well.

Though far from the largest hedge fund, Calloway had a reputation for adamantine, Terminator-esque pursuit of gains that was legendary. It'd become a poster child for the perils, and potential profits, of unchecked avarice in the late nineties, when the dangers of highly leveraged, unregulated hedge-fund activity first became apparent. Entire nations could, it turned out, be brought to their knees by the collective whim of a few dozen math whizzes in monochromatic cubicles in lower Manhattan. The hedge funds themselves weren't impervious either, and many, including Calloway, had been run into near or total bankruptcy in 1998 when Russia suddenly defaulted on all its short-term debt.

A year later, Gabriel's mother published an op-ed in the *Los Angeles Times* that argued for more federal oversight of hedge funds. She mentioned Calloway in the piece, writing that "though small, [it] represents the worst kind of animal in this menagerie. In the ten years since it was founded it has served its tiny group of wealthy clients at the direct expense of stability in the developing world."

So when he took the job at Calloway, he wrote his mother an e-mail saying that he would be working for BellSouth. As lies went, BellSouth was pleasantly innocuous. Who, after all, could complain about telephones?

Her reply was just one word: *Congratulations!* She had learned to shun any discussion of work or politics with him. Although her position was understandable—political ideology was as personal to her as religion was to most of the rest of the world—Gabriel found her inflexibility, her sheer bullheadedness, maddening. Theirs was a tiny family, a family of two, and they could not afford to put a moratorium on discussions of such a large proportion of their common interests.

Intending to defuse the explosive device before she could use it against him, Gabriel opened their conversation that Monday by saying, "Mom, guess *what!* I forgot about Thanksgiving! I mean, I don't know how it happened, but it did! I'm sorry!" He laughed, because it was, he wanted her to see, just a funny blunder, like pouring coffee on your Cheerios.

"Where the hell are you?"

"Bolivia." He was sitting in his boxer shorts on his bed at Hotel Gloria.

"I thought you were dead, Gabo. I called a thousand times on Friday! Nothing! I waited. Saturday. Yesterday I called hospitals in New York."

"Oh Jesus," he said as the guilt latched on. "I'm so sorry. I have a different phone here."

"How long have you been there?"

"Not long. I'm so sorry, Mom," he said. "I forgot, and then I assumed—"

"It's fine, Gabriel," she said. "How are you doing otherwise?"

"I've been busy."

He said that he was "busy" as often as possible to her because she didn't respect him as much as he wanted. Not that her love for him was in doubt. Her love was, in fact, generally suffocating. Still, it was all swaddled in condescending innuendo. It was as though she saw right through the ruse and knew he was a hack, a third-rate reporter, just another shyster who'd conned a gullible editor into hiring him. Then, incapable of hanging in, he'd quit like a quitter and taken some snoozer of a job at the telephone company. This was the narrative he imagined she might construct to explain his professional life so far. Meanwhile, she was the genuine article. Brassy and brilliant, she was a lecturer who could hold forth on any subject for hours, and every sentence would be a mini-revelation; her oration would be grammatically spotless (though English was her second language), its syntax would be lively, and her word choice would be as apt as what Gabriel could produce only after exhaustive editing. His mother regularly gave papers at anthropological conferences. She had been the keynote speaker at a recent conference in Denver. Newspapers to which Gabriel had not been able to sell his freelance work quoted her regularly. So he told her he was busy. He said it all the time. He said it because it gave him a reason for being a deadbeat son who didn't even bother to call on Thanksgiving, and he said it because busyness was a noble state in his mother's universe. Or, more accurately, she believed that noble people were busy, and from this Gabriel settled on the logical fallacy that busy people were therefore honorable.

"BellSouth is in Bolivia?" she said.

It would have been better to know the answer to that question before he called. "Uh—we have some operations here, yes," he hedged. "I'm looking for ways to expand telephony further into rural areas. Farmers need telephones too."

"How else would they get in touch with their stockbrokers?"

"Precisely! Anyway," he said, moving right along, "I've got a date today, with a woman named Lenka, who works for Evo." He needed to score a point and subtlety be damned.

"Oh?" He had successfully piqued her interest. "What does she do for Evo?" she said in Spanish; she always switched to Spanish when the conversation went personal.

"She's his press agent," he said, following her into Spanish. "I'm hoping she'll introduce me to Evo."

"I'm going to write a long essay about him for the *Nation*," she said.

There was a pause while each waited for the other to ask a follow-up. Then, when Gabriel realized that his mother was going to steer the conversation to herself and her piece in the *Nation*, he ran interference. "I met Lenka through a journalist I know who works for the *Wall Street Journal*." There was some truth in all this. He was, in fact, meeting

Lenka later, but it wasn't quite a date. It was supposedly an interview. "She's a single mother," he said.

"Oh, my love, don't take advantage of her!" A single mother herself, his mother had an unending reserve of sympathy for women in her position.

"I'm not going to take advantage of her, Mom," he said.

"Well, of *course* not," she replied, and he could hear a hint of pity, a sentiment born of her cloying, overly maternal side. What made it worse was that her implication in saying "of *course* not" in that way was that he *couldn't* take advantage of Lenka, regardless of his intentions.

Despite his winsome ways and boyish good looks, Gabriel was no Casanova, not by a long stretch. He had dated sporadically in college, and while women were often initially drawn to him, he had a confounding knack for fumbling at the crucial moment. Sometimes, from the back of his mind, he watched himself going astray but was unable to right his course. His timing, for one thing, was atrocious: tepid one minute, overeager the next. He invariably put forward precisely the wrong kind of sweetness (fraternal, adorable), and then cut it with a dissonant brashness (cruel, pouty), so that the whole package seemed both contrived and careless, and he managed to come off as simultaneously overeager, lecherous, and creepily insecure. Maybe if he could relax a little, he would be more successful with women, but as it happened, he'd only been with nine, all of whom came to know him in nonromantic circumstances. They had, in short, been seduced by accident. With Fiona he'd assumed she was out of his league and had viewed her simply as a valuable contact. Only once she was suddenly naked, in the middle of her hotel room, stubbing out a cigarette with one hand and letting her hair down with the other, did it occur to him that maybe her interest wasn't strictly professional.

Gabriel, phone cradled at his ear, said, "Mom, it's just a date. I'm going to be here for a while, and I thought it'd be nice to make a friend. That's all." Sometimes, he liked to ambush her with some shocking burst of candor—she was so excitable!—and he did so now. "But if we end up screwing tonight, all the better!"

"*¡Hijo malcreado!*" she screeched, as if horrified. "I have *not* raised a womanizer!"

"A capitalist and a womanizer!" he said and listened to her holler with laughter on the other end. He stood up and straightened his back. She was relaxing, so he moved to deliver the bad news, "But, Mom, I wanted to tell you that it looks like I'll be here through the New Year."

"*No. Gabriel!*"

"Believe me, it's not what I want."

She groaned. "Gabriel, don't. *Please.*"

"I have no choice. *Really.* It's this new job. Is there any chance you'll come down for your piece on Evo?" He'd said this last bit to ameliorate the situation, but as soon as the idea was aired, he realized that it'd be wonderful. Problematic, too—the lies would have to become more elaborate, unfortunately—but he missed his mother badly and would love to see her.

"You're staying there for Christmas?"

"That's what I'm saying." He said it as flatly as possible, like he was selecting dressing for his salad. If he gave her any room with this, she'd pin him to the wall with it.

"Will I ever see you again?"

"*Drama,* Mom," he said, reverting to a shorthand he'd adopted in high school. It was always a question of tone with her. Although she was someone whose life was steeped in the intricacies of language, so much of their communication was between the lines. She lilted soothingly in Spanish, whereas his experience speaking English with her suggested that the language was most useful for perfunctory mother-son business, or lecturing. "Look," he said, holding firm, "you'll see me when you come down to interview Evo."

"I'm not going to go there, Gabriel. I have classes."

"They're scheduling classes on Christmas Day? That's not right."

"You're hopeless, child. Now, go be nice to that woman." This was in her closing-time voice, and it was too bad. He did miss her. This was, in part, he knew, the sadness of being abroad too long. Even if he spoke the language like a native, the isolation was inescapable. He was simply too gringo-ized to fit in.

About his father, the man who'd provided the whitening influence in his DNA, Gabriel knew virtually nothing, not even the man's name. His mother refused to tell him. The whole subject was something she assiduously avoided. A lifetime of habit had made Gabriel disinclined to discuss him too.

When he did occasionally ask her about him, she replied in a blizzard of ardent and vacuous declarations. "It doesn't matter who he was! We were students! He was a foolish child and so was I and there is nothing else to say about it!" It was a narrative she steered principally by bellowing every single line shrilly, in Spanish. But her resolute imprecision, her insistence on obfuscating every engagement with the subject, conveyed that whatever she might have to say, she wasn't going to say it to Gabriel. For some reason—whether the man had been an abject shithead or something else—she needed him to remain an enigma to Gabriel.

She wanted, ultimately, to be viewed as an idealist. A Chilean exile who'd defected to Moscow, and then defected, once again, to the United States. Her biography wasn't a story of a woman driven to extremes by crude human concerns—in this story, her personal decisions were a series of philosophical gestures. In the United States, she'd finished her doctorate at UCLA and had her child, himself a complex product of the Cold War, born in the United States of Soviet and Chilean stock. She'd propped this wailing infant on her hip when delivering papers at conferences. Her wild and murky backstory made her a favorite at those dreary events.

She published widely: regular op-eds in the *Los Angeles Times* and the *Washington Post*, longer essays in *Boston Review*, *Mother Jones*, and the *Nation*. Few of her publications were in *Anthropology Today*, or *Current Anthropology*, or the other academic journals of her field, but no one in the department seemed especially bothered by that. By the time she was thirty-six, she had tenure at Pomona College and was leading rallies to boycott South African diamonds outside jewelers in Claremont. Her son, meanwhile, was then in the third grade at the largely white Franklin D. Roosevelt Lower School, where he had the language and a name reminiscent of the Mexican immigrants of Claremont's poorer surrounding areas. But he spoke with the precocious eloquence of a professor's child and wore a pigmentation that was, ultimately, neither here nor there.

Growing up, he never considered the possibility that his identity might be a fixed thing, that it might not be something that could or should be adjusted for each situation. He had been born with multiple identities, after all: Californian, Chilean, Soviet, bourgeois, only child of a single mother, Latino, Caucasian. In these, he saw options. He was partially pasty Russian and partially *café-con-crema* Chilean. Despite what his mother seemed to believe, it wasn't as if one race had swallowed the other. He may have ticked the box for *Latino/Hispanic* on all of his college applications, but it wasn't that simple. He ticked *Latino/Hispanic* on most job applications too, except for that one summer-job form in high school when he chose *Caucasian* and was quite sure that was what won him a position as a waiter in a snooty French bistro in Claremont.

If his racial and ethnic complexity had been mostly a burden when he was growing up in Southern California, where he was saddled with the perennial curse of creoles across the world (that is, instead of being a member of multiple groups, he wasn't a member of any), it meant something very different once he got to college. At Brown, he found himself gifted with the versatility he'd always wanted. He was not one person bisected or composed of fractions of other people; he was a person amplified, a many-voiced man.

His mother, sensing this emergent tendency to view his identity as multifarious—a convenient array of masks that he could don as he pleased—chided him on the phone about this once when he was a freshman, saying, "You want to pass for white sometimes, but, Gabo, this is not attractive. Not at all. You should be aware that it says nothing appealing about you, trying to play up one race over another."

"What do you *mean?*" he replied severely. He didn't use that tone with her ever. He could be stern, but he'd never been so harsh. She was understandably stunned. He continued, "Are you saying that I need to pick a side?"

"No. Of course not. I'm saying—well, I don't know." She inhaled sharply. As someone who'd made it her life's business to be one thing and that one thing thunderously, she had never succeeded in sorting out the complex nature of her own son's relationship with this issue. She said nothing else. Despite being obdurate on many scores, she had no trouble spotting true futility and was not ashamed to give in when it was due. So she said, "Fair enough."

And that was that.


Gabriel was in one of the puffy armchairs in Gloria's lobby, watching the two receptionists argue about something he couldn't hear, when Lenka arrived. The dark lobby had the whispering quality of a library, and when the guard opened the door for her, the white light outside seared itself into his eyes so he could not see her well at first. She came into focus: her ponytail yanked so tight that to his still-blotted vision it looked as if she'd shaved her head. He stood. Her face looked scrubbed. She seemed somber, with her thick black eyebrows, her no-bullshit gait. She had on a pair of skinny jeans and a black Adidas nylon jacket, zipped to her chin. Just when he was about to cower, her eyes met his and she lit up, smiling widely. The transition was so abrupt that he blurted, "Wow," and she laughed, leaned in, and kissed him on the cheek. She led the way back out, explaining that she had to pick Ernesto up from school. "I hope you don't mind, but I have to drop him off at home."

He said he didn't mind. In fact, he liked the idea of running an errand with her. He said he liked Ernesto, but she didn't react, so he added that Ernesto seemed smart.

"He gets that from me," she said, but he didn't know her well enough yet to tell if she was joking or not.

"Who takes care of him while you're at work?" he said, intending to find out if she had a boyfriend or a husband.

"My ex-husband's wife."

"You live with your ex-husband's wife?"

"Yes. And I live with my ex-husband. And I live with my brother, my mother, my grandmother, and my son. It's like a comedy. A comedy with no jokes." He laughed and she went on. "Really, we are a big happy family, but it's not simple. My brother and my ex-husband have a company—they are electricians, and they have lived in that house for a long time. My father moved in because he cannot afford to live alone anymore. Ernesto and I used to live in Miraflores, but it became difficult when I started working for Evo, so now we are all together. This is the story."

"That sounds—" He wanted to make a joke, but nothing came to mind.

"It's insanity," she said. "But we are pretty poor here, you know?" She said it in a matter-of-fact way. Like a lot of other Bolivians he'd met, she had a bluntness about the country's poverty that defied him to express an opinion. Were they proud of their poverty? They certainly weren't ashamed of it. It was just there, like that statue of Neptune in Plaza Murillo. He said nothing. It wasn't clear how accommodating she was socially. People in her line of work were typically, at a minimum, hyperactively concerned with pleasing others. She did not seem to be afflicted by that problem. She was just tired. She'd wanted to go on a date with him, but now she was exhausted, and the date itself had turned into an errand. That was his guess. She pulled the keys from her pocket. "This is my car," she said.

The paint on her busted two-door Datsun had lost its gloss and was a dull beige now. She'd put one of those bright red steering wheel locks on—which seemed strange, because no one would want to steal a car like that. The price of the car couldn't be much more than the cost of a tank of gas. They got in, and she tossed the lock onto the floor by his feet and started the engine. He reached for his seat belt, but there was none. The seat belts had already been sold.

She had pendants dangling from the rearview mirror, including one of St. Christopher. There was a sticker of the Virgin Mary on the glove box with a message beneath it: *Nuestra Señora Del Sagrado Corazón, rogad por nosotros.*

She accelerated down the street and turned into a thicket of gridlock. In front of them a howitzer-sized pipe protruded from the grimy rear end of a Tang-colored bus, and when traffic inched forward, a heavy black cloud of exhaust barfed out onto them. Lenka's window was open. Exhaust filled the car. She didn't seem to notice. Down there, at street level, the cacophony was simply astounding.

Watching her drive, he felt even more attracted to her. It made no sense, but he'd noticed that he got turned on by women doing monotonous things: sitting in traffic, sewing buttons on a shirt, cleaning eyeglasses; it was all wildly, weirdly sexy. There was something alluring about the habitual execution of a dull and necessary task—like a preview of married life, but viewed through an enthralling lens of newness.

"What do you want to know about Evo?" she said.

"As much as possible," he said. "Like, what's he going to do once he takes power?"

"He hasn't been elected yet," she said.

"Right, but has he picked his cabinet members? The finance minister?"

She glanced in the rearview at the traffic. "We're going to be here all day," she said and pushed into first gear, yanked the steering wheel to the right so that the passenger side of the car lurched up on the sidewalk, and then accelerated around the car in front of them.

In this way, half on the road and half on the sidewalk, she sped past the traffic and then turned, wheels screaming, at the intersection. The underside of her car scraped against the curb as they swerved back into traffic.

When she turned to him, Gabriel let go of the dashboard. "Sorry, I'm impatient," she said. "So, you wanted to know who the finance minister will be if Evo wins the election?"

"Yes," he said.

"Well, I can't tell you," she said. "Evo wants these decisions to be completely secret. If he wins, he'll announce all of the cabinet appointments at once the week before he takes office."

"We don't have to talk about Evo," he said.

"I don't know how to talk about anything else anymore. You understand?"

"I do."

They pulled up outside a school in a dreary neighborhood halfway up the hill to El Alto, and Ernesto jogged up to the car and leaped into the back seat. He leaned forward and kissed his mother on the cheek.

Gabriel held an open palm up to the back seat and Ernesto didn't do anything for a while, and then he punched it quickly twice. "Well done," Gabriel said.

"How was school?" she said.

Ernesto said it was fine. Lenka asked if he'd spoken to his teacher about Friday, and Ernesto nodded.

They drove in silence through La Paz's congested streets. These were neighborhoods that Gabriel hadn't seen. Some of the streets were so steep they were nearly walls. Messy nests of black wires perched around the tops of crooked telephone polls—all of it jerry-rigged. Homeowners had taken it upon themselves to patch potholes near their houses, but they used different fillers, so the road looked like an asphalt quilt. Still, these were not slums exactly. Gabriel looked at the buildings rolling past: all blocky two-story structures with large rectangular windows. Concrete posts rose like stalagmites from the roofs; rebar poles stretched forth like exposed bones. The rebar represented hope, he knew—it meant another level could be added to the structure, if money ever permitted.

The second time he had visited South America—for a semester of intensive study in Quito in his senior year at Brown—he hadn't wanted to leave. The day before he was to depart, he nearly tore up his ticket. It would sound trite, and it was trite, maybe, but he simply felt more *alive* down there, away from the strictures of the First World. It had been easy to overlook those strictures growing up in Claremont.

Lenka parked outside a huge and bleak house, shaped by architectural shorthand and painted a Soviet shade of pastel blue. Lenka and Ernesto got out and went inside while Gabriel waited in the car. Ahead, he could see a hazy slice of south La Paz, where the upper classes lived. Down there, the rocky hillsides gave way to soft dry soil and clay-rich badlands, which eroded into steep arroyos and vales of hoodoos. The earth beneath those suburbs was in a constant metamorphosis that required sophisticated foundations for the hilltop mansions, foundations that could easily cost twice as much as the buildings themselves. In San Pedro, Lenka's neighborhood, everything was cracked slabs of concrete. There was nothing living in sight. The cinder blocks hadn't even been painted on the more squalid houses.

Looking at it all, Gabriel found himself overwhelmed with a desire for a luxurious and spacious store or restaurant, somewhere in Manhattan at Christmastime, maybe: a sparkling oasis of ravenous retail. And even though he knew the feeling that the place would give him would be a lie — satisfaction imitating joy — the mirage was still tempting.

Lenka returned with her cell phone at her ear. She flung herself back behind the wheel so quickly he caught a whiff of her soapy shampoo. *"Bueno señor, pero, ya"* — she checked the mirror, put the car into gear — *"pero ya estoy con un periodista. Sí, ya."*

She listened, checked the mirror, released the parking brake.

*"Pues, sí — hablamos entonces."* She hung up the phone, shoved it under her thigh, started off down the street.

"The future president?" Gabriel said.

She just smiled. "Gabriel, have you been to Blueberries?"

"Were you talking about me to Evo?"

"Does that make you feel special?" She grinned at him.

She kept smiling quietly, eyes back on the road. They drove through the tunnel connecting San Pedro and Sopocachi, and on the other side Lenka slowed and stopped at a red light. Dusk showed La Paz at its finest: the cool air, papaya sun in a cobalt sky, craggy mountains lit vividly. The comparatively well-heeled denizens of Sopocachi walked past, some muttering into cell phones.

Gabriel asked her if she'd had a lot of press to deal with.

"Yes." She pulled the parking brake, took her foot off the clutch, and scratched her ankle. "There were reporters from every newspaper calling us all afternoon. Fiona called, actually. I told her that I was going to meet you later."

"Oh *God*," he said and rolled his eyes, aware that he was tipping his hand.

Lenka's smile widened and she checked to see that the light was still red. She looked back at him. She had magnificent eyelashes, like palm fronds dipped in pitch and dried in the sun, and when she blinked he could almost feel the breeze. "Why do you say 'Oh *God'* like that?"

He shrugged. "What do you think?"

"Did you sleep with her?"

He grinned guardedly, stuck somewhere between embarrassed and proud. She shook her head. He was surprised by how relieved he was to make the admission. "Does it surprise you?" he said.

"No, it's just funny." Now she was lying. "What was Fiona like in bed?" she asked.

"Do you know what a mechanical bull is?"

She laughed, shook her head. "You are bad, Gabriel."

"That's true," he said.

Someone behind them honked, and she put the car back into gear.

A block later, she parked on the north side of Plaza Avaroa. The plaza slanted slightly to the southeast and was full of knobby, tumor-laden maples that stooped behind worn metal benches. Restaurants and cafés packed the promenades on two sides of the square; the other two were occupied by a mixture of colonial houses and old ministerial buildings. On the distant westerly corner, the American ambassador's former residence, a once stately mansion, was dark and abandoned now. The residence had been too exposed there on the square, too easily accessed by the mobs, and the ambassador had had to move down to the far corner of an obscure neighborhood in south La Paz.

• • •

When she asked him what he wanted to know, Gabriel leaned back and thought it through. The boisterous restaurant was packed with people, mostly leaning over two-person tables and talking animatedly. It seemed as if all of them were smoking at once. He didn't know why they called it Blueberries; nothing on the menu involved blueberries. He said, "It's all deep background right now, nothing for attribution. So, if you could tell me the next finance minister's name, I'd be eternally grateful."

She squinted at him, an expression somewhere between scolding and flirtatious.

"The name of the head of the central bank?" he continued. "Minister of the interior?"

She rolled her eyes. She had made it clear already that Evo would not be revealing the names of these people until January. It was a big deal to Evo. If she leaked one of the names, she'd be fired.

A gambit opened for him. With Lenka, he had little reason left to maintain his cover. Of course, if she let it out that he was there as an analyst for Calloway, Priya would probably fire him. And Lenka herself had little to no reason to want to talk to a hedge fund. She might do it anyway, and she might keep his secret, but these were far from certain; still, she knew everything he wanted to know. And he liked her a lot already, and the feeling seemed mutual, and if he told her the truth, she wouldn't have as much of a reason to withhold that information. He held his course, though. "Is he going to expropriate the natural gas?"

"He has said repeatedly that he plans to do that."

"Right." Gabriel paused, but she offered nothing else, so he said, "But does he mean it?"

She smiled, partially exasperated already. This was turning into more of an interview than he'd intended it to be.

He continued anyway, unable to stop himself. "And what about the mines?"

"Can I ask you a question?" she said.

"Anything," he said. The eye contact was steady, but her flirtation was dimming.

"What kind of questions are these?" she said.

"They are direct questions. If you want, I can ask what he plans to do once he takes control, but if that's what you prefer, then you should just give me a copy of your latest press release."

She had ordered tea, which now arrived. He watched as she drizzled pale honey over the floating tea bag until it started to sink. She put the honey down, and the bag rebounded, returned to the surface. She tugged on the string and the bag bobbed.

"You can be at the speech when he unveils his cabinet picks. It'll be in January, if he gets elected. I'll save you a seat in the front row."

"I'll be there. Look, I'm sorry I've been—" He gestured vaguely.

"Pushy?"

He smiled at her.

"I like you, Gabriel," she said, "and you're pretty, but I can't get involved with some reporter who's just going to leave tomorrow, so I—"

"I'm not leaving tomorrow."

She squinted at him dubiously.

"I'm not saying that I'm staying forever," he said, "but I'll be here for a month, at least. Maybe more."

"You're great, but I don't know what I'm supposed to do with you. I don't even know if this is a date or an interview."

"Can it be both?"

"It can be both," she said.

"I was sent here with the understanding that I would be discreet about my purpose, and I'm finding that it's very hard to do that. Please, I ask you, as a personal favor, don't tell anyone. Is that okay?"

She nodded, her expression amused, almost.

"I work for an investment firm called the Calloway Group."

Her expression didn't budge. She sighed. She nodded. She pushed her cup away. "Thank you, but I should go." She picked up her bag, put the strap over her shoulder, and was about to stand when he reached out and touched her arm.

"*Please.* Please give me a minute."

"You lied to me."

"I lied to everyone. You're one of the only people I've told the truth to."

"Well, in any case, you need to talk to the central bank, not me."

"But who would I contact at the central bank? Who's going to be in charge in two months? *That's* what I need to know."

She took her bag off her shoulder and set it down again, but she kept the strap in her hand. "Why are you in Bolivia?" she said. "What kind of investments are these?"

"I honestly don't know," he said.

She squinted at him.

"You won't tell anyone?" he said.

"Why would I?"

"It'll be in equities," he explained. "Probably betting for or against stocks of foreign companies heavily exposed to Bolivia, mostly in minerals and natural gas, maybe some telephony and basic infrastructure. There are around five to ten companies that will be deeply affected by Evo's decisions in the next month or two."

"Do the other reporters know who you work for? Does Fiona?"

He thought about it briefly before he said, "No, none of them know." And, like that, his foray into candor was over. While he would have preferred not to lie to her from here on out, it was inescapable. He needed her to recognize the sacredness of his secret, and if he admitted to telling others, she would be less inclined to see it as sacrosanct.

"And what will happen to you if the reporters find out?"

"I don't know." He shrugged. "I'll probably have to leave, go to another country."

"And if I don't tell you what you need?"

"The same—I'll leave."

Now she was perking up again, enjoying herself a little more. This was interesting to her. The flirtatious edge returned to her voice. "And what if you find out something and then it turns out to be untrue?"

"It depends on what I tell my boss and what she does with the information. If she acts on it and loses money, I'll probably be fired."

"That's not very nice."

"Well, she's not very nice."

She smiled at him. "And are you betting for us, or against us?"

"We're not betting on anything, so far. And I doubt it would involve Bolivian companies. It's more likely that it'd involve foreign companies exposed to Bolivia."

"Right, but I'm asking which way you will be betting."

"Well, *I'm* not betting," he said, hoping to put some distance between himself and the answer to that question. "I provide them with information."

"You provide them with information. That's a choice you make."

"Yeah. I'm a spy for assholes. It's true. But it's still the coolest job I've ever had."

She laughed, shook her head.

"I'm hoping to find out what Evo will do with natural gas."

"He's going to expropriate! He already said so!"

Gabriel glanced around to make sure no one was eavesdropping. "I know that's what he's saying," he said, lowering his voice in the hope that she would quiet down too. "But a lot of Latin American presidents have said things like that, only to change their minds once they're in power. If you look at the stock prices of the companies in question, it's clear that they don't know what to think of Evo yet. I'm here to help expedite the answer to this question for my boss."

She blinked quickly at him, shaking her head, unsure of whether to trust him or not.

He lifted his glass of wine, and she reluctantly clinked her teacup against it. They each had a sip. "*Salud,*" he said. She grinned at him, just barely, over her teacup.

Lenka was a hard one to read; her confidence was as vivid as her reticence. There had once been, he believed, some brightly spangled joie de vivre about her, which was probably blunted by the birth of her son and her subsequent divorce, or maybe it was just the inevitable drudgery of life. Still, her mood seemed to remain on a spectrum set to measure degrees of amusement, rather than of sorrow or indignation. Peculiarly for someone in the business of dealing with journalists, her bullshit detector did not seem to have an off switch, and she didn't have the self-restraint to keep her opinions to herself.

She was unlike most women he'd been attracted to, who tended to be powerful and sexual in conspicuous ways. Although he could sense some attraction from Lenka, the signals were dampened. She would not, as Fiona had done, strip naked midconversation on a first date. She was not proud or brash in the way people of her professional stature in other countries might be. She was very Bolivian. She was *reserved*, in that she reserved portions of herself and was not impatient to release them all at once. Her demeanor was what he might have expected from the younger sister of a terribly boisterous and adored woman in North America. She paid attention, waiting, and then let loose.

So he toned himself down too. He let her run with her thoughts. She'd had a long day, after all. She talked about Evo, and he listened carefully, admiring her from across the table. She was remarkably attractive. Or, she was quite attractive, and he was remarkably attracted to her. Though he wanted her to like him as much as he liked her, the odds were not in his favor. Still, he did his best. He asked sensible questions and listened carefully to her answers. She didn't reveal anything that he had come to find out, but she did tell him about Evo as a man, about his love of his country and his eagerness to help his people. She had become an expert at describing his difficult roots — growing up impoverished, the child of miners, working in the coca fields, and eventually becoming involved in organizing workers and in public service. She sketched a hero's journey, but tilted it, slightly, for Gabriel's benefit. She made sure it was clear that Evo knew his weaknesses as well as anyone. He hired people who were capable of doing the difficult work of interpreting the data, she said.

Now she was in her element, Gabriel could tell. Her speech was limber and she made adjustments to her narrative to suit his bias. She was playing as well as any of them could: giving a unique and personalized spin to the one tale she had to tell. With Gabriel, she chose an unusually frank tone. Eventually, she stopped and sighed an exhausted sigh. A week ago, she'd been the press liaison for a long-shot presidential candidate in an obscure South American country. Now he was certain to win and she found herself charged with the task of being the voice of the most exciting political phenomenon in Latin America in years.

"Thank you for meeting me, by the way," she said. "It's been nice to talk off the record—to talk to someone who is interested but isn't a journalist, someone who doesn't work with me and isn't in my family."

"It was a pleasure," he said, still hoping to project something like eagerness. "Sorry if I seemed pushy before, I'm just—I don't know." He spoke slowly in a low voice, trying to draw her forward. "I'm new at this too, you know. It's exciting to be here. I used to be a reporter, and I'm still learning what's different about this job."

She tilted her head in a way that he found encouraging. She said, "Yes, I like that about you. We're both in over our heads. We have accepted our lots, because it would be crazy not to accept, but we find ourselves wondering what we've gotten ourselves into. Isn't that right?" She squinted at him, inspecting him.

He nodded. That was a purer distillation of his situation than he himself had managed so far, but he didn't want to get into it with her yet. So he changed the subject, asked her what she had done before.

"I worked at the Casa Cultura," she said.

"Tell me more."

So she did, and they remained there at that little square table, pursuing a line of conversation that moved further and further afield from the designated talking points.

On the drive back, she wove through the narrow roads west of Prado, where the city sloped gently up toward the steeper cliffs. The streetlights gave the city a sickly yellowish tinge. Above them, the gibbous moon was high and bright, the contours of its surface cut vividly. As they drove past the square at San Pedro, she mentioned that she lived up the hill three blocks. Gabriel offered to get out and take a taxi the rest of the way, but she just shook her head.

They stopped at a red light and she pulled the car out of gear, glanced at him. He wanted to kiss her, but he was afraid he might come off as entitled. "Let's meet again," he said. "We don't need to talk about Evo."

"What else would we talk about? You called me because you want to know about Evo. Please don't pretend it's something else. I don't have time for anything, but I especially don't have time for people who pretend."

"I'm not pretending. The truth is that I'd like to see you again, and we don't need to talk about Evo."

She looked at him sideways. "Are you even able to be honest?"

"I think so," he said, which was true. "I hope so." Also true.

She yawned, pulled into the intersection. They sped along and he stared at the city as they flipped through shadows and bright concrete beneath streetlights spaced to conserve electricity.

She parked in Hotel Gloria's taxi stand. He was trying to get up the gumption to kiss her when she said, "By the way, did you hear the news?"

He shook his head.

"One of the vice presidents at the World Bank quit his job yesterday over Bolivia. He said the U.S. was pressuring him to cut off Bolivian aid."

He nodded. "That's weird."

She nodded too, yawned. "An Italian. I think I'm going to invite him here."

Somewhere in the back of his mind, he was still taking notes for his next message to Priya. He didn't want it to be that way, but he needed to keep his priorities in order if he wanted to last there.

He leaned over and kissed Lenka on the cheek. He paused, looking at her up close, but she just turned away and started her car again. She shook her head and kissed him once, slowly, gently, on the mouth. She looked him in the eyes, blinked once, twice, then turned back and looked ahead resolutely, as though she were already driving away. He could see tears starting in her eyes. "Not a good idea," she said and blinked quickly. She let the parking brake down.

He opened the door, got out, and stood beside the car. He leaned down and looked at her through the passenger-side window. Her hand gripped the wheel, knuckles stretching the skin. It was not the pristine, dainty hand of a young woman, but a strong hand, one marked by years of activity in an active life. She glanced back at him. The severity she seemed to want to radiate was undermined by those vanilla specks on her chin. Gabriel grinned deviously. "I'll call you tomorrow."

She shook her head and pushed the car into gear.

A large brown envelope sat upon his bed when he returned that night. Inside, he found a copy of Bolivia's latest Article IV report, with Fiona's kiss, in brownish lipstick, on the top page. She'd gone back to her bureau's office in Lima and had DHLed this from there, apparently after some waffling. Gabriel lay down on the bed and flipped through boilerplate. He skipped to the end and found the phrase "profound fiscal imbalances that will create long-term instability in the macroeconomy." He read on. The diagnosis from the IMF was beyond grim. There was nothing in there that would be useful to Priya, but he wanted her to know that he'd managed to get a copy of the report, so he went down to the business center and sent her e-mail explaining that he had it and it was useless.

Back upstairs, he ordered a ham and cheese sandwich. With the plate on his lap, he watched CNN International. Then he put the plate on the bedside table, lay down, and stared at the asbestos tiles in the ceiling, which were stained gray-brown by decades of smoke. The odor of all that smoke still clung to the room. There were blackened spots on the tabletops too, as if some demon had set a scalding finger down. Gabriel turned off the television, turned off the lights. He rolled onto his side, closed his eyes, and lay there, motionless, listening to the cacophony.

During his orientation at Calloway, Oscar had said, "I have done this job longer than anyone I know, and I've done it for only five years." That had struck Gabriel. It repeated on him. He knew most were fired. Getting fired, and soon, was the norm. He wondered how long he would last before he was fired.

Oscar went on to say that he'd actually known two other analysts —neither at Calloway, but it was the same—who had managed to keep their jobs for several years. They'd both sworn off the industry altogether recently.

"Why?" Gabriel asked.

Oscar appeared surprised by the question, as if the answer should be self-evident.

Oscar wore oval gold-rimmed glasses. He had roughly cut gold cuff links, a gold tiepin, a loose-fitting gold Rolex. He was jowly, pale, of an indeterminate age, though if Gabriel had to guess, he'd say Oscar was in his midforties. He was friendly and subdued, intensely distracted. He had a lot going on, and this other duty, the interviewing of a prospective analyst who would cover the rest of Latin America, meant little to him because he would not be working with the person. By the job's definition, they would not overlap. Still, he listened to Gabriel's questions, and he talked about the life, what Gabriel could expect.

"My wife is a saint," he said. "We met before I took the job. She has the kids to think about, and many hobbies. Tennis. Knitting. This thing called Pilates—you know it?"

Gabriel nodded.

Oscar continued. "She has friends too; I don't know them very well. My wife and I used to talk on the phone often while I was away. Eventually, we accepted that the phone only makes it worse, so we don't do that anymore. When I'm gone, I'm *gone*. Sometimes, after I'm gone for a long time, I sleep in the guest room for a couple nights when I return, because it's as if we don't know each other anymore. My wife used to worry that I had a mistress, but she has realized that it's not possible. Because there is no place that I go. There's literally *nothing* there. When I am out there, I am nowhere. Do you understand?"

Gabriel nodded, although he didn't understand at all, yet.

# 4

# Santa Cruz Gas

*Wednesday, November 30, 2005*

EVO'S POLITICAL PARTY, MAS—Movimiento al Socialismo
—had its headquarters in a large and desolate storefront two blocks up
the hill from Plaza Murillo. Posters of Evo's beaming face and globular
head with its truncated forehead covered every possible square inch of
wall in either direction. The street was narrow, its sidewalk raised two
feet above the street to reduce flooding during seasonal torrents, which
poured through storm drains that fed the Choqueapu River, bisecting
the city from top to bottom.

The Choqueapu, slick with toxic waste and frothy sewage, ran
mostly underground now, where the stench wouldn't bother anyone. La
Paz would never have existed were it not for the profusion of gold that
had once glittered in that river's waters. By the time the conquistadors
had finished wringing every nugget from it, the surrounding city was
developed enough to sustain itself without the gold. And once the gold
was completely gone, the conquistadors focused on silver in the south,
mainly Potosí. The silver helped prop up a century of the Spanish empire. Once the silver was exhausted, the Spaniards' attention moved to

tin. By the time the Spanish ceded control, in 1825, the mountains of Bolivia were honeycombed with mineshafts. Little of value remained.

The plundering of Bolivia came to be known as El Saqueo—"the sacking." For a century and a half after the Spanish departed, Bolivia was led by a colorful array of buffoons, descendants of the conquistadors or the lesser nobility who had been dispatched to manage the country during its occupation. Through a series of lost wars and bungled treaties, Bolivia's borders contracted.

Their stretch of the Pacific was home to a species of bat that painted the sandstone cliffs white with its shit. The bat guano was monetizable, however, as an ingredient in gunpowder. When Bolivia increased its tax on this bat shit, Chile (which harvested and processed most of the shit) attacked, and it was through the ensuing war that Bolivia became landlocked. A still more inglorious moment came some fifty years later when, in 1864, a stupid and vain president named Melgarejo traded a huge swath of oil-rich jungle to Brazil for a single white stallion.

For most of the twentieth century, Bolivia languished in deep but steady poverty.

Finally, in the 1990s, large natural gas reserves were discovered in the jungles to the southeast. True to form, most of the profits from this latest subterranean bonanza also ended up in the hands of the Spanish, in this case by way of the Spanish company Repsol, which, during the 1996 privatization of the gas industry, bought up more of the reserves than any other company did. Once again, El Saqueo: only a fraction of the profit would find its way into the pockets of Bolivians.

Evo and sympathetic liberals around the world, including Gabriel's mother, were furious that Repsol and a handful of other foreign corporations had taken most of the profits from the natural gas discovery. Evo's ascendency was fueled, so to speak, mainly by his commitment to re-appropriating the gas reserves from Repsol and other companies. His plan was to invert the profit-sharing ratio between the companies and the Bolivian people: 70 percent for the companies would become 70 percent for Bolivia.

Gabriel didn't object to Evo's plan. He understood why people were outraged, but he also thought the issue was more complicated than Evo made it out to be. In matters of economics, if the answer seemed straightforward, you weren't looking closely.

In the case of Bolivian natural gas, the new profit-sharing arrangement ran a strong risk of forcing certain companies out of the country. Then Bolivia would have effectively nationalized the industry, and the new Bolivian gas company would likely lose the high-paid (mainly foreign) specialists who brought in, and managed, the complex technology involved. Safety and environmental standards, a given for Repsol, would likely be brushed aside by cash-strapped Bolivia. Foreign investors would back off. Contracts would dry up. Jobs would disappear. Plans for pipelines would be scrapped, refineries would fall into disrepair, and the whole industry would slacken into toxic obsolescence. Also, Brazil, an important Bolivian ally that also held a significant percentage of the gas fields and that imported much of the gas, would be furious.

Gabriel opened the front door of the MAS office and found a worn but capacious space, dun-colored. Overhead, fluorescent lights buzzed; beneath, a flurry of activity within a dense grid of vintage metal desks. He did not see Lenka anywhere.

A zaftig receptionist, her makeup glistening slightly under the artificial light, smiled drearily at him.

Above her a large nylon banner read:

ADELANTE BOLIVIA! MAS!
VOTA EVO!
MAS!

The banner had zero graphic sophistication. It was just that black blocky text on a white backdrop. Gabriel admired the bluntness, that distinctly Bolivian lack of flourish or pretense.

He asked the receptionist in Spanish if Lenka Villarobles was in.

She looked him up and down. Her lips were as glossy as glazed pottery. Her crimped hair looked like the dark tendrils of a sea plant that had dried stiff at low tide.

"She is expecting me," he said.

The receptionist dialed a number, then turned away and whispered into the phone, glancing back at him. Then she hung up. "Please you will wait here," she said in heavily accented English.

He picked up a campaign circular and sat down. On the cover, Evo, visiting a mine, wore a yellow hardhat. In the background little boys spattered in slate-colored mud, burgundy hardhats on their heads, too-big rubber boots on their feet, stared at Evo in wonder. Gabriel flipped the page. More of the mines: a glimpse at a chillier and darker atrium in hell's labyrinth. It was an infinite landscape of gray: pebbles, boulders, and sheets of slate; gentle shale, half mulched, as if attacked by an army of rock-eating termites. There was nothing else. Just as Gabriel began wondering if Lenka had anything to do with this leaflet, she appeared.

He stood and lunged into the greeting awkwardly. She flinched, almost, then leaned in, and they kissed each other on the cheek quickly. Though acutely aware of the many eyes on them, he had no idea if the attention was as a result of something she'd said about him, or if this was just because a young man had arrived and seemed to know her.

"You like that?" she said, referring to the brochure.

"Did you make it?"

"No."

"Then it's just okay."

She smiled at him and he caught a glimpse of warmth.

She led the way across the floor to her office, on the far side of the room. The only window in her office was a floor-to-ceiling sheet of glass facing the main floor. She sat in front of her computer. Her co-workers outside sort of pretended not to stare.

Gabriel looked at the chaos on her desk—piles of paper teetering precariously or, having already cascaded, forming text-filled lagoons on the floor. In the corner of the room, towering stacks of newspaper threatened greater disarray. On the walls, irregularly shaped clippings about Evo were Scotch-taped at haphazard angles, as in a stalker's lair. "So, are you going to introduce me to Evo?" he said.

"I don't think so, I'm sorry," she said and glanced outside. He could tell she was hyperaware of the possibility that they were being watched. He realized that she had not told her coworkers anything about him. To the extent that there was something going on, it was, for her part, on the down-low.

She had to finish an e-mail, she said. He watched her type, her face bunched in concentration. He would have sat, but the only other chair was occupied by a banker's box.

Lenka finished her typing and then chewed the corner of her lip, reviewing what she had written. He loved watching her at this—lost in thought. It reminded him of the expression on her face when she drove.

She grabbed her jacket and led the way outside. They walked up the hill.

"What would you have asked him?" she asked.

He was tempted to say something flirtatious, about how he'd ask Evo where he'd found such a lovely...but he stopped himself. It was precisely that kind of maneuver that had scuttled so many promising beginnings for him. So he decided to be honest. "I would have asked him if he had decided who his finance minister would be."

She shook her head. "Please, Gabriel."

"I know. Believe me, I'm sorry to be persistent," he said. He wanted to back off, but there were no alternative routes. There was information that could result in profit, and there was information that couldn't. Everything else was just filler. It wasn't journalism—and it couldn't be faked. One small victory and Priya might decide he'd passed the test. That's how he saw it. He needed to give her something, and this seemed the most feasible option.

"Evo will not announce the names of cabinet members before he wins the election. That would be crazy for many reasons, maybe most important because it'd be very bad luck."

"This would be off the record."

"That doesn't help. I am his *press* liaison, and you are not the press." She had a knack for conciseness. But she didn't work on people or apply charm like others in her line of work might have, because, regardless of the particulars, she was finally a salesperson. The product she was hawking was not Evo himself, intrinsic Evo, but the perception of him as seen by those whose opinions determined his future (the Bolivian electorate, other politicians, bureaucrats, and so forth). That perception was shaped by the writers and journalists and editors who conveyed news about Evo to those people. So her job was to manipulate the messengers. That she did so without a surfeit of charm might have seemed to a cynic part of the everyman shtick that she aimed to sell. But Gabriel didn't see her as someone who was able to strategize so clearly. Her finest quality was her brusqueness, her sharpness. She was not merely smart-sharp, but cutting-sharp: filleting his argument before he got started. And that was what he adored.

They were walking toward a restaurant Lenka liked, called Cabra, that was near Plaza Mendoza. The restaurant did carryout lamb sandwiches. She said she hoped to seize an empty bench before the lunchtime rush. She walked quickly, apparently concerned that there would not be any room for them.

Against the evident futility of his situation, he said, "I could write a freelance piece about Bolivia. If I actually published something, would you want to talk to me then?"

"No. I know who your audience is. I looked up this Calloway Group. I read about them. You're not going to quit. You're going to do everything you can to stay with them and if you fail here, you'll go somewhere else and try again."

They avoided Potosí, because of protests. Gabriel had no idea who was protesting or what was bothering them, but as they walked parallel to Potosí, he glanced down at each intersection to see the protesters shambling along slowly and chanting, their nylon banners held up high. Some waved the rainbow-colored *wiphala* flags of Tupac Katari's revolutionary army. The country had hundreds of groups that were more than eager to take to the streets for a day of marching. Protest and insurgency were as fundamental to the national gestalt as the concept of liberty was in the United States. Butchers would protest the rising cost of beef beside students marching in opposition to rising tuition bills; some teachers would march in opposition to the students and some teachers would march in support of them; shop owners would hold a rally to protest all the protests.

Lenka had sunglasses on, and Gabriel couldn't see her eyes, though he wished he could. He'd felt warmth from her at first, but now he wasn't sure what she was thinking. He wanted to kiss her again. He worried that he'd repulsed her by talking business. For his part, he hadn't even brought a pair of sunglasses, and the sun was so bright he was having a hard time keeping his eyes open.

They stopped at a light. Midday, and the gridlock persisted. A flatbed truck's engine roared as it edged forward a few feet. Standing on the back of the truck a dozen or so soldiers in black fatigues held on to weathered black submachine guns and stared contemptuously down at the pedestrians. Above, the over-bright sun irradiated them all.

They walked another two blocks in silence and arrived at the corner of Plaza Mendoza. She stopped and looked around. The place was so mobbed there was hardly room to stand, let alone sit down for lunch. "Damn it," she said, anguished. "I'm sorry about this."

"We could grab some salteñas?" he offered. They were only two blocks from his favorite place for salteñas.

She sighed, apparently embarrassed and frustrated that she'd led them so far afield. When she didn't respond, he added, "Or we could go to my hotel and order room service." A naughty/funny flirtatious suggestion, he hoped, on the surface, with a clear option for her to take him seriously, if she were of a mind to.

Her expression didn't budge as she looked around at the droves again. Eventually, she turned back, cocked her head to the side, and gazed at him. "You want me to give you the finance minister's name why? Because it will help you? But what will it do for Evo?"

"Oh." He had thought they were talking about something else. Still, it was a valid question. This was, inevitably, the biggest challenge of his job: unless they were corrupt, which she clearly was not, government officials had little to nothing to gain from sharing information with him. He had, however, detected some insecurity about Evo's reputation as a steward of the Bolivian economy, so he said, "Do you know why there are no other investors looking at Bolivia? You know what they say about this country? Calloway actually sees potential here. Calloway's a powerful firm too; it attracts attention. If we actively bet on Bolivia, other firms might follow. Other types of investment might follow."

"This is not my area."

"I just want to know whom to talk to."

All around them cars honked and pedestrians hurried along, their shoes clip-clopping on the asphalt. She took her sunglasses off and squinted up at him. Shielding her eyes with her hand, she considered him. "I know that it's your job. And I think it's okay. I'm sorry if I seem—"

"It's okay."

"Can we just not talk about it?"

"Absolutely. Honestly, I like you and if we don't talk about this stuff—that's fine."

She continued to shield her eyes and look at him. She seemed relieved to have dispensed with that issue. She said, "We should eat some lunch though."

"Of course! You lead the way—I'm up for anything."

"You mentioned room service?"

"Room service?" he repeated, nodding, not sure that he'd heard her right. He looked at her dark eyes, the overlong lashes curling up toward him, the sad and forgiving look of someone wiser and more sensible than her circumstances required she be. He saw some tiny muscle behind her eyes relax.

"Yes," she said and her eyes narrowed. "Room service."

He nodded at her, biting back his delight. "Billed to the hedge fund, in fact."

She rolled her eyes, as if amused with him and herself equally. She sighed, then turned and started in the direction of his hotel. He followed.

At the next corner, they had to stop because the traffic was moving.

"When do you have to be back?" he said.

She shook her head. She put her sunglasses back on. "Tomorrow morning, at the latest."

She led the way through the traffic. A smile spread until she was on the verge of laughing, and he knew she wasn't joking.

And it was not this realization itself but the look on her face that ruined him. His guilt settled in right then. Giant raptors glided overhead, their shadows sweeping fast across the brightly lit pavement, sweeping past preteen beggars, colossally bored, their outstretched hands cupping nothing.

He followed her through the revolving doors, across Gloria's lobby, her hips popping more assertively at the outer edges of their swing — she was aware that he was staring, he knew — and her shoes clacking on the tile floor harder than they had earlier. He had his room key in his pocket, his index finger tracing the teeth.

In the elevator, he leaned in and kissed her. They paused when the elevator stopped at the second floor, stepped away from each other as a maid entered and pressed the tenth-floor button. The three of them ascended in silence, all watching the numbers above: 3 ... 4 ... 5 ... 6 ... 7, and at 8, the elevator squeaked to a stop. Its doors blundered apart, and the maid stood aside.

Lenka led the way and Gabriel pulled the key from his pocket.

An hour later, they lay side by side on their backs while he caught his breath, which still took a lot longer than it would have in New York City. Lenka pulled down the sheets to get some air on her skin. He sneaked a peek at her cesarean scar again. It had transfixed him while he was on top of her. The scar was crude and jagged and puffy. He rolled onto his side and traced its length with his index finger. She looked at him, shifted her weight, and explained that the anesthesiologist had had trouble administering her epidural. He'd somehow been unable to puncture the ligaments of her spine and offer relief. He had given up in a huff, as if it were her fault. By the time they cut her open, she had been in labor for ten hours and had taken not so much as an aspirin for the pain.

"I screamed for a while and then I passed out. When I came to, I felt supernaturally calm—there was no pain at all. They had opened me up completely and were pulling this purple thing out of me. It only sort of looked like a baby. It looked like they were hauling out my intestines. The next thing I remember I was holding a clammy baby. He looked ugly then, nothing like he does now. He had a face like an angry old man. They had put morphine into my IV by then, and I felt much better. I remember it looked like a bomb had exploded in me. High on those drugs, I watched while they sewed it back up. I had the baby with me. He was asleep, bored by the world already."

"What did your husband do?" asked Gabriel. His arm was asleep, pinned beneath his own torso, so he rolled onto his back and looked at the ceiling.

"My husband stood back. He looked like he was going to faint."

Gabriel thought about it for a minute. "And what happened afterward?"

"Nothing. Six months later we were divorced."

"Isn't that something that you're not—" He held it there.

"Because I am Catholic?"

He nodded.

"It was difficult. I had—"

They were interrupted by a knock at the door. They had ordered a bottle of cheap Bolivian chardonnay and two slices of vanilla cake for lunch. Gabriel went to the door, and Lenka sat up and clapped approvingly when Gabriel returned and handed her her cake. Then she set it down carefully on the mattress, staring at it lustfully. She pulled off the cellophane wrap, and stabbed her fork in. She lay back and chewed, while he poured the wine.

"You were telling me about the divorce from Luis," he said.

She nodded and proceeded to tell him about the last day of her marriage to Luis, about how he slashed the tires of her car in an attempt to keep her from leaving.

"Understandable. I'd cut your tires too," Gabriel said. He sat next to her with his cake and took a sip of the wine, which was awful. He could feel the furnace heat emanating from her body.

"The cut tires didn't stop me." Instead, she said, she got into the car with infant Ernesto on her lap and, clutching her rosary in one hand, shifting with the other, and steering with her knees, drove away as fast as possible, murmuring her Hail Marys as they wobbled noisily at twenty-five miles an hour all the way down from El Alto to the city, a nine-mile trip.

Gabriel had another sip of the awful wine, which somehow deteriorated with further drinking. He gave up on his cake and handed her the rest. Sitting there beside her, he was aware that he had not felt so fully at ease in the presence of a naked woman in years.

By the time she'd arrived at a service station near the market, she continued, all that was left on the wheels were the most meager scraps of rubber. "I could've recited the entire rosary, it took so long," she said, "and Ernesto was screaming the whole way, shrieking like he knew what was happening. He made the sound I wanted to make."

Once she was done with her story, Gabriel pondered his next question. Should he ask? It seemed so. "Was your husband abusive?"

She didn't answer at first. Gabriel turned to face her again. Up close he could see the splattered area of pale, reverse freckles on her chin. He remembered the lines he'd seen on her forehead earlier, lines formed by years of making expressions like the one she was making then.

Eventually, she said, "People often abuse each other when they are married. It happens. There are degrees, I guess. Regret is important to growth, and growth is very important in a marriage. You should learn from mistakes. He did not seem to learn from his mistakes. Or, he did eventually, but it was too late. I know that he is very kind to his new wife. With her he is a saint. And I like to think that maybe it was me, that maybe I taught him how to be that way."

Listening to this, he understood that, unlike Fiona's sadness, which had molted many times and calcified like a spiny shell, Lenka's was simpler, lighter: it was an aura, a weary air. It radiated like her warmth, and maybe that was why Lenka's was, in the end, a softer pain.

When Gabriel's mother brought him to Chile in 2001 for his grandfather's funeral, she made a point of stopping in Bolivia, she said, because she wanted him to see the *real* South America. Her homeland was too Europeanized for her taste. The trip would be his rite of passage. Other children had bar mitzvahs or first communions; he needed to see "the real South America." She took him on a tour of the shantytowns of El Alto, which were as squalid as promised, but he was not affected in the way she'd hoped. He noticed, yes, that people lived in conditions that hadn't been seen in North America in a century. He saw that they inhabited hovels with no electricity or running water. Families had simply commandeered a small section of land, hastily erected a home, and dug two holes: one for drinking water and one for an outhouse. Unfortunately, both holes plumbed the same water table, which had long been contaminated by a dangerous cocktail of fecal-borne parasites and bacteria. Still, what struck Gabriel most was the place's wildness—its anarchic quality. Chaos indicated a lack of structure, which itself implied freedom. Apart from certain mandatory field trips into the lowest rungs of squalor, he avoided his mother's company in La Paz and traipsed around the city alone. He chatted to locals in Spanish, to foreigners in English.

Growing up in Claremont, that little white dot amid the broad, poor, and largely Chicano Inland Empire, Gabriel rarely spoke Spanish outside of his house. Socially, he was in a complicated position: he looked mostly white but had a Mexican-sounding name. If any of his white classmates or teachers implied that he was Chicano, he was always quick to correct them. Yet among his friends and classmates who knew him reasonably well—these were generally white, lower-middle-class kids—he was the comparatively rich child of one of the more prominent faculty members in their small college town. His house was nicer. His friends' parents watched a lot of television, while his non-TV-watching mother was erudite; the walls of their house were insulated by bookshelves jammed with volumes in various languages.

In Bolivia, he found something else. Bilingual and of indeterminate ethnicity, he darted in and out of clubs, cafés, and hostels on Illampu and Sagárnaga, switching between foreign backpackers and the locals. He was amphibious. He danced salsa and talked trash about gringos one minute, helped cute Australian girls explain themselves to a waiter the next. In the course of three days he fell into bed with three women: a pretty local with a lazy eye, an Italian backpacker six years his senior who didn't shave her armpits, and a frighteningly beautiful Israeli, the daughter of an El Al pilot. It was an unprecedented run for him.

While on the flight back to Miami with his mother, it dawned on him that part of what he'd loved about Bolivia was that he was finally completely outside of the range of the pressures of his murky class position—the compulsion to "succeed." More to the point, everyone seemed outside of its range.

Gabriel's mother didn't know what to make of it all. What a treat that he was smitten by Bolivia, on one hand, and that he was as ardent as she had hoped he would be. But he seemed to love it for all the wrong reasons. "This is not a holiday from reality," she said.

He enthusiastically agreed. (They might as well have been speaking two different languages.) He insisted that what he loved was the feeling of being outside the pressure-inducing illusion that he took for granted in the United States.

She tried to steer the conversation back to the miserable living conditions in Bolivia, but it was no use. He said, "In Providence, I'm surrounded by these overachievers who, for all their politically correct talk, are still just as white and privileged as the assholes who run Bolivia or the U.S. Just as privileged as you and I. You know, we're all living with this preposterous falseness..." and so on. His mother stared at him, alternately hopeful and frustrated by his line.

Bolivia did not have a study-abroad program that Brown would endorse, but Ecuador did. He had filled out his application for the program within a week of returning.

Though he didn't have the words for it yet, he would later realize that what had struck him was not Bolivia itself but what it implied about the United States. That despite being one of the safest and most prosperous countries in human history, the United States was actually a very bizarre place. Elsewhere in the world, the unattainability of great fame and fortune was more readily accepted, and so life was less driven by grandiose fantasies. Elsewhere, people wouldn't tell their children that they could achieve anything, because, of course, they couldn't.

When he returned to Providence from the trip with his mother, Gabriel found his peers' obsession with making it finally *felt* as trite as he had always believed it was.

A semester in Ecuador did nothing to dampen the force of his revelation. He returned, if anything, more bombastic than ever. To his college friend Harlan, he'd said, "It's like Morpheus came along and took me out of the Matrix. Now I'm back inside, but I know it's fake. We're all doing laps in the cooling waters of a giant mirage..." Harlan bristled at the suggestion that he was a drone in the illusion, insisting that he knew it was a mirage as well. In fact, to Harlan, it may have seemed Gabriel was finally figuring out what he, Harlan, had known all along. Gabriel, undaunted, tried to tell him that knowing it and feeling it were different, but that was when Harlan checked out, on the grounds that Gabriel was acting like a patronizing fuckface.

In time, he refined his understanding of the issue. The mechanism for capitalism's perpetual rejuvenation was, he came to believe, built into human nature. Economists called it *utility*. *Utility* had a floating definition, which was approximated by something like "satisfaction," or "joy." At the root of all economic theory stood the assumption that human beings' primary motivation in life was to maximize their *utility*. A simple and apparently irrefutable concept: people want to be pleased, and they do not want to be displeased.

But economists also believed that there was a direct relationship between wealth and utility: the more money a person had, the more utility he had access to. The ratio wasn't one to one. A hundred dollars meant a lot more to a poor Bolivian farmer than to, say, Oprah Winfrey. Still, every single dollar a person had would, in theory, increase his utility. To Gabriel, the correlation was somewhat less straightforward. People like him, for example, might be instilled with an initial desire for money, which, in turn, spawned a secondary desire to be finished with that first desire. People might desire to be done with the desire.

In the United States, where the system flourished unfettered, the average workweek got a little longer every year, and the average person's debt grew a little bigger, his vacation shrank, and, in general, the quantity of his time and energy devoted to the acquisition and spending of money grew steadily, persistently. Which was not to say, Gabriel believed, that capitalism was bad and something else was good, but the frame of the system necessitated an illusion of meaning and order that broke down at the margins, in the most destitute parts of the world.

The stratum that Gabriel had been eyeing in the United States, the one he'd worried about his placement within, was, it turned out, a small section of a small section of an immeasurably large canyon. He was fretting over his position, measured in centimeters, at the upper rim of the Grand Canyon. And now that, by traveling to Bolivia, he'd seen this—the narrowness of his perspective, of everyone's perspective—the taut ambition that had been pulling across his throat since he was born slackened, and he could breathe right, at last, and it felt incredible. For a little while. It didn't last. It couldn't last. He had to deal with the life in front of him, not some theoretical life. So he was pushed, daily, a few inches further from his beatific moment, a little further back into a miasma of worry about "making it." Soon, he was trying to keep pace with everyone else, struggling to suppress a spike of envy when a smarmy acquaintance lined up a megabucks job at Amazon over winter break during their senior year.

Caps flew at graduation, and then Gabriel was in New York writing about international finance for *IBI*. In the morning, he shivered on a subway platform, a large coffee scalding his fingers. During work hours, he occupied a taupe cubicle. In this way, a day occurred. And another. Life proceeded. He noticed that he'd become a sidelines man, a commentator. He met the players, wrote about them. He had lunch with them sometimes too, and he never went for the bill, even though it would have been on his expense account. He liked to watch them pay.

After two years at *IBI* he'd developed a tic of Googling himself almost daily. He sought some low-grade immortality. A sign of his own footprint in the desert everyone was wandering.

Another two years like this in New York and any trace of his revelation from that trip to Bolivia was gone. Whatever he'd escaped in that first trip to Bolivia had caught up to him again and was sitting on him now. And it was heavy. And he was suffocating.

So he sent off his résumé to Calloway Group and prayed—silently, obsessively—that they'd call. He checked his e-mail every five minutes. He checked his cell-phone reception regularly, just in case. At last, on a Thursday morning, he had a message in his in box. It was from someone named Oscar Velazquez and the subject heading read simply *Calloway Group interview*. Sitting there in his cubicle, Gabriel emitted a short joyous screech.

"Everything okay?" someone nearby asked.

"Yeah, yeah," he said and bit his knuckle. He clicked on the message with his free hand.

Lenka left in the middle of the night and then Gabriel finally managed to drift to sleep. His body felt well tenderized when he awoke at seven. Though he had not slept more than a couple of hours, his mind zinged with such energy that when he stepped into the shower that morning he might as well have just freebased a two-carat marquise of methamphetamine. Her body was not skinny. It was powerful, athletic; she had an authoritative bearing.

After washing, he dressed and thought about her, about that body, the square shoulders; the wonderful ass, too grand to find its way comfortably into white-girl clothes—it was an ass that in itself made a good argument for settling down once and for all. When she walked, it swung like the pendulum of a clock in need of winding.

Breakfast was spartan: fresh fruit and a glass of purified water. He passed on the coca tea and the coffee—no need. He pissed. He shaved.

He wore an incandescent yellow tie, a bright blue shirt. They had not used a condom and he had not asked her if she was on birth control, and, thinking about the various dangers he had exposed himself to, he felt dizzy with terror and pleasure, in exactly equal measures.

He went down to the business center. The computer took a long time to power up, but he wasn't impatient.

There was only one e-mail. It was from Priya, who wanted to know what the fuck he was up to, and did he have any new information to give her yet?

Yes, he wrote to her, he did. He said he'd send her a report that afternoon.

One thing he did know was that he and Lenka would make a strange couple. But so did most worthwhile couples. He was who he was, and she was who she was—an oblique but apt statement. She was, more specifically, press attaché to the future president of Bolivia, a single mother, and a woman who lived with the father of her child, that man's new wife, and her own parents. Life was complicated. Without even stepping inside that messy house of hers, he knew that she ruled the roost. She was tougher than Gabriel by a margin, but so were all of the women he had ever cared about. It wasn't that he was flimsy; it was just a somewhat predictable Oedipal event: he fell for women who, like his mother, were sturdier than he was. In fact, it was their very ability to run roughshod over him that he found alluring.

She was energetic in bed. The sex seemed to replenish her, somehow, as if the act were her photosynthesis, daylight to a sprawling kudzu. She bit and she scratched, she screeched and pinched; she kicked his backside with her heel as if he were a steed in need of encouragement. For Fiona, it had been a more straightforward thing, a brisk workout. Lenka put everything into it, body and soul, and expected nothing less in return.

A midmorning drizzle misted the window. Tiny droplets banded together into bigger drops, which succumbed to gravity and occasionally avalanched into rivulets as they approached the sill. Working on his laptop, he scoured the Internet for some agenda he could push on Priya to distract her. If he continued to produce nothing, she would fire him within a week, he thought—maybe less.

A quick tally of his track record since he came down was discouraging. So far, Fiona was the only person who had given him anything useful, so he saw little hope that he'd beat the press to the punch on the identity of the finance minister. He needed something else.

Popping around financial blogs, he found an angle that seemed promising. It was a medium-sized Brazilian natural gas company called Santa Cruz Gas. The company had sprung up in the late 1990s. In the aftermath of the privatization, a little more than half of the Bolivian gas operations had been bought up by Repsol and Petrobras, immense companies based in Spain and Brazil, respectively, but Santa Cruz Gas had a 9 percent stake in the market too. It had been founded by a mining magnate based in Singapore. Created with the hope of drawing fast dollars from international speculators, it went public six months after being incorporated. The gas was pulled across the Bolivian border to be refined and consumed by Brazilians. If Evo seized all the foreign gas operations in Bolivia, as he'd promised to do, the company would be eviscerated.

The stock, which traded on the São Paulo market, had been brought to the NYSE on a scantly traded ADR (ticker: SCZG) that waggled around $9 a share now, down $4 since Fiona had published her article about how Evo was going to win the election. The fate of the company had everything to do with Evo's decision regarding the expropriation of foreign gas.

On the phone with Priya later that day, he said, "I'm looking at Santa Cruz Gas. They have one hundred percent of their fields in Bolivia and one hundred percent of their refinement in Brazil. Expropriation would completely destroy them."

"Are you sure that Evo will expropriate the gas?"

"I don't know yet. That's what I'm trying to figure out."

"Right. I'm going to look at this."

She hung up on him.

Twenty minutes later she called back and said, "Okay, Gabriel, if you find out for certain what Evo's going to do with the gas before anyone else does, I'll double your salary this year."

He inhaled slowly, deeply. He sat down on the side of his bed.

"Really?" he said. He had just been trying to placate her and now she was hurling around ludicrous incentives. And, like any good economist, Gabriel knew there would be no free lunch, particularly with someone as astute as Priya.

"People are speculating on Bolivian gas?" he said.

"In a way." She didn't elaborate. He had to assume that she had looked into it and found that Santa Cruz was, in fact, an ideal candidate for speculation. It was that, or it was something else, probably something that he did not, or could not, fathom, some complex mathematical model generated by Paul that hinged on the outcome of Bolivian gas. There were mysteries in the fund's mathematics that Gabriel, despite his training in economics and his experience as a financial reporter, could not begin to grasp.

"You'll double my salary?" he said.

"Yes, if you get it before anyone else does. A full year's wage delivered in January."

"Okay then, um—" He tried to collect himself, think of the best way to handle the situation. It sounded bad. He didn't like the way the potential upside had doubled so quickly. It just didn't bode well for the potential downside.

When he didn't say anything else, she cleared her throat and said, "So, I want an update soon." And then she hung up on him again.

# 5

# Election

*Sunday and Monday, December 18 and 19, 2005*

THE ELECTION TOOK PLACE exactly one week before Christmas, on a gusty Sunday. Clouds bunched up, appropriately dramatic, and scrolled across the sky too quickly. Rain occasionally splattered the window, and the sun emerged once in a while to ignite the drops clinging to the glass. By the time the voting booths opened, Evo's victory was beyond a given. The press gathered at Hotel Presidente to report on the great anticlimax. Potbellied cameramen in cargo pants and baseball caps consulted quietly with unshaven sound engineers, while comely reporters in heavy coats of matte makeup glowed nearby, scanning notes beneath painfully bright lights and tilting their satellite-dish-sized umbrellas into the wind. Meanwhile, small clusters of men with machine guns and full riot gear patrolled downtown, looking for signs of unrest. Some police loitered briefly on the corner by the Casa Cultura, beneath Gabriel's window, eating pink ice cream cones and chatting among themselves. An atmosphere both surreal and abrasively real, almost mundane, pervaded. Still, the city's mood, if such a thing could truly be identified, was hopeful, even joyful.

In Bolivia, voting was compulsory but—in what must have been a practical joke played on the electorate by the elected—driving was illegal on Election Day. So the entire country was out on foot, walking around and searching for their polling places. Absent the automotive section of the orchestra below his window, a very different tune emerged from the city, Gabriel found. Voices, separated from their snarlier accompaniment, came through much clearer. Listening to it upstairs, he noticed it sounded like a stadium just as the team took to the field.

He kept his television on a local channel all day, the volume off. The results came in resoundingly in Evo's favor. At one point, Gabriel turned the volume up and flipped through some channels. Although it had been obvious that Evo was going to win for more than a week, the reporters seemed unable to hide their lingering disbelief. All of them at some point reminded their viewers that Bolivia, which had been an independent republic since 1825 and was over 65 percent indigenous, had never elected an indigenous president.

At dusk, Gabriel watched from his window as the foreign cameramen wandered the streets, collecting stock footage that could be used in future broadcasts about "the situation in Bolivia," whatever that might be, while the rest of their crews got down to drinking Pisco Sours de Señorita Fiona, as they were now officially called, at the Lookout.

For his part, Gabriel stayed in his room, looking on from his window. He had wearied of the press corps in the past two weeks and was spending less time at the Lookout, much more time with Lenka. He could see the lights of the Lookout from his room, could see how much smoke was up there, and from that smoke he estimated that the bar was as crowded as he'd ever seen it. Fiona had probably returned from Lima; she'd be up there leading the charge. He considered going over, but quickly decided against it. He hoped Lenka would come around later, once the hullabaloo died down. They could eat room service, screw, and talk about the day.

In the two and a half weeks since they'd first slept together they had seen each other every night. They'd found a routine. He didn't reveal to her the details of Priya's challenge, but he did mention more than once that he was trying to find out more specific information about Evo's plans for the gas industry. She didn't offer anything, but that made sense to him. He believed that if his situation became dire enough, she would give him something—enough to enable him to keep his job.

Priya, fortunately, had mostly kept her distance since he'd unveiled his investigation into Santa Cruz Gas. According to Paul's calculations, the region's gas industry was pricing in a 60 percent chance that Evo would expropriate foreign gas outright, but Santa Cruz's price was buoyant, reflecting something closer to a 50 percent chance of expropriation. Paul had run the numbers in different ways and hadn't been able to figure out a cause for the discrepancy. It was precisely for situations like this that they had hired Gabriel. The math didn't make sense, so the solution had to be in a human element that they couldn't see from Weehawken.

By seven o'clock, Plaza San Francisco was packed, and the windows of the Lookout were fogged up. Gabriel glanced at the television and saw Evo speaking in front of a lectern in a square in El Alto. He was garlanded in coca leaves and flowers, wearing a black collarless jacket. Lenka was there too, in the background under bright sodium lights. It was windy in El Alto, and she squinted at the back of her boss's head, then glanced around at the crowd as her hair flapped in the gusts. She had recently applied her makeup and looked magnificent. She tried pulling strands of hair out of her eyes and tucking them behind her ears, but it was no good. Evo's microphone picked up the blaring wind in the pauses between his words. It sounded like a bonfire.

Gabriel waited until the speech was over before he called her cell phone and left a message. She called him back half an hour later.

The president-elect and his entourage had already made it back to MAS's downtown office. They were celebrating their victory. She had sneaked off to call him. He asked her how she felt and she mumbled about it feeling like a dream. Evo was, she said, considering a world tour for the two weeks leading up to his inauguration, and she had to look into where he would go and what he would do once there. It would take her all night and she couldn't get away.

Gabriel told her he was happy for her. He asked if he could see her the next day.

"Yes, I have the morning off," she said. "We skipped Mass today. So we are all going at nine tomorrow. I'll call you after I'm done."

"Good." In the background, he could hear people's voices. He could hear laughter and he could hear music. "You should go," he said.

"I have to. I'm sorry. I'll call you tomorrow."

In most branches of the foreign service, the rule was that no assignment abroad should last more than three years. The reason: after three years in a country, people ran the risk of going native. They developed a kind of Stockholm syndrome, whereby they began to care more about the welfare of their host country than of those who'd sent them there. The paradox of Gabriel's job was that to do it well he needed to remain distant enough to keep his allegiances clear, but he also had to keep his ear to the ground. Though not confused about his mission, Gabriel found that being with Lenka put him (problematically) closer to the ground, so to speak.

She usually came around to the hotel after dinner. She never stayed all night, but sometimes she was there until that moment in the predawn when the sun rose from an unseen horizon and was still hidden behind the mountains, illuminating the milky clouds from beneath.

Regarding the state of his career, Gabriel guessed he had two weeks left in Bolivia before Priya pulled the plug. He had whetted her appetite too much to give her nothing. At a minimum, he needed to be the first person to get the name of the next finance minister. His plan was to keep following Santa Cruz Gas, and if he seemed to be getting no closer, he would redirect his focus and beg Lenka for the finance minister's name. She would doubtless give him that much, if it came to it, even though to do so could endanger her career. (If Evo found out that she had helped the agent of a hedge fund, he'd almost certainly fire her.)

In the meantime, Gabriel had continued compiling his dossier on Santa Cruz. It traded on the São Paulo exchange and had, from what he could tell, almost no liquid assets. All of its liabilities were held by subsidiaries of the Odessa Corporation, a mining company based in Singapore. The stock was volatile, lightly traded, owned by no major financial institutions, and it had regular spikes of short interest, suggesting that a few vultures were circling.

It had been founded by a creepy Canadian billionaire named Lloyd Pingree, now the CEO of Odessa. Pingree, one of the shadier figures in what was perhaps the world's shadiest legal industry — mining — had brought together a plethora of wealthy Brazilian investors in Santa Cruz Gas. These board members tended to have connections to Brazilian president Luiz Inácio Lula, who was, in turn, friendly with the leftist wing within Bolivia. Pingree's hope had doubtlessly been that these powerful board members would step in to defend their investments if the deal was queered by shifting political circumstances in Bolivia. That was probably the reason for the unnatural buoyancy of the stock's price.

He'd looked into it and found that while Odessa and Pingree had done well in Santa Cruz's IPO in 2002, they hadn't done *that* well. Odessa still held a majority ownership, with 55 percent of the stock, about $120 million. For Pingree, $120 million would be just one of many chips on his global roulette table. Still, if things went well, Santa Cruz could conceivably generate the kinds of gains that would push him another ten or twenty steps up the *Forbes* annual "500 Richest People in the World" list, on which he had so far languished in the mid-400s.

The day after the election, Gabriel ate breakfast by himself in Gloria's cafeteria, then went upstairs and took notes for a meeting he had the following day with Foster Nathanial Garnett, a junior diplomat from the U.S. embassy. Foster Garnett had been on assignment in Bolivia for two and a half years and would soon be leaving. From what Gabriel could tell, Garnett was in no danger of going native: in a State Department photo, he wore his hair parted and kept the corners of his lips turned down in a smarmy salesman's grin. He looked like an affable frat boy who was excited, if a little surprised, to find himself in such a serious job. Gabriel understood completely. Gabriel had picked Foster to interview not because of any potential for camaraderie but because he knew that departing diplomats had a tendency to talk a little more freely. They were thinking about their next assignments, usually, and feeling a little philosophical about the present ones.

He was still formulating questions when Lenka called. Evo's staff had all taken the day off, and she was going Christmas shopping and wanted to know if he would join her.

"You can just come up to my room and get me," he said.

"No sex, Gabriel," she said, reading his mind.

He laughed.

"You come downstairs."

A new oversize plastic nativity scene greeted Gabriel in Hotel Gloria's lobby, its blinking colorful lights strung about chaotically. Some sort of mini-conflagration—no doubt courtesy of one of those precarious lights—had left a droopy blackened hole in Joseph's shoulder. A long strand of scraggly gold tinsel wreathed the front desk, and Gabriel grinned, seeing it, because it reminded him of the chintzy old decorations his mother used to haul out every year at Christmas. There was no angel on top of their tree in Claremont, but it did have a star, which his mother claimed to have heisted from the cathedral in Santiago where Pinochet used to worship. "It was the last thing I did before I left the country," she said, often enough that Gabriel was prepared to believe her.

Lenka arrived in the lobby and Gabriel kissed her hello on each cheek, then again on the mouth. She slapped him on the ass, hooked her arm under his, and they were off.

They crossed Mariscal Santa Cruz and ascended Sagárnaga to the Witches' Market, where tourists were supposed to buy postcards, alpaca scarves, fridge magnets, and what was without doubt Bolivia's oddest tchotchke: dried llama fetuses. According to a still-popular tradition in Bolivian witchcraft, if a person buried a llama fetus under the foundation of his house, he'd have good fortune while he lived there.

Once above the Witches' Market at the outskirts of the much larger

Black Market, where locals did their shopping, Gabriel and Lenka paused to catch their breath.

"Ready when you are," he managed to gasp.

She tried to laugh but wasn't quite able, so she just shook her head breathlessly. Once she'd recovered, a few minutes later, she led the way down a side street. They walked slowly, surveying goods. Potatoes, native to the region, were ubiquitous. Tiny perfectly spherical ones, like dirty marbles, filled a basket next to a pile of knobby fingerlings streaked with fuchsia. The *chuño*, freeze-dried by exposure on the altiplano and then periodically trampled by barefoot Aymara women, looked like a cross between a morel and dried goat shit. Pretty pyramids of *tuntas* — expensive alabaster potatoes that spent weeks immersed in the icy runoff from melting glaciers before being gently dried in the alpine breeze — caught the eye from a block away.

In the next street, flies buzzed around a row of pungent butcher stalls, where *cabezas*, lamb's heads, a local delicacy, were invariably given the premium spot, from which they could gaze down from hollow sockets at passersby. On that block, mangy street dogs sloped to and fro, glancing sideways at stacks of gutted river fish, which ranged in dimensions from minnowy to a cricket-bat-sized carp with teary, bloodshot eyes. All around, the streets were littered with a carnival-colored assortment of tiny plastic bags that had somehow loosed themselves and were running amok on the asphalt, or just drifting sleepily in the breeze.

She stopped at a dried-goods vendor. Twenty or so heavy burlap sacks ringed the periphery of the narrow store. Lenka filled a flimsy yellow plastic bag with dried fava beans, and a larger one with coca leaves.

While the woman weighed and tallied her *bolsitas*, Lenka turned and asked Gabriel if he had plans for Christmas Day.

He said he did not.

"You should come to our house."

"Well, I wouldn't want to impose."

"Don't be stupid. I ask you to come because I want it. If you don't want to, just say so."

Gabriel nodded. "Well, if you put it that way."

She grabbed his hand and kissed it. It was settled; he'd spend Christmas Day with Lenka and her family, and it might be awkward, but so would spending Christmas alone in his hotel room or, worse, with whichever orphaned foreign journalists were at the Lookout. They walked on and Lenka reassured him that it was no big deal. The major holiday party in Bolivia was on Christmas Eve. He'd be one of sixty or so non–family members, she said.

Lenka had to buy a suckling pig. That was her main mission that day. The problem was that everyone in La Paz who wanted to have a traditional Bolivian Christmas Eve dinner also had to buy a suckling pig. The pork butcher had carcasses stacked up as high as Gabriel's shoulder. The pigs were all facing the same direction, making a wall of floppy pink ears, smashed snouts, and fleshy eyelids pinched shut. A few of the pigs had plump violet tongues protruding. Their pink skin looked grotesquely human. Blood pooled between the cobblestones and ran down the street for half a block.

Across the street from the butcher a living crèche filled an open storefront, complete with a real lamb, costumed people, and an actual newborn. The infant nursed at the Virgin Mary's breast while a few dozen pedestrians gawked, whispering among themselves. A sign said that the display had been organized by the Maria Santa orphanage. Gabriel didn't know what to make of it. He tried to read the other onlookers, but he got nothing from them. Lenka was busy vying for the attention of the butcher.

Once she had paid for her pig, the butcher wrapped it in plastic, cinched the plastic at the top so that the blood would not spill, and handed it to Gabriel.

Gabriel slung it over his shoulder and they set off for her car, which was parked, unfortunately, all the way back at Hotel Gloria, half a mile down the steep hill.

By the time they had made it to the bottom of Sagárnaga, he was perspiring, panting, and doing everything in his power to avoid letting his distress show.

"Do you want me to carry it for a while?" she said.

He wiped the sweat from his forehead and switched the pig to the other shoulder. "No, I've got it." He wasn't going to make her carry the pig.

At her car, he put the pig on the back seat and got in the front.

They said very little as she drove through the narrow streets. Her entire family would have returned after their Monday-morning Mass. They'd all be there, pretending it was Sunday, dressed to the nines, eating *changa de pollo*. Officially, he would be there to help carry the pig, but she'd clearly engineered the situation so that she could show him around to her family and collect reviews.

"What about Luis?" he said as they edged through stop-and-go traffic. Her ex-husband would also be at the house.

"What do you mean?"

"Is there going to be some testosterone thing? Muscle flexing and so on?"

"That's not for you? You are not a muscle person, is that right?"

"Well, I was an only child, so I never had that early training in fisticuffs. Is Luis macho?"

"Luis?" This was a hoot. "Of course he's fucking macho: he's *Bolivian!*"

"Well, if it looks like he's going to clock me, I'm going to deck him with the pig. I just want to be clear with you about that."

"Be my guest, please. I'd *love* it."

She took out her phone, called the house, and asked her mother if she had cleared enough space in the refrigerator for the pig yet. A pause. "Because we're almost there!" she said. She hung up, plonked the phone down onto the floor.

It must have been disorienting to everyone in that house when Lenka's career took such a hard turn into the limelight. Six months earlier she had started working for an outlying candidate; now he was not only the president-elect but one of the most talked-about public figures on the continent. And she was still there beside him, managing his newly outsize image.

They parked directly in front of the house in San Pedro. With the pig slung over his shoulder, he followed her to the door, into the claustrophobia-inducing foyer. Low-ceilinged rooms and hallways, devoid of windows or any decorations, ran off in every direction like a plaster dungeon that had been decorated in the mid-1970s. Sickly light seeped from tired fixtures in the ceiling. Cheap parquet hardwood tiles covered the floor throughout, except for the linoleum kitchen at the far end of the hallway. The house was redolent of simmering chicken stock and potatoes, old rags. Queerly small icons of saints and of the Virgin Mary dangled from nails planted in the hallway walls. Gabriel, taking it all in as swiftly as possible, followed her through to the capacious kitchen. On the far side, through another doorway, the family were in a massive sitting room, chatting animatedly, laughing, and drinking tea, while children were scattered on the floor playing with toy cars, and the men pretended not to stare at a soccer game on a small television in the corner.

In the kitchen, a robust woman with steel-wool hair and a grape-colored polyester dress knelt in front of the refrigerator, digging around. In that position, her ass stretched the threads in the seam almost to the breaking point. Cartons of milk and packages of cheese, along with one of the refrigerator's wire shelves and a number of cellophane bags of vegetables, littered the floor around her. On the old white stove a huge battered vat of chicken soup bubbled gently.

"Damn it, you're here already?" the woman huffed, turning around. This was Lenka's mother, Gabriel supposed. Lenka had told him that her name was Mirabel. There was only a passing family resemblance. The woman had a face like a tuber. Her eyes were wet flakes of siltstone.

Mirabel shuffled out of the way and Gabriel attempted to cram the piglet into the refrigerator. It was too long bodied, though, and the spine was too stiff to bend. The three of them stood back, surveying the situation: food scattered in front of the gaping refrigerator, its door propped open by the stiff pig wrapped in heavy plastic, its two dainty-hoofed feet dangling out. Dark brown blood dribbled through the cinched end of the plastic onto the yellow linoleum.

"What an impressive swine!" said a man in a brassy baritone that sounded as if he were speaking through a trombone. This was Luis, Gabriel knew.

Gabriel turned around and found a stocky battler, with a scar from where he'd had a harelip crudely sewn up. Though he was as thick and brutish as an Incan foot soldier, his eyes had a bright and even playful twinkle as he squinted at Gabriel. Despite the burliness, the man's resemblance to Ernesto was evident, particularly in his conspiratorial glint. He squeezed Gabriel's hand hard and shook it once, firmly. "A pleasure!" The voice was uncanny. The depth surpassed something that would seem manly and came off almost inhuman; it reminded Gabriel of the groaning bison he'd heard at Yellowstone when his mother took him there as a child.

The two men had barely broached the niceties when Ernesto materialized. Luis picked him up, kissed him, and asked if he knew Gabriel. Ernesto nodded: "Yes, Gabriel is a friend of my *mami*."

Luis chuckled and, much to Gabriel's surprise, handed over the boy, who seemed too old to be passed around like that.

Gabriel had seen Ernesto several times since their first meeting in Plaza Murillo, mainly at Pollo Copacabana for fried chicken after school, but he had never held him. He didn't quite know what to do with him now and found himself gripping Ernesto by the rib cage. He felt embarrassed, and was further embarrassed by the fact that he was embarrassed—as only a gringo would be—but Ernesto and Luis didn't seem to notice. Ernesto just slung an arm around Gabriel's neck. He was heavy too, and Gabriel realized he couldn't hold him like that for long. He hoisted him up to get a better grip and said, "How are you, kid?"

Ernesto beamed and pointed at his own beaming face, and Gabriel kissed him on the cheek and then plopped him down on the ground. He looked back at Luis, who patted Gabriel on the shoulder firmly, winked. He indicated Lenka with his ogre's chin—she was bent over the refrigerator with her mother now—and whispered, "Good luck. She's fucking insane."

"Oh?" Gabriel said.

Lenka glanced over her shoulder at her ex-husband. "What'd you say?"

"Nothing!" Luis replied, and winked at Gabriel again. The madness of such a union, that they had ever believed that they were well suited for each other, required a special kind of shared craziness.

Luis took two steps over to the refrigerator, brushed his ex-wife aside, reached in, and pulled the pig out by the hooves. "I should break its spine," he suggested helpfully, addressing his former mother-in-law. "If I do that, it will fit, right?"

"How?" Mirabel said.

He ripped open the plastic and pulled the pig out, set its damp body down on the nearby kitchen table, dropped the bloodied plastic onto the floor, turned, and yanked open a thin metal drawer nearby. He snatched up a rusty claw hammer from a mess of metal tools inside, shoved the drawer closed.

"Here," he said. "I'll break it here." He tapped the pig once in the center of the spine, and then swung hard and fast. A direct hit! The bone cracked. There was a small dent in the flesh.

He hit it again, just as hard. This time the hammer left a deep imprint slightly beside the spinal column, but close enough that the outer edges of the spine were clearly visible through the stretched skin. He hit it again, even harder. This one landed directly on the spine. The skin split, exposing a mixture of gristle and crushed bone, a crunchy and gelatinous substance like half-frozen yogurt at the back of the refrigerator.

"That's it," Luis said. He put the greasy-tipped hammer down on the table.

Clutching both front quarters with one hand and both hindquarters with the other, he lifted the carcass and pulled the two sides together until the remaining bone fragments in the spine buckled and cracked noisily. He stopped only when the pig was completely doubled over. The gash at its back had split another inch on either side, exposing tender flesh, pink as the inside of a baby's mouth. Once the pig's snout was lodged neatly between its stiff hindquarters, he brought the animal back to the refrigerator, pushed it in, and swung the door shut.

Mirabel applauded and said, "Very good, Luis!"

"That's impressive," Gabriel said, because it was impressive.

Lenka shot Gabriel a short, dissatisfied look. "Come. I want you to meet the rest," she said and led the way into the next room, while Luis and Mirabel remained behind to clean up the mess.

There, Gabriel met the rest of the brood. They were evenly distributed across the generations: gurgling toddler to milky-eyed patriarch who couldn't manage to stand up in greeting; their coloring likewise ran a broad spectrum, so broad, in fact, that Gabriel wasn't entirely sure they were all related. In greeting him, each of the men stood and shook his hand, gave a warm welcome, and managed to abstain from allowing the match on the television to pull his gaze away. A little while after, everyone settled back down and resumed watching the match and talking among themselves. Gabriel and Lenka were sitting at the back of the room near a scrawny elderly lady named Leti, who instantly started rambling about her deceased husband, an inventor, who she claimed had come up with the blueprints for a perpetual-motion machine but had been unable to locate the funding to make it a reality. "Then he died," she said and patted Gabriel on the knee, as if to say: *Do yourself a favor and try not to die before you finish building your invention.*

He glanced at Lenka questioningly, but she just smiled back at him lovingly.

A little later her mother entered, griping about Luis's treatment of the pig. Not satisfied with their earlier introduction, she beckoned Gabriel to his feet again and kissed his cheek. Then she clutched his shoulders and gazed at him appraisingly for a moment. She sighed and turned to Lenka, her hands still on his shoulders, and said, "Why didn't you say that he was so pretty?"

Everyone laughed at that. Gabriel blushed and shook his head.

Lenka stood up and put an arm around his shoulders. "Stop," she said to the assembled, "he's shy — don't make him blush!"

Leti cleared her throat and said, "But he looks *even prettier* when he blushes!"

That sent them into hysterics. Gabriel shook his head again, laughing, then plopped back down in his seat, waving them all away.

He looked up in time to see Luis swagger in from the kitchen and say, "What is this?"

"Luis," Gabriel said, "can you do that trick with the hammer on people too?"

And the room went wild.

In his hotel room at Gloria that night, he and Lenka recalled the meeting in detail. She assured him that they had adored him, and he told her it was mutual.

They ate two baked trout from Lake Titicaca with white rice and the kind of neatly cubed vegetables often found in TV dinners. This was room service from Gloria. They had yet another bottle of cheap Bolivian white wine. The ritual of ordering and eating room service had become a major part of their relationship already. They knew the menu by heart. The room service, like the room itself, was a manifestation of their relationship's organizing principle. Being at her house today together, however briefly, had been a violation of that principle. Apart from a few odd hours with Ernesto once in a while, they spent no time together with other people. What they had, instead, was a kind of nocturnal hermitage in Gabriel's room. By day, their lives were blindingly public and relentlessly social. She was on the phone for hours, talking with scores of people; her meetings were stacked up tidily, constructed of ten-minute increments. Gabriel was out in the city, making the rounds, meeting political figures and bureaucrats in their offices, reporters at cafés; he was still trying to make use of his crummy freelance-journalist cover. It was, for both of them, a brutally public existence. They spent most of their days talking to strangers, navigating a familiar series of motivations. For both of them, it was new, and it was alienating. For Gabriel, it was all the more acute because he was so far from his country and from everyone he knew, and was further isolated by his moat of lies. Lenka felt to him like a refuge from all that.

She didn't have it much better, he could see, having been blindsided by her boss's abrupt elevation; she was suddenly spokesperson for the biggest celebrity the country had had in a generation. And after a long day, she was supposed to go back to her overcrowded house and play normal. Now that he had seen the inside of it, Gabriel knew why she was eager to spend her nights away.

Together, they had a sanctuary in his room. She arrived usually just after the cars and pedestrians below Gabriel's room had shut up. They would lie side by side in silence in the dark and for a while the pressures of the day receded. This had been a sudden, swift vertical climb for them. They were both, in their own ways, blasting toward the stratosphere, far above their expected orbits. So they understood each other's situation in a uniquely personal way. And, like any good love affair, it felt as if they were in on some intimate experience together that no one else could understand. There was them, and then there was everyone else in the world. They were both floating in the miraculous, if airless, stratosphere, far above everything and everyone they had ever known. Up there, they had only each other.

After the waiter dropped off their trout and the bottle of wine that Monday night, he lingered by the door. He was youngish, wore a bowl cut, like Ernesto. Nametag: *Alejo*. Alejo had a severe countenance, the harsh and gallant expression of a teenager who supports himself through hard work and has done so for some time. He lingered, scowling at them, wanting to say something but too shy to speak.

"Is there something else?" Gabriel said.

"I saw you on television," Alejo blurted. He was addressing Lenka.

"Did you?" she said.

"You were with Evo on the stage yesterday."

"That's right."

He nodded. "Tell him congratulations for me, please."

"I will," she said.

Alejo nodded again, staring at the carpet, and then, without another word, he left.

Gabriel set the tray down on the table and leaned over. "I think he likes you." She nodded, kissed Gabriel on the forehead. "I saw you too, you know," he added.

"Really? What did you think?"

"The same thing he thought, I suppose."

"Really, and what's that?"

"'I wonder what she's wearing under that skirt.'"

She laughed and punched him hard in the shoulder. She shoved him onto the bed. "Here," she said as she straddled him, "I'll show you."

Later, with the bones and skins of their trout strewn on their plates, they made love a second time. The first time had been furious, but the second time, a couple of hours later, it was softer, slower. Gabriel was sore already. The pain helped him focus, and he found that he actually hoped the pain would linger, because he loved the moment enough to want to capture it and sear it into his mind.

Approaching climax, he paused and kissed her on the eyelid, and she whispered into his ear, "*Te quiero,* Gabriel."

"*Te quiero tambien,*" he replied.

And it occurred to him then that maybe they really did love each other. If not, they could always try to love each other. He could start going to church with her. She could overlook the chasms between them. She could try to overlook his hunger as well, and its attendant vices, namely his comfortable way with deceit. They could work at seeing each other in a better light. And maybe that was, after all, what loving another person meant. Love required, above all else, a capacity for hope, some faith that the future would—given enough effort—improve upon the present. In any case, staying together for the rest of their lives couldn't be harder than spending the rest of their lives alone. Which might have seemed a callous thought on another night, but with the two of them in his room—lost in the cold and dark of their extracelestial orbits and temporarily out from under the burdens of their ambitions — it felt sincere, even sweet. But then, when the virgin light started to glow above the eastern peaks of the Andes once again, the voyage was already ending. They were falling back through the atmosphere, back down to the ground to rejoin the rest of the world.

He was still awake when she got up and dressed. He didn't move. He listened as she wrote a note in the bathroom, set it down on his laptop, which lay clamshelled on the desk. She bent down and kissed him on the forehead. Her lips lingered for a tiny extra moment, an aching moment, and in that moment he knew that she felt for him what he felt for her.

When she left, he let himself fall asleep.

He awoke a few hours later, at eight. He brushed his teeth, showered, got dressed. He picked up her note, written on Hotel Gloria stationery. It read:

> *The next finance minister of Bolivia will be Luis Alberto Arce Catacora. Good luck with that!*
>
> *And ... burn this note, please.*
>
> *XO — L.V.*

He was stunned, first, then struck with powerful relief. But of course this was merely an opportunity to survive, if it came to that.

If he played this well, it could boost Priya's estimation of him, but it wasn't the kind of thing that she could turn into money, so it wasn't going to win the day for him. His best hope, as he saw it, was to track down this Luis Arce Catacora and interview him under seemingly innocuous circumstances — a young freelance reporter talking to a _____ (whatever Catacora's current job happened to be). Under that innocent premise, Gabriel might be able to cajole Catacora into hinting at the administration's real position on the natural gas question and, possibly, on Santa Cruz Gas in particular. It was a solid opportunity. His best lead so far. No officials wanted to talk to Gabriel, but Catacora wasn't an official yet.

Still in his pajamas, he grabbed his laptop and went out to the elevator. Holding his open laptop with one hand, he touched the button.

He rode down to the business center on the second floor and entered. It was, fortunately, empty.

While the computer searched for the wireless connection, he decided that he wouldn't tell Priya yet. For one thing, he didn't want to burn Lenka by just blabbing about her leak right away. He should use it only in the event of an emergency, and then he would have to use it in such a way that it wouldn't get back to Evo. It had to be handled carefully.

Still, there would be no harm in planting a seed of interest in Priya's mind now. Although Priya had claimed that she wanted valuable information, when he had handed her the exclusive that Evo was set to win the election, she hadn't been as impressed as she should have been. So he needed to cultivate within her the desire for something specific, and only once the desire had achieved the correct ardor would he indulge her appetite.

After his computer had connected to the hotel's server, he wrote Priya a short e-mail:

---

TO: priya_singh@calloway.net
FROM: gabo_de_boya@yahoo.com
SUBJECT: evo's economic team

I might be able to find out the name of one of Evo's picks for his economic team in the coming days. If so, I'm hoping to meet with that person before anyone else does and glean something about the future administration's intentions regarding natural gas.

In the meantime, I continue my research into Santa Cruz.

—Gabriel

---

After he'd sent the e-mail, he Googled the name Luis Alberto Arce Catacora.

Catacora was a professor of economics at Bolivia's largest university, Universidad Mayor de San Andrés. He worked in the Central Bank of Bolivia in the 1980s but had been in academia for the past sixteen years. He was an ideal target; an academic might even be flattered to be interviewed by a freelance reporter.

Gabriel sat back, picked up his phone, and dialed the university.

A receptionist answered.

"Can you put me through to Professor Luis Alberto Arce Catacora?" he said.

The phone rang five times before the answering machine picked up. After the beep, Gabriel spoke, in Spanish. "Hello, Professor Catacora, my name is Gabriel Francisco de Boya, and I am a freelance journalist. I'm writing about Bolivia's changing economic situation, and I would love to talk to you." He gave his room number at the Hotel Gloria, along with his phone number.

Gabriel checked his e-mail. No reply yet from Priya. Then he opened his E-Trade account. The markets weren't open yet, but he checked the account anyway. It was a funny tic. Like opening the refrigerator to check that a new bottle of champagne was still there.

Since he had started working at Calloway, Gabriel, who had been living paycheck to paycheck before, had socked away $54,000 in the stock market. His initial deposit of $24,000 had all gone into a risky double-leveraged Latin American fund. If Latin American stocks had a bad day, Gabriel had twice as bad a day, and if Latin American stocks had a good day, he had twice as good a day. So far, he was up 12 percent on that buy.

He checked the account constantly. He stared at the balance as it fluctuated during trading hours, refreshing every few minutes when he was at his computer. He did some light research, but it wasn't really significant. Really, he didn't *do* anything. He rarely bought or sold shares. He just stared at the account. On days when his holdings grew by more than 2 percent he felt awash with euphoria and confidence. On days when it sank, he was crestfallen. It wasn't that much money, really. The account had grown by about $5,000 so far. It was worth $59,422 when the market opened that morning. At her base salary, reportedly $9 million, Priya made more than half that when she showed up for work. On the whole, Gabriel's account grew more than it shrank, but that was beside the point. The issue was how much he *cared* about the account. What, precisely, was he seeking when he refreshed his browser again and again on an inactive trading day? Other people were addicted to gambling, work, sex, but Gabriel was mesmerized by the fluctuations in his brokerage account. It was trite and it was a waste of time and yet somehow Gabriel suspected that he was not alone in this.

In Theravada Buddhism, the cause of all human suffering is identified, very succinctly, as *craving*. *Tanha*, it's called, and it gives rise to the parasitic defilements of greed, hatred, and delusion. But the root of our problem, the cause of all human misery, is *tanha*: our insatiable craving for *more*. Economists have come to a similar judgment of the human condition, although they don't levy any value judgments. To them, it simply is.

Still, the capitalist paradigm is predicated on an acceptance, if not a passionate embrace, of that craving. When Gabriel first went to Bolivia, young and callow, he wrote in his Moleskine, "The American dream has turned out to be just that: a *dream*. It is an impossible fantasy." How revelatory it felt! It had seemed sublime and easy, as if the diagnosis were also the cure.

After ten minutes gawking at his E-Trade account, Gabriel checked his e-mail again — still nothing from Priya. Then he resumed researching Santa Cruz Gas and its founder, Lloyd Pingree, who turned out, ironically enough, to be a devout Buddhist. While a student at Berkeley in the 1970s, Pingree had been convicted of selling marijuana. He dropped out of college to spend some time as a Buddhist monk in the Himalayas. He eventually moved back to Canada and began trading penny stocks on the mineral exchange in Vancouver, where he acquired for almost nothing a supposedly defunct gold mine that turned out to be bloated with gold. He used the capital to pole-vault into further ventures, including one at the Blind Elk mine in Wyoming. There, one of his cyanide-heap leaching pits seeped into local waters. By the time the EPA shut down the mine, in 1991, the damage was done. Blind Elk was declared one of the worst environmental disasters in American history. Pingree picked up the nickname Leachy Lloyd, and the EPA more or less chased him out of the United States.

There was, of course, no shortage of opportunities abroad. He made Singapore his new base. By the mid-1990s he was owner of the world's most prolific nickel mine, located in Canada. Directly or indirectly he had major excavations under way on every continent on the planet except Antarctica, which was protected, for the time being, by a shield of glacial ice.

A recent article pictured Pingree, like some over-the-top supervillain in a James Bond movie, in his personal helicopter hovering above a vast crater in Inner Mongolia, surveying a gash he'd recently cleaved into the planet. This despite the fact that a couple of decades before he'd been a few hundred miles away, clad in saffron robes, barefoot, his pale head shorn, begging door to door for alms. These days, up there in his helicopter, the man who still identified himself as a Buddhist gazed at the world laid out beneath him and pondered his options.

# 6

# Altitude Sickness

*Tuesday, December 20, 2005*

LUIS ALBERTO ARCE CATACORA was smallish, with tiny hands that he folded across a yellow legal pad on his desk. His wedding ring was scrawny and silver; his fingers effete. He looked reptilian — not metaphorically, or pejoratively, but literally lizardlike: angular features, broad mouth, eyes set far apart, a nose that did not protrude but simply seemed a part of his face's overall arrowhead structure. He wore a pale gray suit with a black shirt, oval eyeglasses. Gabriel didn't have to look under the desk to know he was wearing black loafers with tassels. His office, on the third floor of the Monoblock, was boxy and petite, proportionate to the man, really. A narrow window offered a view of some stained rooftops. It was midmorning. The office reeked of stale coffee and a heavy mélange of microwaved leftovers.

Catacora said, "Evo is the first rebel who stands a chance of survival here. This is, historically, an unfriendly place for rebels." Catacora was speaking in English, although Gabriel had initiated the conversation in Spanish. Catacora was understandably proud of his English. According to Gabriel's research, Catacora had earned his master's at the University of Warwick, in England; he must have been fluent when he matriculated.

"Great rebels come here to die," Catacora went on. "In 1781, Tupac Katari's heart was ripped from his chest and burned in a square up in El Alto. In 1908, Butch Cassidy and the Sundance Kid were shot to pieces near the salt flats in the south. Che Guevara was captured and executed, also in the south, in the 1960s. And those are just the very famous ones. We've had dozens of martyrs and rebels killed here in the past hundred years. The most famous Bolivian novelist, an outspoken dissenter named Marcelo Quiroga Santa Cruz, was tortured and killed by Meza in the 1980s. They incinerated his corpse in a tin smelter near my brother's house."

"And Evo is different how?" Gabriel was trying to move it along. He had stopped in on his way down to interview the diplomat Foster Garnett. Catacora's rhetorical style reminded Gabriel of his mother's. Incredibly digressive, he killed time skillfully, methodically, with his words. Gabriel had been there half an hour and had enjoyed a very compelling survey of twentieth-century Bolivian history laid out in baroque megaparagraphs, but he had nothing remotely useful to show for his time. And his time was running out. He was supposed to meet Foster at the Tennis Club in ten minutes.

"Well, Evo is going to be in charge, for one thing," Catacora said. "None of the others were actually in a position of power. Evo will be president. Despite our rich tradition of rebellion, we have never managed to give a rebel real power. They have set fire to the presidential palace many times, but they have never inhabited the place."

"Isn't that just the thing? I mean, in the last ten years South America has elected its share of leftist reformers, but none of them have stood firm once they took power. It is easy to make grandiose promises when you're stumping, but governing a country like Bolivia doesn't leave you with a lot of viable options. So I guess my question is: what makes you think he'll hold his positions once confronted with the realities of the job?" The question was aimed at Catacora as well, of course, an attempt to gauge his appreciation of the practicalities of the position.

Catacora shook his head and readied himself to unfurl another monologue, which began, "He won't change because—"

"But what about the consequences?" Gabriel stopped him short. "If he does what he says he'll do, the World Bank and others could cut off aid; foreign investors could flee. If the foreign aid stops, what then?" He was pushing toward his point. Trying to modify the question until it contained enough complexity that it couldn't be answered with a digression about history. "Bolivia isn't rich enough, like Venezuela is, to reject that aid. If Evo allows the economy to sag, he'll be kicked out. Don't you agree?"

"That is one view. I think he will have the support of the South American countries, no matter what. Chavez, as you just pointed out, has lots of money."

"Well, not *that* much—not enough to replace the aid supplied by the World Bank."

Gabriel had downloaded and read Catacora's master's thesis that morning. Written in 1986, just after the debt crisis had concluded, it was a survey of the monetary policies of the various Latin American countries affected, but it focused mainly on Mexico. Catacora had also written an extensive addendum in 2003, which studied the monetary policies of countries that had gone through credit crises in the late 1990s, and it would probably have been more revealing, but Gabriel couldn't get his hands on it. He did find an abstract. From what he could tell, the first paper showed a somewhat standard devotion to Milton Friedman; the second demonstrated a sharp departure. Catacora's grasp of the issues had become more sophisticated. He had, by then, been present for several miserable new chapters in the country's history. He had seen Friedman's ideas backfire, spectacularly. He admired Chile's approach in the mid-1990s. The Chilean finance minister had instituted a temporary levy on short-term investments; foreign investors who committed to Chilean companies for more than a year paid no tax, but speculators had to pay heavy fees. In this way, Chile kept warm by globalization's hearth but had enough distance that it was not scorched when the embers lit its neighbors' more ostentatious houses.

It seemed to Gabriel that Catacora was an academic economist, most comfortable writing long papers on events that had already happened and analyzing other economists' failures under the generous illumination of hindsight. He didn't often make pronouncements on how to proceed. Like any historian, he preferred forensic analysis of the deceased to diagnosis of the living. Still, and despite his years in the academy, he very much inhabited the weasel-like mindset of a midlevel Third-World bureaucrat. He was insecure about his station. His allegiances lodged uncomfortably between a passionate sympathy for the poor—he had grown up in poverty, and had been one of the very few to make it out—and an appreciation of the rewards of upper-middleclass life.

Fortunately, he did not seem to find anything odd about Gabriel's line of questioning and earnestly endeavored to answer whatever questions came his way. Gabriel knew that as long as Catacora was still just a professor, his schedule would be wide open. So he decided not to push too hard that first day. He had to go to the Tennis Club, anyway, so he apologized for having to leave so soon.

He stood and shook the man's small hand. "May I come back and talk to you tomorrow?"

"I won't be here tomorrow. How about Friday?"

Gabriel nodded. "Noon? I'd like to take you to lunch—if you have time."

"I'd love that," he said, escorting Gabriel to the door.

After orchestrating the successful revolution in Cuba, Che Guevara wrote in his journal:

> I've got a plan. If some day I have to carry the revolution to the continent, I will set myself up in the jungle at the frontier between Bolivia and Brazil. I know the spot pretty well because I was there as a doctor. From there it is possible to put pressure on three or four countries and, by taking advantage of the frontiers and the forests, you can work things so as never to be caught.

He made many flawed assumptions about Bolivia's readiness for his revolution, the most crucial being his belief that Bolivians were as outraged by their condition as he was. When he got to the spot he'd identified, he found that few locals were interested in taking up arms. Most believed that they had already had their revolution, in 1952, when dynamite-toting miners revolted. So in the 1960s, when Che pointed to the direness of their living standards, they were, if anything, offended. The locals turned on him. They gave him away to the CIA.

He had a small, poorly armed force. Their position was not ideal, as it had been in the mountains of Cuba. It was marginal, and it was impossible to defend. Che's last stand took place in the early days of October 1967, at La Higuera, in the jungles of southern Bolivia. He was captured, briefly tortured, and then shot by a firing squad.

Félix Rodríguez, the CIA agent who had followed Che to Bolivia and who was there in La Higuera during Che's final days, still wore the watch he'd pried off the dead revolutionary's wrist. Rodríguez had been there when a doctor sawed off Che's hands. The hands, preserved in jars of formaldehyde, were sent to Argentina for fingerprint analysis. Once their identity had been confirmed, the hands were forwarded to Cuba, as a message.

In 1781 Tupac Katari was ripped apart by four horses in El Alto, and his severed limbs were sent to the outlying Aymara villages, also as a message. Katari, like Guevara, would take on a mythic status in Bolivia once executed. Total failure had come to be seen as a badge of honor in the country where only villains won. The country's history was itself a litany of defeat, plunder by foreigners, and further defeat, so it made sense that all of the national heroes had failed to accomplish what they'd set out to achieve. On the Plaza Avaroa, near Gabriel's hotel, a statue of General Eduardo Avaroa commemorated the man who had been roundly beaten in the battle for the Pacific, when Bolivia lost its coastline to Chile. The statue showed the fallen general with his hand outstretched — either to keep fighting or to ask for help, it wasn't clear.

And yet, now it finally looked like the country was wresting control of her fate from others, striking out for victory. That was the narrative favored by left-leaning intellectuals anyway, who were keen on erecting Evo as an avatar for some kind of liberal resurgence. But how many Bolivian leaders had been elected in order to fight corruption? More than half. And how many had eventually been kicked out for becoming corrupt? Almost all. Gabriel, and many other onlookers, had been leaning toward a pessimistic view of Evo at first, guessing that he'd backpedal once in office, but Lenka had successfully convinced Gabriel that Evo was the real thing. Investors, meanwhile, put a 60 to 65 percent chance on the likelihood of Evo's sincerity. How long would he last? Estimates varied. Most of those in the business of prognosticating regional political and financial shifts were not yet prepared to speculate on whether he would survive his first year in office.

As far as Gabriel was concerned, the question of whether Evo would last or not was secondary. The real question was whether Evo's commitment to his ideals would yield the desired results. Could the country find enough footing to begin building sustainable economic growth under Evo? Gabriel was completely undecided on that matter. A good economist would argue against Evo's anti-market ideas, but Gabriel believed that good economic theory didn't function very well in all situations. Piloting an impoverished country through such intense macroeconomic chaos was like flying a tiny airplane through a hurricane: the laws of physics could, in the immediate term, be overruled by meteorological circumstances.

In any case, Evo would be the first Bolivian president to claim power with the passionate support of the poor and the opposition of the rich, which counted for something in terms of his potential life span. The Bolivian poor might never have managed to elect one of their one before, but they had certainly ejected their fair share.

The story, cited often in Bolivia, was that just before Tupac Katari was drawn and quartered, he said, "You can kill me now, but tomorrow I will return, and I will be millions."

When Gabriel had stood at his hotel-room window on Election Day watching those thousands of people milling around on the streets below, it had occurred to him that Katari's prophecy might yet be realized.

• • •

Gabriel hailed a taxi outside of the Monoblock and continued down the hill to the Tennis Club for his meeting with Foster Garnett. Memberships at the club were de rigueur among well-heeled expatriates. A foreign diplomat could have a temporary membership for $250 a month, while a Bolivian had to either inherit a membership or pay $18,000 to initiate one, along with the $250 monthly fee. Foreigners stationed in cities like La Paz didn't have that many options socially and were happy to pay dues for the ability to congregate daily with their peers. They needed somewhere with tennis courts, a swimming pool, a bar, and a serviceable restaurant. It had to be kid friendly. So places like the Tennis Club could be found hiding behind tall walls in most major Third-World cities, and in every such club at least half of the members were foreigners.

The Tennis Club was tucked away in a crevice at the southern end of the city, where the upper classes lived. Because of its altitude, La Paz had an upside-down layout. In most cities, the wealthy inhabited the peaks, and the poor pooled in the valleys. But in La Paz, the rich filled the deepest ravines, where the altitude was less oppressive, while the shantytowns were splashed on frigid, windblown perches.

At the front desk, Gabriel announced himself in English lest he be mistaken for a local by the guard. He gave the Americanized version of his name too, with the broad *a* and no trill on the *r: GAY-bree-el.* That was what he liked most about his name, the versatility of it. When speaking to a gringa at Brown, he'd use the Spanish version. With Latinas he could do either, depending on the context. A heavily lipsticked girl in a discotheque in Bogotá would get the Americanized name, whereas a tattooed indie rocker Chicana at the Glasshouse in Pomona would get the Spanish: *Gah-bhrri-el.*

The guard glanced over a list and found him. There was a note: Foster was playing tennis and would not be available for another hour, but Gabriel was free to make himself at home.

Gabriel walked through the lobby and out to the grounds, where Aymara governesses clad in boxy maroon uniforms chased giggling children around the pool while somber-faced parents in mirrored sunglasses dozed in the blinding sun, occasionally waking to sip colas and paw at bowls of peanuts. A robust lawn rolled away from the pool to a series of tennis courts, delineated by tall hedges. A squad of leathery men in coveralls misted the clay of the empty courts with hoses while members in gleaming tennis whites lunged around in nearby games. Apart from the sounds of grunting players and their *thocking* balls and the splashing children, the place had a hushed tone, a dreamily serene quality — like a singular somnolent oasis in that coarse terrain.

Gabriel loosened his tie and wandered. It occurred to him as he walked that thanks to the layout, a person, once inside, could not see any evidence of the city of La Paz in any direction. What he could see was a gigantic pale swath of sky, some burly shrubbery, the jagged peaks of a few mountains. Gabriel hadn't realized how tense the poverty was making him until he got away from it. Now he felt a little drowsy and decided to go inside to wait for Foster. Upstairs, the restaurant was empty. Adjacent, a handful of graying gentlemen were gathered at a bar, which had a sign gently explaining, in cursive, that under-twenty-ones were not allowed. Gabriel sauntered in, eyed his options, and selected a stool at the bar. He looked over the questions he'd planned to ask Foster, which he'd arranged into two categories: mild and aggressive. None of them were going to do the trick, he sensed. His attention wandered.

The walls were paneled wood, stained a rich, if improbable, mahogany. The furniture was bulky, embellished with too many brass buttons, which pinned the burgundy leather down tautly. On the wall by the bar, he saw a deeply contrived series of paintings of English fox hunts, red coats on the riders and all. He asked for a glass of water and the bartender poured him one from the tap. Gabriel asked if he could have a bottle of water. The bartender explained that the water came from a well and was purer than bottled water. Gabriel accepted the glass and had a sip. It tasted like stagnant pond water, an amoeba velouté. He thanked the bartender and put the glass down.

The other men in the bar were conferring in whispers. They drank cognac from bulbous snifters. Taking it in, Gabriel found that all of it—the brazen excess, the fierce allegiance to the patrician pretense—made him miss the actual cushiness of the north even more.

For most of his adult life, he had not cared for cushiness at all. He had scoffed at the comfort of hotel rooms and preferred the two-dollar-a-night flea-ridden bed in Quito's Taxo hostel, where slugs held sway in the kitchen and laced every surface available in their silvery tinsel trails, so all the guests had lived on takeout pizza and cheap beer. He'd stayed there happily for two months. A year or two ago, though, Gabriel had undergone an elemental transformation. Everything he had desired before, everything he had coveted, had been surreptitiously replaced by other things. His daydreams themselves had molted while he wasn't paying attention. Now he came to a place like the Tennis Club and, though he still felt a light scorn, instead of wanting to retreat into the dingy alleys of La Paz, he pined for genuine luxury. This would have seemed a gross turn to the person Gabriel had been two years before, but he wasn't that person anymore. He didn't even know what he would say to that person if he met him. Life was, finally, too haphazard for such straightforwardness, for such clarity.

He looked at his notepad and was about to go over his notes again when he felt a tap on his shoulder. "Gabriel?" It was a familiar voice.

He turned to see Grayson McMillan—ruddy, stubbly, reeking of musty cologne. "Hey!" Gabriel shook the hand, motioned for him to sit. "I wasn't expecting to see you here."

"I'm a member." Grayson sat, ordered a martini from the bartender. "I wasn't expecting to see you." Grayson remained savagely handsome, remarkably fit; he wore an untucked oxford, the top three buttons open and the shirt splayed, exposing a hearty swath of chest hair. He was a marvel: a sort of well-tanned mascot for Gabriel's evolving ambition. Grayson's smile started hard and judgmental, but warmed quickly. "So, what the hell are you doing here?"

"I've got a meeting with Foster Garnett of the U.S. embassy, but he's playing tennis." Gabriel smiled at Grayson; it was good to see a familiar face, even if it was one he so disliked.

"I know him. Wife is perky and pleasant, as they go—he's on his way out, I believe, lucky fucker." Grayson cleared his throat, glanced around, then tilted his head to one side and regarded Gabriel appraisingly for a moment. He said, "Have you seen Fiona since she returned?"

"Not yet."

"Me neither."

Gabriel glanced out the window, saw a nurse in black scrubs wheeling an oxygen tank out toward the gym—for guests who felt lightheaded, no doubt. While he had Grayson, he might as well try to solve one of Priya's other questions. "I was wondering if the World Bank or the fund is going to cut programs here; do you know?"

Grayson shook his head vaguely. "What, you heard about the Italian?"

"Yeah." This is what Lenka had mentioned the night that they went to Blueberries. It had been in the news for a week or so afterward: an Italian vice president at the World Bank had very publicly resigned over the fact that he was being pressured by the United States to cut aid to Bolivia. The story had flared briefly, and then gone away.

More recently, Lenka had mentioned that the Italian had accepted the invitation she'd extended, on behalf of Evo, to come to Bolivia. Evo was going to have a party in the Italian's honor on the thirtieth of December, the day before she and Evo set off on the world tour, which she had been busy arranging.

"You think that'll affect the bank-fund approach to Bolivia?" Gabriel asked.

"I don't know. Off the record?"

Gabriel nodded. "Absolutely."

"I honestly don't know, but the way I see it, these days—with Wolfowitz already drawing a lot of fire at the World Bank—I doubt they'll want to appear to be accepting pressure from the U.S."

"And the Italian put Bolivia into play in that way."

"So if any of the aid institutions acts unilaterally against Morales, or Bolivia, everyone will assume that it's in response to pressure from Bush, and the scandal will flare up again. So, for now, Bolivia has a reprieve. It won't last, but I think it's too hot an issue for anyone in the aid community to take an interventionist position. Again, that's just my guess."

Gabriel hadn't thought of it that way. "They care?" he said.

Grayson shrugged. "Probably."

Gabriel looked around. Grayson seemed to pick up on his disdain somehow. "You think poorly of this place?"

"It's fine."

"Yeah, right," Grayson said. "But it feels good to be inside, doesn't it? Go on, admit it."

"It does."

Neither one of them said anything for a moment. Then Grayson, perhaps bothered by Gabriel's possible disdain for the club, said, "No doubt it's easier to turn your nose up at it if you don't live here." Gabriel hadn't expected him to be so defensive. Grayson had somehow convinced himself that Gabriel was an anti-elitist. Grayson wasn't as dexterous at his art as his reputation suggested. Reportedly a lethal diplomatic sniper, he was instead armed with a blunderbuss. Gabriel didn't quite know how to respond, so he just shook his head. "No, I'm just not really a country-club guy."

"So you're not a little bit of a socialist?"

Gabriel laughed. "No, no, I'm not a socialist — trust me."

Grayson squinted at him. "Where are you from?"

Gabriel shook his head. "Southern California."

"And how was that?"

"It was fine. I wouldn't want to move back, but —"

"You're family is from Mexico?"

"No. I'm not — I'm half Chilean and half Russian." He hadn't been asked that question in years and it knocked him off balance. He'd been too adamant in his reply, he knew, but he couldn't stop himself. Grayson's burst of contempt had been strange, but then this quizzing about Gabriel's ethnicity — Gabriel wasn't quite sure how to proceed. He knew he hated the condescending undertone, though. He hated it a lot, and he was tired of encountering that tone with men of Grayson's stature, so he decided to try turning the tables. "What about you? How was Belfast?" he said.

Grayson hesitated, as if slightly surprised. "How did you know that I'm from Belfast?"

"From your accent, I suppose." This was not true at all. Grayson had no hint of an Irish accent. The truth—and Gabriel knew it, had read it in a profile on the International Monetary Fund's website—was that Grayson had studied at the terribly posh Dulwich College, in London, before matriculating at Cambridge. Grayson's parents had sent him to Dulwich doubtless for the express purpose of purging him of his brogue.

"You can hear it?" Grayson smiled stiffly.

Not wanting to push it, Gabriel backpedaled. "There's just a hint. I didn't mean to—"

"No!" Grayson shook his head. His face lingered between expressions as he tried to dig out the hidden insult that he apparently assumed was buried in Gabriel's reply.

He did not find anything, because there was nothing, but he shot back anyway. "Your family? Where are they from?"

"My mother's Chilean." Gabriel decided not to give him anything more than that.

"She was there during Pinochet's rule?"

"Sort of. She left in 1973. She—" Gabriel hesitated. He knew it wasn't wise to confess personal details to Grayson.

"Driven out by Pinochet?"

"No, not really," Gabriel lied. He didn't want to make it an issue. Out the window, he saw the emblem of the club had been carved into the bushes by an overeager topiary artist. The sun made a dramatic show in the west: the light fractured like a laser shot through a prism, each individual color parceled out and shining naked, alone. Eventually, he said, "Can I ask, what's with the map on your office wall?"

"It shows the infant-mortality rates of the countries of the world," Grayson explained. "I put it there when I arrived; it reminds me of the weight of these problems that we're looking at."

"Right." Foster would be done soon.

Gabriel was about to bid farewell to Grayson when Grayson said, "You know, it's not an easy job, representing the fund here. We're hated ninety-five percent of the time, and we're treated better than Christ risen the other five percent, when they need us. The truth is, I think we can really help them." Grayson accepted his martini from the bartender, had a sip, put it down on the bar. "People your age tend to see the world in absolutes, because it's easier. But we're not bad people." After a pause he added, "Anyway, that's why I put it there."

"Plus, it goes well with the de Kooning," Gabriel said.

"I really hadn't thought of it that way."

"Well, it's true." Gabriel stood up, took his wallet out.

"That's quite cynical of you, Gabriel." Grayson was tickled.

Gabriel pulled some bills out and put them on the bar. "I guess so." That was supposed to sound flip, but the incidental valences multiplied right there before him, fanning out colorfully, a terrible array of ways he could feel bitter without any good reason.

That night, Gabriel sat alone in his room with the television. He could have gone over to the Lookout, but it would have only made him feel worse. Lenka was at home with her son, her ex-husband, his wife, and the rest of the brood. She was sleeping alone as well. He pictured a narrow bed in a tiny room, glossy white walls. Though tempted to call her, he resisted. There was nothing good about how much he missed her that night. It didn't bode well for his ability to survive at Calloway. He thought about Oscar, who had said, "I have done this job longer than anyone I know, and I've done it for only five years." He knew that the real trick was merely to survive for as long as possible.

It wasn't unheard-of for a quant's hair to go white in his first year, and the pressure was much the same for analysts, it turned out. But if you could hang in for as long as Oscar, you'd probably be able to give each of your eight grandchildren a new Jetta on his or her sixteenth birthday without a problem. It was a different scale of reward. It was so outsize that Gabriel could not see how to convince himself that something like his relationship with Lenka—sublime and wonderful as it was turning out to be—could take priority.

The interview with Foster Garnett had not been as interesting as the conversation with Grayson, to say nothing of the one with Catacora. Foster did, to his credit, spill the beans about the United States' five-point agenda in Bolivia, but there were no surprises there:

- Total elimination of coca cultivation
- Increase free and open trade (minus the aforementioned coca)
- Preserve representational democracy
- Fight poverty and improve wealth distribution
- Help improve environmental standards

Gabriel had tried to get Foster to talk about the snafu with Vincenzo D'Orsi at the World Bank, but he just shook his head. He was still in his tennis whites. He had blond eyebrows, blond eyelashes, blond leg hair. He had the build of a jock but the social polish of a person who'd been to Exeter or some other American equivalent of Dulwich. Gabriel did his best not to stare at his prodigious Adam's apple—it looked as if he'd swallowed a golf ball.

"If Evo starts seizing foreign assets, what will you do? No reprisal? No reduction in aid?"

"He'll feel a pinch," Foster had said. The Adam's apple bobbled slightly.

"Will there be any change in policy from the World Bank and IMF?"

"We will put the matter to the executive boards of both institutions; we will lobby for punitive measures, but we don't have final say," he said, reciting double-pasteurized talking points. The message was there though, and it connected with what Grayson had said. The scandal with the Italian at the World Bank had killed any chance of a quick change in World Bank–IMF policy at the management level; the United States could only hope to rally support at Bolivia's next review by the board, some nine months away. But as long as Evo didn't make a scene, the United States would not likely find any backing. Ultimately, the

State Department was prepared to just shrug at the defeat and move on. It didn't care to fight over a country like *that*.

Gabriel was in his pajamas watching CNN International, trying not to think about Lenka, when he heard a light knock at the door. Assuming it was Lenka, he bounded over, but when he opened the door he found Fiona.

She wore a black dress with a wide crimson bow wrapped around her midsection, its knot sagging. "Merry Christmas," she said. Her lipstick matched the bow, almost.

He stepped aside.

She entered. She was wearing black stockings, a black jacket. Her hair was in a chignon; it looked different somehow. Better. "Where's your girlfriend?" she said. She took off her jacket and tossed it on the chair.

"What girlfriend?" he said, but it stung him to say it, so he added, "She's at home with her ex-husband and their son."

"Really?" she said. She sat down on his bed, looked around at the room. "This is horrible, Gabriel," she said. "You live here?"

He turned off the television, twisted the blinds shut. "Do you want a bottle of water?"

"Why don't you move to Hotel Presidente? I'm sure Priya would be happy to spring for it."

"I'm trying to be discreet."

She laughed; she winked. "Your secret's still safe with me." She lit a cigarette. He didn't say anything, so she went on. "And Lenka? How much does she know?"

"Why are you here?"

"Ouch," she said. Smiling at him fondly, she kicked off her shoes, had a drag, exhaled. "Do you know how vampire bats feed?"

"No, I don't."

She stood, undid the red bow at her waist, let it fall to the floor. "They come into your room at night and crawl along the wall like huge black spiders. They don't fly because the commotion might wake you up." She put her cigarette down in the ashtray on the bedside table.

"They sneak up like that and then burrow under the covers and suck the blood from your big toe. Gently, so you won't wake." She untied her hair, turned, unzipped the back of her dress. "Because all bloodsuckers, as you surely know by now, have as their biggest problem — their number-one threat to survival — the question of how to do their thing without their host realizing what's going on. Mosquitoes weigh close to nothing, and their feeding tube is thinner than a strand of hair — you shouldn't even feel it enter." She dropped her dress to the floor. "Leeches actually anesthetize the area with their saliva." She stretched across his bed, crossed her legs at the ankles. "Did you know that?"

He shook his head.

"Well, that's what I'm here for, to enlighten you." She picked up her cigarette and had another drag, then stubbed it out, exhaled smoke at the ceiling.

He glanced down at the milky breasts puddled on her chest, her tan aureoles; he looked at the lacy fringe on the sides of her purple thong; he looked at her tiny curly navel — flat against a wall of muscle, it looked like a mollusk that had been stepped on. Looking at her face, the faded freckles, her too-big mouth, the wicked expression in her eyes, he knew this was not a good idea. There was nothing about this that was a good idea. Still, it was necessary. What was required was a wedge to split his feelings apart.

She laughed uncomfortably, and he realized he was staring.

"Sorry," he said.

She looked at him searchingly. She seemed aware of his guilt somehow. "Can I do anything for you?" she said.

He thought about it. "No." He shook his head. "You can do nothing for me."

Then he flicked the light switch off and, fingertips grazing the wall, felt his way across the room until his shins touched the edge of the bed. He sat down in the total darkness and started to undress.

# 7

# Mistakes Were Made

*Friday, December 23, 2005*

AS LUCK WOULD HAVE IT, Alejo had come to the eighth floor to deliver breakfast to a neighboring room that morning; he'd knocked on that door and was standing there, in the grim light of the hallway, at the exact moment that Fiona and Gabriel exited his room. Alejo kept his eyes down, but the hall was small and it was just the three of them. There was no confusion about whom Gabriel was with—or, more to the point, whom he was not with. Nor was there any ambiguity about where they were coming from. Alejo knocked on the door in front of him again. He had a battered aluminum cart with a single plate on it shrouded in its tin cap: breakfast for one.

Fiona, oblivious to the complex personal scenario under way in that corridor, pushed the down button at the elevators. "What are you doing later?" she said.

"I'm—I don't know," Gabriel muttered, glancing at Alejo's back.

Then the guest opened the door and Alejo pushed the cart inside.

Fiona, picking up on the direction of his anxiety, gave a curled smile. "Feeling guilty?"

"Yes."

"Well"—she pushed the down arrow again—"you should get used to that."

"Yeah."

The elevator arrived.

Inside, he pushed two buttons: one for the ground floor, for her, and one for the second-floor cafeteria, for him. Last night, after she had fallen asleep, he had decided that he should see if he couldn't get her to give him something else. But he didn't want to leave with her now, in case anyone else saw them, so he needed to quickly set up his request. "Are you going to speak with Evo again?" he said.

The doors jerked shut. "I have a meeting with him tomorrow," she said. The elevator began its squeaky and unsteady descent.

Spotting an opportunity, however slight, to locate some information, he said, "Have you heard of Santa Cruz Gas?" There was no time for foreplay.

"If you're going to ask me to ask him about this Santa Cruz—"

"No, no, but if he says something about gas, or Santa Cruz Gas, you'll tell me?"

"Oh yeah, of course"—here, sarcasm—"you'll be the first to know." Despite her tone, he wasn't sure that she wouldn't tell him. She was, above all, a swift hand with the conversational whipsaw; all he could do was hope, against the evidence, that she would see fit to help him. She had no professional reason to share, none that he could think of, and she wasn't really the type to conflate professional and personal agendas.

The doors opened at his stop. He leaned in and kissed her quickly near the mouth and ducked out toward the cafeteria, as if trying to squirm away from a toxic odor.

He'd experienced a similar uneasiness at his circumstances when he'd come down to Bolivia a month ago, but the feeling then had at least been tempered by the thrill of being on his first assignment for the Calloway Group. The job had seemed to carry an air of espionage, at first. His first week there he'd been ensconced at the Lookout, yukking it up with the international press, embellishing his aliases, and generally enjoying the gamesmanship. Now, the aliases were a nuisance to maintain. The thrill had been replaced by fear and confusion.

On the bright side, that uneasy guilt had slackened and the lies came easier. He had never felt especially conflicted about lying to his mother about Calloway, which he considered necessary in precisely the same way that lying about premarital sex to a Catholic parent might be necessary. But he would be lying without hesitation to Priya now, or at least withholding information from her. He lied to all of his sources without a second thought. He'd even be lying to Lenka soon, about Fiona. He would rather not have had to lie to Lenka, at least. Part of him felt that it was inevitable, because such were the vicissitudes of his career. Lying would be, from now on, part of his life. The lilies were fine, but a little gilding wouldn't hurt. The work itself necessitated a certain amount of subterfuge, and he was getting better at the work. As Fiona had suggested, if he was going to let himself feel guilty about deceiving people, he would do well to resign and go back to writing copy for *IBI*, back to the long slog through the dreary middle.

That wasn't an option. But that didn't mean that he needed to be *wholly* corrupt. He could retain some measure of poise, and he should.

So when he sat down to his rank breakfast—the scrambled eggs wafted queer and fishy that morning—Gabriel decided he would call Fiona later and tell her not to come around like that again. He would say it had been fun—wonderful, even—but it wasn't appropriate, not when he was dating Lenka. It was not just that Lenka would be heartbroken if she found out; somehow, because of the unusual nature of their relationship, the question of fidelity was all the more important. It was precisely because they spent their days dealing with connived half-truths, a mess of people (themselves included) trying to maximize some professional angle, that the honesty and faithfulness of their partnership, such as it was, needed to remain pristine. At least, his thinking went, there could be purity in this *one* corner of life.

He abandoned his breakfast after a last bite of stale toast, washed down with coca tea. He stood and thought about the forthcoming conversation with Fiona, dreading the awkwardness.

*No,* he realized, it was a bad idea to do it that way. He was right to call it off with her, it had to happen, but to do so that afternoon would be premature. Better to speak to her about it after she'd had her interview with Evo. Just in case she came up with something he needed.

There was a protest on Prado, as usual, and the streets were clogged. Gabriel had been up to the market again to buy Lenka's Christmas present, and now he was back in the valley, and the whole city center was jammed up around the protest. It was the miners. They had no specific gripe; they just wanted to let Evo know that even though he was an indigenous peasant, like them, they weren't going to make it easy for him. Among the many powerful labor groups in Bolivia, the miners held a special place. They were numerous, truculent, did horrendous labor that generated a sizable portion of the country's GDP, and they wielded sticks of dynamite. In terms of sheer numbers, merchants beat them, but the merchants were poorly organized. The bus drivers had the most effective tool—buses parked across the country's major roads—for twisting the government's arm, which was why the Bolivian government persisted in spending so much on a gasoline subsidy instead of on things like education, health care, and infrastructure.

Today, though, it was just the miners. They tossed quarter- and half-sticks of dynamite periodically, and the explosions jangled windows throughout the valley. Cabdrivers refused to go anywhere near them, and traffic came to a standstill.

So Gabriel had to walk all the way down to his meeting with Professor Catacora. He steered clear of Prado, sticking to Potosí. Explosions lapped up and down the narrow streets, each making a staccato cracking sound. The sound sliced the air like the sonic boom of a low-flying fighter jet. Gabriel remembered that sound from September of 2001. He had graduated from Brown and gone down to New York City that June. He had his job at *IBI* by August. He'd been on his way to work one morning when he saw a huge mob of people gathered by the L stop at Bedford. They were all looking toward downtown. Someone said that the World Trade Center was on fire. "Jesus," Gabriel said and craned his neck to see. He noticed that it was, in fact, on fire, up at the top. Then he skipped quickly down the stairs, swiped his card, and headed down to the stinky platform. Standing there, he realized it must have been a huge fire. He'd been up on one of the towers that summer and had a sense of the scale, and by his estimate at least twenty floors were burning. Maybe it'd been a bomb? He rode into Manhattan, thinking about that fire. By the time he emerged at Union Square, the entire city was outside, staring, stunned. They crowded on the west side of Sixth Avenue, from where they could see the towers. He was walking up the side that was empty, enjoying an unimpeded rush-hour sidewalk, when he heard the mob across from him gasp as one. Unable to see what they were seeing, he watched the crowd. A blond woman spun around and vomited into the street—an image that would soon come to centerpiece his personal narrative of that day.

Nine hours later, rattled and exhausted, he walked over the Williamsburg Bridge with tens of thousands of other Brooklynites. For the next month, a noxious odor—like burning plastic—blew occasionally into his apartment. And F-16s screamed overhead sending thunderous ripples through the neighborhood's tight grid of shallow gullies. Not until that morning in Bolivia with the miners' dynamite, four years later, had he heard a sound so baleful and monstrous and immediate.

Twenty minutes late, he arrived at Catacora's office in the aptly named Monoblock, and the two of them set off up the hill for pizza at Eli's. Catacora, expansive once again, held forth in a lecture on Katari's siege of 1783. "It's about geography," he said in English and waved at the hills, "and nearsighted urban planning. La Paz was born and raised around the Choqueapu's gold. But from a defensive standpoint, the location couldn't be worse. It's easy to besiege. We still have only one real highway in and out. And do you know where it goes through?"

"El Alto," Gabriel replied, through gasps.

"That's right. So the peasants in El Alto, they live in a very cold place, but they also have a tactical advantage over the elites. They can easily block off access. They do it all the time now, with buses. And that is what Katari did. He was there"—Catacora pointed at the ridge—"and the Spanish were here, starving. They boiled their shoes."

Gabriel got the point. He urged the conversation back to the situation at hand. "What will stop them from throwing out Evo?" he said. "I mean, I know he wants to be a completely different kind of president, but will he be able to do that?"

"Why not?"

"Well, it's one thing to cut off the road to La Paz and force the leader's hand, but it's another thing to be the leader yourself. If he tries to expropriate Brazilian gas companies, he could lose the support of President Lula. Of all countries, Bolivia needs to be on good terms with its neighbors."

"True," Catacora said. Eli's was on the far side of Plaza del Estudiante, a hazardous spot for pedestrians to reach because they needed to cross multiple lanes of speeding traffic. Catacora paused, weighing the best route. A garbage truck ambled past, one of the men on the back clanging the truck's giant bell. Storeowners rushed out with their garbage, tossed it into the back. Catacora, seeing an opportunity, led Gabriel on a dash through the noisome wake of the truck, and through a temporary blockage in the traffic. By the time they got to the other side, Gabriel had lost his place in the conversation.

They settled into a small table in Eli's, a dive-y pizza joint that claimed to sell New York–style pizza, although it was very much Bolivian-style pizza: a thick pelt of white cheese over a puddle of slick marinara on a pale, doughy crust. Customers could have their pizza garlanded with a variety of canned vegetables and/or desiccated lunchmeats.

Catacora and Gabriel shared a twelve-inch pie, and Gabriel did his best to redirect the conversation. "Have you heard of Santa Cruz Gas?" he said.

"A Brazilian company?"

Gabriel nodded. "An editor asked about it." Gabriel was aware that in theory, he should have an advantage in this conversation because he had more information about the state of affairs than Catacora did. But finding a way to exploit his advantage was proving complicated.

He had written to Priya the previous afternoon to say that he was making a little progress on Santa Cruz, and he was hopeful that he'd have more soon. Taking a step toward specifics, he'd said that he should be able to find out the identity of the finance minister in a day or two.

She had fired off a reply stating that this was good, and she was eager to hear more.

He'd replied that he'd know more soon. He planned to tell her Catacora's name that day. He hoped that by the time he sent her that e-mail, he'd have more on Santa Cruz, so that he'd have something else to dangle in front of her for a few days. He needed to keep one move ahead: promising only what he'd already achieved. This next step, finding out about Santa Cruz, didn't look encouraging.

Priya was eager for *something*, though, and he hoped that giving her the name of the finance minister would hold her for a little while.

"Why does your editor want to know about that company? It's very small."

"I don't know. It was just an e-mail. She said, 'What do you know about Santa Cruz Gas?' and I said I knew very little. I suppose people want to know how Evo will actually go about expropriating these companies. Like, is he going to treat them all the same?"

"I wouldn't know."

"Right, but if you were Evo, how would you do it?"

He shrugged. He thought about it. "I would talk to my counterparts in neighboring countries before I did anything, I suppose."

Gabriel nodded. "Oh?"

"What? You look surprised."

Gabriel shook his head. But he *was* surprised—surprised that Catacora had let that slip. Judging by what he'd said, it seemed likely that Evo was, in fact, planning to wait. He would clear the expropriation plan with Lula and other foreign leaders before he went through with it. Gabriel wasn't positive of this, but assuming Evo and Catacora had already discussed the matter, surely Catacora wouldn't say anything that contradicted their official plan.

While walking up Prado toward his hotel after lunch, he stopped at a narrow cybercafé and sent an e-mail to Priya:

---

TO: priya_singh@calloway.net
FROM: gabo_de_boya@yahoo.com
SUBJECT: finance minister

The name of the next finance minister is Luis Alberto Arce Catacora, a professor at the University of San Andrés. I just had lunch with him. He hinted that Evo will consult with his neighbors before doing anything. I'll pursue further and give you more after Christmas.

—G

---

He clicked Send and then logged off.

He continued trudging up the hill. The grade of the street's incline was so subtle he wouldn't have noticed it at sea level at all, but up there, it was obvious.

He stopped for a breather in front of the city's main post office, which was on the ground floor of the immense Comibol building (Corporacion Minera de Bolivia). The miners had migrated there, at the intersection in front of Bolivia's mining headquarters. There were maybe a hundred of them. Some carried signs, but not many. They wandered around listlessly, muttering among themselves. The riot police, clad in green and black, had set up across the street and were now leaning on their plastic shields, which were the approximate size and shape of Roman centurions' shields. They wore helmets, the plastic visors up. Some had grenade launchers—loaded with tear-gas canisters—slung over their shoulders.

Gabriel had seen a lot of protests in the month since he'd arrived, and this seemed no different from any of the others. Most of the miners had lumps the size of walnuts in one of their cheeks, from wads of coca leaves. The quantity of drug released by chewing it that way was not insubstantial and Gabriel thought the men seemed keyed up and agitated. They were frowny, clean-shaven.

The mountains were latticed with an endless series of mines, and the regional mutation of Catholicism had it that those mines were part of hell itself. The earth was the realm of the goddess Pachamama, the heavens were God's domain, and the mines were Satan's. At least while they were under his jurisdiction, the miners should worship Satan. The miners needed to honor the correct deity when they were underground, so they burned candles to Lucifer at makeshift altars at the intersections of their tunnels.

Gabriel noticed to his alarm that the miner nearest him, who was maybe fifteen feet away, had lit the fuse on a half-stick of dynamite and was waving it around. He wore coveralls, huge Wellington boots, and a sky blue helmet, just like the rest. He was possibly drunk, because he was hollering a diatribe in what sounded like Quechua but might have been very badly mangled Spanish. Gabriel took a step back, not wanting to be too near, but he lingered, out of curiosity. Other than a handful of pedestrians who hurried past, there was no traffic on the normally very busy street. Gabriel was contemplating leaving and heading back to his hotel for a little work when the ranting man's hand exploded.

The blast tackled Gabriel, shoving him onto the pavement.

It knocked the wind out of him, and it took him several moments to catch his breath. It felt as if he'd been sucker-punched, hard. It felt like the time in eighth grade when Terrance had thrown a basketball at his face, point-blank, during lunch. He'd had a black eye after that, and Terrance had been made to write a letter of apology. Now, Gabriel rolled over and opened his eyes and saw yellow and red. He blinked and saw a plume of smoke swirling airily in front of firm packs of cumulus clouds. It smelled a lot like fireworks. He was reeling, lying on his back, too stunned to make out the circumstances. A bell rang in one ear and he couldn't tell if it was an alarm from a nearby building or if it was in his head.

He staggered up, shot straight into idiocy. It was bad. He knew that much. Bad enough that he thought he might have lost his hearing or something, he didn't know what. The miners had been shot aside. They'd been scattered. It was a mess there. There was still smoke in the air. The man who had been holding the dynamite lay on the ground awkwardly, face-down, his legs splayed behind him. He was wearing only one boot now. The other one was gone—elsewhere. He had one arm beneath his torso and the other…it was gone. Gabriel looked at him a few seconds more to verify. There was an image and he needed to be sure it made sense. The top of the arm was still there, but it came to a ragged and fleshy end a few inches below the shoulder. Gabriel could see white bone in the damp meat. The skin hung in sloppy flaps. His face had a black smear. The man's eyes were wide open and he looked thoroughly dead.

Gabriel glanced around. No one else seemed hurt. The others who had been nearby were standing up again. Did this mean he was fine too? Probably. As his wits slowly returned, he felt a spike of panic at the possibility that he was hurt. His ear was still ringing and it ached. He reached up and touched the ear. It was wet.

"Oh *shit*," he muttered. Something was wrong. He touched his cheek. Wet too. He couldn't hear anything from his left ear at all. He checked looked down and saw his legs were there. Everything that was visible was okay. But his face was numb. It was his cheek. Through the numbness, he felt a burning, as if his face were on fire.

"Fuck," he said. He told himself to remain calm, but it was no use. "Oh my God. Oh *fuck!*" He said it aloud. His breath was suddenly ragged. He was too jacked up on adrenaline to really cry. He glanced at his fingers and saw blood.

He stumbled over to the police, who were all tensed, their visors down. One of the cops saw him approaching and lifted his visor, came around the barrier to speak. The policeman said something, but Gabriel couldn't hear.

He shook his head and turned his good ear to the man. "Are you okay?" the man asked.

"I don't know. Am I hurt?"

The policeman nodded.

"Really? My face?"

The policeman nodded again.

"Oh, goddamn it," he muttered, in English.

The cop said something else, but Gabriel didn't hear him. Gabriel shook his head. His face hurt more now. He felt a lump in his throat. "Um —" He didn't know what to do. Back in Spanish, he said, "Should I go to the hospital?"

The cop led Gabriel to a paddy wagon and helped him inside. Gabriel sat on the bench. He took a deep breath. He noticed he was panting. He tried to calm down and catch his breath. It was no good. He could feel his pulse in his head, in his face. He took another deep breath and held it, watching as a few policemen brought over the dead man, the one who'd been holding the dynamite. They hoisted him up the back stair and laid him on the bench opposite Gabriel.

One of the policemen entered and sat beside the miner's feet. The side with the arm that had been blown off was, fortunately, out of view. "¡Vamos! ¡Vamos!" the cop yelled and banged the metal wall behind him.

They drove with the back doors open. The doors slammed shut and swung open at the turns, wavered in the middle at times, randomly, each door drifting one way or another. Gabriel watched everything out the back of the truck. He felt sick, sort of like the way he felt sick before he had to speak in public, but worse. La Paz rolled along behind them. The siren droned too languidly to convey appropriate urgency. Pedestrians looked at them and then vanished behind a swinging door.

He glanced at the cop sitting opposite him. The cop shook his head, with a jeez-this-is-crazy expression. Gabriel nodded. He couldn't muster a smile. He didn't look at the miner lying on the bench. He turned and looked out the back.

He saw blood dripping slowly from his chin onto his thigh. There was a big dark blotch on his jeans. It was dripping quickly. As they slowed at the clinic, Gabriel stole a look at the man on the bench opposite him and was surprised to see that he seemed to be alive after all. He was very pale, and he didn't appear to be looking at anything in particular, but he was breathing quickly, with an expression of concentration on his face. The truck stopped and the cop leaped out, offered Gabriel a hand. Gabriel took the hand and stood up. The cop, indicating the floor, told him to be careful. Gabriel looked down at the lake of blood under his feet.

"*Gracias,*" he said.

He stepped gingerly down to the bumper. Standing there on the street in front of the clinic, he immediately felt like he was going to faint, so he steadied himself against the truck.

Despite a rising urge to vomit, at the insistence of the policeman Gabriel took the miner's feet—one barefoot, one in a rubber boot—while the policeman took his blood-drenched torso. In that way, they carried him into the clinic, taking short quick steps, exactly as if they had been carrying a bulky piece of furniture. At one point, because of the blood on his hand, Gabriel dropped the man's booted foot, but he picked it back up, gripped it firmly, and continued. The man was definitely alive. He was mumbling as they carried him. Gabriel gazed at the exposed bone again. The stump looked false—something from a war movie, maybe. The miner's one exposed foot was enormous in proportion to his body, a big slab of half-dried clay. Besmeared toenails were overgrown and yellow.

Inside, they set the man down on a gurney. A doctor was there. The doctor didn't say anything to them. He and a couple nurses rolled the gurney out of the room.

Gabriel lingered. A woman behind a counter looked at him and said, "I'll get you a doctor too."

He nodded. Saliva flooded his mouth. He retched a little, but caught himself. The policeman from the back of the truck helped him into an old wheelchair. Gabriel felt enormously grateful and patted the man's hand. He squeezed it. He said, "Thank you, thank you." He was feeling feverish now, and he was starting to cry, at last.

The man said it was no problem.

Gabriel sighed, wiped away tears, shook his head, and then turned and retched again. His diaphragm convulsed hard and he puked up a soupy splatter of red-and-white half-digested pizza. The brightly colored vomit pooled beneath his wheelchair. He could smell tomato sauce. He hiccupped, retched again, and drooled onto his bloodied lap. His throat felt scratchy, and his brain was not his brain. Dropping away, he groaned and blinked at the painful blur . . . a sharp pain somewhere . . . the room sparkled like out-of-focus tinsel, like a gauzy dream about a Christmas party . . . his mind slipping, he enjoyed weak relief as his bladder emptied slowly, warmly.

He woke in a narcotic stupor. His head still hurt. His ear still hurt, but his hearing was improved. He could hear a woman somewhere in the hospital shrieking and begging people to stop whatever they were doing to her. Her voice didn't diminish from her hollering. It seemed to grow stronger. At last, as she was exhausted or drugged, her screams dimmed to a sad howl, the plaintive and resigned braying of a cat being forced to take a bath.

A nurse came around and put a tray of food beside him. He was sozzled on pain medication, and food didn't interest him. Then she explained that she was going to give him a tetanus shot. The serum came in a glass vial with a narrow neck that could be snapped off, thereby exposing a jagged glass opening. It was into that opening that the nurse carefully inserted her needle. The technology seemed positively Edwardian.

He was not upset. He was not upset about much, thanks to whatever opiate they'd spiked into his IV. He felt, instead, a light euphoria, bolstered by the thrall of posttraumatic bliss, and the knowledge that he'd managed to survive. He gazed at the nurse when she inserted the needle into his arm. The needle prick came at a remove, like a description of a sting rather than a sting itself.

She was flirty, or wanted to be, but he was too doped up and confused to know how to really engage. She smelled strongly of soap and had a face quite like a dagger: the chin participated as much in the impression as her nose and cheeks; it was all blade. Beneath, her neck was pale and elongated, swanlike — it looked precarious next to such a face.

He asked what had happened.

She explained that there had been shrapnel, of a sort. Fragments of the man's hand, of his bone and tendon, had been hurled into the left side of Gabriel's face. Gabriel's ear had ripped, horizontally, and his cheek had several deep puncture wounds. His skull had done its job as built-in helmet: it had prevented the shards from piercing his brain and killing him.

He'd been in shock when they brought him to the hospital, she said. But he was not in any danger now, she added. They had removed the shrapnel, such as it was, from his face and stitched up each of the three punctures. The doctors had stitched his ear back together again too. The ear had been pretty well mangled, though, and they were not sure it would hold together well. He had to take it very easy on the ear for the next few weeks, at least.

"Will I have a permanent scar?" he asked.

"Yes," the nurse said matter-of-factly.

She added that although he had bled a lot, it had been more or less all surface damage. Still, they had swaddled the left side of his face in bandages. They had given him a powerful antibiotic, which would precede a two-week barrage of oral penicillin. The biggest threat was infection, she said. She didn't elaborate. She didn't have to. Gabriel knew that there was nothing hygienic about having someone else's bone blasted like buckshot into one's face.

Incredibly, the other man — who had at first looked so dead — was actually alive. He was in serious condition, the nurse reported, but he'd probably survive. Apart from losing his arm, he would be blind in one eye, deaf in one ear. He had lost several teeth too, broken two ribs, and his lip had torn badly. The skin on half of his torso had been ripped and burned. He was, however, in the parlance of doctors, "lucky to be alive," as if luck had anything to do with it. There was bad luck all around, and maybe some good luck too; but mostly Gabriel saw a lot of madness.

The sun was low. He didn't know if it was dusk or dawn. The clinic took up three floors of an old building. The machinery and instruments were bulky, chrome and dreary teal. It was all cheap—hand-me-downs from hospitals in wealthy countries.

Measuring poverty has always been difficult. According to the theory of purchasing-power parity, in a perfectly operating market, the cost of a given thing should be the same everywhere. But markets are, it turns out, decidedly imperfect. Gasoline can change price from one block to the next. A Big Mac in Norway costs twice as much as a Big Mac in Mexico City. The cost of things makes a problematic barometer, so economists have had to look elsewhere to quantify comparative wealth and poverty. Life expectancy is one effective measure of so-called *real* wealth, as is a country's infant-mortality rate. Death, it turns out, is a symptom of poverty. From the inside of that dilapidated clinic, this made sense. In the world's poorest countries, death is everywhere. If civil war doesn't get you, famine, cholera, or a pinkie-toe hangnail that gets infected and then goes haywire will. A sixty-five-year-old Rwandan is as statistically improbable as a one-hundred-year-old Canadian—such is the danger of poverty. And, although Bolivia was nowhere near as afflicted a place as Rwanda, there could be no escaping death's proximity. People were aswim in it.

Miners set off dynamite in the middle of the day on the capital city's main drag, yes, but there was more to it than that. To Gabriel, the shadow of death was implied, somehow, in the beggars' diseased eyes, and in the vintage equipment at the clinic; it was there too in a lurid old bus's shaky rear wheel, and in the lack of expiration dates on perishable food. The threat tried to be flippant on the Death Road between La Paz and Coroico, a popular destination for daredevil mountain bikers who were supposed to be delighted by the fact that more than a hundred people were killed on the road every year. Death, in that ubiquity, seemed to beg for intervention by a sense of humor. Take the oft-encountered carcasses of street dogs, furry legs protruding from bloated torsos: cold nightmare or black comedy? A person's response might depend on how many times he'd seen one. The first time he might retch; the second time he'd probably just avert his eyes. Eventually, after he'd seen enough, laughter would seem like the only sensible answer. To take it seriously, to give it that much meaning, would be unthinkable.

Amid such violence and chaos, death came to seem an impatient mistress. The danger had never bothered Gabriel before. When he fell in love with Bolivia, he didn't consider himself a potential object of death's caprice. A common misbelief in the young, and one inevitably corrected. Now Gabriel was afraid. It wasn't just the obvious things, either, that spooked him. He worried about contaminated water, feebly constructed buildings, nests of live wires that teetered atop telephone poles—the precariousness of everything astounded him.

In January of 2002, his mother had sent him a clipping from the *Los Angeles Times* about how on the last day of 2001, a vendor inside Lima's fireworks market had demonstrated one of his wares for a customer and the whole building had ignited in a multicolored inferno. Within an hour 276 people were dead, and the whole market, the size of a city block, had been reduced to ash. Scores of people had been incinerated in their cars as they sat in gridlock out front.

Gabriel and his mother had been to that market when they went on their tour of the region the previous year. Lima had been their last stop, after Chile and Bolivia, and they had stayed for only two days. On the second day they took a tour of the city, during which they stopped at the fireworks market, where eager salesmen lit matches and ignited fuses to entice the gringos. That they might be in danger did occur to Gabriel, in a way, but it seemed theoretical.

His mother had not recoiled either, although he'd expected her to. She had wanted, he understood, to be close to the danger. Or, more to the point, she didn't want to be seen as afraid. So they lingered, standing stiffly to the side, their nostrils full of the sweet, nostalgia-laced smell of burning black powder, paper, and sulfur, their eardrums tickled by arrhythmic explosions. They watched until a bandolier of crackers began rattling off nearby and she suggested—pretending to be bored by it now, or mildly annoyed by the racket—that they might step outside and wait for the others in the fresh air.

He'd never deliberately enter such a place now. Now, he liked his fireworks to have prominent warning labels. Exclamation points were a plus. He liked seat-belt laws too, and rules about air bags. He liked his Food and Drug Administration, with its random sanitation checks and obsessive rules. He liked his milk thoroughly pasteurized. All of this would have seemed priggish to him once, but now it made so much sense.

More than anything, he liked that in the developed world, even though it was equally voracious finally, death appeared less indiscriminate. Death made sense. It was, as it should be, an orderly, rational affair.

When he called his mother from the hospital to tell her what happened, she said, in Spanish, "I'll be there tomorrow." Gabriel had opened the conversation in Spanish, in order to communicate to her posthaste that things were *not* okay.

"Don't come down tomorrow, Mom. It's not an emergency. The doctors tell me I'm going to be fine. I'd love for you to come, but—please don't come tomorrow. If you want to come, what about, I don't know, maybe later in the week. I have obligations."

"Obligations? Why do you need to prepare for me? What are you doing down there?"

"I'm working."

"Working? BellSouth?"

He held the phone against his good ear and waited. Gaping silence sometimes had a way of registering as a cautionary note with her. It gave her time to collect herself and realize that he had a reason for his position, whether or not she understood it.

At last, she pulled back, saying, "Well, I'm going to call you twice a day until I see you next. If I'm not allowed to come down, at least let me do that."

"Okay," he said. "You can do that."

"I'm worried about you, Gabriel."

"I know." He didn't have the heart to lie to her that night, so he didn't tell her not to worry. "I'll leave soon," he said. "In a week, I think. I have to go now. My batteries are dying."

"Fine. Be careful."

Later, the pain sneaked up on him, and the nurse upped his dose of painkillers. Then Lenka arrived. There was a television in the corner, up high, and it played a fuzzy local channel. He'd faded in and out, watching dubbed *Saved by the Bell* and *The Simpsons*. Lenka sat down and he gazed at her, blissed out on Percocet. She kissed him on his good cheek. The bad cheek pulsated. It felt hot under the bandages. *"Te amo,"* she said.

*"Te amo a tí,"* he said and nodded, opened his eyes. He hadn't even realized they were shut. The opiates had made him itchy all over. They muddled the boundary between consciousness and unconsciousness so that he could drift in and out of his nods without ever quite knowing he was one way or the other. It was all just easy. Still, despite his creamy beatific feeling, his gentle sweetness, his airiness, he began to cry a little. He whimpered feebly and tiny teardrops formed, just big enough to blur his vision. He frowned at her. "I want to go home," he muttered in English. He'd never spoken to her in English before and didn't know if she spoke the language well enough to follow.

"I know," she said, also in English. She held his hand, kissed him on the cheek again. She was, of course, used to ministering to tearful boys. And if it hadn't quite been clear to him before, he could tell then, even in the blur of that moment, that he was in love with her.

A little later he opened his eyes again and looked up at her. Some time had passed, he didn't know how long. He held her hand firmly so she wouldn't move. With his free hand, he reached over and had a sip of water from a plastic cup. His mouth was pasty, his tongue thick and awkward, coated in salty foam. He put the water cup back. He didn't know if it was tap water or bottled water but he didn't really care. His eyelids drooped shut and he forced them open.

"Are you going to leave?" she asked in English. Her English was good, apparently.

He shook his head. "I can't. It was..." He closed his eyes for a while. His mind flickered, dodging shadows that ran along in dark spokes, clicking as they passed. The spokes of a bike he'd owned when he was young—he saw them spinning in shadow on the asphalt in the setting sun...An itching area crept up his arm and he scratched it, opened his eyes again. "This was such a mistake," he slurred in Spanish.

"You couldn't have known—" she said, also switching to Spanish.

"No, no, no—no, not that," he said. "Not the dynamite. *You.* You are the mistake. You're going to ruin this for me."

She blinked slowly, fanning him with her eyelashes. She grinned in a way that he didn't recognize. "You too," she said. "You are my mistake." She kissed him on the nose, and brushed his hair off of his forehead. She kissed him on the temple.

He closed his eyes.

"Do you want some tea?" she asked later. His eyes were still closed.

He nodded, but didn't bother opening his eyes. He felt queasy. He had too much saliva in his mouth. "Please," he said. He opened his eyes and saw the outline of his own legs in the blanket in front of him. His knee itched. He scratched it. Then he turned and saw, to his tremendous relief, that she was still there.

# 8

# Them

*Saturday, December 24, 2005*

A TAXI DROPPED GABRIEL OFF at the hotel the next morning and he went up to his room and took a shower, careful not to get his head wet. They had replaced his bandages before he left the clinic and the new ones would be good until that night, when he'd have to change them himself. He plugged his phone in—the batteries had died —and lay down on his bed, turned the television on. He watched CNN International for a while before one of the anchors, a pretty Indian woman, mentioned in passing that it was Christmas Eve. It hadn't occurred to him.

Once the phone had charged, he turned it on, dialed the office. Markets were closed, but he was pretty sure that wouldn't stop Priya from showing up.

"I had a problem," he said.

"Got drunk and spilled champagne on your laptop?" she quipped.

"Uh." He was too wiped out to cope with her weirdly cheerful tone. "No, I—"

He was about to explain what had happened when he heard a knock at the door. "Can you hold on?" he asked, and answered the door. It was

Alejo, slouchy in the cheap black blazer with satin lapels. It looked like an old recycled tuxedo jacket. It was his uniform, along with a white shirt and a battered burgundy bow tie, black slacks. Very grand.

Alejo said, "Mrs. Lenka Villarobles called. She wanted you to have this." He held out a bottle of Bolivian wine. "She wanted you to know that she would be around later tonight."

"Thank you."

Gabriel could tell Alejo was looking at the mountain of bandages on the side of his face. Alejo expressed no surprise at all, though. Resentment radiated brightly from his face.

"Thank you," Gabriel said again. He took the wine, swung the door shut in Alejo's face. How incredible that the biggest threat to his relationship with Lenka—and therefore his work in Bolivia itself—would be a bellboy in an ill-fitting tuxedo jacket and lopsided bow tie.

"Are you there?" Priya said.

"Yeah, I'm here."

"So, what happened?" she said.

"Oh." He sat down on the side of the bed. "You're not going to believe this."

On March 17, 2000, the day after a team of forensic archaeologists working in conjunction with Amnesty International discovered Gabriel's grandfather's body in the Atacama Desert, his mother called to inform him that he *would* be accompanying her to Chile for the funeral in two weeks. "I'm in school, Mom. I can't just leave when I want."

"I know. I'm in a school too, in case you forgot. I bought your ticket. It's in the mail already." She didn't mention that she had also booked an extra three days in Bolivia.

She enclosed in the envelope with his ticket an article she'd clipped from *La Nación* about the discovery of the mass grave ninety miles from Santiago. According to the article, there had been eleven bodies. The desert had parched them out before bacteria or insects could get to work, so they were well preserved, neatly mummified. There were three women, eight men. They had been picked up and killed on a Sunday, and they were mostly in nice suits and frocks. Their hands and feet were bound. They had been gagged as well, which meant that they would have been speechless in the back of the DINA van as it drove out through the cooling summer evening toward the desert. Eventually, the van would have pulled off the road and the prisoners would have had to wait in the back, listening to their captors dig. They would have sat there quietly in the dark, aware that they were all going to share the experience of death together.

The exhausted guards eventually led them out. The guards probably would have been sweaty, even in the cool night. Their hands would have been blistered from the shovel handles. Overhead, the stars and the moon would have been bright enough to illuminate the desert. The prisoners were made to kneel in front of the hole. At the last minute, their gags were removed and thrown into the pit, presumably so that they could all say their last words. And then they were shot, one by one, in the back of the head. When it was done, the weary soldiers put down their rifles, picked up their shovels again, and returned to work.

The forensics team could not tell in what order they had been shot.

In the weeks after the discovery but before they went down for the funeral, Gabriel's mother called him regularly and wept on the phone. He did his best to console her. He said that her father had died honorably, one of the fallen heroes of the resistance. She didn't disagree. "But what was he thinking in his last moments?" she asked. It was almost as if it hadn't occurred to her until then — twenty-seven years after he'd vanished — that he might have died in this way. It was the story she'd told Gabriel his whole life, but now she seemed surprised by it.

"Why haven't you had a funeral yet?" he asked.

"We didn't know for certain that he was dead," she said. Then, "He might have been in some secret CIA prison."

When she said that, he recognized what was going on. It had always been a sort of unacknowledged subtext of the story. If her father had not been killed, the likelihood was that he was in Buenos Aires with a mistress, rather than in Guantánamo Bay with a hood over his head. She wept so violently now not just because she had to accept that her father was, in fact, dead, but also because she had to accept that she had, partially, at least, always both hoped and feared that he had just abandoned them and was alive and well elsewhere. Later, when he thought about this more, Gabriel would come to see that this uncertainty was one of the primary cruelties inflicted by the disappearances. The uncertainty warped people's minds, made them wish for terrible things. It turned a funhouse mirror on the survivors' innermost feelings about the disappeared person and in so doing made monsters of them until they turned against one another.

In Santiago, Gabriel and his mother stayed at his uncle Horace's house. Gabriel spent his time with two male cousins who were around his age. Having never had siblings, he often wondered what they might have looked like, and here was an answer. They got along fine, but the differences ran deep. They wore starched white shirts opened almost to their navels and they reeked of cologne. Gabriel wore a too-small vintage YMCA shirt, ancient jeans, and a pair of scuffed wingtips he'd harvested from a bin at the Value Village in Pomona that still stank of mothballs.

Once, the three of them were at a hookah bar drinking Turkish coffee, and the young women at the next table kept casting glances at Gabriel but not his near-identical cousins. Walking back to the car later, his cousin Nico speculated, "Maybe they heard your accent?"

"I have an accent?" Gabriel said.

Diego, the other cousin, laughed. He was the more furious of the two, the more political. Even his bitterness had a bitter edge. "It's not *that*, brother," he said. "He looks like a gringo."

"Bullshit! He looks exactly like us!" said Nico. Nico was the younger. He was the more handsome and more charming.

"Would you wear those clothes?" Diego replied.

Nico bit his lip and laughed. "Sorry, Gabo" — he looked at Gabriel — "but no fucking way! He looks like a bum!"

"*Exactly!*" Diego said.

"Exactly *what?*"

"Jesus." Diego shook his head. "You know what it says about a guy that he comes from a place where it's considered rebellious to dress like he's poor? He's so far in the other direction that he's going backward."

The funeral itself was as surreal as all funerals ought to be. It took place in a large old church in central Santiago, but there were only a few dozen guests, mostly family. Immediately before the service, Gabriel accompanied his mother to a brief viewing of the body in a rear room of the church. It was a small space with a tiny stained-glass window. Gabriel stood, his arm around the shoulder of his crying mother, staring at the desiccated cadaver. He was amazed that they had decided to have an open casket. The body looked simultaneously fake and all too real. The skin was deep umber, glossy; it looked like a dark resin had been painted on the withered body, like some macabre papier-mâché sculpture. A ragged hole the size of a golf ball in his cheek, directly below his left eye, marked the exit wound. Leathery wrinkles rippled around the sharper points in his skull. The skin around his mouth was pulled taut in a horrific gasp. Blue cloth covered everything beneath his jaw. What else could there be to hide? Gabriel wondered.

After the service, they went to Tío Horace's house. Gabriel was the only foreigner there, the only real outsider. He took a glass of wine and ducked out to the veranda at one point. It overlooked Bellavista's near-Parisian streets. The whole city was fantastically Europhilic; all the neighborhoods were named after countries in Europe. No wonder his mother wanted to take him to Bolivia as well. She followed him outside a little later.

"What do you think?" she said. It was one of the few times she'd addressed him in English since they'd come down. Just as Spanish functioned as a code between them in North America, so English functioned as one in South America.

"It's nice."

"Nice?"

He shrugged. "What else am I going to say? Look, thanks for bringing me here, Mom, but I'm looking forward to getting back to school. You know, I'm in the middle of a semester."

"I am too."

"Right, but he wasn't my father. I don't know these people and I don't know this place."

"But this is your country too, which is why I'm asking what you think."

"I don't know," he said.

Aware that she wasn't going to let him off the hook, he thought about it a little and said, "I don't think this is my country. The people are different from anyone I know. The cousins—I don't get them at all. They're *weird*." There were other words he wanted to use, but he didn't want to offend his mother. The truth was that the cousins' obsession with the grandeur of their social station was embarrassingly naked. It was cheesy and it was coarse.

"*Weird?*" She shook her head, admonishing him for this lack of verbal specificity that she had been endeavoring to rid him of.

He thought it over, tried to find a better way of saying it. He had a sip of wine. "They're eager to seem white, for one thing."

She shook her head lazily, in the way she did when she had hoped he'd be more interesting. She said, "Aren't you too?"

"What? Eager to seem white?"

"Yes."

He laughed. "I *am* more or less white," he said.

"You look maybe seventy-five percent white," she said, shrugging. She was prodding him now. "Eighty percent? Do you think that white people, when they meet you, round up?"

He sighed noisily, as if she were just being silly now.

"Well, it's probably easy for you to scoff at them," she said, "but you don't know what it's like to live here. People, you know, they come *down* here. You hear that? What's the operative word?"

He groaned. "Down," he recited, rolling his eyes. He'd heard this one before. He'd grown up with a world map on the wall of the kitchen that was "upside down," with the South Pole above the North Pole, because, of course, the universe did not actually have a top or bottom, so neither would the planet. The map was also a Peters projection, which, unlike the more common Mercator projection, did not distort the world horizontally and enlarge the Northern Hemisphere. In the Peters, which was slightly more accurate than the Mercator and which was stretched more vertically, South America was enormous, steam-rolled long and narrow, while Greenland, that frosty behemoth in the Mercator, was *petite*.

"What if you had grown up here?" she said. She was working him into the kill zone. He had to evade or fight back, but he'd never done well fighting back with her.

So he went for something between honesty and humor and said, "If I'd grown up here, I guess I'd be like the cousins: Drakkar Noir cologne, shiny black shoes, designer jeans, and" — he winked at her cheesily and popped his hip — "a lot of salsa."

She laughed, threw her arm around his shoulder, grabbed the scruff of his neck, and shook him firmly. He knew he had said something very good that time. Still smiling, she said, "Is that really what you think of them?"

He shook his head. "C'mon, Mom, have you *met* them?"

She laughed again, shaking her head.

When Gabriel arrived at the Lookout, he recognized no one. Fiona was not there yet, so he made his way to the bar. Severo poured him a Pisco Sour de Señorita Fiona as soon as he sat down, and Gabriel thanked him, aware that Severo was staring. The nurse had unceremoniously, if effectively, affixed a huge piece of gauze to the ear with a couple of yards of white medical tape. It looked bizarre, like an enormous home-made earmuff. Underneath it, his face was swollen and bruised; several puncture wounds had been sewn up with black sutures. His ear had been more or less ripped in half horizontally. They had sewn it back together with black sutures, which now looked like tiny crushed spiders in the moist red lesion.

"What happened to you?" Severo waved a hand around his own face.

"An accident," he said.

Which was true, in a sense, but so much seemed accidental or arbitrary. Of the many overly simple assumptions built into economics, the most egregious, as Gabriel saw it, was the idea that individuals were rational and aware of the costs and benefits of their decisions. It simplified the mathematics but could not allow for reality's madness. All the integers were shimmering, skewed in ways no one could comprehend.

Fiona entered and crossed the room briskly, stopping to greet a table of journalists on her way. When she sat down beside him, she said, "Yuck."

He didn't say anything.

"That's dynamite?" she said.

"Sort of." He didn't feel like talking about it with her. He didn't feel like dealing with her reaction. "So, how did your meeting with Evo go?"

"What did you say?"

"What did I say?"

"Yeah, what did you say?" she repeated. Severo put a cocktail in front of her.

"I said, what happened with Evo?"

She slapped her hand on the bar and laughed a bit too hard. "Wow!"

He looked away from her. This wasn't starting well. He'd known it might get messy, but he hadn't expected her to get punchy so quickly.

"Well, that's my Gabriel!" She patted him on the back, very friendly, very sarcastic. "He may be wounded, but his focus is laser sharp!"

He wasn't sure how best to proceed. It would be fruitless to backtrack, since he planned to break it off with her anyway. The best way forward, the only way, was to plow ahead with cold honesty. "Fiona, I have to ask—"

"Right, right, right, right, okay, I know, my little darling. It's fine, please don't get sensitive. Really, of all things: *sensitivity*? It doesn't suit you, Gabriel." She lit a cigarette. "The truth is that I didn't get anything for you. It slipped my mind. Sorry! Maybe next time. No, actually, I won't. I don't know why I'd ask something on your behalf."

"Fair enough," he said.

"No — really, *why* would I?" She put the cigarette down. It smelled good. Gabriel had never liked the smell of cigarettes before, but he liked it that night. Normally, it was as though he could smell the poison in the smoke, but that night it smelled soothing, satisfying.

"I don't know," he said. "You might ask something on my behalf because maybe, one day, you'll want something from me."

"I would have laughed at this a month ago," she said. "Now, I don't know." She tapped her cigarette firmly, had a drag, looked around. "With you — I wouldn't be surprised if I did end up asking you for a favor one day."

"Okay. Is that it?" he said.

She shook her head, had another drag. She seemed keyed up, pugilistic, and he wanted to be away from her. "What is your problem?" he said.

"What happened to your subtlety, Gabriel? Everything is so — since you met Lenka, you've been just ignoring me. That's fine, but it's blunt. And now *this?*"

He hadn't realized she'd expected to hear from him. "Look," he said, hurrying after this opportunity to transition to the more unpleasant business at hand, "I have to tell you that this —" He shook his head, hoping that she would anticipate his direction and settle down.

"Wow!" she said, not settling down. She put her cigarette in the ashtray, ran her fingers through her hair. "If this is how you treat friends —" She stopped.

"I'm sorry if it seems blunt, Fiona, but I had bone fragments blown into my face yesterday, and I don't want to act out some verbal tango with you tonight. I don't want to joust it out. And I'm not going to snort a couple lines, make nice, and then let this slip later. You want the truth. This is the truth. I'm sorry, but I can't do it anymore. I've got a girlfriend here, and things in my life are a little crazy right now, so" — he shook his head — "and they've got me on these pills, so I'm pretty —" He stopped and looked down at his cocktail.

"Okay. That's fair enough. I'll chalk this up to your injury and your medicine," she said.

He glanced at her, unsure of what she meant by that. "Look," he said, "I accept that I could have handled this better, but the message remains the same. I'm sorry, but I'm serious."

"Oh, I know you're serious, Gabriel, please don't feel like you have to reiterate *that*." She had a drag, glared directly into his eyes. Her face was pinched. He hadn't realized that she cared about him. Not that it was the first time he'd missed such a signal. The way women cared for him, it was easy to miss the message. He had no idea why, but their affection was forever cloaked in a veil of indifference.

"Are we done here?" she said.

He nodded.

"Good," she said. She gestured to Severo for her check.

"I don't want to hurt your feelings," he said.

She leaned in and, with her breath warm on his ear, whispered, "I get it, Gabriel: you don't want to fuck me anymore because you're fucking some woman who's something more useful for you. That's fine. I get *that*, believe me. We all have that day at some point, and maybe it's kind of shocking to you at first, but I promise, Gabriel, it's completely normal. The thing you've got to realize is that this is just a sea of bullshit—I'm bullshit, you're bullshit, and even she's bullshit—we're all full of bullshit and we're all swimming in bullshit."

"I get that," he said, staring at his cocktail again.

She leaned back and looked at him. "Yeah, good. There you go. There's the bullshit. And don't worry, by the way, it wasn't special for me either." Severo brought her the check and she stood up. She patted him on the shoulder hard, like he was a good chum, then she bent down and signed the check. "My treat, " she said.

He nodded, glanced at her.

She drained her cocktail. "And, by the way: merry Christmas." She walked away, leaving her cigarette burning in the ashtray.

Gabriel took a deep breath. He hadn't been told off in years and it was an alarming experience. It took a moment for the warmth to drain from his face.

He glanced at the cigarette. It smelled good at the Lookout that night, so he lifted it and had a drag. The smoke scorched his lungs and they seized. He stifled a cough, exhaled slowly. The smoke scraped his throat. His bronchi tingled as the nicotine slipped through the unblemished membranes. He downed the rest of his pisco sour, took another short drag, and then stubbed the cigarette out ineptly, so it broke in half and continued to smolder. Then he stood up quickly and waited for the dizziness to overcome him. It didn't take long.

He wound up in Plaza San Francisco later that night, plumb drunk. There had been other bars. He'd flirted for a while with a startlingly attractive Bolivian woman, who'd been pleased with things all in all, as she should have been. She flirted in a Catholic way, leading him on. She wanted to see his wounds and he let her peek under the bandage. She clearly had no intention of sleeping with him, and he couldn't have faced her by the light of day. The problem was her joy. He'd have relished that joy a couple years ago, but now he wouldn't have known what to do with it.

Later, he stumbled along the lines of low-wattage light bulbs that hung on black wires between vendors' booths in Plaza San Francisco. In the plaza, the smell of stewing chicken intermingled with the heavy odor of frying pork and boiling corn and grilling river fish. It was revolting, delicious, and he wanted to hug someone. It was Christmas Eve!

Weaving around the thicket of pedestrians, angry with them for being so plentiful, so in his way and in one another's way, he found that he wanted to levitate above them all, wreathed in flames, and dish out Old Testament wrath on them: pulverize the bodies and turn the moist pulp into pale ash.

"This is depressing," he said in English to a man with a coppery face who was also visibly drunk and who was trying to sell blue and pink balls of cotton candy. The cotton candy was threaded, puffy and pastel, on a white lance twice as tall as the man himself. The cotton candy man didn't hear Gabriel and wouldn't have understood anyway. Gabriel nodded firmly at him. "I'm sorry," he said, again in English, and trundled along.

Well, was it Christmas? Yes. It was Christmas. It had been Christmas Eve before, and now it was after midnight, so it was Christmas.

Gabriel's face hurt, despite his steady ingestion of Percocet. There was a war of attrition under way between his pain on one side and his painkillers on the other. He retrieved the bottle of pills from his pocket and popped another. Too huge to dry-swallow easily, the pill got lodged halfway down his esophagus. His throat muscles churned, trying to massage it downward. There was no bottled water nearby, none that he trusted, so he tried to work up some saliva. He stood there amid all those warm bodies, smelling their breath and feeling their thick muscles brush against him, focusing on the pill. At last it settled in an esophageal nook just above his stomach. Close enough. It'd get there eventually.

He shook his head and thought about what would have happened if he'd choked. Would anyone have noticed? Maybe, and maybe not. He might have lain there dead, his maimed face locked in breathless surprise, while Bolivians wandered around, stepping over him.

In front of him, the centuries-old church of San Francisco was grand, the color of parched bones, terrible against the sky. If divinity did exist above, he might be seeing it now. La Paz was so high it might have punctured the purplish sheet hiding the heavens, and now he was seeing the real thing, a hollow chasm, all limpid negative space. The depth of the space, up there, it began to make sense. There was nothing. Up there, he saw an *infinity* of nothing.

A crudely drawn sign indicated that midnight Mass was under way inside the cathedral. Gabriel pulled out his phone, checked the time — it was 12:33; he had missed thirty-three minutes of midnight Mass. The church had been designed by missionaries in the 1600s for the purpose of luring nonbelieving heathens into the fold, which explained why it was decorated with such a curious hodgepodge of Catholic and Inca iconography, including images of the goddess Pachamama carved into the exterior walls. He saw flourishes from Tiahuanaco side by side with details borrowed from the Almudena Cathedral.

Gabriel bought a cigarette from a young boy, lit it, and had two puffs as he walked up to the giant doors, but it didn't taste that good, so he flicked it away. He entered as the beginnings of a headache started at the back of his brain.

He stumbled up the narrow stairs that cycloned up beside the door to the small balcony at the rear. It was not so crowded up there. A small wooden cot had been planted, awkwardly, by the top of the banister. A plaque above it explained that it was where a certain infirm monk used to lie in the 1700s in order to hear the day's Mass. Gabriel stood at the banister beside a transvestite, who was kneeling, pinching and twisting her rosary ardently. Below, at the far end of the great yawning nave, a broad-shouldered Franciscan monk with a long white beard and long white hair, light alb, and flowing white chasuble stood with the Eucharist, chanting. He had a thin leather band wrapped around his head. He didn't look like anything Gabriel would have expected from a priest, to say nothing of a monk. He looked like an extra in a movie about the life and times of Christ.

The man intoned in a remarkably sonorous voice toward the domed ceiling, and his voice reverberated with surprising power, but the echoes crisscrossed until they made mud of his words. The vast church was packed, except for the upstairs. Up there, they had lots of room. Was Gabriel with the repentant squad, those who didn't have the audacity to show up in the nave and refuse communion in view of the congregation? No. That was too easy. Gabriel saw all manner of people up there. If they had anything in common, it was that most were alone.

Below, he saw one of the witches from the nearby Witches' Market. Those *brujas* wore a black-on-black version of the traditional indigenous attire; from the petticoat to the hat to the stockings—it was all black. Gabriel stared down at her while beside him the transvestite prayed, intensely, kneeling on the stone floor and not on the padded ledge. The transvestite pinched the beads of her rosary, her hands quivering, as she hissed prayers toward her boyish breast.

It was approaching time for Holy Communion, and a few of the people in the balcony sneaked downstairs. The priest said something, stopped speaking briefly, and the congregation replied in a muffled indecipherable chant. Then the priest asked them to give the sign of peace and, to Gabriel's surprise, the transvestite stood up and extended her undainty hand to him.

Gabriel reached out, took the hand, looked at the face: the full lips, plump and redolent with grief, painted industrial red; the dark, beady eyes lost beneath gargantuan fake eyelashes. The cheeks were sweat-moist. Gabriel smiled as sincerely as possible at her face, so festooned with tragedy. The sorrow had bureaus in which further misery lingered, expressing itself in ways he had not ever seen before. The shape of the nose somehow implied tragedy too, a drooping hook. The hand was clammy, its grip predictably feeble.

She said, "Peace be with you," and he knew that she meant it.

He knew she had wished him well more sincerely than almost anyone else he had met since he'd arrived here. Other than Lenka, no one in Bolivia seemed to want him to really be okay, not that vividly. And for that alone, he wanted to kiss her face and apologize for thinking unkind thoughts about her.

But he was stumped, and replied only, "Peace be with you," and then he turned and wished the same to another man, also to a woman. He felt their hands. He looked into their eyes, and—for a fleeting moment—he knew that he had made a very bad decision when he chose to accept his job at Calloway. He had made a bad decision when he had agreed to come down to Bolivia. There were decisions that scattered away behind him, and most of them were wrong. Since he had arrived, he had made bad decisions daily. He had made scores of them. The epiphany flew quick and bright into view, where it lingered, briefly, awfully, for him to appreciate. It began its retreat before he turned and hurried down the winding stairs to the ground floor. By the time he ran out, the realization had evanesced completely.

Outside, he sat and caught his breath, leaning against the jamb of the doorway. Before him the mob was a blur, the voices were fuzz, the smells foul. A smear of senses. Fondly, he thought of the crowded streets in New York before recent Christmases, the harried bluster of Midtown near *IBI*'s offices, where he sometimes loitered with a coffee while on a break, observing the ravening shoppers. He remembered the scent of chestnut smoke and how it had already seemed freighted with nostalgia the first time he smelled it, and he remembered the stampede of clopping heels and the hypnotic blur of giant shopping bags swinging in the chilly air.

A finger tapped him on the shoulder, and he looked up, expecting to see the sad transvestite—hoping to see her, really; there were things they could talk about—but it was not her. It was a man.

Standing, he shook the wee simian hand—recognizing, with a little ruefulness, that it belonged to Alberto Catacora, the finance minister in waiting. He was with a woman, presumably Señora Catacora. Gabriel hastily attempted to recover a more sober version of himself. No luck. Aware that, with a kind of belly-flop slow motion, he was already wavering, cockeyed, he said, *"Eshtoy borracho."* He swayed as he stood, as if in demonstration. He hoped to kill the issue by putting it right out there. Such was the nuance of his game that night.

"I see," Catacora said, in English. "What happened to you?"

"Oh—Jesus. *Dynamite!* Can you believe it?" He could hear himself slurring. "Very horrible. This is—it was this miner, this guy, he blew his hand up. *Boom!*"

"I'm sorry."

There was a long pause while Gabriel nodded steadily.

"Were you inside?" Catacora asked and pointed at the door behind him.

Gabriel continued nodding, a little more quickly. "With a—there was a transvestite! Jesus! Have you ever seen a transvestite in there? I mean—" He shook his head.

Catacora took a deep breath, shook his head quickly, embarrassed, eyebrows crushing toward the center of his face.

"No," Gabriel blurted, in order to clarify what he, belatedly and incorrectly, saw might be Catacora's misperception, "the transvestite wasn't *with* me. I mean, she was—I don't know—just *there*. You know?"

"You should get to sleep."

Something about Catacora's tone said that he didn't, in fact, understand what Gabriel had meant. So, to make sure Catacora understood, Gabriel said, "I just found her there. It was a surprise to me."

Catacora nodded and turned toward his wife as if to leave, and Gabriel said, "It was nice talking to you." Then embarrassed that he had flubbed the conversation so badly, he added, "Are you—are you going to be an official—"

Catacora turned back. "What?"

"You—are you okay with being a *politician?*" Gabriel hurled the last word like an epithet. He managed a wink.

"No." Catacora turned and murmured something to his wife, an apology perhaps.

"A *finance minister?*" Gabriel muttered, because he wasn't going to let it go like that. He didn't want to come off both unknowing and drunk. "That's—is that *you?*"

Catacora's face went severe. "Where did you hear that?"

"I just think that—well—*no*." Gabriel shook his head. "I've had too much to drink." This was, by his dim reasoning, a deft maneuver. He'd raised the issue and ducked its consequences.

The man didn't move.

Gabriel said, "Let's talk tomorrow. Right?"

"It's Christmas, but I will call you." Catacora turned without another word and led his wife into the crowd.

Gabriel sat down on the church's steps, satisfied that he'd handled that well. His headache was worse and he thought it might be because he hadn't been drinking for the last half hour, so he decided he'd drink a little more. He caught the attention of a young man hawking *chicha* and waved him over. The man ladled the viscous fermented-corn drink into a plastic cup and handed it to Gabriel. It was warm through the plastic. The man said it was five bolivianos.

Gabriel reached into his pocket, pulled out a messy wad of bills. He tried to sort through it one-handed, tried to organize the bills and to make sense of the numbers. Eventually he found that the smallest bill he had was fifty bolivianos. He handed the fifty to the man. "You keep the change."

The man started counting up bills for his change. Gabriel repeated, "Please, keep the change! It's for you!"

The man paused briefly and stared at him, and then he shook his head, threw the fifty back at Gabriel. "Fuck you," he said and walked away.

Gabriel nodded. He thought, *Fuck it!* and glanced down just in time to see a little boy's hand reach out and snatch up the discarded bill. "Good for you," he mumbled. With the cup of warm *chicha* in his hand, he weaved back through the crowd in the direction of his hotel.

Every time he bumped into someone he stopped, bowed, and said, very politely, *"Permiso, por favor, disculpe, permiso..."* No one replied. One woman laughed, thinking it was a joke, but that was the only response. He sipped from his cup until, halfway done and too sickened to continue, he handed it to a nearby legless beggar, who glided noisily around the square on a wooden plank affixed with wobbly metal wheels. The man bowed, thanking him, grinned toothlessly, like a fledgling chick: big dark eyes, beak abridged and fixed in a terrible grin, wings wooly and crooked, pegged to a warped torso. Disturbed by the man's visage, Gabriel moved on and was quickly bumbling through the horde toward his hotel again. Among them, he too was a shuffling phantom, one of the many slurring together in that plaza, a shadowy and slow-shifting thicket that wandered, in unison, nowhere in particular. Together, they made a great sad swath of tottering and blinking humanity.

He briefly muttered curses at them in English, things like "I think I understand why GIs shoot pedestrians in Iraq." He said these things to people and either they didn't acknowledge them, or they nodded back at him, as if in appreciation. And the further he got through the crowd, the harder he pushed against their stocky, sauntering bodies.

Soon, he put away the ethnic slurs, out of guilt, and—despite how much he hated them all by then—was back to the more sane and polite refrain of someone traversing a thick crowd. *"Perdoname, por favor, discul-pame, con su permiso, por favor..."*

Eventually, he neared his hotel and his impatience returned. He felt frantic. He banged into the people in the crowd by accident at first, and then deliberately, jamming his elbows into their ribs. He began surrep-titiously shoving them aside, into others. In that swarm, no one could identify the source of aggression. And still, he continued with his litany of apologies. It came like a sweet benediction; he muttered, *"Con per-miso, señor, por favor, lo siento..."* Inside, it was all bile and wrath and burn-ing blood—inside, he was wishing the horrors of hell upon them—but outside, he begged their pardon.

"Forgive me," he implored. "Please, I'm so sorry, *please...*"

In his hotel room, Gabriel took the heavy, blood-drenched gauze off of his head and dropped it on the bathroom counter. He stood, star-ing at himself as he listed in front of the mirror. His cheek had swollen and was mottled colorfully, like half of an overripe mango. The punc-tures sat moistly, stitches pulled taut on the surface of the distended skin. He recalled the beautiful girl from the bar earlier that night, who had peeked under the bandages and then continued to flirt with him. He thought of her kindness, her perfect beauty. She had given him her phone number. He had thrown it away when he left the bar.

That night, he brushed his teeth with tap water. He was never go-ing to successfully avoid those germs and it was pointless, finally, even to attempt such a thing. If it wasn't an ice cube, it was the beads of water on a leaf of lettuce, a still-damp plate in a restaurant. Sooner or later, the germs found a way in. It was a shame, but the sickness wouldn't last long.

# 9

# Christmas

*Sunday, December 25, 2005*

TINY SPECKS OF BLOOD dotted the pillow in the morning. In the bathroom mirror he saw that the swelling was down, but the bruises had darkened. The pain was worse, a dull ache all over the side of his face that resonated through his skull. It itched too. It itched furiously. After showering, he reapplied the ointment and put three large Band-Aids over the sutures. The ear was still a problem, though. It was just too gruesome to leave uncovered. He tried to construct a less gigantic gauze earmuff than the one the nurse had made for him yesterday, but his lighter application of medical tape wouldn't hold it. Abandoning that approach, he gently applied a few oversize Band-Aids to the offending area, which looked weird, but he concluded that it was better than any of the alternatives.

He brushed his teeth, again with the tap water, and pondered his illbegotten conversation with Catacora. Magnificently stupid. He blushed just thinking about it. He tried to eject the thought from his mind, but it was no use. It had slipped in like a splinter.

Gabriel mulled over the potential consequences. He bypassed a number of benign or even pleasant possibilities and tucked into the most mortifying possible outcomes.

One specific nightmarish scenario played out in his mind on a kind of loop, repeating incessantly, as if to confirm that it was, in fact, possible. The pieces fell with a horrid logic: Catacora would find out that Gabriel was working for Calloway, and then he'd discover that Lenka had been sleeping with Gabriel. He'd be able to deduce that she'd fed Gabriel sensitive information. She'd be fired on the spot. Catacora and Evo might well go to the press with the story — both to advertise the potential investment opportunities being created in Bolivia and to show that they were not going to tolerate scheming foreigners — at which point Gabriel's name would work its way through the newswires in a story about hedge-fund subterfuge in Bolivia. Priya would make a big show of firing Gabriel. His mother would disown him. Lenka would (justifiably) blame him for ruining her life.

After breakfast, Gabriel called his mother. It was one thing to forget Thanksgiving; it would be quite another to forget Christmas.

"I'm glad you called," she said immediately. "I booked a ticket. I'll be there in two days."

"You're kidding."

"No, I'm not kidding. And *feliz Navidad a tí también*, Gabo."

"Merry Christmas, Mom. But, look" — he paused, letting her acclimate to his less-than-cheerful tone before continuing — "this isn't a good time for me. I just want you to know that."

"I know," she said. "That's why I'm coming..." As she went on, he recalculated the lay of the land and it struck him, straightaway, that it was hard enough to maintain the one lie — that he was a freelance journalist — while in Bolivia, but it would be almost impossible to simultaneously sustain his mother's belief that he worked for BellSouth. There were other considerations too, but he couldn't do all the calculus right then. In his good ear, she was saying that she was worried, and that it was Christmas, and that she was going to write a profile on Evo, who had agreed to an interview.

Gabriel understood that had he not managed to get himself blown up, she wouldn't be en route—all he'd done was stop and take a look at the miners' protest, and now his life was derailed and rolling down some hill. "You got an interview?" he said. "How did you set it up?"

"What do you mean?"

"The interview."

"I don't know—I just called his office." She was, if not exactly rocking back on her heels, trying to deflect his tone. "What's going on, Gabriel?"

What was going on was that he was wondering if his mother had spoken to Lenka, and, if so, had either of them put it together? He didn't want to get into it with her though. There were other, more pressing issues. He said, "I've just got a lot going on here."

"That's why I'm coming down. I'll be there on the afternoon of the twenty-seventh. Where are you staying?"

"You're not staying here."

"Why?" She'd moved to Spanish.

Resisting the autopilot impulse to reply in Spanish, he stood firm, saying, *"Mom, please."* The unspoken anger was more chastening than anything he could have said.

"What's going on, Gabriel?" she said, still in Spanish.

"Things are very complicated here. How long are you planning on staying?"

"If you don't want me—"

"I want you to come, but you're not going to stay at my hotel."

"What's this about? Is it that girl?"

"Which one?" he said.

"Oh my . . . *Gabriel,*" she said, as if unsure whether to be impressed or shocked.

He sat down. "Look, it's not that. I'm working very hard here right now. If you're at my hotel, in my space all the time, it'll be chaos. It's great that you're going to be here, but I need space to work, and so on."

"And so on?"

He laughed at her scandalized innuendo.

"I don't know, Gabriel."

"What don't you know?" He then repeated his message, nearly verbatim.

When he was done, she sighed loudly. "So, where do you want me to stay?"

Nearing Lenka's house, still a little early, he wandered in Plaza Sucre awhile, rehashing the stages of the most disastrous scenario in his mind. It wasn't inconceivable, especially with his mother down there to entangle herself in events. Evo would have every reason to fire Lenka if he found out, and he would have just as much reason to take the story to the press.

The plaza was largely abandoned on that sunny Christmas Day. The only people in sight were the guards around the huge wooden doors of San Pedro Prison. An attractive old building, at least from the outside, the prison had been an unusual tourist attraction for many years. Until a change of policy earlier that year had outlawed casual visitors, inmates had held a daily bazaar in the courtyard, where they sold everything from homemade sweaters to cola and sandwiches. The inmates could pay rent for a better room and were allowed to have their families share the cells with them, if their families were so inclined. That all came to a halt when it became clear that many of the "sandwiches" and "crafts" they were selling were actually cheap, disposable vessels for homemade bazooka, a gooey form of crack cocaine.

Plaza Sucre itself was serene, shaded by evenly spaced umbrella thorn trees, whose leaves shushed in the gentle breeze. Opposite the penitentiary stood Lenka's family's church, the Iglesia San Pedro, built in 1790, just after Katari's uprising. San Pedro had been an indigenous neighborhood until the past few decades, when the country's caste system began to erode. Now, the neighborhood was generally mixed. As with the United States, the gentrification didn't amount to much real change. Racism was rife, and the Indians remained segregated from the mestizos; the only difference was that they had been pushed up higher, to El Alto. It was still unheard-of to see an indigenous person in the upscale restaurants around Sopocachi—unless that person happened to be the president-elect, of course.

Gabriel was still sauntering around, taking it all in and considering his options, when his cell phone rang. It was Oscar Velazquez. "Merry Christmas, Gabriel," he said.

"Right, right—you too, Oscar. What are you up to?" Gabriel sat down on a bench and stretched his legs out, crossing them at the ankles. He was suspicious. This wasn't a social call—not on Christmas—but he had no idea what was up.

"This a bad time?"

"No, no, if I sound winded, it's just the altitude—I was strolling through sunny La Paz. Looking at a prison right now and thinking it looks much nicer than my hotel." He resisted the urge to scratch his cheek.

"That's Bolivia for you. So, you're still there!"

"Astonishing, right? I'm starting to wonder if I'll ever get out."

"Understandable. You had an accident too. Some dynamite."

"Yes, *some* dynamite." Gabriel looked around. He gave in, scratched his cheek furiously, briefly, then quickly stopped because it hurt and he was afraid of breaking the stitches.

He'd taken two Percocets before he set off from the hotel and was feeling quite good now, all things considered. He'd smoked a cigarette after he got off the phone with his mother while he finished off his morning cup of maté. The hangover had initially been brutal: a bright bolt of pain had bounced inside his brain and lit up a wide grid of nerves. By the time he'd finished his conversation with his mother, the pain had focused on a particular twisted nodule in the base of his skull. He got dressed and fantasized—drearily, unimaginatively—about not being hung over. Then he'd remembered about the Percocet.

"Look, I—uh," Oscar was saying, finally getting to the meat of the matter, "I think Priya's not sure what to do with you anymore."

"Not sure?" That sounded like a euphemism for "completely sure." He girded himself.

"I just wanted to give you a heads-up on that, so it's not a surprise. I think she was hoping you'd have sewn this Bolivia thing up by now."

"She's the one who upped the ante."

"I know."

"And I'm on track. I've just been trying to work around the holidays, the election, and this dynamite thing. But I'm making progress. Two days ago I gave Priya the name of the next finance minister."

"Oh, really? She didn't mention that. That's good. It really is, but I'd just try to figure out what you can tell her about that gas company that you mentioned."

"Yeah, I understand." Not exactly a surprise, but he'd hoped that giving her the finance minister would tide him over for a while. Then again, the finance minister's name wasn't monetizable.

"You really piqued her interest when you brought it up, but none of us have been able to find out what's going on, so now it's up to you. So you're making progress?"

"Of course I am," Gabriel said. He had his report. It wasn't going to cut it, evidently.

It was obvious now that he had made a mistake bringing up Santa Cruz Gas with Priya. It had been a critical mistake. In his attempt to placate her by simulating progress, he'd inadvertently sparked sincere interest. Now she had very concrete expectations. She wanted real answers, and though the stakes were still low for her, they had become high for him—never a desirable situation in a negotiation. He said, "What if I don't succeed? What then?" He knew the answer, but he needed to double-check.

Oscar didn't say anything right away. He dragged the ensuing pause out long enough that Gabriel, not wanting to force him to say it, said, "Okay, okay, don't hurt yourself, Oscar."

"I know it's not the kind of thing anyone wants to hear on Christmas Day," Oscar said, "but I thought you'd want to know as soon as possible."

"It's fine, Oscar. Thanks for the heads-up. I'll see what I can do. Enjoy your Christmas."

"You too."

Gabriel hung up and walked around the square, trying to sort out what this meant. It didn't mean anything—really, it simply confirmed what he'd suspected all along, that the life expectancy of his career at Calloway was, in fact, quite short.

He knocked on Lenka's door and scratched the wounds on his cheek one last time while he waited. Mirabel answered and cooed a vowelly declaration of maternal affection. Then she reached her plump moist hands out and gently cradled his jaw. *"¡Pobrecito!"* He kissed her cheek. "Such a beautiful face," she said. "I hope you're not too badly hurt!"

"Oh, I'm sure I'll be even more beautiful once it's all healed," he said. She laughed. He thanked her for letting him come.

"Agh!" she harrumphed, waving at him. "You sure you're okay?"

"I'm fine. More than fine! They gave me these pills; the worst that will happen is that I'll fall asleep on the sofa in the middle of the party."

"Ha!" Mirabel hooked her arm through his and led the way down the long hall. "You can take a nap in Ernesto's room, if you want. Anytime. Just give me a sign"—she tapped the side of her nose with an index finger—"and I will show you the way. No one will care."

He thanked her. She looked only vaguely like Lenka, mainly in the hypnotic, oversize eyes and her vivid chin. She was grandly proportioned, though, and she kept her hair, which was flecked with springy steel strands, cropped short. She waddled, slightly bowlegged, and wore cheap sandals that looked as if they'd been grafted to her feet some decades prior. The air around her was full of a beguiling and profoundly maternal kindness. She gave the impression that she'd seen so much of the world's crap, whatever crime you confessed to would not damage her opinion of you. Her love was not going to be swayed so easily.

She said, "Your mother must be worried about you."

"Oh, my mother!" He rolled his eyes. "She's actually coming down. She just told me this morning."

*"Aí!"* She stopped walking and turned and hugged him. She looked up at his eyes and said, "I want to meet her. You'll bring her here?"

He nodded. "I'll bring her around."

"Any woman who raised such a wonderful young man by herself would have to be a miracle worker."

"Yes, she is that. It's a difficult job, I see, raising boys alone. Lenka's doing it well too, I think. Ernesto is a wonder. Of course, she has you to help—"

She shrugged. "But she takes care of him." She continued steering him down the hallway. "He says he's going to be president now too. Ernesto"—she shook her head—"he is even better than you, I believe."

"Oh, I'm sure," Gabriel replied. "I've seen: he's a better dancer. Smarter. More handsome."

She laughed.

In the kitchen, she said, "I'll be right back to introduce you to everyone," and then she shuffled to a tiny patio beside the sitting room where a group of smokers were standing around a small grill stacked high with ears of corn. The smell of grilling corn and cigarettes drifted directly through the kitchen window, and it pleased Gabriel greatly.

Dozens of people stood in every room of the house chatting. Gabriel lingered in the kitchen, glad that he had come. One way or another, he'd have to shake every man's hand and kiss every woman's cheek. Bolivia, antique in so many ways, was also atavistic in its formality, its attention to decorum. Still, he didn't mind. After spending the morning pondering the dangers of his situation (Catacora, Santa Cruz Gas, Fiona), dealing with his mother on the phone, and then receiving that call from Oscar, part of him wanted to retreat to his hotel room, but he truly was relieved to be amid the warmth of Lenka's family. He looked forward to shaking the hands. He looked forward to being paraded around by Mirabel, or Lenka, to seeing Luis and Ernesto.

Thanks to the pills, Gabriel wasn't hungry at all, but he knew he'd be practically force-fed. Nearby, the charred remains of the pig now straddled the kitchen table, its legs outstretched, as if it'd seized, midleap. The head remained largely intact, its pudgy eyes pressed shut, its mouth open, almost grinning, but not. The ears were gone—to the dogs, probably. Its skin had turned amber; it looked as if it'd been shellacked. Apart from a few tufts of shredded flesh and gristle still clinging around the joints, the hindquarters had been more or less picked clean, leaving a pair of tan bones and blackened hooves. Its midsection had been ravaged as well; half of the torso was simply gone, and the other half had been fairly well decimated, revealing the ribs, like long witchy fingers clawing at the hollow cavity.

Luis entered the kitchen, midconversation with another man, and started idly picking at the meat piled beside the carcass. He snarfed it with his hamsterish, repaired-harelip mouth. It was an indistinguishable meat pile, a brownish heap of fat, charred skin, bone, and shredded flesh. When Luis looked up and noticed Gabriel, he interrupted his conversation and beckoned Gabriel casually with a greasy hand. "I didn't see you arrive," he said. Gabriel was glad to see him. Then, in his eerie baritone, Luis introduced him to Marco, a deacon at the San Pedro church.

Gabriel shook the man's hand, which was parched. He wore a baggy, pilled blue cardigan and a cheap digital watch, well-worn light gray slacks. He was gaunt, his expression pinched and dour. He said nothing and barely made eye contact.

"I heard about this," Luis said, gesturing at his own cheek, "I'm sorry. They drink a lot of *chicha* up in the hills, and then they come down with this dynamite and it is not good!"

"So I gather!" Gabriel said. "If I'd been standing an inch or two in another direction I'd have lost my eye, maybe even been killed, so I guess it could have been worse."

"The other man is dead, no?" This from Luis still.

"Actually, I think he's going to survive," Gabriel said.

"Too bad!" Luis guffawed, slapped Gabriel on the shoulder with his clean hand.

"Well—" Gabriel shrugged, scratched his cheek. "It was an honest mistake, I think."

Marco just shook his head, glowering at it all. "We have some very angry people here," he said. "They are very angry and very poor," he added, in case Gabriel hadn't picked up on that.

Gabriel inferred that Marco inflected principally with his eyebrows, like a bad actor. He spoke in a cheerless monotone and his expressions ran drearily between condescending acceptance and condescending denunciation.

Gabriel said, "From what I can tell, distressed people all over the world are blowing themselves up these days. It's the new thing."

Luis laughed heartily, pleased that Gabriel was gibing with the deacon. Marco himself just wrinkled up a concerned eyebrow.

Not wanting to push it, Gabriel said, "Sorry, they gave me these pills, and I have absolutely no idea what I'm saying."

That was when Lenka's mother poked her head in the room and commanded Luis to introduce Gabriel around because she was busy with the corn.

"As you wish," he said. Then he cleared his throat, wiped his hand on a dishrag.

The following ten minutes were spent processing around the rooms, Gabriel catching faces and names as he met everyone, catching their scents and then losing them all as soon as the next person came into his line of sight. He kept glancing around for Lenka but couldn't see her. Despite the confusion of it, and the inherent awkwardness of running through so many surface-level conversations, and despite the fact that he still hadn't seen Lenka, it was, as he'd hoped, a warming experience. And he wondered why he hadn't been spending more time among these people all along. Apart from the curmudgeonly deacon, Gabriel was awash in kindness, a feeling that was only amplified by the gentle euphoria he'd been given by the pills. All of his concerns about his mother coming down seemed a little trivial. Of course he'd bring her around here! And his job? So what if he lost it? There was more to life!

Somewhere in there, Gabriel kissed the cheek of Luis's new wife, who said that she'd heard great things about him—he waved off the comment, as if modest, and said, "No, really, it's all true." And she laughed, touched his shoulder. Then he was on to the next cluster of people. He had no idea who lived at the house and who didn't. The web of relations was byzantine. It didn't matter anyway. The point was not to memorize names, it was to touch each of them, one by one, and to smile and say something nice, or funny, or generous, and then move along to the next.

Mostly, Luis introduced him as a *friend* of Lenka's. Occasionally, he said *friend* in a semiconspiratorial way, and then the man Gabriel was being introduced to—Luis did this only with men—grinned at Gabriel as if Luis had just said that Gabriel was legally blind but aspired to be a commercial pilot. One of the men actually pointed at Gabriel's face and said, "Did she do that to you?"

"No, not this," he said. "This was dynamite. The wounds she's inflicted—I can't show you those, not here."

Luis and the other guy were thrown into hysterics by this—they howled, tearing up, shaking their heads. Gabriel laughed too, scratching his cheek, vividly aware that it'd been a long time since he'd had so much fun.

Lenka had been ensconced at the rear of the house so he didn't spot her until he'd almost exhausted the rest of his hellos. She was talking to a woman and gazing at Ernesto, playing with toy cars on the floor. She wore a prim brown pantsuit and a lavender blouse, and although it was one of the least sexy outfits Gabriel had ever seen her in, he found it intensely arousing. She was lost in conversation, unaware that he was even there, and it was one of those moments—like watching her handle her car—when he felt he could peer into a wonderfully mundane portion of her life. It was, by all measures, totally unremarkable, and that was exactly what made him sick with love. When she eventually noticed him, she grinned conspiratorially and stood up. She had a great body, and the pantsuit, despite its dowdiness, showed it off.

Luis excused himself and Gabriel thanked him, still looking at her. She was beaming as she approached. They kissed cheeks and she said, beneath her breath, "Thank you for coming."

"No, thank *you* for inviting me. I'm having a great time."

"I'm glad."

"A warning, though: I might have offended your deacon. I couldn't help myself."

"He deserves it. And how was Luis?"

"He's my hero: a human bazooka."

She rolled her eyes. "Well, I'm glad someone likes him. Have you eaten?"

"Not yet. What do you have left, some pig face?"

She cast him a wicked look. "I saved the eyeballs just for you."

"By the way," he said, lowering his voice still more, "my mother is coming down."

"Wow."

He nodded slowly, eyes cranked open in shock. "You didn't speak to her, did you? She somehow arranged an interview with Evo, and I was thinking..."

"Oh," she said, when she realized what he meant. "Who is she with?"

"The *Nation*, I think."

Lenka thought about it and then sighed, shook her head. "I would have to look it up. Maybe? That's crazy. You know, I'll probably meet with her. Does she know about—"

"Oh yeah. She's thrilled about you. Me, she could do without, but you sound like a dream come true to her."

She smiled.

"But I still haven't told her about Calloway," Gabriel whispered.

"Eek." Lenka screwed her face up. "Maybe you need a Scotch?"

He nodded in mock solemnity.

"This way."

She poured him a whiskey and they went to the entranceway where they could talk in peace for a minute while he drank up.

"When does she arrive?"

"Tuesday. Two days."

"Evo and I will be gone then."

"I know. She's here for a while, then leaves Friday, before the reception."

"Maybe it's good that you'll have a chance to be alone with her for a couple days before we return?"

"Maybe." He drained the rest of his whiskey. "You want to introduce me to anyone I might have missed?" The way she looked at him then, he swore he could see love in her eyes. He leaned in and kissed her on the mouth, once. "Thank you," he said.

Hours later—after Gabriel had met another dozen people, had let their names enter his mind and then leave; after he had eaten a plate of the shredded pork, an ear of smoky corn, and a couple of chalky wedges of boiled cassava—he and Lenka sneaked off to Ernesto's room for some privacy. Maybe it was the Percocet working its way out of his system, or maybe it was all the small talk, but he was weary.

"Do you regret coming here today?" she said. They were sitting side by side on the bed. Ernesto's room was a tidy rectangle, like all of the rooms in the house; a plain rectangular window offered a view of a row of boxy properties across the street.

He shook his head. "I love it here. I love your family." Battered, brightly colored toys—Buzz Lightyear, Thomas the Tank Engine—had erupted across the floor near the closet. Ernesto'd made his own bed, Gabriel guessed; the sincerity of the attempt was matched only by the awkwardness of the execution. He felt woozy, but he knew he needed to snap to attention; she was trying to talk about something of importance. He needed to convey, most of all, that he adored her and her family. "You know that this isn't"—he gestured in the downstairs direction—"it's not me. The charming guy who buys toys for your son, comes over to dinner all the time. That's not me, but I like it here, and I was thinking that I shouldn't be so, you know, limited."

"Are you going to start coming around for dinner every night?"

"No. But, I mean—" He scratched his stitches and wondered how he could say what he thought he should say, that all the sweet norms of romance—the bashful presentation of flowers, the holding of hands in a dim cinema—did not seem appropriate for them. But their relationship was alive and passionate and it thrived *especially* in the absence of any of that pro forma schlock. Their place was up in his hotel room, with cake and wine, at a slight remove from the messy world below. Still, there was more—or there was potential for more. He loved her and she loved him and he was even falling for her family, and if they—he and Lenka—were an unconventional couple, so be it. Maybe it could be strange and wonderful. But he didn't know how to say these things. Instead, he said, "I really like it here. I really do." And he nodded earnestly as he said it, staring at the toys on Ernesto's floor.

She draped an arm over his shoulder and they sat in silence. His wandering attention settled on a crucifix above the bed. He'd seen it when he entered, but he took a moment to stare at it now. Like other crucifixes he'd seen in Latin America, it presented a much gorier picture of Christ than you'd find in the North. Jesus was pulped, scored with oozing lacerations, his emaciated body painted in blood. The seam of skin at the lower edge of the wound in his chest sagged open like the bottom lip of an idiot's mouth, exposing the pale ribs beneath.

Lenka, aware that he was staring, stood up and retrieved it from the wall. And from the way she held it—cradled it, really—he could tell she was a true believer. She handed it to him and sat down.

He held it, not sure what to do. Did she want him to talk about religion? He didn't believe and would rather not lie about it. He preferred to lie only out of necessity. He blew some dust off the cross. "It's intense," he said, for lack of anything else. He handed it back to her.

"Yes," she said. This was disappointing to her, maybe. She stood up and put it back on the wall.

"I don't mean any offense," he said.

She sat back down. "You know, this is supposed to be a very happy holiday."

"Christmas isn't happy for you?"

She shrugged. "He was born to suffer so horribly, so brutally. His gift to us is his suffering. You know, in four months, Paceñas will be dragging crucifixes through the city streets on the anniversary of his death. Some of them crawl—and by the end of the day their knees are raw and covered in blood." She shook her head. "The suffering continues. We do it to ourselves. Did you know that they say that Bolivia is a donkey on a gold mine?"

"I've heard that. I don't think of it that way."

"I know, Gabriel," she said. She was trying to be kind to him, but something was wearing thin for her. She shook her head and he wished that he could explain better what he meant and how he felt. He wished he could explain how much he adored her family, and how crazy it was for him to care that much about them, considering what he'd come to Bolivia to do.

"I just found out that I will probably be fired from my job," he said. "And my mother told me she's coming, and—I wanted to tell you that the most remarkable thing of the day has been spending this time here. I really—I don't know how to say this..."

"It's okay, Gabriel, you don't have to," she said.

That would have to do. He couldn't bring himself to explain the rest.

She leaned in and kissed him on the eyelid. "Thank you," she said. "I love you."

He nodded and stared at the toys on the floor, feeling awful.


Lenka helped Gabriel sneak out of the party without all the goodbyes. He asked her to apologize to her mother for him, and to say that he'd bring his mother around.

Kissing slowly around the corner from her front door, he ran his hands down the back of her pantsuit and felt where the coarse fabric grew taut across her hips. He leaned in to her ear and said, "Will you wear this tonight?"

Staring at him, she nodded slowly, her mouth open. He could see that her lower lip was wet from their kissing. He leaned in and kissed her beneath the eye.


When he got back to Hotel Gloria, he stopped at the front desk and asked the petite woman if he had any messages. Yes, he did. Catacora had already left a message saying that he wanted to meet at his office the next morning.

"Did he say anything else?" Gabriel asked the woman.

"No."

"Really?"

"Really."

"Ugh." Vexed, he lingered. "Okay. Thanks."

He went to the Lookout, half hoping to find Fiona, half hoping not to find her. She wasn't there. She probably wasn't even in the country anymore. He sat in a booth in the corner, near the window that looked across at Hotel Gloria. There were a handful of journalists at the bar, none he knew. He gazed out the window and tried to figure out which window in the Gloria was his. He narrowed it down to two, but he wasn't sure which floor was which.

Then he opened his notepad and glanced over his notes on Santa Cruz. He had nothing so far. He'd never been fired before, and he didn't look forward to the experience.

He dialed Oscar, whose phone was off. It was, after all, Christmas evening. He didn't leave a message. He knew he was supposed to call his mother, but he couldn't bear to do it. The conversation would go on and on, he knew. And the last thing he wanted that evening was to talk to anyone for a long time.

Severo wasn't there that night. It was another bartender. The bartender came over to the table and asked what Gabriel wanted.

"Coffee with cream, please."

When the bartender brought him his coffee, he took the cup downstairs to the casino and quickly burned through two hundred dollars at the blackjack table. He tipped the dealer his last two chips and left his coffee, tepid and untouched, on the table and went back to his hotel.

That night he and Lenka didn't order any wine or any trout. He wasn't in the mood for trout or wine and she wasn't talking. He wasn't in the mood for sex either. They just sat on the edge of his bed, fully clothed. He had cleaned the ashtrays out, but the smell lingered.

Eventually she said, "When are you going to leave?"

She and Evo would be in Sucre for a few days that week, but back on Thursday, the day before the party in honor of Vincenzo D'Orsi, the

Italian former vice president of the World Bank. Evo wanted to portray the man—and, by association, any sympathetic European or American—as a heroic rebel. The narrative, which Lenka was helping to sculpt, went that D'Orsi was the kind of person who was prepared to put his personal needs aside in favor of the greater good. The man had deliberately lost a very plum job because he'd been a stoic defender of the Bolivian people. Gabriel knew it was more complicated than that. Everything in life was more complicated than that. The day after the party, Evo and Lenka would set off on Evo's world tour. Gabriel would probably leave then too. In a week, he'd be back in New York and she'd be off touring the globe with Evo.

Seeing no need to adorn the truth, he said, "I'll leave when you leave on that tour with Evo, next Saturday." He pushed his fingers through his hair. "Unless my boss fires me first."

"I'm sorry about that. I wish I could help you."

He nodded. Time was running out for him. He didn't want to ask anything else of her, but he was short on options. In a sense, he was looking forward to getting fired. He was ready to be liberated from the stress.

Neither one of them said anything for a while. They just sat beside each other staring at the other twin bed, where he had thrown his medical supplies, including the large box of gauze, the white medical tape, three boxes of adhesive bandages, the antibiotic ointment, both bottles of pills, and an ice pack, now at room temperature. The boxy and colorless flotsam of the wounded.

"Would it be so bad if you lost this job?" she eventually said.

He was about to shake his head, but stopped to think about it. He envisioned New York and his life there; impressions flashed of late-night subway rides and of a glistening breakfast in Greenpoint at the Polish deli that smelled of old dishwater and was always full of cops and of the annual *IBI* staff party at Faddo's, a tiny Irish bar in Chelsea. He remembered walking backward into a cold wind one winter night with some friends; all of them were walking backward and emitting a chorus of groans at the gusts. They had ended up in the loft of a friend of a friend of one of Gabriel's suddenly wealthy college friends—Vic, a quant at D. E. Shaw. The woman who owned the loft looked like a young Yoko Ono. Her husband was a bigwig at Geffen Records. She served them cashews and champagne and they talked about a recent rash of exploding manholes. Gabriel wanted to take the subway home afterward, but Vic insisted on their taking a taxi. Gabriel gave in, and when he got out of the cab he handed Vic fifteen dollars, and Vic, who no longer thought about money in the way that mortals did, accepted the bills absent-mindedly. Then Vic continued to his new brownstone in Park Slope, and Gabriel walked up to his studio apartment.

So to Lenka he said, "Yes, it would be bad if I lost my job." It was lovely to be in Bolivia and to stand comfortably outside the local class structure, but he wasn't going to be in Bolivia forever. Sooner or later, he would be back in New York. He didn't want to lie to her any more than was necessary; actually, he didn't want to lie to her at all, so he didn't say anything else.

"Is your job that satisfying?" she asked.

"*Satisfying?*" He shook his head. "No, it's not satisfying. I'm afraid it's only rewarding in one way: the most straightforward way."

This last part wasn't quite true; there were more perks to it than that —the thrill, the illicitness, its espionage quality, to name a few—but the spirit of the point remained. Working for the hedge fund might even be as exciting as working for Evo, but in the end a very large part of the allure had to do with the crazily outsize paychecks.

Understandably, she didn't like what he was saying. And that was the problem. She didn't respect people who would work for the sole purpose of making heaps of money. Not many people did. It seemed to require a base value structure, something that was, if not outright corrupt, at least a little cold and nihilistic. And while that position did resonate on a deep level with Gabriel, who was, after all, his mother's son, he believed that there was more to it than that.

Assuming, for the sake of argument, that he was pursuing profit to the neglect of everything else, at least the work wasn't as harmful as people seemed to believe. For one thing, the profit in question wasn't coming at the expense of the inhabitants of any poor countries, as his mother had claimed in her opinion piece in the *Los Angeles Times*. It turned out that the point of his work was not to extract money from Bolivia—there was, frankly, not enough money there to attract his employer's attention—but to find some way to outgun the competing hedge funds. He was in Bolivia because it was an angle the others weren't pursuing. The point was to somehow achieve better gains than the other hedge funds did. It was a straightforward race, but it was sprints, all the time. There were four sprints per year, one each quarter. The object was to beat the others on your quarterly statement. Ultimately, the goal was to generate a record of such impressive gains that risk-friendly people seeking a place to plant a few million would be willing to accept your high fees. The fees themselves were nice, but it was imperative to always lure new clients to your shop. With those kinds of small hedge funds, there was no point in marketing, really. Anyone with the means to participate was not going to look at the company's logo. Interested parties would study the quarterly results alone. The best hedge fund generated the best results, and, in so doing, did the best job of appealing to the greedier instincts of those in the position to play with millions of dollars.

Gabriel had noticed that of all the cardinal sins, greed was the most uniformly maligned. A glutton might be merely an overzealous bon vivant; a lustful person might be too passionate; and a slothful person could be simply over-mellow. Envy, wrath, and pride flared once in a while in everyone, and so they were easily appreciated. Greed however held purely pejorative implications. Unlike the rest, it wasn't seen as spawned of heart—of passions. It was seen as a cold and cerebral sin, a schemer's sin, one that had to be committed knowingly. But Gabriel didn't see it that way. To him, it was just as complex and obsessive a vice as lust, envy, or wrath.

When Hernán Cortés encountered Montezuma's emissaries, in 1519, he reportedly said, "Let your king send us more gold, for I and my companions have a disease of the heart, which only gold can cure."

Crucially, he spoke of the heart. What else but passion would propel a group of men on such a journey? What else could enable them to

commit such deeds? A look at the many swelling and popping financial bubbles of the past century indicated a culture overcome with fits
of mass hysteria and delusions, a culture *passionately* obsessed with the
acquisition of wealth. It was all heart. And the enemy of wisdom was a
taste not for vice but for certainty. This was Lenka's failure, her unam-
biguous moral clarity and the attendant proclivity for judgment. It was
what made her a brilliant spokesperson for Evo, and it was what made
her incapable of understanding why Gabriel sincerely wanted to work
for the Calloway Group. Lenka's own mother, though, seemed to stand
at the distant opposite end of this spectrum. The wise aura she emanated implied not an adamantine moral confidence but an acquaintance
with (and an appreciation of) human frailty.

Gabriel was hoping to appeal to something similar in Lenka when
he said, "My job is not about the things my mother told me mattered.
It's about money."

"But you think that money does matter."

"Look around you, Lenka. What do you think?"

"I believe that life can be about more than that."

"I do too. Or, I hope so. My problem is that I am in a very strange
situation, and it's a good situation. It's a great situation, actually. I have a
job right now that, if I can manage to keep it for a few years, will put me
within striking distance of very early retirement."

"Right."

He took her hand. "I just need to survive at this job for two or three
years and then I will be done. This is my chance. If this doesn't work,
I'll go back to some other job, and I'll be a slave to some paycheck. And
that's not the end of the world, it's normal, obviously, and it's what I'd
expected life to be like. But I've managed to locate a secret passage out,
and I've just entered that passageway."

She looked at him and, in the next moments, he watched as she
gave in. The part of her that had been resisting—he could practically
see it collapse. "Fine," she said.

"Fine?"

She took a deep breath. "Yes, fine. I'll ask Evo what he has planned for Santa Cruz Gas."

"Thank you," he said. He said nothing else. He wanted her to speak next.

Eventually, she said, "I'll do it tomorrow."

There was no harm in her asking, of course, but if Evo told her something major and she told Gabriel, she would be committing a serious breach of Evo's confidence. Giving information about the president-elect's economic plan to an agent of a hedge fund would be nearly an act of treason. Evo would almost certainly never find out. Even if his administration figured out that a hedge fund had been betting on Bolivian gas, it would be more or less impossible to locate the source of that hedge fund's information. Still, she was risking everything that she had achieved for Gabriel's future in an industry she reviled.

"Thank you," he said again. There would be no way to thank her sufficiently.

She kissed his forehead, stood up. He pulled her back down.

"Thank you," he said, once more. He kissed her shoulder.

She stood up and started to resume her trip to the door but he pulled her down once again and pushed her back on the bed. He straddled her and leaned in, kissed her. She smiled up at him a little halfheartedly. She stared at his eyes so close that he could feel her eyelashes tickling his forehead and he could almost see the reflection of his own eyes.

"I should go," she said.

"No. You should stay." He had never ravaged anyone before, to the best of his knowledge. He hadn't quite known what it meant. But now he did know, and he planned to ravage her that night.

She gave a vulpine smile and said, "How much money do you actually make?"

"A lot. And if things go well here, I get a two-hundred-and-thirty-thousand-dollar bonus."

She blinked at him in disbelief, her mouth open. She was blushing.

• • •

That night, they slept embraced, their bodies pressed completely together. He'd never managed to sleep that way beside anyone before. And while he awoke often, sometimes with her breathing or snoring softly in his neck or at his chin, he never pulled away. He kissed her sleeping face, brushed strands of hair from her eyes, and let himself absorb the heat burning off her body.

In the morning, wearing his bathrobe, Gabriel stood with her by the elevator door and kissed her neck. It was eight thirty. She had spent the whole night for the first time. When the elevator bell dinged, they kissed once more. The doors slid open and there inside stood Alejo—of course, that lurker, and witness to Fiona's recent early-morning exit—in his black and white uniform, with his bowl cut and grimace-etched terra-cotta face.

"Hello, Alejo!" Lenka said as she swished inside, guileless.

"Mrs. Villarobles," he mumbled. He didn't even look at Gabriel.

If he'd been a different kind of person or had trusted his instincts a little more, Gabriel might have intervened in the seconds that remained. He could have stuck his arm out, stopped the doors. He could have gone down with them, supervised the interaction, and then walked her out. Or he could have pulled her from the elevator altogether, free of Alejo's venomous gossip. But he did nothing. He just stood there dumbly and waved goodbye to her. And she, standing there beside Alejo, smirked flirtatiously back at him, waving slowly.

And then the doors slid shut abruptly and Gabriel was alone in the dim corridor again, which stank of mildew, industrial carpet cleaner, and stale cigarette smoke.

# 10

# Gambling on Boxing Day

*Monday, December 26, 2005*

THERE'D BE NO MORE breezy chitchat with Catacora after Gabriel's drunken performance Christmas Eve. Still, he hoped he could salvage the situation somehow, and maybe even turn the blunder into something worthwhile. So he showed up early at the office, clutching his notebook, and shook the man's hand firmly, making direct eye contact. He sat down, apologized for his behavior. "The alcohol," he said, "it affects me much more at this altitude," which was true, if somewhat beside the point. "And I was upset about this." He pointed at his still-swaddled face.

"That's fine," Catacora said. Gabriel had the notebook open on his lap, having learned from his initial interview with Lenka that people might find him suspicious if he didn't take notes. As expected, Catacora skipped the small talk and said, "So, how did you find out?"

"I can't reveal my source, but I will say that your appointment isn't a very well-kept secret." Gabriel emanated blaséness as studiously as possible. This was a bluff he'd thought up in the taxi on the way to the Monoblock. He hoped to direct suspicion away from Lenka.

"I actually thought it was a well-kept secret. It hasn't been in the press yet."

"I'm the only reporter who knows." By now, Gabriel was practiced enough with this kind of deception that the irony didn't even touch him.

"Why haven't you written about it then?"

"I wanted to talk to you first." Gabriel saw an opening developing for him in the conversation and thought he might be able to make a move for it after two or three more steps.

"Who are you going to sell the article to?"

"Probably a wire: Knight Ridder, AP, Reuters—I have no idea. I'd prefer to have it in the *Wall Street Journal,* but I'd need something extraordinary." He was getting into position.

"What do you want to know?"

"I'm interested in your thoughts on how to change Bolivia's fiscal policy."

"I have not yet been—"

"But you must know his plans." There, it was almost done. Catacora shrugged and Gabriel continued. "I want to know what Evo has planned for the foreign gas companies. That's the million-dollar question, and the *Journal* would find my piece a lot more attractive if I had some information on that."

"As you know, Evo has—"

"I understand he's promised to renegotiate the contracts with foreign gas companies, but you know it's not that simple. I've read your master's thesis, Professor Catacora, and you're attentive. Evo wouldn't be hurting only Repsol or some huge multinational conglomerate that could absorb the loss. There are a lot of companies invested in Bolivian gas. Brazilian companies would be the most damaged. Petrobras would survive, but Evo would be killing Santa Cruz. What would Brazilians say? You mentioned that Evo would clear it with Lula, but why would Lula agree to something that has no benefits for Brazil? And if he refused, would Evo just do it anyway?"

Catacora squinted, and Gabriel knew that he'd pushed too hard and aroused his suspicion. He wasn't acting like a freelance journalist. He knew too much, for one thing—not just that Catacora had been selected to head the finance ministry, but the contents of his master's thesis—and he'd passed on an exclusive, supposedly holding out for something better. It was odd. "I don't know," Catacora said. "Honestly, we haven't made it to that level of specificity."

Gabriel scribbled the word *nada* on his pad. If he'd had more time, he might have called it a day and circled back later, but he didn't have more time, so he looked up and said, "The inauguration is approaching quickly."

"Yes. We just had the election and then the holidays and now Evo is preparing to leave on this journey. He and I have barely had a chance to talk. We are trying to figure these things out as quickly as possible, but it might not be solidified until after he takes office."

"I can wait a couple days."

Catacora leaned forward, pursed his lips, and frowned at his desk in contemplation. Gabriel sensed that Catacora was about to turn the questions on him and he readied himself.

"Can I read your most recent article about Bolivia?" Catacora said. "I Googled you, but there wasn't anything recent."

"I haven't published anything since I came down."

"You're not—do you work for one of the gas companies?"

"*What?*" He hadn't seen that coming. "No, not at all. God, I wish I did. I could use the money. That would be tremendous! I'm not—you do realize I'm staying at Hotel Gloria."

"I know. It just seems strange. You're not with the U.S. government either, right?"

Gabriel was relieved by the craziness of the accusations. He shook his head, sincerely amused. "Like the CIA? That would be nice too. And I won't complain if you decide to spread *that* rumor! I'd be the talk of the town. But, really, would I be asking these questions?"

Catacora shrugged. "I suppose not. I've just never met a journalist who is not in a hurry to publish his exclusives."

"I need something bigger. When I was at *IBI,* I wrote a lot of hundred-word briefs, and I'm done with that. Knowing the name of the

Bolivian finance minister a few days before the rest of the press isn't all that remarkable. I'll do it—I'll do that brief if I have to, but I hope I don't have to do it. Look, I'll give you a few days, and if I don't hear from you by the end of the day on Thursday, it'll go forward like that."

"And what will you write?"

Gabriel didn't reply. This was his opportunity to twist the man's arm. He gave a look that indicated that he considered it a regrettable thing, but he was willing to do it.

Catacora absorbed the implication without any help. He considered the situation for a moment and then spoke. "You'll write that we don't even have a plan for our fiscal policy?"

"It's the truth, right? You say you want to nationalize gas, but there's no plan."

Catacora shook his head dismissively, but it was a lost cause. He was cornered. Gabriel had something that was newsworthy enough to get his article sold, and all he knew so far was that they hadn't even formulated a vague plan of action. Not the kind of news that an incoming administration wants publicized.

"You'll call me in the next couple days?" Gabriel said.

"By the end of Thursday I will call you."

"No problem. But if I don't hear from you..." He let it dangle like that.

Catacora blinked quickly, nodding. It was understood.

In his second year at Brown, Gabriel had become interested in game theory. Particularly, he was interested in the argument about its efficacy. Marooned between the social sciences and mathematics, advocates of game theory are often conflicted about their purpose: to study human behavior or to study the mathematical models themselves.

Game theory is built on fictional scenarios, or games, which require the adoption of assumptions that ensure that the fictional players are competing on a set playing field; the precise assumptions about the playing field vary from game to game. The assumptions are known as the Nash equilibria—named for John Nash, the schizophrenic Nobel Prize–winning mathematician.

Game theory's most famous example is the Prisoner's Dilemma:

Two suspects are arrested by the police. They are put in separate cells, and each one is told this: "If you testify against your partner, and your partner remains silent, you will go free and your partner will go to jail for ten years. If you both say nothing, you'll both go to jail, but only for six months on a minor charge, since we don't have enough evidence to convict either of you of a major crime. If you both testify against each other, both of you will receive five-year sentences." Each prisoner must choose to betray the other or to remain silent.

What should the prisoners do?

The playoff matrix looks like this:

|  | Prisoner B doesn't talk | Prisoner B testifies against the other |
|---|---|---|
| Prisoner A doesn't talk | Each serves six months | Prisoner A: gets ten-year sentence<br>Prisoner B: goes free |
| Prisoner A testifies against the other | Prisoner A: goes free<br>Prisoner B: gets ten-year sentence | Each serves five years |

The assumption is that each prisoner is interested only in minimizing his own jail time and couldn't care less what happens to the other. If all the equilibria are in place, the dilemma produces a *non*-zero-sum outcome; that is, the gains and losses will not balance. Each prisoner is better off betraying his partner no matter what the other does. However, the result is counterintuitive: If each prisoner acts in his own best interest, each will get a five-year sentence. But if the prisoners cooperate with each other, each one gets a lighter sentence.

In the more complex Iterated Prisoner's Dilemma, the prisoners are repeatedly confronted with the same situation and can learn from their mistakes. In these repeated games, players can adapt and change their strategies, leading to better outcomes. Certain iterated games show that what looks like altruism is actually purely rational and self-interested behavior.

Of course, the assumptions in the Prisoner's Dilemma and all of its variants are fictitious. The fact that the equilibria don't match up with real-world circumstances is, according to game theorists, beside the point. They work with models analogous to the models used in physics. To game theorists, their models describe perfect human behavior. The results are prescriptive, not descriptive.

In the mid-1960s, an unpopular group of social scientists tried to develop *descriptive* models for classic game-theory schema. They presented actual people with the situations from game theory's games and found that their subjects almost never chose the rational response.

These empirical studies often debunked basic Nash equilibria, including, crucially, the notion that people always aim to maximize their individual wins. The results became statistical and varied—best organized on vast spreadsheets, rather than in tight mathematical formulas. The work remained unhelpful, if not an affront, to traditional game theorists.

In an abstract for a paper criticizing the findings of some of his empiricist peers, Yale mathematician Niles Gilbert wrote, "While it might be entertaining to see how individuals handle these games, it is the work of psychologists. Mathematically, I see nothing of use. The data appear intended to point out the real-world fallibility of the Nash equilibria, as if that were ever in question... More to the point, their methodology, I'm sorry to say, demonstrates a complete misunderstanding of our very enterprise."

Gabriel had continued to be interested in game theory during his years at Brown, and had even written two papers on the Closed-Bag Exchange game as it applied to the problem of moral hazard in bailout packages during credit crises. He'd followed the mathematics. He'd un-tangled the formulas and pursued the issue to the limit of his curiosity.

Later, when he started digging into the skewed results of theoretical economics in his senior year, specifically the inflexible CPI basket that was used to measure inflation, Gabriel grew wary of the more strictly mathematical version of anything in economics. When it came to for-mulating actual policies and grappling with real phenomena, theorists were working with broken assumptions. The empirical side might be less pure—might even be unhelpful to theorists—but Gabriel wasn't a theorist. He wasn't, finally, a quant.

For better or worse, he dealt with real people. The tangible and messy world interested him. He wanted the place where players' infor-mation was forever imperfect, their motives inexplicable; where if you wanted to play well, you had better get used to working with blurry integers.

Gabriel stopped in at MAS's office on the way back to his hotel. Lenka was leaving for Sucre that afternoon. She and Evo would be in Sucre for the next two nights. The banner had come down, and the desks were mostly cleared. A handful of employees helped direct movers. Other-wise, the office was empty. He walked across the room and peeked in the window of Lenka's office, but she wasn't there.

Gabriel went down the hall, looking for her. He heard voices ahead, from a conference room. He opened the door, knocking as he did so.

Inside, he found Lenka, Evo Morales, and a few others around a ta-ble. They stopped talking and turned to stare at him. He saw newspapers stacked on the conference table. He hesitated—would it be a mistake to indicate that he knew her? Before he could finish his calculations, Evo said, "Can we help you? Are you looking for someone?"

"I didn't mean to interrupt," Gabriel said. "I—" He was dumbstruck.

"Are you a journalist?" Evo said.

Gabriel glanced at Lenka. "Yes," he said. "I—" He hesitated.

"I was supposed to talk to him," Lenka said. She glanced at her watch and said, "If you want to go sit at Café Presidentes, I'll find you there when I'm done. Sorry I'm late."

He nodded and was about to turn away, but then he paused, stepped forward, and extended his right hand to Evo. "Congratulations, by the way," he said.

Evo shook his hand. "Thank you." He had a powerful grip, meaty hands.

Evo released his hand, and Gabriel looked at the other faces: Lenka's coworkers, all of them. Maybe she'd mentioned a freelance journalist, but it was unlikely. Some had probably seen him come around that day for lunch, but they wouldn't remember. To them, he was just another journalist who was there to talk to Lenka.

He hurried back down the carpeted hallway, his right hand tingling at his side.

His mother would be shaking Evo's hand too in a few days. Or would she kiss his cheek? Gabriel played out possibilities, outcomes. Would someone—maybe Lenka herself, unwittingly—point out to Evo that he'd met the woman's son recently?

*My son? The one who is here working for BellSouth? I hadn't realized he...*

The rest was too unpleasant even to consider. The awkwardness. The overturned expectations. A presidential interview postponed. Or would his mother continue with the interview? Would she be able to successfully compartmentalize Gabriel's betrayal? Probably. She'd be stoic, if visibly heartbroken. She'd get through it. Gabriel's life, however, would explode. It would be thunderous—a slow-motion action-movie explosion, a grandiose fireball explosion. And when that was done, Gabriel's life would be done. Not even a flake of ash would remain.

In the game Gabriel had focused on in college, two people meet and exchange closed bags. It's a simple transaction: the sale of something illicit, maybe. It's conducted in public, where neither person can open his bag. One person is supposed to give a bag of money, and the other person is supposed to give a bag with the goods. Because the bags are closed, each player can choose to honor the agreement, or he can "defect" from the deal by turning over an empty bag weighted with something worthless. If the exchange goes as planned, both players come away with a reasonable profit. If only one player defects, he gains hugely, because not only does he not forfeit his prize, he gains the prize of the other player.

The payoff matrix:

|  | Player B gives the expected item | Player B defaults |
|---|---|---|
| Player A gives the expected item | Both players win modestly | Prisoner A: loses much<br>Prisoner B: wins much |
| Player A defaults | Prisoner A: wins much<br>Prisoner B: loses much | Both players lose modestly |

When all the appropriate Nash equilibria are in place, the rational player will turn over an empty bag. The rational choice is to defect. The game is *truly* zero-sum.

The players should lie to each other, each promising to deliver on his end. Then they should meet up and exchange empty bags.

The correct scenario is lose-lose. That is the only rational outcome.

The café was empty. Gabriel ordered a cappuccino and salteña. The metal steamer wailed as the barista foamed a jug of milk. At the window, Gabriel stood on a chair to get a better view of a small demonstration outside. A line of police guarded the palace. Behind him, the espresso machine reached a shrieking crescendo and then went abruptly silent. He picked up his cappuccino. They served the best cappuccino in La Paz. The place was called Café los Presidentes Ahorcados, which meant "the hanged presidents." A colorful mural behind the counter showed the hanging of President Gualberto Villarroel in 1947, a pigeon perched on his head, the Neptune fountain splashing in the background.

Gabriel returned to the window and monitored the crowd. Who were they and what were they protesting? He had no idea and he didn't care. He'd given up trying to decipher their motivations. They had won, fair and square, and yet there they were, back in the plaza, the day after Christmas, braying some new complaint. He knew they had reason to be upset, maybe more than anyone else on the continent, but the ceaselessness of it, especially considering the recent election, made no sense to him.

His mother would arrive the following afternoon and he needed to find the best way to resolve the conflicting stories about him: BellSouth versus freelance journalist versus Calloway Group. It was clear that he couldn't convince everyone he knew in Bolivia that he actually worked for BellSouth, so that was out. Which meant that he'd need to confess *something* to his mother.

Freelance journalist would backfire sooner or later because his relationship with his mother was long term. When he never published anything, she would spot the lie. It was an iterated situation, in game-theory parlance: the winning solution for game one would not necessarily work in the long run.

He ate his chicken salteña there, staring out the window, and thought about the problem. There was no simple answer. He took another nibble, careful to keep the juices from spilling. It was delicious. And this problem he was facing was just this problem, he assured himself—life would go on, either way. There'd be salteñas in the future, regardless. The salteña was a glorious invention. From Lenka, Gabriel had gathered that they'd emerged somewhere in Argentina, then migrated around South America. The dish was now fairly widespread, but it was most popular in Bolivia. Since he'd tasted his first one, a few days before he'd met Lenka, he'd been an avid devotee. For the past month, he'd never hesitated when he saw one on offer—the sweetness and spiciness, the crust that was tender in the yellowy skin, crisp along the blackened ridge. After the sweet juice had leaked all over his lap once, he'd realized why people stood when eating salteñas. Only native Bolivians had the dexterity to eat them without making a mess.

His mother didn't know about salteñas. Or, if she did, she'd never spoken of them to him. For all her posturing on behalf of the poor, she didn't really do street food. She didn't really do working-class delights: no television, no cans of Budweiser, no turning the music up too loud in the car. In the end, she was just as prim as any other upper-middle-class mom.

Lenka, meanwhile, knew all about salteñas. She had tried to teach Gabriel the art of eating them. She held one upright, nibbled off the tip, slurped the liquid out, then chewed half an inch down and slurped up more liquid. In that manner she'd worked her way down the length of the oblong pastry. It was noisy and conspicuous—the whole mouth needed to be involved. She held it with the dark glossy seam facing out, toward him, used her tongue to move around moist strips of chicken breast inside. Gabriel attempted to imitate, but it didn't work.

There at the café, he tried again, but the liquid dribbled on the floor beside his shoe. It leaked all over his fingers. He scarfed the rest and then hurried off to wash his hands in the bathroom. He dried them on his pants and then observed himself in the mirror. The bandages were in place. He had figured out a system: he put three across the three holes in his face and then put a smaller one horizontally across the ripped seam of his ear, wrapping the adhesive around the back of the ear. It would do. Soon, he'd just stop trying to hide the ear. The bruises had begun to dim, slightly, but they'd also migrated. Now it looked almost like he had a black eye. On seeing himself there, he was struck by how exhausted he looked. His mother would be shocked. She'd be worried. She'd be right to be worried.

When Lenka arrived, he offered her a salteña, but she wasn't interested.

"I'm sorry about interrupting your meeting," he said.

"It's fine."

"He seems nice, I think. Magnificent handshake."

She smiled at him faintly. Still, she was not herself.

"You okay?" he said.

"Yes. I have just had a very long day. And we leave in two hours."

"I'll miss you," he said, which was true.

"I'll miss you too," she said.

She lingered there, in the pause, and he could see that she was considering her next move. He had learned to read her well enough to know when she was contemplating something. It looked as if she was doubting some decision that she'd already made, and he knew it was possible that she'd found out some information that might be useful to him but was reluctant to tell him, so he pressed her. "Did you have a chance to ask him?" he said.

"I'll tell you," she said. She looked pained about it.

"Do you want to walk?"

She shook her head. She looked almost as drained as he did. She sighed, hesitating, and then gazed at him in a strange way for a moment, almost sadly. Then she said, "He's going to save the Brazilian companies, including Santa Cruz, at least for the first year or two. And then they'll get a better deal. He needs to keep his ties with Lula intact. With Repsol, Total, Exxon, with all of them it'll be different. He'll demand that they renegotiate their contracts immediately or Bolivia will begin seizing their installations by March."

"Jesus. Thank you so much." He kissed her. He held her close.

She shook her head and pulled out of his arms. "Sorry, I'm tired."

"It's okay. Thank you. This is incredibly helpful, it's—"

"You have everything you need now?"

"Yeah. So, when will I see you next? My mother's interviewing Evo right after you return. But I hope you can meet her before that."

"Me too." She gazed absently at his chest. He'd never seen her so exhausted.

"Thank you so much," he said again. "You have no idea how much this means to me."

"I do know. You talk about it all the time." She smiled wearily and shook her head. "I'm sorry, I have to go soon. I'll see you on Thursday."

He nodded.

"Take care of yourself," she said and left.


Gabriel's new knowledge was probably the most valuable thing he had ever owned. There were two aspects of the knowledge. The first was more straightforward: he knew what Evo planned to do about natural gas. The second was equally important: he knew the *timing* of Evo's plan. Models in game theory generally required players to have equal information, because the point of the games was to study optimal strategy, and the games lost all of their complexity if one player had a clear advantage. In this case, Gabriel had access to two vital pieces of information that no one else knew. The range of options presented to him was daunting.

His information could functionally lead to what would be considered insider trading, which was a felony. But what he did with it would not be illegal. If the same information emerged from inside of Santa Cruz Gas, it would be tainted, and Gabriel would not be able to use it legally. But all he had really was a tip about changing political policy that came from a purely political source. It didn't pertain directly to a specific corporation, and that made it legal. Opportunities like this did not come along often. But what would he do?

Still at the café, he took out his notebook and made a list of his immediate options:

1. Tell Priya right now, and let her do what she wants with the information
2. Hold off on telling Priya
3. Buy Santa Cruz stock and wait for the price to spike on this news
4. Do #3 and simultaneously do either #1 or #2
5. Do #4 and then circulate word about the rumor in the press, thereby inducing the spike in Santa Cruz's stock price and accelerating the whole process.

For the next half hour, Gabriel paced around in front of the café's window, mulling over these choices. If he chose number 3, 4, or 5 and didn't tell Priya, he could be fired. Ultimately, number 5 was probably the best option. It was a bit daring, but it was good. Still—considering the value of what he knew, it didn't feel quite satisfactory. This was a tremendous opportunity, and to take full advantage of it, he needed to take tremendous steps.

He began to consider another, more elaborate option. He didn't write this one down. It could be called option number 6. It would involve all the risks of number 5, but it would also involve breaking the law. It would be significantly more profitable for both him and Priya, and both of them could convincingly claim (she, truthfully) that the illegal portion of the transaction had been done by accident, which would, in this case, nullify the criminality. Option number 6 was more complicated, though, and the risks, from an investment standpoint, were greater.

So many large multinational investments seemed to reside in the gray areas of legality anyway — particularly in certain sectors, such as mining and commodities. Pingree himself had made his first millions manipulating penny stocks on the Vancouver exchange, a famously shady stock exchange known as "the scam capital of the world."

Gabriel didn't have time to think it over. If the trades occurred over the course of a few days, and he wanted to finish the entire process before the week was out, he needed to have it under way within twenty-four hours, at the latest. One of the most important benefits of attempting the scheme that week, the one between Christmas and New Year's, was that those were some of the most lightly traded days in the market, which meant that the markets would be more volatile than normal. Prices tended to overreact in both directions. There were fewer people manning the trading floors and there were fewer people to verify rumors, so a well-placed rumor could have an especially powerful effect.

Back in his hotel room an hour later, he cracked his window and smoked a copious number of cigarettes. He ran through the scenario again and again. He jotted down a list of potential problems, but none of them was too threatening. When he looked up, the sun had set.

He tore the relevant pages out of his pad and took them through to the bathroom. He burned the pages over the toilet with the ceiling fan going. Once all of the pages had burned and the ashes had drifted down into the toilet bowl, he flushed. The black stains remained around the rim of the water, so he flushed again.

An hour later, too nervous to eat and too amped to stay in his room, he went down to the small casino in the basement of the Presidente and lost money at the blackjack table. He played badly: hit on seventeen, stayed on thirteen. He was all over the place. He drank Johnnie Walker Black on the rocks, and smoked Marlboros. A cocktail waitress who smelled like papaya shampoo emptied his ashtray. An hour later, she did it again.

After losing a few hundred dollars, he moved to the little bar in the corner. Vegas, this was not. The room was low ceilinged, musty, almost mildewy, its walls covered in dark mirrors. He opened his steno pad and jotted down the steps for option number 6. He needed to retrace them clearly — to suss them out kinesthetically, via the pen — just in case he was missing something.

1. Open the short on Santa Cruz stock
2. Tell Priya to do the same
3. Disseminate (false) rumor
4. Wait for the price to tank
5. Close short and buy all long with the gains
6. Tell Priya to do the same again
7. Correct rumor and apologize to reporters for the mistake
8. Close position after short spike has subsided
9. Reap gains

It checked out. It really did. And it was elegant, in a way even beautiful, if such a thing could be called beautiful. The risks were, nevertheless, significant.

To begin with, step three was a solid felony. It was absolutely illegal to spread rumors to generate profit in the securities market. Still, he would be "correcting" the rumor swiftly, claiming that he'd made a mistake, which (if it were true) would absolve him of the crime. It wasn't a crime to disseminate a false rumor that you believed was true. More to the point, there would be no evidence that Gabriel had known that the rumor was false.

Gabriel finished his drink and headed for the door. He needed to pace around his room. As he was crossing the casino, though, he spotted Grayson McMillan at one of the blackjack tables. Gabriel kept going for a few paces before he paused. He didn't need to spend any more time up in his room driving himself crazy. Grayson's company, despite its shortcomings, would do him good, he assured himself, so he changed course.

He patted Grayson on the back and sat down, saying, "Cards? I had no idea you played."

"Well, hello, Gabriel. How are you?" Grayson put his cards down for a moment and glanced at him. "What in hell happened to your face?"

"Long story. Clumsiness, basically."

Grayson grimaced, picked his cards up again, and studied them gravely, chewing the corner of his lip. "Well, it doesn't look good."

"Not as bad as what happened to me here tonight." Gabriel waved at the table.

Grayson grunted in amusement. He squinted at his cards, hit again, and won a hand.

"Good for you," Gabriel said.

"Not really. It's rigged, you know." He glanced back at Gabriel and tapped the felt. "It's a very poorly choreographed grift." He received two cards. "Here, watch. I'll lose this." He held on nineteen. The dealer drew twenty-one and then pulled Grayson's chips. "See?" he said.

"This sure is the life, huh? Boxing Day alone in an underground casino, playing a rigged game?"

Grayson smirked, more sincerely this time. "It'll do," he said and tapped the felt again. The dealer served two more.

Gabriel noticed Fiona approaching. She was there with Grayson, he realized, and he regretted his last comment immediately. She'd been in the bathroom or somewhere. Had she seen him at the bar taking notes?

Probably. What were they doing there? Gabriel knew that she didn't gamble, had no interest in it. Was this some sort of dreary date? Gabriel dreaded what was to come, but he couldn't escape now. Instead, he projected as much innocent cheer as he could muster.

She chose a chair on the far side of Grayson, understandably. She looked marvelous: her hair seemed especially impressive, it looked effulgent; her makeup did the trick of underscoring everything beautiful and disguising the rest. She sparkled, nearly. She seemed even more alert than normal. "Hello there, Gabriel," she said.

"Fi-fi, is that you?" he said and accepted her hand, kissed a ruddy knuckle.

She grinned at him dangerously. "Your face looks better."

"I wear damage well. And I'm happy to report that I have no gangrene. Dodged that, at least. It seems that, cards aside, my luck knows no bounds. You? Any new wounds to report?" Gabriel glanced at Grayson, who was lost in his hand, and she squinted at him in warning.

She was wearing the black dress that she'd worn to his room the other night, when it had been cinched with a red ribbon. Seeing her there now, punchy and amused, he knew that nothing quite compared to the ego-death of encountering a former lover like that, strutting in all her plumage and on the arm of a far more desirable man. "Gambling too?" he said.

Was she amused by him or angry? He had no clue. Whatever vulnerability he'd accidentally elicited the other night would not be making a return appearance. Never again. For all her many frailties and lousy habits, he could tell she was not a person who suffered the same ignominy twice. True to form, she replied, "But isn't gambling your thing, Gabriel?"

An allusion to the hedge fund, probably; she was dangling the secret, reminding him to keep in line. She wanted to lead in a brisk waltz, showing off for Grayson. Gabriel didn't want to deny her anything, not that night, so he straightened his back and tried to keep up. "Grayson," he said, "I think that's meant to be a double-entendre."

"My antennae picked that much up," Grayson said. His eyes were still fixed on the dealer's hands, the cards, and the felt. He held on eighteen and the dealer hit blackjack, pulled away two more chips. "Fuck me," he muttered. "Right," he sighed. He shook his head at the dealer. "That's me." He turned to face Fiona. "What's the famous Warren Buffett credo about mitigating losses?"

"Mitigating losses?" Fiona thought about it. "Well, I'm sure he doesn't have one—losses aren't really his problem."

Grayson spun around to Gabriel. "What about you? Any wisdom for a losing gambler?"

Gabriel groped through his memory and then said, "'Severities should be dealt out all at once, so that their suddenness may give less offense.' Does that work?"

"It does. And the severities have been dealt with all at once, I guess. That's not Buffett," added Grayson, master of the obvious.

"It's Machiavelli," Fiona said. "Right?" She sent Gabriel a sly look.

He gave her a mischievous grin. "Oh, is that who it is?"

"He's being funny, Grayson," she said. And then, turning to Gabriel, she asked, "But do you know the rest of the quote?"

"'And enjoy your winnings when they come'?" he guessed.

She rolled her eyes. "Yeah, something like that."

"Oh dear!" Grayson groaned, amused. "Am I boxed in by a pair of Machiavellian journalists? This reminds me of a nightmare I had recently!"

"No, no, no," Gabriel said. "Claws are all away." He shot her a look to assure her he meant it. "Now, let's get a drink."

With that, the three of them wandered back to the small bar where Gabriel had been earlier. The bartender lurked nearby, sporting a grave unibrow and a slightly baffled expression, his tremendous bow tie cocked at a steep angle. The place was brownish, in an almost succulent way, and looked like a Chesterfield advertisement from a vintage *Playboy* magazine—except for the fixtures, which fell decidedly short of the promised glamour. Up close the details were scuffed and artlessly distressed. Sepia mirrors reflected a constellation of feeble bulbs. The carpet had been worn down to weedy twine not just by feet but by decades of hot vomit and cold cocktails.

They settled into uncomfortable chairs and Fiona lit up. Gabriel withheld, not wanting to unsettle her by lighting a cigarette himself. She didn't know he'd picked up the habit.

"You play poker?" Grayson said.

"No, no, never." Gabriel shook his head. "I'm a numbers person. I like blackjack."

"Really?" Grayson said, surprised. "You don't seem like a numbers person. You're so — what's the word?"

"Daft?" Gabriel suggested.

"Treacherous?" Fiona offered, ostensibly in jest.

"Alert," Grayson said. "Alert to the human element. So I assumed you'd play poker."

Fiona giggled and Grayson arrived at an expression midway between amused and offended. "Are you laughing at me?" he said.

"No, she's laughing at me," Gabriel explained. "Anyway, even if she were laughing at you, you shouldn't feel too bad about it. She's often amused at the expense of men who sit beside her. It's part of her charm."

From Fiona's look, Gabriel gathered that she hadn't liked that. She no longer wanted to continue playing. Fine. It was hers to direct. She thrust the focus back onto Gabriel. "How's it going with your girlfriend, by the way?"

"She's in Sucre with Evo."

"You're dating one of his staff?" Grayson said.

Gabriel nodded. "His press attaché."

"I met her," Grayson said. "What's her name?"

"Lenka Villarobles."

"Yes. A fascinating woman," Grayson said. "Very beautiful too."

"Yes," Gabriel said. He resisted the temptation to glance at Fiona again. It was best to avoid anything that could be interpreted as gloating.

Fiona was ready to move on anyway. "See, Gabriel?" she said. "It's like I said. In La Paz, everyone knows everyone. There are no secrets."

"Are you keeping secrets, Gabriel?" Grayson said.

Gabriel winked at him. "A few."

"Anything I'd like to know?" Grayson said, quite earnestly.

Gabriel shrugged and checked in with Fiona, not sure how best to proceed.

"He's full of shit," she said and so resolved that question while also diminishing the brief allure Gabriel had summoned for himself.

Grayson just shook his head, mildly confused but still enjoying the show they were putting on. He remained fiercely unflappable, a fountain of jolly curiosity. He was happy to watch, prod with the occasional question. It was, after all, a rough game, and he'd spent enough time playing to know that sitting on the bench was the best position one could hope for.

Fiona was also done sparring. "Let's go," she said to Grayson.

Grayson's glee dangled there as he stared at Gabriel for another moment. He rapped the table with his knuckles. "Well," he said, loitering, unwilling to let the moment go.

Gabriel shrugged, not wanting to step in the way of Fiona's request.

Sensing that Gabriel was deferring to Fiona, Grayson relinquished his interest, thrust out a hand. Gabriel shook it firmly. The eye contact came steady, appreciative. There was something different in Grayson in that moment; something had changed in the way he looked at Gabriel. The expression indicated respect, Gabriel realized, even admiration.

"You should rethink poker," Grayson said. "I think you'd do well."

"Oh, that's funny," Gabriel said, without really smiling. "Isn't it?" he said to Fiona dourly, harshly. He was overplaying and he knew it.

"Okay," she said to Grayson, standing up. "Let's go."

Gabriel watched the two of them walk to the elevators on the far side of the room. He might have stung her at their last meeting, but now it was different—the shame was mutual, it was just some swampy sadness between them, and it favored no one. That she'd somehow managed to care for him spoke not to any quality in him but to the extent that loneliness had perforated her life. He lit a cigarette as she and

Grayson approached the elevator bank. He watched her push the button. She was talking. Grayson was lost in an assortment of rising and falling shades of hilarity. At last, Fiona glanced at Gabriel and he raised his cigarette in salute, winked at her. Seeing the cigarette, she smirked, barely, and then turned back to Grayson and continued with whatever she'd been saying. The moment was over. The elevator arrived and the two stepped inside, turned, and faced the open doors. She reached out and pushed the button. For a brief moment, no one did anything.

Then the doors slid shut.

Gabriel got up and went back to the blackjack table. He'd had enough already, but he sat down anyway. He pulled his wallet out and set it on the table, rapped the felt gently with his fingertips, beckoning fresh cards.

# 11

# Gambit

*Tuesday, December 27, 2005*

IT WOULD BE option number 6, after all. If it hadn't been decided the night before, it had certainly been decided by the time he awoke. It was ludicrous, but he couldn't think of a better way to play it.

He could do option number 5, of course: just invest in the market in a straightforward way, tell Priya what he knew, disseminate the truth. That would be great if things played out well, but it wouldn't help him when and if—and the *if* seemed unduly optimistic—he was fired. Sudden dismissal by Priya, which had seemed a vague danger of the job, now felt imminent, nearly inevitable. It was the golden rule of investing that if you had the time, you had to play for the longer term, where gains compounded. In this case, there was no long term, so he did nothing for himself by nurturing a career that was irrevocably moribund. Accepting that his position at Calloway—and in the lucrative industry itself—would soon be gone, he needed to be especially aggressive in the short run. He had to maximize his winnings at every turn, even if that meant that his moves would be riskier. So went the logic. The deceitful and illegal option was the only option. He did not see another way. More to the point, he saw little to no chance that the plan would backfire.

The plan would go like this:

He would establish a short position, then spread a false rumor, and then, soon after (as soon as the rumor had gained traction, which might take a day or two), he would eliminate his position and begin backtracking. Within as little as twenty-four hours, he'd be telling everyone he knew that he had been mistaken. It had been a simple mistake. If all went according to plan (statement to retraction) the whole thing would be over in two days, at the most.

The SEC wouldn't investigate because the money involved would be too small to raise concerns. Even if they did investigate, they could never mount a case. There would be no evidence. Then there was the question of jurisdiction: Gabriel would be a U.S. citizen in Bolivia circulating a false (and then subsequently true) rumor about a Bolivian political situation that affected a Brazilian company that was owned by a mining firm incorporated in Singapore and run by a Canadian. Crucially, because Gabriel planned to quickly correct his "mistake," it would be impossible to prove that he had intentionally committed fraud. Without testimony from Lenka—which she would never offer, not only because she loved him but also because if she did it would be damning to her too—there would be no way to prove that he hadn't made an honest mistake and then simply corrected it.

In the meantime, Gabriel would ride the price of Santa Cruz. First, he'd ride the price down on a short sale, as the stock price plummeted. Then he'd close that short position at a profit, probably not quite as much as 100 percent, and then put everything toward a long position and ride the price back up. The price would likely spike above its starting point on a so-called short spike, triggered by automated buy orders set up by hedge funds to cover their own short positions. For Gabriel, the trip back up would be where he really cleaned up, doubling or tripling on his already near 100 percent gains. He would aim to sell out within the short spike.

Finally, the price would settle somewhere near, if slightly above, where it currently stood. Even if the timing of his personal trades was somewhat off, he'd come away with gains measured in the hundreds of percents.

Still, he hesitated. Prosecutable or not, it was securities fraud, a serious offense. It was white-collar crime to boot, which had especially unpleasant implications for Gabriel, the son of a liberal firebrand. The dapper uncle of clubfooted larceny, this kind of fraud was the domain of the sweaty and bespectacled accountant who sneaked off to the Caymans with someone's grandma's retirement savings. The mascot of this sleazier side might be Dennis Kozlowski, ex-CEO of Tyco: florid, bald, a complexion of braised poultry. He wore the ill countenance of a Nazi captured by the GIs who'd been trying to pass himself off as a prisoner at the concentration camp he'd been guarding. So Gabriel hesitated. But he couldn't hesitate for long. The shelf life of his information was remarkably short, so if he planned to use it he needed to make his move now. He had to act that day. Indeed, he had to act that morning, before he went to the airport to pick up his mother.

By the time the stock market opened, at nine thirty, he had made himself stop hesitating.

He rode the elevator down to the second floor, entered the business center. He lit a cigarette while the computer booted up and reminded himself that he needed to buy some gum to hide the smell of cigarettes from his mother. Her flight arrived at 3:40 that afternoon.

He tapped the cigarette, blew away the smoke that snaked in his direction. Icons appeared slowly on the screen. Outside, shafts of misty yellow light burst majestically through a carpet of clouds, shooting neat blotches of light onto the bare countryside. Once the computer was fully awake and had connected to the hotel's server, he opened his E-Trade account.

He liquidated 92 percent of his portfolio within five minutes of the opening bell, which left him with a cash balance of $62,017.11. He guessed that if he played it right, he'd be able to turn that balance into something in the area of half a million dollars by the end of the following day. Peanuts to someone like Priya, but to Gabriel, enough to set him up for a while in New York after he was fired. Or, if he wanted to move to Bolivia, say, he could coast for the rest of his life without difficulty. Not that he was thinking, directly, about moving to Bolivia. But the idea had alit somewhere at the back of his mind, where daydreams spawned, and was settling in.

Once he was ready to begin, he felt such a surge of anxiety that he thought he might vomit. His heart, that organ so often anointed with mysterious powers, envisioned as the seat of emotion, was quite clearly nothing other than a knot of muscle embedded in his chest cavity, pumping and sucking blood through a nest of tubes. It did this herkyjerky labor vigorously, steadily. Feeling it that morning, he knew that his blood pressure was up and that his heart was straining with its work.

He picked up his phone and dialed E-Trade. The market had been open for ten minutes. He refreshed his browser and watched Santa Cruz's price dip two cents.

An automated voice asked him to punch in his account number. Next, he was asked to provide his birthday, his Social Security number. He keyed through more questions until he arrived at the options desk. The phone rang twice before someone picked up.

"Good morning, this is Tim Nester, may I ask whom I'm speaking to?"

"Gabriel Francisco de Boya," he said. He stubbed out his cigarette. He refreshed his browser, and the price of Santa Cruz Gas lifted three cents. The spread was wide, because trading was still light.

"Okay, let me pull up your account information," he said. Tim was probably Gabriel's age. Gabriel pictured a doughy guy with a crewcut. He pictured the office, some three-story building on the outskirts of Omaha. He saw something drab and awful, a slightly more deadening version of his former job at *IBI*. "How's your day?" Tim eventually said.

"It's been pretty crazy already, actually." It occurred to Gabriel that E-Trade might be taping the conversation. He should act blasé.

"Oh?" Tim said, seemingly just happy it was something different. "Where are you?"

"Bolivia."

"Bolivia? Wow."

"What about you?"

"We're in Atlanta." Tim sighed. "Sorry, it gets kind of slow this close to opening."

"That's fine." Gabriel refreshed the browser. The buy price ticked up one cent, but the sell remained steady. He refreshed again. The buy ticked up another cent, the sell still didn't move. These were just the normal palpitations of a lightly traded stock. The direction was favorable to Gabriel, but negligibly so.

The crime he was about to commit wasn't victimless, exactly, but Santa Cruz's shareholders—those who held on to their stock—would be unharmed, as would the employees. The only people hurt would be those who speculated against Santa Cruz Gas or other companies exposed to Bolivian natural gas based on the rumor Gabriel planned to circulate. The losers, for the most part, would be other hedge funds and a handful of adventurous day traders. On the whole, it was a pristine and lovely stratagem: he profited, it hurt other speculators, and it left the *true* investors in the company largely unaffected. Even the company's founder, Lloyd Pingree, would be unharmed (unless he sold out too, in which case he'd lose more than anyone). The perfection of the scheme lay in the fact that it was profiteering for Gabriel, but it was also a morality play, because those who lost the most would be those who bet against the future of Bolivia. So went the logic.

Gabriel called Priya just after he'd opened his own short position. He said, "I have your answer on Santa Cruz Gas. It's not confirmed at this point, but I have it on good authority that he's going to sack all of the foreign companies at the same time, most likely in the first couple months of his term. So I'd short-sell Santa Cruz Gas. The news is probably going to hit this afternoon, or maybe tomorrow morning."

"How do you know when the news will hit?" she said. The skepticism was not disguised. She was an expert appraiser of odds, if not of people. So while she might have trouble locating innuendo, she could spot bullshit from a mile off.

"Well, I heard it from the finance minister–designate," he said, trying to make himself sound weary, not rattled. "Also, I gather that people were talking about it at the bar here where the journalists hang out, those people know—"

She cut him off. "If I do this, you know that it's your ass on the line."

"Yeah, I know." He said it quickly, to underscore his confidence. The fact that his ass was *already* on the line—that Oscar had phoned him to clarify the precariousness of his situation—was beside the point. This was a zero-sum gambit: if he gambled and won, he won big; if he gambled and lost, he lost big; but if he played it straight, he lost outright. Therefore he had no choice: he had to gamble.

"I'll talk to you later," she said, and hung up.

He went back up to his room. He could feel his heart flexing with mechanical efficiency. He hadn't felt that way since he'd shoplifted a Snickers from the Exxon on the corner of Foothill and Upland, in Claremont, when he was fourteen. He and Nico had each grabbed one candy bar. After, they leaned against a pinkish wall beside the nearby strip mall, chewing, dizzy with adrenaline. Now he felt the same as he stood in his room, on the verge of hyperventilating, staring at his bandaged face in the mirror above his desk.

At ten thirty, he was back in the business center, where he fired off an e-mail to Edmund at *IBI,* who had taken over the Latin America desk:

---

TO: Edmund_Samuelson@IBI.com
FROM: gabo_de_boya@yahoo.com
SUBJECT: Off the record

Hi, Edmund,

Hope you're well. I just had a tip, and Calloway is taking a position on the basis of this tip. Now, we don't know when the news will trickle out into the public, and Priya would rather not wait weeks before the move pays off, so I thought I'd let you know. If this turns out to be untrue, please let me know. As of now, I think it's true.

Long story short: I've heard from two sources close to Evo that he intends to seize all of the foreign gas installations within his first year in office. He'll offer them a chance to renegotiate their contracts, but he's talking about turning the Bolivian share of the profits from around 30% to around 72%. Anyone who doesn't cooperate will be booted out of the country.

So, I just thought I'd give you a heads-up. Thanks for forwarding the e-mail about this job at Calloway, by the way. I love it.

— Gabriel

---

At the Lookout at noon, he ordered a pisco sour and went over to say hello to Craig, a midcareer reporter for the Associated Press.

Half an hour later, he went to a different table, said hello to Sandra, the cute, young Scottish woman from the *Economist*. She was freckled and thick, ginger-haired, bawdy as a roughneck. She was all glint, no glare.

As he'd done with Craig, Gabriel told her that, regrettably, it all had to be completely off the record. "Oh, I love secrets," she'd breathed huskily. In a simpler era, Gabriel would have lingered to flirt with her, but these were not simple times.

At three thirty on the dot Gabriel was downstairs again, tilting after two pisco sours. He glanced skyward but didn't see any silvery airplanes cruising toward the airport. Despite his mother's insistence that he not meet her at the airport, he knew that with his being newly and gruesomely injured, and with his Thanksgiving no-show hanging freshly in the air, to say nothing of the fact that he'd forced her to stay at a hotel one mile distant from his own, he needed to be there at that airport when she arrived. He could do *that much*, at least. Petulant italics were implied within the idea itself. So he'd go pick her up and escort her to her lodgings, safely outside the rings of orbits in his strange solar system.

He'd have to tell her an updated lie. What he'd decided on was, like most good lies, a half degree from the truth. He'd tell her that he was writing freelance reports for a private equity firm. He'd say that he was working for Big Thunder, which was a teddy bear of a firm, despite its awkwardly macho name. Based out of Tahoe, it sought to replicate the returns of a frosty hedge fund like Calloway by buying direct stakes in startups through providing venture and angel capital. The group remained aggressive on tech, but it had also diversified into forward-looking green companies. Gabriel could tell her that he'd lied to everyone in Bolivia because he didn't want to tip them off to Big Thunder's Bolivian agenda. It was ecotourism, he'd say—and solar power; also, there was interest in finding a socially and environmentally responsible way of tapping the lithium in the salt flats for use in the batteries of electric cars. It was all very hush-hush, he'd say. Mostly, he'd keep it as vague as possible.

He opened the door of a taxi parked right there outside the Hotel Gloria, got in, and lit a cigarette. They were off before he remembered that he was supposed to buy gum. He said, "Excuse me, sir. Before we get to the airport, can you remind me to buy some gum?"

"Yes. Of course." The man caught Gabriel's eyes in the rearview and said, "You have no bag—are you picking up a girl?"

"Oh, no, no, no." Gabriel chuckled and rolled his eyes. "It's my mother."

The man tossed his head back, laughing. Gabriel smiled. "She's coming here to destroy my chances with any girls."

The driver kept on laughing.

Gabriel's mother's plane had already landed by the time he arrived. The driver didn't remember to tell him to buy gum, and Gabriel thought of it only once they'd seen each other by the baggage claim. Seeing her, despite himself, despite all his grumbling, he felt a fantastic relief. He found himself smiling—beaming—involuntarily, immensely reassured.

She was staring at his bandages, of course, but he didn't want to dwell on that. They hugged first, and then, when they kissed cheeks, he held his breath, aware that keeping her in the dark about his smoking was probably futile. She was not the type to be so easily deceived.

Half a foot shorter than he, she looked up at him in wonder; there were tears in her eyes. This was because of his bandages, he supposed. Not the cigarettes, he hoped.

She was what people sometimes referred to as a "well-preserved woman." She had a pretty face, much like Gabriel's, if a little more elfin. Skin collected uncomfortably around her neck now, and she was slowly losing her battle against the bulk that had been trying to gather itself in the lower half of her body for several decades. She looked, finally, like a middle-aged woman one might encounter at Whole Foods on a Thursday evening pushing her cart through the store after her weekly yoga class.

"Good to see you," he said. He tried to hold his breath back as he spoke. "You like the look?" He turned his bad side to her. She needed to understand that he was not going to allow it to be a big issue. If she'd come down to minister to her baby's scrapes and bruises, she'd come for the wrong reason. The wounds would be subjected to the same kind of acid humor that she applied to his writings on finance.

"Gabriel, you look—" She just shook her head, tears shimmering in her eyes. "You look wonderful." She was, mercifully, speaking English. She knew she was on his turf. It was a strange alchemy, the way a person came to belong to a place, or a place came to belong to a person. Bolivia, once hers, was now all his. She might have been a scholar of the place, and she'd spent more time there than he had, but he'd been scarred by it. It was literally in his blood. So Bolivia was his now and, whether he liked it or not, he was Bolivia's.

In the taxi, they kept things broad and nonaligned—they discussed her flight, an angry e-mail she'd received from a colleague at Pomona, and so forth. He tried not to think about the churning rumors that he'd kick-started that morning. Horrific possibilities presented themselves: the rumor had already been corrected and had been traced back to him;

Lenka's connection to him had been exposed too. As firmly as he was able, he assured himself that such fears were pure paranoia. In any case, it was out of his hands for now. He had his mother to cope with. He sat with his bad side to her, and he could feel her staring at the bandages, could feel her wanting to peel them back and look at the wounds. Emanating as much diversionary energy as possible, he ushered their conversation toward Evo. They spoke English to evade the curiosity of the driver.

Sitting in the loud, uncomfortable back seat of the taxi, Gabriel's mother administered a concise verbal abstract of her essay on Evo. He listened as carefully as he could. He noticed the highlights in her hair; a bit too coppery, he thought. She'd been darkening out the silver for as long as he could remember and had kept her hair short, in the style of suburban moms everywhere.

Seeing that they were approaching the city and would soon be in less tightly confined spaces, Gabriel pounced on a short pause. "I haven't been completely honest," he said.

"Oh dear." She drew a quick breath and glanced once again at the bandages, as if they were covering the misplaced truth or as if the truth about his wounds were in doubt.

"It's nothing too bad, but I don't actually work for BellSouth."

She nodded at him, guarded, her forehead fully furrowed.

"I've been doing consultancy work for Big Thunder, the private equity firm."

"Oh." From her nonresponse, he guessed that she hadn't heard of Big Thunder. So he explained who they were, where they were located, explained too about his projects there: the solar-power panels, which he said seemed unlikely to work (he added this just to give it a realistic flavor, the wariness of a skeptical insider); the salt flats, which Evo was not likely to share with foreigners—

"Nor should he!" Gabriel's mother interrupted.

"Of course," Gabriel said dismissively, and then he talked briefly about the ecotourism, which he claimed to consider a far more promising investment than either of the other two. "It'd be indirect," he said, "bundling projects together and providing a single loan to all of them at once. So we'd be creating a network too."

Whether she was actually relieved or not, he couldn't tell, but her response was infinitely better than what it would have been if he'd told her the truth. She asked a few questions, but they were trite. And he, relieved by how well the lie was holding up, went on to explain that he'd been telling everyone that he was working as a freelance journalist.

"Why?"

"Well—we don't want to alert people to our interest in Bolivia. Not yet, anyway. There are other firms that are trying to replicate our strategy, and they'd follow us here. So, if anyone asks why I'm here, you need to tell them that I'm a freelance journalist."

She scowled, looked away. "Oh, I don't like *that*," she said.

"Me neither." It was true, he didn't.

"What about the girl you're seeing? Does she know?"

His gut told him to say that yes, she knew, so when the two women met, Lenka wouldn't have to lie much—she'd just have to switch out *Big Thunder* for *Calloway Group*. But, ease of use aside, he couldn't risk telling *anyone*—not even his mother—that Lenka knew that he was an investor posing as a journalist. It was too risky for Lenka, so he said, "No. She thinks I'm a journalist. We don't talk about these things much."

"Is this why you want me at this silly hotel?"

He just shook his head. "No, no—it was everything." He paused, casting around for a way to explain it. He found it harder to do this in person. He was truly grateful that she was there, but it wasn't simple. The architecture of his scheme was such that each piece of information had to be marshaled along carefully. His mother liked to dig into the methodology of his thinking and so was a dangerous person to have around. As long as she was there, he'd do well to cultivate an attitude of stony mystery with her. "I can't explain," he said.

He could feel her looking at his bandages again. Clearly, the wound was personal for her. He remembered how, when he was a teenager, she would sometimes watch him eat his cereal in the morning and whenever his spoon approached his mouth, her mouth would open. Her empathy was purely kinesthetic. She was concerned about his emotions and his mind, about his career, but she *felt* for his body.

Not breaking her gaze, she said, "It might be hard for me to keep a low profile."

"I know. When are you interviewing Evo?"

"The day after tomorrow, noon." She held it as long as possible and then said, "Will she be at the interview?"

"Probably. They're in the south right now. They'll be back the morning of your interview. I'm sure you'll meet them both then." He tried to imagine the two women meeting—what would they say? They might have a few minutes together before the interview with Evo began. Would Lenka want his mother to be clear about the connection, or did Lenka want her relationship with Gabriel kept secret from her boss? If Lenka was supposed to keep it under wraps, could his mother handle that? Maybe Lenka would just skip out on the meeting.

They'd made it down to the plangent city already and were lurching and stopping in a thick braid of traffic. With such a crowded and turbulent city, he should have been able to stow his mother somewhere out of range of his social circles, but it wouldn't happen. The occupants of the calmer spaces above the mess were scarce, which was why to foreigners and the wealthy, La Paz was a tiny village, while to the rest of the city's inhabitants, it was a seething metropolis.

Then, fully out of the blue, she said the most surprising thing to him. She said, "Would you like to meet him?"

"Who?"

"Do you want to come with me to my interview with Evo?"

"Are you serious?"

"Sure. You could come along. If your girlfriend's there, you could introduce us."

"Oh—well, if she's there, I need to ask you to please be discreet."

"Of course I'll be discreet."

"Yeah, well, I'm not sure she'd want people to know that she's been dating the weird freelance journalist who never publishes anything."

"Fair enough."

"Why are you asking me along?"

"It sounds like you're working for a well-meaning firm, as these things go. So I don't see any harm in having you there. You could maybe even ask a question or two. Would you have questions for him?"

"Evo? Yes, I would." He was dumbfounded at first. But it made sense: his mother held the keys to the kingdom, so it wasn't strange that he might sneak inside behind her.

"Take a couple minutes, if you want. I don't mind." Then, ever the professional, she clarified, "You're not going to publish some feature on the event, right?"

"No, absolutely not." He held the eye contact for as long as he could manage.

"Why are you so surprised?" she said.

"I don't know. I just—he's kind of a hard guy to get a hold of."

"Even when you're dating his press liaison?"

He nodded. This, he saw, had embarrassing implications—all the more so considering that in the version of the narrative he'd given his mother, Lenka actually believed he was a journalist. Still, there was nothing to be gained by explaining his difficulties. Stony silence was best. "I'd love to come along," he said. To divert her, he added, "I'd like to ask him about ecotourism."

She looked at him askance, briefly, her forehead tilted. Maybe she could tell he was running calculations in his mind. Even if she didn't know what he was up to, she could see he was working toward something. He felt her expression relax as she decided to let it go.

He glanced at the time on his phone. It was four fifteen. The market had closed fifteen minutes ago. He was desperate to know if his rumor had circulated yet, but there was nothing to be done about it. A good strategist knows when to be a receiver of ongoing events and when to wait and be an actor in events to come. Now, he was a receiver of actions he'd already taken, and an actor in events unfolding with his mother.

After she'd dropped her bags in her large suite at her hotel, they ate a light dinner at the Ritz's upscale dining room, and then, while they waited for the check, she cast a weary look at him. He asked if she was feeling the altitude yet, though he could see she was.

She nodded.

It would probably only get worse for her in the next twenty-four hours. The Bolivians called it *soroche*, and it was totally indiscriminate in whom it afflicted the most. In rare cases, people died from cerebral or pulmonary edema. The only known treatment was to get to a lower altitude, so if a person continued to deteriorate, he or she needed to hurry to the nearest automobile or helicopter or airplane and go somewhere lower.

His mother wasn't dying, but she wasn't that well either. Gabriel had, for his part, dodged the worst of the altitude sickness. Looking at her in discomfort, he felt a surge of love for her and concern for her well-being. That kinesthetic empathy might work both ways because he found there was nothing like the sight of his mother in pain to bring out his most protective and loving side. "Drink water," he said after he brought her back to her hotel room. "And if it gets worse tonight, call me. Especially if you start feeling really dizzy or nauseated, then you need to call me immediately. It can be dangerous, Mom. Do you know that?"

"I know, I know." She was wilting before his eyes. Though she still wore her makeup, it was as if he could see beneath it. The only times she actually appeared without her makeup was before her morning shower and after she brushed her teeth at night, and to see her at one of those times was always an arresting experience—like seeing a man you know well suddenly lose the toupee that you hadn't even realized he wore.

Gabriel kissed her on the cheek and told her that he was glad she had come down. "I'm sorry I'm going to be so busy," he said. "Don't think I'm trying to avoid you if I'm not around—it's just that I've got a lot on my plate."

She smiled at him wearily, and he knew that she understood. He squeezed her hand and then closed the door and walked quickly toward the elevator.

Downstairs, he got into the nearest waiting taxi and pulled out his pack of cigarettes, his lighter; he rolled down the window and said, "Hotel Gloria."

At the business center, he saw that there was nothing new about Santa Cruz Gas. The price of the stock had fluctuated all day, unremarkably. Maybe the news just hadn't made it out yet? Time was not on his side. He considered recontacting the journalists that he'd already contacted, but he didn't want to push it. He didn't want to raise anyone's suspicion.

By the time his worry slackened enough that he could think about doing something else, it was almost eleven. He turned the computer off and went back up to his room.

He watched television for an hour. From his window, he could see that there were people up in the Lookout. Fiona was probably there. He dialed her number and she answered on the fourth ring.

"Gabriel Francisco de Boya! My favorite lout!" she exclaimed. He could hear from the background noise that she was at the Lookout.

"You're at the bar?"

"That's right. And I gather that you were skulking around here earlier, spreading rumors about Bolivian gas."

"Was I?"

"Aw, you'll tell other people but you won't tell me? Is that how it's going to be?"

"No, no, Fiona, it's not that." The truth was, he hadn't told her because he didn't want her to use the false rumor. It was one thing to give some rumor a minor existence, and it was quite another to give a false lead to a journalist from the *Wall Street Journal*. She'd smell a rat or she'd go with it; either way he'd be in trouble.

"Well then, what is it?" she said. "Do you know something, or are you just juicing an angle?" The noise had dimmed, so Gabriel knew that she had stepped away for the conversation. She was probably at one of the windows on the other side.

"It's not that simple. Priya's making a play on the basis of a rumor that I heard. I believe it's true, but I'm not sure. That's what I've been telling people. I've been clear with them about it. Look, my ass is on the line, so I wanted to push the story forward."

"You're juicing an angle."

"I just can't afford to wait until it trickles out. I'm not exaggerating the angle, I'm just expediting it. If I don't have results by the end of this week, I'm done."

"Jeez, Gabriel. *Really?* You're already that close to getting fired?"

"I'm afraid so."

"Maybe you're just not cut out for the hedge-fund world."

He cleared his throat. "I'll be fine."

"Of course you will."

"People are talking about the rumor?"

"Oh, yes. All night I've been hearing that Evo's going to expropriate the foreign gas. But it's still just a rumor. As soon as someone gets confirmation, it'll hit the wires."

"I'll look into it. If I can find out more information, or some confirmation, I'll tell you."

"I hope you didn't just make it up, Gabriel."

"I didn't just make it up! I heard it from two separate sources, but Evo—he just doesn't seem to have formed his decisions completely yet. He has these plans, but he hasn't quite imagined what carrying them out will involve. Look, I'll call you about this tomorrow."

She groaned dubiously.

"And about last night at the casino—"

"What about it?"

"Nothing," he said. "I think he's an okay guy."

"Grayson? An *okay* guy?" She laughed. "Gabriel, he's twice the man you are."

Gabriel was tempted to say something small, something about how Grayson was at least twice the years Gabriel was, but he thought better of it. He needed to play it cool for now. She should be as comfortable as possible. So he'd let her lead. He'd let her tamp him down too, if that would help. In his best eye-rolling tone, he said, "Sure, he's twice the man. Anyway, I'll talk to you tomorrow, midday, unless I hear from you before then."

"Right." She was circumspect, understandably.

"Seriously. From here on out, you've got the exclusive on this."

"How exciting," she droned. He'd find a way to make her change her mind about him.

He lay in his bed for another hour running through the possibilities and then, still unable to sleep, went back down to the business center. He opened his e-mail. Nothing. He wanted, more than anything, to call Lenka, but it was very late. He just wanted to hear her voice. He opened his brokerage account, looked at the sum. He wouldn't sleep that night. So he stayed in the business center, surfing the Internet in another window and then returning to the brokerage to click on the refresh button occasionally, although the sum of money didn't budge — couldn't, not when the markets were closed. At some point, he checked for news about Santa Cruz Gas on Google News, but there was nothing. He smoked a cigarette by the window, looking out at Casa Cultura, and he wished that he had, at least, a photo of Lenka.

His mind wandered back to the danger at hand. It wasn't so bad. He knew he wouldn't be arrested. Still, he was sick with it. There was something else, in the pit of him. It was the stomach-wrenching part of vertigo, with something rotten in it too. He was doing something *wrong*. It felt that way now, felt cold. The first time he'd had a one-night stand, when he was a freshman in college, he'd felt sick afterward in a similar way. It'd seemed reckless and wretched. By his fifth one-night stand, the feeling wasn't so bad. These things did get easier with repetition. Still, that night in the business center, missing Lenka and grazing on dreary news, he felt simply hollow. He was scooped out.

He checked his brokerage account one last time at a little after three in the morning. The figure was $62,219.01. He'd made a couple hundred dollars that day on what remained in the leveraged Latin American fund. He looked at the number and felt nothing but a fantastic loneliness. Then he went back upstairs and slept.

A little after nine, he awoke. He went through to the bathroom and put on a new set of bandages. The scabs were still a little moist, but there was no blood anymore.

Still in his pajamas, he stumbled back down to the business center and checked Google News. Nothing. The price of the stock was unmoved in premarket trading. He hit refresh. Nothing happened. Tears filled in his eyes. He blinked them away. "Fucking Christ," he whispered, and refreshed the browser again. Still nothing. He wiped away more tears and felt a lump in his throat. He wanted to hurl the monitor out the window.

Then his phone started ringing.

It could be Priya, or it could be Fiona, or it could be his mother, and if it was any of them, he didn't want to answer. He dreaded those conversations. There was only one person in the world he wanted to talk to, and she was in Sucre with Evo Morales.

# 12

# Maneuvers

*Wednesday and Thursday,*
*December 28 and 29, 2005*

IT WAS HIS MOTHER on the phone, wanting to see if he was available. He told her that he was. If the rumor didn't take within the next day, he'd be fired. The precariousness was sickening, but there was nothing else he could do, so he needed to get away from it. "What do you want to do?" he said.

"Nothing. I can work if you want me to leave you alone." A great deal of hay had been made over the Catholic compulsion to feel guilt, a trait that his mother — lapsed or not — exhibited, but Gabriel had not heard nearly as much about the equally powerful Catholic compulsion to martyr oneself. If his mother were merely self-lacerating, that would be one thing, but she frequently hurled herself on metaphorical coals, asking people to walk across her.

"You don't need to leave me alone," he said. "How are you feeling today?" He knew he sounded tetchy; he didn't want to, but he did.

"My headache persists. You?"

"Oh, I'm fine." He made it sound breezy, despite himself.

When he showed up at the Ritz later that morning, his mother was trying to recuperate from the altitude's assault.

She grimaced at his face when she opened the door. Then, despite her weakened state, she managed to cajole him into showing her his wounds.

He stepped in front of the mirror in the bathroom of her suite, peeled the bandages back from the top so that they hung off his face like flaps of skin that had been flayed incompletely. The scabs beneath were dark, nearly black; the surrounding skin inflamed and swollen and moist. His ear remained the most grisly. It had hardly changed. He came back out of the bathroom.

She nodded stoically, staring. She produced a grin — her lips pressed firmly together — that was meant to be reassuring, but he could see that tears were not far behind. Her whole face seemed to be flexing, straining for the expression. Mostly, though, her forehead gave it away. He knew he should be more sympathetic about the effect on her, but it was *his* face, and it was his life that had been upended. It was her decision to foist herself on him in this troubling situation, a decision made against his protestations. Despite himself, he felt like saying that he'd told her to stay away. He resisted, though. Still, he couldn't muster the kind of sympathy he knew he should have.

"It looks worse than it is," he said.

She nodded and then the tears started to well up.

"I'm sorry, Mom." He sighed and looked out the window, where the yellow light shone a little blurry in a lingering, thin, midmorning mist. He looked back at her. She pulled herself together, wiped away the tears with her fingers. He nodded. He went back into the bathroom to fix the bandages.

"What do you want to do today, Gabriel?" she called through.

He craned toward the mirror, pressing the adhesive strips back. They were never as effective on the second application. He'd probably have to change them by midday. "I was thinking we could go visit Lenka's mother. She said she wanted to meet you."

The two mothers squeezed each other's arms affectionately and pecked kisses and then Mirabel steered Gabriel's mother, him trailing behind, down the long hallway to the kitchen, in the belly of that huge blocky house. Water was boiled for tea while they stood around under fluorescent lights. Gabriel was acutely aware that he was supposed to be enjoying this more, that he was supposed to be attached to it more, but his mind was elsewhere.

Once the tea had been made, Gabriel ferried a tray of mugs and vanilla cookies to a front room. They sat around a bleak coffee table. It was one of the few rooms with a window that had a view. There were bars over the windows, but still...

The mothers chatted between themselves mainly, fortunately. They griped about how their children worked too hard (Mirabel initiated that idea) and were often absent (courtesy of Gabriel's mother).

"Mine is away now. She leaves her son with me!" said Mirabel.

"Gabriel didn't even tell me he was in Bolivia!"

"No!" Mirabel covered her mouth and stared at Gabriel. She smirked. "Is this true?"

He shook his head and rolled his eyes at the same time and managed to come off as both ashamed of his mother's griping and suspect.

Mirabel tsk-tsked and then returned her attention to her counterpart. Gabriel's mother segued into an extended summary of her complex life story, which was always a crowd pleaser: Chile and the tragedy there; her wild idealistic youth in Moscow; bearing a child as a single mother in California; raising that child alone while working as a professor. It was epic, but it had the elements of a good yarn: difficult beginnings lead to more difficult middle years, a willful woman fighting her way to happiness. The whole narrative felt laboriously manufactured to Gabriel by now. He'd too often seen his mother embellish the story one way or another for a given audience. Visions of herself in ghostlier incarnations, she was the artificer of her numerous worlds. That he did the same with his own life was, if not beside the point, certainly not the point itself—the point was that she proudly staked out territory above such manipulations.

Although she normally never talked about her romantic life in front of Gabriel—he vaguely knew that she'd been on dates here and there all his life, but nothing of substance ever developed—she spoke of it now. And it was startling to hear. The subject had been cordoned off in the way that many families deal with certain issues that are, for whatever reason, deemed out-of-bounds. Now, inexplicably, she was volunteering information about her romantic life to Mirabel. "There are men I meet," she said, "but none that I admire. Maybe now that my son is so absent from my life, I will need to go on more dates, though."

"I think that's a great idea," Gabriel said.

"Your mother loves you," Mirabel said, maybe having interpreted his mother's lack of interest in men as an indication of her fidelity to Gabriel. A pretty thought.

Throughout, Gabriel—shunting off his fears about his scheme, which was unfolding all the while—did his best to play the part of the aw-shucks son, feigning exaggerated protestations against the essentially harmless criticism from his adoring mother. "Not true!" he'd yelp, grinning as if in spite of himself.

His mother eventually maneuvered the conversation to politics and there she hunkered down. It was here that the two women found their true point of connection. In South America people demurred when it came to politics, but only until they opened up, and then there was nothing else in the world they wanted to talk about. The matriarchs shared their disgust for the notable Bolivian political catastrophes, and their admiration for Evo; they expounded on their hopes for the future.

Two hours passed in this way, bouncing around between politics and anecdote, the women commiserating in turns and then moving their focus to Gabriel. By the end, they had established a kind of maternal buttress. They ganged up on Gabriel in alternately cooing and scolding tones. He did his part, but it was painful. He needed a cigarette. He needed to get back to work. He wished at least that Lenka were there to buffer the awkward environment.

At noon, Mirabel offered them lunch and Gabriel's mother looked at him searchingly.

He grimaced and shrugged, explained that there was work to do. He suggested his mother remain behind, but she wasn't having it.

• • •

He directed his mother to an Internet café three blocks from Lenka's house. She bought a bottle of water and took another aspirin. She'd been gobbling aspirin all day to fight off her headaches. She sat down at the computer beside him. He could feel her eyes sweep across his screen. He turned to her and said, "I think I might—" He gestured at the screen.

"What?"

"This is personal."

She gazed at him blankly.

"It's private," he said.

"Right," she said. The absence of affect was palpable. Then she looked away, back at her own screen. She was blushing, shaking her head. "Of course." Had she thought he was talking about sex? That he was going to read a pornographic e-mail? He chose not to clarify. He moved two computers away, opened the browser, and checked his e-mail. In a second tab he opened finance.yahoo.com and checked on the ticker SCZG, and in a third tab he launched a Google News search, narrowed to "Previous 24 Hours," for "Santa Cruz Gas."

He waited while the three screens assembled themselves.

The e-mail landed first. One from Priya: *News?* As subject lines went, it didn't bode well, but it was better than, say, *Fired*. He opened the next browser. The ticker showed that the price had risen five cents. The story had probably not made it out. If it had made it out and there was no change, he was completely screwed. He opened the browser for Google News. Nothing, as expected. Back to the e-mail tab. He opened the mail, but there was no message. The message was the subject line itself: *News?*

He wrote back:

---

TO: priya_singh@calloway.net
FROM: gabo_de_boya@yahoo.com
SUBJECT: RE: News?

Tomorrow. Talked to journalists and I believe they're verifying today.

—G

---

There were other e-mails too — an announcement that Harlan's band was playing at the Living Room in SoHo, two trade confirmations from E-Trade...He read none of this. He just logged out. Then he checked CNN, a reflex, but there was nothing happening in the world.

He checked his E-Trade account. A few percentage points down: unimportant.

He glanced over at his mother. She was typing away brusquely, smiling to herself as she did sometimes when writing. Her fingers swept into a line of thought aggressively and then her right pinkie stabbed the backspace, as if transmitting a message in Morse code. There was a short pause. Then her fingers rattled off another burst, some recalibrated declaration. There was no particular musicality to it, but there was muscularity, some assertiveness in her handling of the keys that indicated a maestro was at work.

Once she was done, they walked down Prado. They ate ice cream cones in the gloaming afternoon. Gabriel looked around at the throngs, and at the whitewashed façades of the old buildings, at the black wrought-iron balconies, and he felt in love with the place for the first time. He'd never quite managed to love Bolivia, but he did now. Maybe it wasn't pretty, but it was *his*, and he felt pride of ownership. Here, not two blocks from where he'd been blown up, eating chocolate ice cream in the afternoon with his mother, he knew that he'd fallen in love with La Paz. He hadn't quite gone native, but there were stages to these things.

That night he and his mother ate at a fancy restaurant at the top of another hotel. The food was mediocre and the views astonishing. The city glittered on three sides through giant, tinted floor-to-ceiling windows. The restaurant was as hushed as a church, and the city lights around them flickered like votive candles at the perimeter of that church. They talked about Evo Morales, and Bolivia, because there was so little else they could talk about. They talked about Gabriel's injury. About the terror of it.

Then, to comfort him, she said that she would be there for him, no matter what.

He smiled at her. But until she'd said it, he hadn't quite realized—not consciously, anyway—that he didn't believe that she would be there for him no matter what. She was not like other mothers. Just because she loved him more than anyone else on earth did not mean she would be his steadfast supporter. He didn't speak any of this; were he to approach it even obliquely, she'd be hurt and defensive, and she was dangerous when she was hurt. He sipped his white wine. She was drinking tea still, trying to rehydrate enough to wash away her headache.

Afterward, he walked her to the Ritz. It hadn't been very difficult to keep her away from Hotel Gloria and the Presidente after all. Tomorrow, though, she had her interview with Evo, and the tidiness of her separation from him would begin to crumble. At least she was leaving before Evo's party—unless she managed to change her mind about that. He could see that happening. If Evo invited her, she'd probably stick around.

As they walked down Arce toward her hotel, Gabriel kept an eye out for muggers. He'd been robbed many times in Latin America. There were, by all accounts, very few thieves in Bolivia, despite the poverty. It wasn't surprising actually, what with its genteel, proud people. If they'd kept their navy intact despite having lost their coastline, they'd manage to maintain nineteenth-century propriety in the face of crippling twenty-first-century poverty.

"Why don't you tell me more about Lenka?" his mother said in Spanish. The sidewalk was wide and empty there on Arce, and he was grateful that they were walking side by side and not facing each other across a table anymore.

"Sure. What do you want to know?" he replied, also in Spanish. "Should I tell you about our sex life?"

She rolled her eyes and clucked her tongue, then shook her head.

"She likes to bite—"

"Oh my God, Gabo—*please*, no more!"

He laughed.

"Do you love her?" Her voice tilted up at the end, as if to make it sound like a perfectly normal or perfectly straightforward question.

"Yes." He didn't even think. It was true. He wished it weren't, but it was. Even her family, whom he had found too alien at first, too bleak—now he wanted them to adore him as much as he adored them. He wanted them to like not just him, but also his mother. When he thought about going back to New York, he was distraught about leaving Lenka behind. When he thought about the fact that he'd almost certainly be fired within twenty-four hours, he felt relieved. Would he stay in Bolivia? It didn't even need to be asked. Of course he would. For how long? Until the relationship broke one way or another. With the money he'd earned in the last couple months at Calloway, he could coast in Bolivia for years.

His mother was grinning, he could feel it. She was amused.

"Why are you so happy?" he said.

"I don't know." Maybe it was what it was: maternal glee at her son falling for someone who was not unlike herself. Or maybe she was seeing the death of his career at Big Thunder in this development—maybe she was seeing his staying in Bolivia as a freelancer, or possibly even on staff for Evo. Wouldn't Evo appreciate a young bilingual man with an Ivy League education who wrote about finance? If daydreams were really just the mind's mechanism for giving space to a miniaturized version of life where things were the way they *should be*, then, in his mother's glee, Gabriel recognized the extent of her discontent with his life as it was.

"Is this job competing with her?" his mother asked. Despite a tendency toward conversational subterfuge, when she wanted to be perfectly blunt, she could be perfectly blunt.

"I guess so." Not a lie. "The job wins because it has to." He said this, he knew, like a soldier repeating an oath under duress. The thing to know, the only thing, was that the oath had been arranged specifically for moments like this. The particular circumstances didn't matter. And while Gabriel might not have believed just then that the job would win, now that he was beginning to feel that he loved Lenka enough to abandon the promise of the Calloway Group for her, he knew that once he got back to New York, life would remind him of the point of the oath.

"This job means that much to you?" she said.

"I think so. I really wish it didn't. I believe that even though I love her, I can love another woman. I don't believe that I will ever have a work opportunity like this again. And maybe she and I can find a way to stick it out or to get back together when I'm done."

"Oh? When will you be done?"

"Two or three years. I want to save a lot of money, Mom. They're paying me very well. I want to save such a heap of money that I don't have to think about money so much."

"So, you want to live like I do?"

He nodded. His mother was not stinking rich, by any means, but she'd been earning six figures for a long time, had paid off her debts dutifully, and probably had fewer money concerns than 99.9 percent of the people on the planet. To her, money was largely a nonissue now. She couldn't buy a Rolls-Royce or an enormous yacht, but she wouldn't want such things anyway. She had enough money to do more or less what she wanted.

He said, "I don't know what to tell you."

She replied with what seemed, at first, like a platitude. "You can't let yourself become your job." This was beneath her, he'd thought, but then he saw what she meant: *Don't break your back trying to impress me, or anyone else, because I have managed to win those kinds of battles and I'm here to tell you that the payoff is poor.*

"So I should quit my job and move to Bolivia?" He said it like it was a joke, but he was really looking for her permission, her stamp of approval on the potentially ridiculous notion. That he was doing what she had just recommended he not do—seeking her approval—was inescapable. He needed advice on this.

"No," she said and it smarted slightly. It was disappointing. Maybe she was just trying to placate him, or trying to make him feel better about his ambitions? Neither, apparently—she went on: "I'm glad that you love this woman, but you can't just quit every new opportunity in favor of something more shiny. You have to see this through. If on the other end of it you decide to come back and be with her, great. But you can't be reckless with these things that the fates offer. They offered you your job first. Respect it."

"So, if I were to get fired, then maybe I should consider doing something like that?"

"You're not going to get fired, are you?"

"Of course not. I'm just saying —"

She nodded. They were near her hotel now.

After dropping her off, he rode home in a taxi and processed her message. He was overly vulnerable to her advice, he knew — one of the hazards of being the only child of a solo parent.

By the time he made it to his hotel he'd managed to convince himself that it was basically beside the point. He'd made his move. Now it was a question of how the dominoes fell, and they did not seem to be falling in his favor. So he was looking for a plan B, an indefinite stay in Bolivia and some kind of life with Lenka.

That his mother had not unequivocally embraced this option bothered him, naturally. The problem was with the mechanics of his lie to her; she might disrespect a job as an analyst for a cuddly equity firm contemplating installing solar panels in the desert, but she wouldn't have disrespected a feral animal like Calloway, a company that whipped giant sums of money around the globe based on a secret mixture of cold math and lukewarm leads.

In the business center, Gabriel checked the news and saw no story about Santa Cruz Gas. A glance at after-hours trading showed that the numbers were unchanged. He was losing. He went upstairs and lay in bed, trying not to think about what he would do once he was fired. Specifically, he tried not to think about moving to Bolivia, but he found himself mesmerized by the question of what kind of apartment he could rent for a thousand dollars a month.

He called Lenka's cell phone, and when she didn't answer, he left a message:

"Hey, I realize it's late." He spoke in a low, gentle voice, trying to mask his excitement. "I was calling because I wanted to know if you had any thoughts on how much it would cost to rent an apartment in La

Paz. Also, I wanted to know if you were going to be at the meeting tomorrow, because it turns out that I'll be there with my mother. So, anyway—I suppose that's it." He paused, tried to think if he was missing anything. "I'm excited for you to meet my mother. I hope you've had a great trip. I love you. Good night."

He hung up.

An hour later he got a text message from her:

> *pleased to hear everything is good. wont be at meeting. bring yr mom to my house l8er? xolv*

His reply:

> *will bring mom @ night or b4. cant wait 2 c u 2mrow. xxxx*


Still unable to sleep, he went back downstairs at four thirty and looked up apartments in La Paz. It turned out that one could rent a very nice house, fully furnished, in a gated community in south La Paz for $1,400 a month. If his scheme somehow worked and he was nonetheless fired in the next couple months, he'd have made off with $500,000, and he could easily earn 5 percent, or $25,000 a year, on that. He could live comfortably, indefinitely, in La Paz on the interest. It wouldn't be quite the way out that he had sought, but it would be, nonetheless, a way out. Even if the scheme didn't work, he could coast for a couple years. Maybe he could write a book?

The first light of day was already itching at the sides of his eyes when he noticed that it was 5:47. Beyond the window, the city was gasping awake, its earliest engines grinding in their labors. Furtive horns hiccupped below the window.

Upstairs, he showered, shaved, and dressed. Newly spruced and back in the elevator again, only a little delirious from the lack of sleep and still hopeful that he could present a healthy image of himself, he noticed that his right eyelid was quivering. Oh well.

After he'd picked up the largest cup of coffee available from Café los Presidentes Ahorcados, he returned to the business center. He sent his mother a text message saying he'd be at her hotel at ten, two hours before they were due to meet Evo. They'd get a bite to eat, maybe.

Once more, he looked at his e-mail. Nothing. The news: there was none. Drearily, woozily, he grazed on information from cnn.com and nytimes.com and the rest, while his stomach squealed and bleated in the background. He lay down on the carpeted floor for a moment. Closed his eyes, but didn't sleep. Then, in the minutes leading up to the opening bell, he checked the futures on SCZG one last time.

It was down 7 percent.

He blinked. Befuddlement yielded to disbelief, which yielded, in turn, to bright hope. He was wide awake now. The digit was red: 7.0%. He exhaled a groan and then refreshed the browser. The number held. His itchy eyeballs trained on the screen and his eyes opened wider than they had in days. He hurriedly typed in the tickers of several major multinational gas companies. They were set to start flat, or barely down. He raced over to other websites to verify the numbers. It was true. His follicles tickled across his neck and arms as thousands of hairs stood up in unison; he stood up too, and covered his mouth. His mind ran blank for the first time in days.

He ran his fingers through his hair, sat down again. Refreshed the browser. The price had ticked down a few more cents in the last minute. It was at negative 7.6 percent. He leaned back in his chair, wiped tears out of his eyes.

It had worked.

# 13

# Endgame

*Thursday, December 29, 2005*

THE STOCK OPENED 12.6 percent below the previous day's closing price as insiders continued unloading shares. Judging by the size of the initial drop, Lloyd Pingree himself must have been dumping his shares. The selloff picked up speed in the first half hour as other hedge funds started shorting the shares.

Gabriel's phone rang. He glanced at the screen and saw that it was his mother calling from the Ritz. She wanted, no doubt, to arrange plans for their breakfast. He didn't answer.

After she'd left her message he sent a text: *Work probs, not available, c u @ evos @ noon.*

He stayed in the business center for another hour, refreshing his browser periodically. The price continued steadily downhill. Prices of other companies overexposed to the Bolivian situation, including a Chilean silver mining company called ANVI that had about a third of its operations in Bolivia's Oruro department, were also sagging more than their multinational competitors'. Any business that drew a signifi-cant amount of income from Bolivian natural resources was now considered toxic. Investors who'd been indirectly betting on Bolivia's long-term prosperity were fleeing en masse on Gabriel's rumor.

At 10:32 Edmund published a brief on *IBI*'s website saying that there was a run under way on companies exposed to Bolivian mining and gas operations; it was a result of reports that Evo had developed a workable plan for expropriating foreign gas within his first year. Though it was only a couple of paragraphs long, the online editor recognized that they were breaking the story, so it was given a prominent spot on the site.

For Gabriel's purposes, that signaled the tipping point. Anyone with an indirect interest in Bolivia would be dumping shares by now. Automated trades would be triggered by the falling prices too, spurring further and more automated sales, forcing the price down even further. The rest of this adventure would be brief. It would be over by the end of the day. From here on out, his performance would depend on timing. He needed to pay close attention to the moments.

Within twenty minutes of the posting of Edmund's piece, the price of Santa Cruz Gas had tanked so far that the spreads on E-Trade grew to more than 10 percent. There had been an avalanche of sell orders. Investors were looking for a floor and not finding one.

By eleven o'clock, shares were down 76.6 percent. Gabriel was due to meet his mother and Evo in an hour.

Seven minutes later, when the price started bouncing erratically, Gabriel picked up the phone and called E-Trade. As quickly as possible, he keyed through to the options desk. A woman answered this time.

"Good morning," she said. "How can I help you?"

"I'd like to cover a short position."

"Well, I'll be happy to do that for you. Can I verify your account number, please?"

In six minutes, he was out.

At the end of the conversation, the woman said, "Congratulations."

"Oh." He cleared his throat. "Thanks." He hung up, refreshed his browser once more, and stood; he stuffed his hands in his pockets, stared at the screen while the computer processed his request. The page materialized once again. The balance was $110,762.55.

He'd made almost fifty thousand dollars in less than two hours. And he was just getting started. The real profits were still to come. At this rate, he'd end the day near five hundred thousand dollars. All he had to do now was reverse the direction of the rumor. All he had to do was correct his "mistake."

First, though, he needed a moment. He needed to do this interview with his mother and Evo, for one thing. He had forty-five minutes before he was supposed to meet them. He'd be back by one, at the latest, and then he'd buy Santa Cruz, all long, and call Edmund and the others.

He could buy long now, of course. That was what he was supposed to do. If someone were to find out that the rumor was false and word of the mistake were to circulate, he (and Priya) might lose out on the re-ascent. But he worried that it would seem more suspicious, from a legal standpoint, if he went directly from a pure short to a pure long. In any case, the stress of this was too much for him. He was sweating, practically hyperventilating there in the business center. He needed to collect himself.

Up in his room, he did twenty pushups, pounded a bottle of water. He caught his breath for a minute, staring out the window at the Casa Cultura, Lenka's former employer. It was a squat concrete building that looked like an aboveground bunker. He was excited to see her now: the scheme was paying off, thanks to her. She wouldn't be impressed, so he'd hold it back, if he could. What it meant, though — that he'd be wealthy when and if he was fired, when and if he moved to Bolivia — well, he couldn't explain that to her either. She'd be repulsed by what he was doing. Better to just shut up about it. The outcome would be the same, either way.

He lit a cigarette and cracked a window. He put on a suit and a nice shirt, no tie — Evo wasn't interested in ties — and went downstairs.

In the business center, he found that the price had bottomed out at an 81.08 percent decline and then bounced to a loss of 72.99. By now, dozens of investors in New York and around the world were trying to get in touch with Evo's people to confirm or deny the rumor. The press might be pursuing the rumor too, but not with anything like the ferocity of those investors. By the time Gabriel met with Evo, he'd likely have heard the rumor himself.

Gabriel was due to meet his mother at the palace in twenty-five minutes. He was supposed to go back in and buy as much Santa Cruz stock as he could afford, then ride the return lift all the way back up past its starting price. But he hesitated. The first half of his ploy had gone off so well, and it was such a relief to be in the clear for the time being, that he decided to wait. He could do it after the interview. It was a difference of an hour or two, assuming the rumor wouldn't already be corrected by Evo or Lenka or someone else. If it was corrected, he'd just say he'd been wrong. He'd lose the opportunity to ride at least part of the return bounce to parity, but there were worse things. And, honestly, it had been exhausting so far. He felt in the midst of a spiritual marathon.

He called Priya. "Are you seeing this?" he said.

"I am." She sounded remarkably calm.

"Look," he said, "I think you should cover the position. I just spoke to someone else in the cabinet, an economist, and I have some reason now to believe that this rumor might have been false. I'm not sure, but they might be lying. Not lying maliciously, maybe, but they really don't have any idea what they're doing. So just close out now and I'll get back to you when I know more. Is that okay?"

"No problem at all. Hold on." There was a short pause. Gabriel could hear muffled voices as she and Paul spoke. She returned. "Okay."

"You're out?"

"That's right."

He didn't want to linger in the business center. "I've got to walk and talk, so if we cut out—"

"Fine."

"I'm going to look into this and I'll be back in touch soon."

"Great." For the first time since he'd met her, she seemed in no way impatient with him. She seemed serene. She'd made—well, he had no idea how much money she'd made so far that morning, but it was probably in the millions.

He exited the door by Hotel Gloria's cafeteria and headed uphill, still on the phone. He'd been pacing long enough that his feet hurt. He had a headache, and his stomach was churning. He'd barely touched food since Lenka had told him what she knew, and it wasn't because of the arrival of his mother, it was because of this. As he huffed around the corner into the alley that led to Plaza Murillo, he said, "Priya, tell me, is every day like this for you?"

"All day long."

He said, "I don't envy you."

She grunted, amused. "Sure you do, Gabriel."

"Yeah, well, I'll be back in touch soon." He hung up. Ahead of him men in polyester shirts clutched fistfuls of sunglasses, their lenses glinting in the sunlight.

He walked quickly toward Calle Jaen. Jaen was an old street that had been preserved in its colonial glory and was now a popular tourist destination. It emptied out onto the square with his favorite salteñeria. Gabriel stopped at one point to catch his breath on a quiet back street. He'd been charging for the last three blocks, and his lungs ached. Then he ambled on, more slowly now, between ochre colonial houses with wrought-iron balconies. The headache was brutal, so he stopped in at a pharmacy. He bought two ibuprofen and swallowed them with a tiny cup of tap water that the pharmacist handed him.

Jaen was a narrow and curved street, inaccessible to cars. It had been laid, painstakingly, with millions of smooth rocks, each embedded into asphalt. Like cobblestones, but the size of a golf balls. The stones massaged his feet through his shoes as he walked up the road. The sky was dreary, and the street quiet and empty. The doors and windows were shuttered; the narrow balconies lingered aloft, unadorned. He passed a plaque indicating that one of the houses was the former residence of Don Pedro Domingo Murillo, for whom the plaza had been named. The residence was now a museum. Various other museums filled the narrow road, which was supposed to be a tourist hot spot. It looked exactly like a narrow street in some antiquated and gorgeous Iberian town, picturesque, if somewhat unremarkable by European standards. In Bolivia, it was absurd. It was an isolating and lonely place to be, a narrow gorge hidden in the city; it looked nothing like what surrounded it. Not that it was contrived. The buildings were real, hundreds of years old, but it was ludicrous regardless. If it looked strangely European, the reason was that the alley had been created by and for the wealthy Spanish occupiers of centuries past, who lived there when gold still tumbled down the icy waters of the Choqueapu. Though himself a resident of that grand road, Murillo had broken ranks to fight for independence, and being a proper Bolivian hero, he'd lost. Before he was hanged in the plaza on January 29, 1810, he uttered his final words, which—like those of Tupac Katari half a century earlier—would become ingrained deep in the national consciousness: "Compatriots, I am dying, but I left a fire that never will be put out. Long live freedom!"

Gabriel had to get to the palace soon, he knew, but he didn't want to deal with it. He could just call it a day and be done. It had been a winning day. The problem, of course, was that he needed to correct the rumor or run a much greater risk that his manipulation would be discovered. If the truth came to light with no help from him, the SEC would be more inclined to say that he had circulated a lie in order to manipulate the stock price. He needed to "find out" the truth and correct the mistake, not just for reasons of profit, but in order to cover himself.

He'd made it halfway down the hill when his phone rang. He looked at the number. It was Catacora. He'd forgotten that Catacora had promised to give him a sense of Evo's plan before Thursday. He sat on the curb and answered.

"I'm sorry I didn't get back to you before," Catacora said.

"It's no problem," Gabriel said, "but I've seen that there's a rumor circulating on the Internet today that Evo is going to expropriate gas in his first year. Have you seen this?"

"Yes, I heard. I'm amazed that it's out already. Who leaked it, do you know?"

"What do you mean? It's not true, right?" he said.

"Well, no, it *is* true, in a sense."

"*What?*" Gabriel felt his stomach drop. "What do you mean?"

"That's why I am calling. I'm sorry I didn't tell you earlier, but Evo was gone, and—"

"Wait, let me get this straight: Evo is going to seize all of the national gas, including the Brazilian companies, in his first year?"

"He's not going to *seize* them, of course. We can't do that. And it's not going to happen at once, but we will announce an offer in May. We're going to give them a chance to renegotiate their contracts by the end of the year. In the meantime, between May first and the end of December, they will take seventeen percent of the profits—assuming they want to cooperate."

"And if they don't want to renegotiate their contracts?"

"They will have to leave."

"That's not what I heard was going to happen," Gabriel said.

"I don't know who you were talking to, but that person either doesn't know or is lying to you. I talked to Evo about it this morning after the rumor surfaced."

Gabriel didn't say anything. His mind scanned the possibilities, trying to see how it could be. Maybe Lenka had made a mistake? He thought about it a little and understood that it wasn't likely. No. It wasn't possible. Rather, she had lied to him. She had lied to him when they met at the café. He couldn't guess why, but that was it. He was so astonished that it didn't even sink in, emotionally. It ricocheted off his heart.

"Oh my God," he said. He said it aloud by accident.

"What?" Catacora said. He waited a moment and then said, "Are you there?"

"Yes. Did—" He had no idea what else to ask. There was nothing to say. He needed to try to comprehend the thing, but he was supposed to meet the president-elect and his mother, and possibly Lenka herself, in ten minutes. It seemed like it should be funny. He wanted to laugh about it, but on some level, he knew it would have deep repercussions. And it was horrendous.

"Did *what?*" said Catacora.

"Nothing." He took a deep breath. "What, um—what about Brazil? Won't Lula—"

"Evo already talked to Lula this morning. Lula is not happy, obviously, but our countries have a lot of common interests, and I think Lula respects that this is Bolivia's most important resource and that we are in a dire situation economically. He understands how important it is for us, and for the region, that we are able to lift our country up."

Gabriel didn't say anything. He was searching for an angle, trying to see how Catacora might be attempting to deceive him—looking for some way that meant Lenka had been telling the truth—but it didn't make any sense. It began to dawn on him what it meant. It began to dawn on him how serious it was that Lenka had tried to sabotage him.

Gabriel stayed quiet. Catacora said, "Is that what you were looking for?"

"Not exactly," Gabriel said.

"Excuse me?"

"Yes, I mean. It's fine. Are you *sure*?"

"I'm *sure*. It's going to be a secret for the first couple months of the year, and the policy will be officially unveiled on May Day and effective immediately. I'm sorry if this rumor has already made it out. You can still have the exclusive on the story of my appointment."

"Thank you. Excuse me, I need to go."

He hung up the phone, turned around, and walked back up the hill.

At the crest, he found a plaza and sat on a bench. He had a few minutes. The palace was three blocks away. A young boy in a black ski mask offered to shine his shoes and Gabriel accepted, adding that he was in a hurry. Gabriel looked at the boy's blackened fingertips rubbing inky liquid into his shoes. He'd bought those shoes, narrow oxfords with chunky heels, before he'd started working at Calloway, and they'd seemed expensive then. They were made by Hugo Boss and had cost eighty-five dollars at the Loehmann's in Sheepshead Bay. He'd bought them on a Sunday and had taken the bus back to Greenpoint afterward, listening to his iPod and making eyes at a waifish pixie hipster nearby. It was a warm spring day. She wore a tank top and had lovely breasts.

On the back of her hand, a new tattoo showed two skipping dice—the dice were green and the surrounding skin puffy and inflamed.

Now, a couple years later, sitting on that bench in La Paz and having his shoes shined, Gabriel reached back for the moment, and although he remembered the day vividly and fondly, it was completely foreign to him. He looked back and he couldn't identify with the person he had been. When he'd left Claremont for Brown, he'd looked back at life in Claremont with a similar detachment, as if it were someone else's memories that had become misplaced and ended up in his mind. The experience was absolutely inaccessible. He could not put his finger on a single way in which his outlook had changed in the last two years, yet it was obvious that everything about him was different. It had all somehow changed when he wasn't paying attention.

Though the inauguration was weeks away, Evo and some of his core staff had been given a section of the palace's second-floor offices for the purpose of organizing a smooth transition. Gabriel showed his passport at the door and was waved along to a desk, where a scrawny bureaucrat with a thin beard took down Gabriel's information. At an adjacent desk, Gabriel spotted the zaftig receptionist from the front of MAS's office typing away on a computer.

One of the guards escorted Gabriel through the palace, which was, Gabriel could tell, really just an immense brownstone. Upstairs, he was directed into an elongated reddish room with a window facing the bright square. From across the dark room, the air outside appeared to be ablaze. In the dim foreground, he saw Evo and his mother seated in the center of the room, beside what looked like a nonfunctioning fireplace. Another man, some unfamiliar assistant with a dreary gaze, sat on a nearby chair with a folder on his lap. He might be security or he might be a secretary or he might be something else. Gabriel's escort announced his name before ducking out. Gabriel approached, apologizing for being late and saying it was no one's fault but his own. "I got lost," he said. "It's a beautiful city, but it's confusing too."

They were seated on dainty Georgian furniture. Evo looked at Gabriel uncertainly. It was an odd place to encounter a man like Evo, who was nothing if not down-to-earth—down-to-earth in such a way that the cliché itself seemed damaged by his sincerity. Being a farmer and the child of miners, he was *genuinely* of the earth, as connected to terra firma as a person could be. Gabriel had supposed, though he'd never say it to anyone, that Evo was the inside-out version of George W. Bush: overreliant on a political persona both ballsy and blue collar. Evo too *felt* his way to his conclusions instead of thinking his way there. Both men were defiant cowboys who trafficked domestically in a kind of folksy populism that won them huge majorities among the ill-educated. Looking at Evo now with his mother, Gabriel knew Evo was genuine, and he knew what it said about his mother that she so ardently supported this man.

"My son," she said, "I was just telling you—"

"It's a pleasure," Gabriel said and extended his hand to the still-seated Evo.

They shook hands and Evo didn't stand up. He looked a little curious, as if he half recognized Gabriel.

"We met the other day," Gabriel explained. "I interrupted your meeting at your office around the corner."

"An interview with Lenka?" he said, remembering.

"Yes. I'm a freelance journalist." Gabriel could feel his mother look away when he lied to Evo; he could feel her horror.

He sat down on the sofa beside the unnamed adviser. Lenka was nowhere to be seen and Gabriel knew why, now.

And if she showed up, what then? Would there be a scandal? Would she make a scene and tell the assembled the truth about Gabriel? No. To do so would be to condemn herself too. Would she mind ruining her own career? Definitely. It didn't make sense—she had too much riding on this to sacrifice it all. Still, what would happen if she did out him? He pondered it quickly, tried to organize some probable outcomes. Some were obvious:

a. Evo kicks him and his mother out of the offices, and then bad things occur.
b. Evo kicks him out of the office and keeps his mother there, same outcome.
c. Evo has him arrested (was this plausible? He didn't know. Probably not. No, certainly not).

Nothing else came to mind right away. Except that maybe, just maybe, Lenka had somehow made an honest mistake. Or maybe Catacora was misleading him. Could Catacora be wrong? Someone was wrong. But this was not a normal mistake. How could two people so close to Evo have such different stories about his plans? Unless Evo was telling different advisers different stories, which seemed unlikely. The only thing Gabriel knew for certain was that one of the two, whether by design or accident, was wrong. And if that was true, then why had Gabriel chosen to believe Catacora so quickly? Only Evo could sort out the confusion, and fortunately he was handy. Unfortunately, proximity aside, Gabriel wasn't in a position to ask Evo whatever he wanted. He was tagging along with his mother, and there were expectations.

She questioned Evo for almost an hour without pause. Gabriel, vigilant of the time, didn't exactly listen—he leaned forward with a thoughtful expression on his face, nodding once in a while, and directing his gaze at whichever one of them happened to be talking. Meanwhile, he silently ran through the questions and problems he'd encountered. His thinking was circular, and like all circular thinking it served mainly to elucidate the particulars of the situation rather than illuminate a solution.

A clock somewhere chimed the quarter hours, sonorously, helpfully. After he heard a third chime, he knew that his mother would pass the questions to him soon. And although she expected him to ask about ecotourism, solar power, or some other featherweight issue, he'd have to ask questions about natural gas, the same ones that had been vexing him since he'd arrived in La Paz. It was unfortunate, but it had to be done.

The conversation between Evo and his mother had probably been quite interesting. From what he heard, she had pressed Evo on a few issues. There were predictable queries about coca production, and whether Evo would grant proper representation to the wealthy and politically/geographically isolated people in gas-rich jungles, and about a slew of items that meant nothing to Gabriel. As he sat and circled through his thoughts again, he began wondering what would happen with Lenka in the long run. Even if she didn't burst into the room now, she still might do something. Would she have him barred from the party tomorrow? He thought it likely. Even if she didn't attempt anything else, she'd do that, he guessed. Or maybe not?

"Gabriel, that was your concern, right?" he mother was saying now, gazing at him. She was finally punting the ball in his direction, and he'd completely lost track of their conversation.

"You mean the solar—" He looked at his mother questioningly.

"And *ecotourism*, right?" she said, her face reddening.

"Yes, those are both my questions, in a way. Ecotourism and solar power. I guess the question behind those questions is about the sustainability of Bolivia's fiscal situation, because those plans, you know, are fiscally difficult. All of those other issues are subordinate to that question. So I know you have great plans, but how can you finance those plans if you don't nationalize the gas?"

Evo shrugged. "I will nationalize the gas, I have been saying—"

"No, no, I know—I know you will, but when and how will you do it?"

Gabriel's mother was staring at him now, surprised by the questions. Alarmed by the seriousness of his line, perhaps. He couldn't help her with that.

"I gather that the rumor is out already," Evo said.

"I heard it this morning, something about May first—is it true?"

"You can't write this—neither of you can—because I will not officially announce my plan until then, but we are letting the companies know now."

"You're going to break the contracts and make them renegotiate?" Gabriel said.

"Well—yes, those contracts were signed by an administration that was a puppet of the United States government."

"I know," Gabriel said, if only to cut short the train of thought before it got moving. "And you're going to give the companies until the end of the year?"

Evo shot a look at Gabriel: not quite affronted, but not so benign either. He was surprised that Gabriel knew so many of the details. Maybe that aspect hadn't been leaked yet. Gabriel's mother gave him a similar look—he could feel it torching the side of his face.

Eventually, Evo nodded. Gabriel sat back in his chair and took a deep breath; he glanced at his mother, then back at Evo. He was done there now.

The silence didn't last long. Evo's unnamed assistant pointed out that Mr. Morales had something else scheduled in five minutes. Gabriel's mother flipped to a new page in her notebook. "So I—um—do I have time for one more question?" she said.

"Of course," Evo said. He looked as before: as if he were mildly upset about something but wouldn't do anything about it. His face was unlined but weary; his expression was limpid. She asked her question. He blinked once or twice, thinking, and then replied. This was a nuisance for him. Already, he was thinking about the rest of his day.

Outside, Gabriel resisted the overwhelming urge to light up a cigarette. His mother was upset and he had to deal with that, and then he had to deal with all of the other, more urgent, problems ahead of him. They walked into the center of the plaza. He could feel her staring at him. He could feel an argument taking shape in her head, but he didn't know where she'd take it. He stopped and turned to face her by the lamppost where Villarroel had been hanged.

"What was that about?" she said.

"What do you mean?" Playing stupid was an easy if not especially effective defense with her. It bought him time, at least.

"I thought you wanted to know about environmental subsidies or something. I thought you were going to ask about ecotourism."

"I was—in a way. I was wondering if he's going to be able to pay for such things."

"I didn't hear you ask about his interest in the projects. I just heard you ask about his fiscal situation."

"It's the same thing, Mom."

"No, Gabriel, it's not the same thing." She switched to Spanish, saying, "And where is this Lenka woman? I thought she'd be here. I was looking forward to meeting her. Are we going to see her and her mother this afternoon?"

"I don't know." He was in Spanish too now. Lenka had invited them over in last night's text message. But if she'd intentionally told him that lie, she might tell his mother the truth. She might tell anyone. Or not quite anyone—she wouldn't want Evo to know the truth, which might have been why she skipped the meeting. "I think we've broken up," he said.

"Oh," she said and her face softened. "I'm sorry to hear that." She switched gears as best she could at that velocity. "What—um—what can I do?"

"You can't do anything. I'm sorry. Thanks for offering. But we shouldn't go and see her or her family. Look, can I meet you later? We'll get a nice dinner at this place I've heard of that's near your hotel. It's called La Comédie. It'll be great. I've had a horrible day, Mom, and I've still got a dozen stressful appointments ahead. I just need a few hours. Is that okay?"

"I leave tomorrow."

"I know. I'm sorry, Mom, but I told you that I'm very busy here."

"*Busy?*"

"Yes. Busy."

"BellSouth? Or, wait, you're a freelance journalist? Or, no, maybe you're working for an investment firm in California? Are you still living in New York, Gabriel? Or have you moved to Palo Alto? When was the last time you were at their office in California? Why are you not telling me—"

He shook his head and waved his hands at her—it was way too much. "I have to go, right now. I have an urgent telephone meeting. We can talk about all this later, but I just don't have time now. This is too important. I'm sorry. I'll pick you up at seven."

"How much of what you've told me is true?"

He leaned in and kissed her on the cheek. "I have to go. I love you." He walked briskly away from her and didn't look back. There were a million things he could have said to soften it, but he didn't have the time.

He turned the corner and headed toward Gloria, trying to organize his next steps. He had to communicate with all of the people he had supposedly misled before. He'd have to explain that he had been more or less right after all. It would be a more awkward, if considerably less stressful, task than it would have been if things had gone according to plan and he had lied to them successfully. His mother would remain furious for a while, but he could make amends that night at dinner. He'd make jokes and play the rascal. She'd get over it. She had no choice.

Priya was first. He called her by the time he made it to Potosí. "False alarm," he said as he crossed the street at the courthouse. A bus ground its gears as it churned up a nearby hill. A child inside gawked at the bandages on Gabriel's face.

"Good," Priya said. It was the response that he'd hoped for.

"The specifics are slightly different from what I'd heard," he continued.

"How so?"

"It turns out he's not going to begin the process until the first of May, but it's going to be an open secret until then. From May until the end of the year, companies will be invited to 'renegotiate' their contracts with Bolivia."

"*Invited?* Ha! As in 'We'd like to invite you to get twenty percent instead of eighty'?"

"That's the idea. Except I think it's seventeen percent."

"And if they refuse to go along with the new plan, they're out of the deal altogether?"

"Right."

"Well, that's that," she said. "Thank you."

He waited, but she said nothing else. So he said, "That's it?"

"Yes, that's it. You're done there."

"Just like that?"

"Yup. You're done. And you did surprisingly well, Gabriel. It paid off. I hadn't expected anything to come of this, but we did well this morning and it was a terrible morning otherwise, so we owe it to you. You earned your bonus, at any rate. What was it? Two fifty?"

"My salary is two thirty-four."

"Two thirty-four. I'll let Anne know. Bonuses are delivered the second week in January."

"Second week in January," he repeated.

"Do you have an accountant?"

"No," he said. "Should I?"

"Yes. You'll need to file quarterly. Most of us use a Norwegian named Life, of all things. Odd guy, but he's very astute, very meticulous. I'll refer you if you're interested."

"I am, I guess." When she'd mentioned referring him to her accountant, Gabriel apprehended that he'd truly passed whatever test she had had in mind for him. From now on, he would be viewed differently by her. He was inside now.

She said, "So, you'll return tomorrow?"

"No. I have some things to tie up here." No need to mention his mother, much less Lenka. "I'll fly back on Friday." He turned the corner at Potosí.

"Fine. Once you get home, take a long shower and replenish the mothballs in your closet, haul the junk mail out to your recycling bin.

Treat yourself to some good food and get a massage. I know a fantastic masseur named Ofir. Jordanian, hands like an orangutan. He does house calls. I can give him your name."

"Right. Okay, thanks. I might need that, I don't know. I'll think about it." He was approaching Gloria now.

"Good. In the meantime, you should start looking into Televisa. Have you heard of it?"

"No. Is that with an *a*?" he asked. He stopped walking, took out his pen and pad, flipped to a new page, and set the pad against the wall of a nearby building.

"Yes, with an *a*," she said. He jotted it down on his steno pad. "It's Colombian," she continued. "Media production and distribution. Television, radio, and film, and some print, but only in Colombia. It's family owned, for now. They're headquartered in Cartagena. Have you ever been to Cartagena?"

"I've never been to Colombia." He put the pen back in his jacket pocket.

"Cartagena is supposed to be a very pleasant city. Oscar's been a few times. He'll recommend a hotel."

"Right," he said. He continued walking. "Fine."

"I'll see you soon," she said.

"I'll be in the office on Saturday," he said, and then hung up.

He called Fiona next and told her the same information: his rumor was true, but he'd been a little off in the specifics.

"You sound disappointed," she said.

"I am, slightly," he admitted.

"Why?"

"I'd rather not explain. It's been an awful day. My mother's here."

"Eek."

"Yeah. She thinks I'm working for Big Thunder. It was the only workable lie."

"Double eek."

"Yeah, I know."

"It's kind of yucky too, I must say."

"Yeah, I know that. But you're the only one who knows everything." This hadn't occurred to him until he said it aloud—that Fiona, finally, was his most trusted confidante. "I have something else for you," he said. "I don't know if you care, but the next finance minister of Bolivia is currently a professor of economics at the Universidad Mayor de San Andrés named Luis Alberto Arce Catacora. He speaks English fluently, eagerly; he earned a master's degree at University of Warwick in the late eighties, and he seems pretty sensible, all in all. Will probably break in the next forty-eight hours, but I thought you might find it useful."

"Wow, Gabriel. You realize that you're giving me your leftovers, don't you?"

"It's all I have."

"I know, and it's sweet of you."

"I'm a saint."

She laughed and laughed at that, and he listened for a long time.

A bellhop opened the door for him, and he entered the lobby and then paused there to call Edmund at *IBI*. He told him as well. Standing in the lobby and speaking as quietly as possible without whispering, he explained that he'd been slightly wrong about the specifics. "Sorry about that."

"No problem at all," Edmund said. "It was a great tip. Thanks."

"My pleasure," he said. "I have to go. I'll talk to you later." He hung up.

He was in front of the elevator doors, listening to the squeaking pulley inside, when he spotted the hotel manager, Dorotea, by the desk.

Looking at her, he put it together at last. He understood what had happened and why Lenka had done it. The morning he'd deposited Lenka in the elevator with Alejo, Alejo had told her about the day after Christmas, when Fiona had exited Gabriel's room at dawn. Could it be that simple? Was Lenka that jealous? Of course it was that simple, and of course it wasn't *just* that she was jealous. That one cardinal deceit had, for her, opened up an array of possible subsidiary deceits.

Maybe Gabriel was CIA after all. Certainly he was just gaming them all, to her mind. She found out about his infidelity and it didn't mean what infidelity normally meant—that he was narcissistic and/or sexually greedy—it meant that he was an utterly diabolical double agent. He was just using her for information. It had probably taken all of her willpower for her to contain herself the morning they'd met at Café los Presidentes Ahorcados.

Looking at the manager now, Gabriel briefly considered going over to complain to her about Alejo. They might fire Alejo if they found out he'd been spreading rumors about a highflying customer to that customer's girlfriend. Even if they didn't fire him, it would certainly stir up a scandal among the staff, which couldn't possibly be good for young Alejo. But in the seconds that remained while he waited for the elevator, Gabriel decided against it.

In the end, Alejo couldn't be blamed for running that angle. It was the best angle available, so he did what he could with it. Presumably, he'd thought he might somehow curry favor with Lenka. It had looked like the play to make, so he'd made it. It was all very natural. Once upon a time, Gabriel might have done the same thing if he'd thought it would impress the right woman.

On his last errand of the day, Gabriel went up to the Lookout and told some of the journalists that he'd managed to confirm the rumor he'd circulated the day before, though a slightly different version of it. They were grateful for the addendum and, maybe sensing that he was a bit overwhelmed by something or other, tried to buy him some cocktails, but he refused. The sun was setting over the Andes by then, and he knew it was over.

The scheme had not played out as he'd hoped, but it had played out well enough. Despite his intentions, Gabriel hadn't broken the law. He'd set out to commit securities fraud and had failed, had accidentally behaved lawfully and told the truth. There would be no investigation. He'd emerged a hero in the eyes of the reporters he'd tipped, and he'd emerged a hero in the eyes of Priya. The only people who were hurt were those who'd held on to the stock—those whom he'd intended to spare.

He wondered what else he could expect from Lenka. Misleading him had been a subtle move; still, she could sabotage him in other clandestine ways: tell his mother, for example, or tell the press. But she wouldn't want to go too far. If she made too much of a show of his story, she'd implicate herself. And while Gabriel might survive the accompanying scandal, might even benefit from it, she'd be ruined. As he considered the issue, he felt a sting of sadness at the way things were shaking out. There was no anger on his side; he understood why she'd done what she'd done. It was, instead, a sorrowful stinging, the sick feeling of having lost a real shot at love. The sadness swirled in with his cyclone of schemes and calculations.

He headed downstairs, aiming to play blackjack for a few minutes before he went and picked his mother up for dinner, but as soon as he got there he realized he was famished. He hadn't eaten all day. He needed food, and he had earned a good meal, so he set off for his mother's hotel. He'd be a little early, but that was no problem. He planned to take her to La Comédie, a French restaurant in Sopocachi that was said to be one of the few excellent restaurants in town. He'd never been. Lenka had recommended it to him once and they had planned to go but had never gotten around to it.

In the taxi on the way to the Ritz, he thought about the situation. Lenka had definitely lied to him. It had been deliberate. It had been unforeseeable. The thought arrived horribly to him. Lenka had tried to scupper his plans. There was no other explanation. As the taxi wended its way through the choked city toward Plaza Isobel de la Catolica, he tried to think of another one, but nothing came to mind. Why would Evo say one thing to her and something else to Catacora? Catacora wouldn't lie—intentionally misleading a journalist or an investor would be a disastrous for a future finance minister.

In Lenka's eyes, by sleeping with Fiona, Gabriel had screwed Lenka in every way possible; he'd pretended to care about her while covertly arranging to enrich himself and his employers. To Lenka's mind, he'd just used her. It wasn't the fact that he'd slept with Fiona, really—Lenka might have recovered from straightforward infidelity, or at least not lashed out—but Fiona was also a source of information for Gabriel. So it must have seemed to Lenka, as it had to Fiona, that he'd been scheming when he went to bed with each of them. To Lenka, he'd turned out to be nothing more than a cold-hearted villain.

The irony was that the reason he'd survived was that he'd tried to lie. The two lies—his and hers—had canceled each other out, and Gabriel had inadvertently told the truth. If he had told Lenka's "truth," as she had doubtlessly expected, he'd have committed securities fraud and wrecked his personal portfolio. He'd have lost his job at Calloway. Lenka had lunged and she'd missed, because he was lunging in another direction. The lesson was fantastically cruel to everyone involved. He'd arrogated to himself a victory, but that victory had (fatally) been built on the assumption of her fidelity.

He'd always known that this was why game theory didn't survive studies of real people. Real people's motivations were too complex and flawed to be fathomed by any mathematics.

When Gabriel arrived at his mother's hotel room, her neatly packed bags were lined up at the foot of her bed ominously, like a pair of paunchy forest green tombstones. She'd packed early and then put her bags there, a visual reproach to Gabriel for his having ditched her earlier; whether she'd done this intentionally or not, the effect was the same. She kissed him on both cheeks. She seemed subdued in a way that he understood was supposed to induce guilt, as if she were too sad to be animated. She wore a flowing brown dress and shawl, and he saw that she was wearing the turquoise earrings he had sent to her for her most recent birthday.

"I'm sorry I fled." It was better to just have it out. He could repeat the lines about how busy he was, but she'd known he was busy. She'd flown down anyway. She'd done what a good mother should do, and now her bags teetered next to the bed.

"It's fine."

He nodded. Maybe it was this way for all grown children and their parents, but he found that whenever he saw her, the whole interaction was shot through with ruefulness. Or at least, the start and end of each visit were heartbreaking. They hadn't done enough, once again, hadn't said the things that they should have said. His gratitude had not yet found voice, and her kinder feelings about him hadn't managed to find voice either. Instead, they had disappointing fragments. "Well, I should have made more time for you," he said. "I'm really sorry about that."

"It's a question of priorities," she said.

He couldn't have said it better. It *was* a question of priorities. Lenka and he could very well have loved each other and might have lived a wonderful life together. But if empirical economists had learned anything in the past hundred years, it was that people were deeply irrational. An irrational fear of loss drove them to make seemingly ludicrous decisions.

If Lenka and the Calloway Group were mutually exclusive, then Gabriel, who had spent so much time in recent years pining after the kind of life Calloway offered, had simply chosen the option that would be hardest to replicate in the future. He could find another woman he'd love, he assumed. He could not find another job like the one he'd been hired to do. And though it might seem awfully cold when it was rendered so bluntly, he felt certain that most people—good people, great people—made decisions that were equally cold on an almost daily basis. It was simply how people viewed life: there were thousands of decisions to be made, and every one of them involved weighing the likely outcomes against each other.

For example: A young couple is thinking about buying a house in a neighborhood they like. The house is small, but they are not expecting to have many children. It's close to friends and family, and they believe the house will appreciate in value. They could wait, but mortgage rates may rise, in which case they wouldn't be able to afford this house anymore. A more pleasant calculus than Gabriel's, but no less methodically calculated.

What about the young couple's marriage? Was it altruism that brought them together, or did each one look at the other and decide that this person would likely bring more happiness than anyone else currently available? Emotion might have swept them away in the moment, but behind that emotion lay a methodical weighing of pros and cons. To an economist, it would make sense: Every decision someone makes is aimed at maximizing his utility. Utility can come from strange places, even from giving anonymously to a charity.

To Gabriel's mother, this was all heresy. To her, there were different classes of desire.

At the restaurant, Gabriel asked for a table in the corner. The restaurant was small, candlelit, and almost empty. It looked authentic, an actual extravagant restaurant, with pressed white linens, dark wood, leather, scowling staff. A smoldering stack of wood in a nearby fireplace exhaled a shrill whine. Gabriel opened his menu. Although nothing cost more than five dollars, it was the most expensive restaurant he'd seen in Bolivia.

He had no idea how far Lenka would go. And did she fear that he would try to get back at her? He could only guess at the extent of her anger. It was a horrible situation. The nightmares competed for his attention. On one hand, he had the acid terror of the professional horrors that she might wreak on him. On the other, he had the heartbreaking knowledge that she despised him. The temptation was to run to her house and pound on the door so he could explain it all—or try to explain it all. She might understand...she was ambitious too. But there was no point. Anything he did would look like an attempt at damage control.

The waiter returned, and Gabriel realized he hadn't been reading the menu at all. Quickly, he glanced at the wine list and asked for a bottle of the same Bolivian white wine he had been drinking in his hotel room since he arrived—the cheapest wine on the menu, by a long shot. His mother ordered lake trout, and he asked for grilled llama tenderloin, medium rare, with blackberry demi-glace.

Dinner was fine. The conversation remained stilted.

They passed on dessert but ordered coffee. He wanted a cigarette. She read his mind and said, "You can smoke if you want to."

"I don't smoke!" he said and chortled.

Her expression didn't change. "If you get cancer, I'll cut your lungs out myself."

He pulled his pack out of his pocket and lit one. He soldiered through the awkwardness of it. She was fixated on the cigarette, purely contemptuous, as if she'd anthropomorphized it into a herpes-ridden Ukrainian harlot who was trying to finagle a green card out of her son. Time was running out and she couldn't really lay into him about it. She and the cigarette grudgingly agreed to be civil during the rest of the visit. She didn't ask how long he'd been smoking. Maybe she didn't have to; maybe she could read him that well.

They finished their coffees and he stubbed his cigarette out. He moved the ashtray to an empty table nearby. She was talking again about the article she was going to write on Evo. She thought Evo was marvelous, of course.

"History doesn't bode well for him" was all that Gabriel said.

She just looked away, her lips pressed together. "Well, we'll see." That was the end of that. Then she said, "So, when will you be back in California?"

"California?" He realized that she was likely wondering when he would next be at Big Thunder's headquarters. So he added, "I don't know."

"You're still renting the same apartment in New York?"

"I am. My plants are probably dead by now," he said, to get off the subject of California.

"Have you had anyone in?"

"I asked Harlan."

"That one with the beard?"

He nodded.

"Then they're dead," she said and grinned.

There were other things they were supposed to be saying to each other. Kind things. But they had old habits to contend with—old inertias. The acting out of stale, well-rehearsed arguments, like opposing generals in dueling late–Cold War drills intended to affirm the effectiveness of their warheads. The machinery for devouring each other was intact, even if the reason for it had disintegrated.

Back in her room later, conspicuous luggage still aslant at the foot of the bed, they worked their way through a preliminary goodbye. He'd be around in the morning to see her again for half an hour before she left for the airport. Still, he felt like he needed to get started now, so he thanked her, in Spanish, for coming down.

"Thanks for letting me come," she replied. "I'm not going to worry about you."

"You shouldn't," he said abruptly, already crouched, fists up. It was inescapable. Backpedaling, he sought a way toward something sincere and kind. "It was great to see you," he said. "I mean—even if it seemed like I was dodging you, it meant a lot to me that you came."

"That's sweet." She grinned, guileless, as if that were all that it took to soothe her. As if she were that kind of mother.

# 14

# The Party

*Friday and Saturday,*
*December 30 and 31, 2005*

AFTER BREAKFASTING in Gloria's revolting cafeteria, he headed to the Ritz, where he rode the elevator up to the fourth floor. The hotel's logo, emblazoned everywhere, was a three-spiked crown, like the top of a chess queen. Cousin, in motif at least, to the emblem from real Ritz-Carltons: the head of a lion, in profile, atop a crown. Royal-themed insignias aside, this Ritz was, he now saw, a total pretender. At his mother's door, he collected himself, remembered that his duty was to keep it sweet and simple, before he knocked. The last few days had been so stressful, but now it was over and he would be able, in theory, to actually connect with her.

After a minute, he knocked again. *"¿Madre mia?"* he said. No answer. He glanced at his cell phone and saw that he was five minutes early. So he went back downstairs.

At the front desk, he said, "Do you know where my mother went? She's in four-oh-seven."

The man behind the counter shook his head. "She checked out."

"Really?" It sort of made sense, since she was leaving for her flight in half an hour. "We agreed to meet here this morning. Did she leave a note for me?"

The concierge glanced at the counter. "I don't think so."

"Well, she must have left her bags —"

"Let me see."

The man went to a back room and returned with another man, this one in a spiffier jacket and tie — probably the manager. The manager looked not unlike Catacora, though a little duck-faced. Gabriel, beginning to feel exasperated, blinked at the man and said he was looking for his mother. The manager opened a drawer and pulled out a receipt, looked it over.

"She was the only guest so far to check out today, and she checked out an hour ago," he said. "She got into a taxi with her bags."

"Maybe you've got the wrong person," Gabriel said, irritation giving way to nervousness. Had he flubbed the time? Had she? In either case, why no note? Why no call?

"No, I dealt with her myself" — this from the manager — "a Chilena woman..."

"Yes, but she's here from California."

The man looked at the piece of paper. "Yes, Claremont, California."

Gabriel could see her upside-down signature.

"She went to the airport already," the man said.

"Well —" Gabriel lingered for a moment, not sure what to do.

He walked away and tried calling her cell phone, but it went straight through to voice mail. He returned to the desk. "If she comes back, can you tell her I came by as planned, and she should call me?"

Gabriel wrote his phone number down and walked outside quickly. Standing there and looking at a line of taxis, he pondered the situation. He knew that his mother was one of the only people to whom Lenka could speak about him without seriously compromising herself. Still, it would be dangerous for Lenka, because Gabriel's mother might write about it, or it might infuriate Gabriel enough that he'd lash out at Lenka. Anyway, surely Lenka wasn't *that* bent on getting even. But no other plausible explanations for his mother's sudden, premature absconding presented themselves.

• • •

There was no call, text, or e-mail from her that day. He tried calling again, but no luck.

He showered and shaved and put on a well-starched shirt, its collar sharp as a cleaver. He wore a rich purple and gold tie, a pressed charcoal suit, and his freshly shined Hugo Boss shoes. He checked himself in the mirror behind his desk—dapper, apart from the wounds. The cuts had scabbed over and the bruises were beginning to dim, slightly. Some new bruises had surfaced though, in paler yellows and greens; it was as if, in waning, the bruises needed to spread out. With his new bruises, he looked like a commando who'd unsuccessfully tried to wipe off his camouflage makeup. Regarding himself in the mirror, dressed so sharply, he decided he wouldn't wear the bandages that night. It'd be better to brandish the wounds. They might provide a kind of armor for him at the party. More to the point, they might create a humanizing, if not outright pitiable, distraction.

Twenty minutes later, he knocked on Fiona's door. She answered, barefoot, in an elegant aubergine dress. "Whoa," she said upon seeing the exposed wounds on his face. "Sexy."

"Should I cover them?"

"Nah, you're fine." She turned around and stomped over to her laptop on the desk in front of the window. The back of her dress was unzipped, revealing a V-shaped swath of pale skin intersected by the strap of her lacy violet bra. She sat in front of the computer and arched her back, stretching, as she examined a message.

"You zip me up?" she said and started typing.

Standing over her, he could smell her hair. She used a distinctive shampoo, an expensive one, no doubt. It was a wonderfully botanical smell, like something that might waft from the open door of a small florist in late spring. The smell summoned physical memories of her on top of him, hair draped over his face. He was sure they would never have sex again. "We have time for a cocktail," he said.

She sent her e-mail and then turned and grabbed a pair of shoes, slipped them on.

Upstairs, they sat at a table far away from the rest. Severo wasn't there and the pisco sours weren't any good. The ice separated from the liquid and floated on top in a bland and crunchy buffer.

"You might have to give another tutorial," Gabriel said.

She shook her head. He offered her a cigarette and she accepted, he took one himself. She lit them both with a single match, exhaled smoke out of the side of her mouth. Her eye contact was unusually precise that night. "How's your mother?"

"Gone."

"Oh, that's too bad. I thought I'd have a chance to meet her tonight."

He shook his head.

"And your girlfriend?"

"Ex."

"Well, that's not too surprising. She's told everyone about you."

He had a drag and it scorched his lungs. "I was afraid she might be doing that."

"For what it's worth, people are scandalized to hear that you've been a double agent."

He appreciated that she was trying to make light of it. "In a good way?"

"Well, they're talking, anyway. And it's not embarrassing. What will Priya say?"

"Nothing. That thing is not an issue anymore. I'm done here. And she likes me now, apparently. I passed some test. I'll be in Colombia next, and there'll be nothing very secretive about my purpose there. I think she just wanted my identity under wraps in case I made an ass of myself."

"I figured as much. You sure you want to go to this party? Won't Lenka be there?"

"That's why I'm going."

"A dozen roses?"

He smiled, had a sip of his pisco sour, chewed on the ice pebbles. "No. A million roses wouldn't cut it. I just want to see her one more time."

He turned and glanced again out the window facing east. A view he'd often enjoyed at dusk, when the setting sun lit up the mountains gently, in warm light. He wondered if he'd ever come back to La Paz. If so, he hoped it would be under different circumstances. Once he'd summited his current professional climb, he could maybe return under more favorable auspices — a humanitarian mission or something. What would Lenka say then? This fiasco could eventually become a wonderful anecdote for them to tell. The rift would begin to seem small in time, and they'd become friends again...

Gabriel didn't think about it too hard. It wasn't the kind of fantasy that was well served by serious consideration.

Fiona held his arm lightly as they walked along the sidewalks leading toward Plaza Murillo. The party was at the national museum, a block south of the Palacio Quemado. Gabriel had never been. He hadn't been to any tourist destinations, actually. On the walk over, he suggested that it might not be wise for him to use his real name at the door. She agreed.

At the entrance, Fiona introduced herself to a woman with a list. She said that she had brought a date, "Oscar Velazquez." The woman asked them for identification, and Gabriel patted his jacket pocket and then, in his best bad-American-accent Spanish, said that he had forgotten his passport at the hotel. The woman hesitated, and then, maybe pitying him (what with all of his exposed wounds), let him pass.

The interior was confusing. Almost like some architectural metaphor for Bolivia itself, it was quite large, square-footage-wise, but had no large rooms, so the guests had to disperse throughout the warren of chambers. Half of the museum was the centuries-old Mediterranean-style villa of a former colonial official; that portion was built in a figure eight around two small courtyards. Each courtyard was surrounded by rooms full of colonial and precolonial art. An adjacent, newly refurbished building was fully modern: white walls and pale hardwood underfoot, contemporary Bolivian art on the walls. The art was pleasant, from what Gabriel could tell, which wasn't much.

A couple hundred people browsed the many rooms, taking in the art and chatting. Gabriel and Fiona snatched up some tiny *humitas* from the buffet and then meandered off in search of drinks. They located a bar in one room, but it was too packed, so they moved on. The next room, also off one of the courtyards, was less crowded, so they got their wine there.

They wandered for a while and then returned to the courtyards for cigarettes.

In their reconnaissance, Gabriel and Fiona had discovered that the main event — Evo's thanking of that former vice president of the World Bank who had resigned over an argument about Bolivia with a representative of the United States — would take place in a long narrow room near one of the buffet tables. Though the largest room in the building, it wasn't be large enough to accommodate everyone. Guests had to have a special pass in order to make it into the main hall. The rest of them would listen from the atrium. The obvious irony was that Evo's people — Lenka herself, no doubt — had had to stratify guests by their *importance*.

They were smoking again when Gabriel noticed Catacora. "Finance-minister-to-be at ten o'clock," he muttered.

"Mine or yours?"

"Uh," Gabriel said, seeing that Catacora was approaching. He looked mightily amused, which Gabriel knew meant that Lenka had talked to him as well as everyone else.

"Gabriel." Catacora extended his teensy hand.

Gabriel shook the hand firmly, gave him a full blast of confident eye contact, even winked. "You look happy, Mr. Catacora," he said. "This is my friend Fiona Musgrave, of the *Wall Street Journal.*"

Catacora kissed her on the cheek, told her it was a pleasure.

Then Catacora returned his giddy expression to Gabriel. He had all of the subtlety one might expect from a person who spent much of his day either crunching numbers or lecturing people about those numbers. "It's funny," he said.

"You're talking about me?" Gabriel said.

"Yes. Funny that you have been pretending all this time!"

"Right." Gabriel wondered whether Lenka had owned up to the fact that she herself had been the one to tell Gabriel about Catacora's appointment. He presumed not. "What did she tell you about me?" he said.

"Just that you work for the Calloway Group."

"Did she say how she found out?"

He shrugged, as if it were beside the point. "Only that you interviewed her many times as well. I should have known when you were in my office so often with such strange questions. But Lenka"—he chuckled—"she figured you out."

Gabriel smiled. "Well, she's awfully sharp."

Catacora laughed and looked around. "They haven't kicked you out of here yet?"

"No, not yet," Gabriel said and scratched his face. "I keep moving around, so I think they can't get a bead on me. In fact, if you'll excuse me, I need to go put more wine in this glass."

He left Catacora and Fiona to talk between themselves, fetched another glass of Bolivian merlot from one of the bars, and then wandered awhile alone, looking for Lenka. He couldn't yet believe that she hated him enough to risk herself in betraying him. He needed to see her to test this idea.

The fact that neither of her schemes had worked out as she'd planned—that one had actually boosted Gabriel's position—only made the whole thing sadder. She was a lousy schemer and he loved that too. She flailed energetically, but landed no punches.

Gabriel dawdled in the modern atrium along with a few dozen others who were also waiting for the speeches to start. The atrium looked like it had been papered with oversize confetti. On closer inspection, he saw that the entire colorful history of Bolivian currency had been put on display. Bills were pressed between quarter-inch slabs of Lucite and mounted on the walls. Six crystalline slabs full of money hung from the ceiling too. Each bill was labeled with the year of its production and the name of the leader who had held office. The currency came in every imaginable hue and varied from tiny sheets of what looked like Monopoly money to clownishly huge bills that would have fit only in a wallet the size of a coffee table.

While Gabriel couldn't imagine a better place for the former vice president of the World Bank and the future president of Bolivia to talk to each other, he could see how the display might prove distracting to members of the press and others not inclined to appreciate the irony. So he and the rest of the unanointed would have to linger outside the hall in this spacious atrium decked with the hard evidence of the country's catastrophically botched monetary policy.

The crowd swelled and a familiar dull roar filled his ears. Gabriel lingered by the back of the room until he saw D'Orsi, the former World Banker—he recognized his face from recent articles—enter with Lenka, who was resplendent in a lemongrass-colored suit, her hair pinned up, her mouth glossy with lipstick the color of blood. She looked dazzling. He'd never seen her dressed up before and it felt alienating to watch her like that, so steely and formidable, outfitted for battle.

A few minutes later the first of three speeches began.

The director of the national museum, whose voice was radio-ready, spoke briefly about Evo and the art on display, about the country's rich history of rebellion. He mentioned the exhibition of money too—"A display that was developed with the help of the World Bank and IMF"—at which the crowd laughed so raucously that it was hard not to sense some ruefulness. They laughed with a kind of fuck-it-all gusto. Then the director introduced Evo with some full-throated verbal genuflecting, going so far as to say he was "the most important and exciting leader this country has had since its independence."

Evo, for his part, kept his remarks brief. His phrases were shorter and more direct, and, listening, Gabriel understood why Lenka and the others had decided that their candidate would opt out of the debates. He had left school when he was fourteen, and it showed. Still, he had an undeniable passion, and it was clear he had the charisma necessary to turn a straightforward statement into a swelling speech. People applauded after almost everything he said. What he actually said, in the end, was beside the point. The point was the context, the solidarity, the pride of the moment when a native person finally wrested control of the country from the intruders.

As he listened, Gabriel thought he recognized a few rhetorical tics as Lenka's handiwork. Evo used the Spanish word *estupendo*—"stupendous"—twice, a word that she'd said to Gabriel several times. Then again, maybe she had picked up the word from Evo.

Evo concluded by thanking D'Orsi for "championing this little country. For too long we have been food for the globalization animal." He praised his forfeiting his own career for the well-being of Bolivians and added that if more people at organizations like the World Bank were so selfless, the world would be a better place. Then he beckoned the man to the stage.

In broken Spanish, so heavily colored by his Italian accent that the words might as well have been Italian, the man said, "Thank you, President-elect Morales, for inviting me to Bolivia. I have been only twice before, and I have always found this country very beautiful; the people are some of the most lovely people I know. Modest and proud—nothing like us Italians." He paused for the audience's obligatory chuckle.

"I worked at the World Bank for a long time, since I was in my twenties, and I enjoyed the work. When I was hired, Robert McNamara was in charge and the World Bank was a different institution. We were smaller, for one thing. But, ahm—" He hesitated, as if he'd lost his place. Then, after a brief pause, he said, "I'm going to skip ahead." Another pause. Gabriel could hear pages ruffling. He wondered if it was a speech that the man had written for a different occasion. It almost sounded like something he'd have read at his retirement party.

"It's, ahm—okay, here: the World Bank was conceived in 1944 by the Allies, because they needed..." He paused again.

The awkwardness spiked. Gabriel blushed as the horror congealed. It was just too painful. After another false start, D'Orsi gave up and said, "I'm sorry, I can't read this."

The crowd chuckled uncomfortably. Some people applauded. The man didn't speak for a while. Gabriel and the others in the atrium exchanged agonized looks.

Then D'Orsi pressed on. "I quit the World Bank because I hated what had become of my life while I worked there. It wasn't the job, per se. I know that this won't be a popular thing for me to say here, but I think that the World Bank is a good institution. It's more useful than NATO, probably. Everyone who works there, including the president of the World Bank, Paul Wolfowitz, who I and many of my colleagues was prepared to hate, means well. Believe it or not, Paul is a good person. He is a smart person, and he cares about the world more than most people. He works hard. He—well, I don't know. All of my colleagues there worked hard. Me too. I did it for more than two decades."

Some in the audience were hissing. Most, though, were too stunned to move.

"But I worked too hard. I gave too much of myself to this thing. And I came to resent it when my life fell apart. I'm middle-aged now and I—I am very angry. I thought that we should be doing better. And when this man, this representative of the Bush administration, came up to me one morning and asked how 'we' were going to respond if Evo Morales won the election, I was infuriated. I was more than that. I was so upset. I felt—I was not *with him,* this man. I hated him and I hated his boss, George Bush."

Gabriel heard scattered laughter, applause, and wished he could see the man's reaction.

"But I'm here to tell you that the World Bank is a big and complicated animal. You know, many of my colleagues..." He stopped for a moment again, then said, "I congratulate Evo Morales on his win. I hope he can do more for this country than those who have come before him. His job is very difficult. I wouldn't wish it on *anyone.*" He paused for effect. "The odds against him making it a full four years are substantial, but I know he means well too. He is here because he cares about Bolivia. He has said he's going to slash his own salary by half, and I believe him. I spoke to Evo earlier today. We had lunch together and he is a very kind person and he is sensitive, and I know he means what he says. That means something. It should, anyway. I've met quite a few presidents in South America, and most don't mean what they say, not in this way. He is *real*. I hope—I hope that doesn't change. I hope that it makes a difference."

The crowd hovered, motionless, uncertain of what to do now. The applause began inside the narrow room and spread out to the atrium. Gabriel whistled and howled overenthusiastically; he applauded over his head, laughing and hollering more.

When the applause finally settled down, Gabriel wiped his eyes, still grinning. Then he pulled a cigarette from his pack and started pushing his way through the crowd in search of one of the courtyards.

An hour later Gabriel saw her. She was upstairs in the atrium, talking hurriedly to assistants about something. He put his glass of wine down and rushed for the stairs, hoping to catch her before she moved along to her next battle. By then the crowd had started to thin. He'd seen the Italian ex–vice president of the World Bank leave, semi-disgraced for failing to embrace the party line with proper gusto.

She looked preoccupied in a way that reminded him of how she'd looked on Christmas, at her house—how much seeing her there that day, in that pantsuit, had turned him on—and he wished he could go over and kiss her, help her relax. He wished he could offer to get her some food or some wine. He couldn't. Still, he approached.

She saw him and averted her eyes, continued talking. She looked serious. In a subsequent pause, she chewed the corner of her lip. This was Lenka at work, apparently. She was an intense presence; she was powerful and alert. Newly in charge, she was a senior officer in the army of Evo. Gabriel stood back and waited his turn. Meanwhile, he admired her preoccupation, the severity of the angles of the elbows on her crossed arms as she addressed her assistants.

Eventually, when the two hurried away to do her bidding, she looked at Gabriel, and her look said it all. She wasn't angry. She wasn't confused about him. She didn't feel conflicted because she secretly loved him. He saw hatred, and nothing else. There was no uncertainty there. It was all very straightforward. Still, she did stay long enough for them to speak once more.

"You leave tomorrow for the tour?" he said. She said nothing, ignoring his attempt at small talk. She was concerned only with the business that remained between them. So he said, "I gather you talked to my mother."

She just looked at him, and he could see some sadness in her eyes. Was it regret? Probably not. She was simply sad that she had had to break his mother's heart, but she knew she was just the messenger. The message itself was Gabriel's responsibility.

"And you've been spilling my secret to people?"

"Yes, to whoever would listen."

"For what it's worth, I didn't do that to you. I didn't tell anyone about us. I just spoke to Mr. Catacora and I didn't tell him that you'd been the one to leak his job title to me."

"Am I supposed to be grateful?" she said.

"No. I just wanted you to know. I didn't tell anyone about you."

She nodded, staring at him. "I understand."

"You look beautiful too."

As if she had not heard him, she said, "I wanted you removed from the guest list, but I am not that surprised that you found a way inside."

"I made a tunnel from Hotel Gloria."

She didn't even start to smile. "Did you lose your job?"

"No." He wasn't sure if he should tell her what had happened, that her scheme had backfired. He decided he might as well, as long as they were being honest. "Actually," he said, "it was quite the reverse. Before, I was just simulating. Now, I am a real employee. Thanks to you."

"Thanks to me?" She shook her head, incredulous. He noticed the reverse freckles on her chin. He'd stopped noticing those after a while. But now, he knew, it was time to pay attention again. "Gabriel, I don't know what you've done. Whatever it is, you owe your place to no one but yourself. Thank yourself. Don't thank me. You made this for yourself."

"I'm not as bad as you think I am."

"No. You are worse than you think you are."

The fact was that she'd parlayed her decision to tell people about Gabriel into a point-scoring moment for herself. Catacora had been impressed by her intuition, her ability to ferret out Gabriel's true intentions. In fact, she'd lied to them all, while using Gabriel as a professional stepladder. He could have pointed this out, and maybe it would have bought him a redemptive moment, but it also would have killed the conversation faster, and he wanted to prolong it, so he lingered. "It's not so simple," he said.

"I'm sure it's not simple," she said. She checked her BlackBerry. It was a new phone. It was not unlike his phone, a slightly older model, but close. It was an appropriate phone for the press secretary of a president. She tucked her hair behind her ear as she stared down at the screen, and in that simple gesture, he was reminded of their drive through traffic during their first interview. He remembered how distracted she'd been, the way she'd steered her Datsun with her knee.

There was nothing to be done about it. It was a loss, a straightforward loss. There were no more plays left. Still, there was time left—time to stretch the encounter out a few moments longer. "The speech was interesting."

She put her phone down, looked at him, and said, "Your people —they would never *really* invest here, would they?"

"Not in the way you mean, no." She glared at him, so he went on. "They would, and they *have* invested here, actually, but not in a way that"—he searched for the right words—"not in a way that *contributes*."

She stared at him for a while. He could see the halogen lights dangling nearby reflected in her black eyes. Her expression was harder than he'd ever seen it before. It killed him to see her like that. It was visceral, an aching in his chest; it rang out in his collarbone, specifically. He scratched at the stitches on his cheek. No one had stared at his wounds all night. No one even seemed to notice.

In the end—and this was the end, he had to admit—both he and Lenka had survived. They had each been tested by circumstances grand

and unforeseen, and they had each survived. There had been damage inflicted along the way, but they'd made it through, more or less intact. She seemed, in fact, to be thriving. Maybe he was thriving too.

She blinked, and he admired one last time the too-long eyelashes. He glanced at her shoulders and knew that she had the most perfect shoulders he'd ever seen. He knew already that whenever he saw a woman's shoulders from that point on, he'd compare them to Lenka's. And although there were a million different ways he wanted to apologize, to explain, he knew there was no point. It was done.

Her phone rang and she checked the number. She looked at him. "While Evo Morales is president, you will not be allowed back into this country. If you try to come here, you'll be arrested on charges of espionage. Do you understand?"

"Espionage?" he said, stunned. He'd been devious — obviously — but he wasn't a spy, and she knew it. He felt sick hearing her say that. He shook his head. He hadn't been disappointed by her until now. "Are you serious?" he said.

She just glared at him, quite comfortable with her new power, it seemed.

Bewildered, he looked across the room and shook his head again.

She put the phone to her ear and walked away.

Back at the hotel, Gabriel put his name into Google News and saw that the story hadn't broken yet.

He went upstairs and packed. He smoked a cigarette and watched CNN International. The television's aqueous light flickered on the walls. He called the front desk and asked for a bottle of red wine.

Alejo arrived with the wine and two glasses ten minutes later.

Gabriel opened the door and let him inside. He stood by in silence and watched Alejo uncork the bottle. Once the bottle was open, he said, "I'll need only one glass."

Alejo poured him a glass.

"Do you want the rest of the bottle?" Gabriel said.

"Excuse me?"

"I'll take the one glass and you can have the rest, if you want."

Alejo shook his head and set the bottle down.

"Fine." He regarded Alejo for a second, and then said, "I just want to ask you something."

"Yes."

"Did you really think that if you ruined her feelings for me, she'd run into your arms?"

Alejo frowned and shook his head. "No, I never thought that. I was not trying to impress her, or whatever you think it was. This is the problem with you gringos: you are so used to being concerned about shallow things that you think everyone thinks this way. She is an important person for this country and I have seen you, and I think you are dangerous. This is why I told her what you did. It has nothing to do with her beauty, or my love for her, or any of those *huevadas*."

This was utter bullshit, but it was heartfelt bullshit. Gabriel nodded, not caring to explain about the outcome—that Alejo's move had accidentally spared Gabriel and expedited the destruction of some companies that had invested in Bolivia. He picked up the full glass of wine and then turned to Alejo and said, "Are you sure you don't want it? I'm just going to dump the rest down the drain."

"You are a shitty person. Do you know that?"

"I do, actually." He lifted his glass in salute.

Alejo turned and headed toward the elevators, then stopped and turned back for a parting shot. "I'm not like you," he declared with the conviction of a true believer. Gabriel envied the earnestness and purity of that perspective, the tender idea that the world was a place where good people and bad people were locked in an epic struggle—

What a gorgeous notion!

The following morning, Gabriel Googled his name again. It wasn't that bad, but it didn't have to be that bad to be fatal. There were a handful of articles that mentioned a Gabriel Francisco de Boya, analyst for the Calloway Group, who was in Bolivia. One was on a liberal blog, FDR Opines, and the rest were near-clones of a Reuters brief about investors seeking opportunities in politically unstable countries. The original piece had been published by Horace Calloway, whom Gabriel had met twice at the Lookout and who, other than his rigid blandness, had seemed like a pleasant enough guy.

In any case, Gabriel's name was out now. If his mother had doubted Lenka, this would erase that doubt. He could try to head it off, call her and tell her this rumor was just the crazy manifestation of some lovers' quarrel, but it was too much. He could be honest, say he'd lied because he didn't want her to write him off. But it was going to be too many lies. It would only make it worse.

He walked up to Café los Presidentes Ahorcados for a cappuccino and one last salteña. As he walked, it dawned on him that he'd not done any touristy things. When he'd come to Bolivia with his mother five years earlier, they'd gone to several museums and seen the hoodoos in the Valle de Luna. They'd had a tour of San Francisco Church, with its second-story garden and its dozens of portraits of malnourished saints and monks. In colonial Latin America, they'd been told by their guide, Saint Francis was always shown holding a skull, a symbol of poverty. It had seemed odd to Gabriel then — in the first days of his youthful, rapturous infatuation with Bolivia — that the skull, symbol of death, would also symbolize poverty. That confusion had been resolved for him now.

On the tour, they had also learned that those disembodied babies' heads with wings hovering around the edges of many devotional paintings were cherubs who had enjoyed the pleasures of the flesh too much and had therefore been deprived of their bodies. Their guide at the church had been a beautiful young woman with a frightening cough. Gabriel and his mother had been the only ones on the tour, and his mother had been relentlessly inquisitive. She'd badgered the ailing woman with questions and had extracted everything she deemed interesting from her. Still, the questions persisted. She picked the bones clean. During the final minutes of the tour, the guide knew almost none of the answers to his mother's questions.

In the past six weeks, however, Gabriel had not once gone to take in a view of the city or to appreciate some cultural attraction. He hadn't even brought a camera. He hadn't sent a single postcard. Other than to occasionally check out a restaurant, he hadn't opened his *Lonely Planet* guidebook since the flight down. He'd had grand plans, initially. He foresaw that the new job would help him develop a rich and detailed familiarity with the best of Latin America.

On the flight down, he'd dog-eared pages for Cusco, Potosí, Copacabana, Coroico, and the rest of Yungas, for Cochabamba, and for Santa Cruz. He'd hoped to come away from the assignment a minor expert on Bolivia's many splendors. Instead, he knew the staff at a couple of hotels by name and he knew his way around central La Paz, but he didn't have delightful recommendations to share. He had no madcap tales of Third-World misadventures that might make for charming dinner-party chitchat. He decided he'd ask his taxi driver for information about the country.

Gabriel packed. After depositing his bags behind the front desk, he went upstairs to the business center one last time to check his e-mail.

There was only one message. He knew who it was from even before he saw the name. He clicked on his in box and confirmed that it was from his mother.

The title said it all: *Calloway Group*.

He felt an aching lump in his throat right away. He coughed but couldn't clear the knot. He took a shuddering breath, set his mouth firmly to stop the crinkling in his chin, and clicked on the message. It was in English.

---

Dearest Gabriel,

As you probably know by now, Lenka told me about your secret. That's why I left so suddenly. I'm sorry I didn't leave a note — I just couldn't think of what to say. I thought of calling you to have you tell me that she was wrong, or that she was lying, but it was clear to me who was lying. My fears have been confirmed now.

I have to say that I am both dismayed and impressed, but mostly dismayed. More than anything, I am sad that you lied to me. But you know that. You know it all before I can even say it. I wonder if I brought you up this way, or if you learned it from someone else? Don't answer that question, please.

I wish you had taken this job to spite me, as some act of rebellion, because then at least it would be personal — from the heart. But it's not that way and I know this. If you were trying to defy me, you would have thrown it in my face. But you hid it, carefully — lied about it and then covered that lie with another lie. You lied because you joined with these people for private reasons. With them you are feeding a desire that you are ashamed of.

Most of all, it makes me sick to realize that I might have unknowingly aided and abetted your work by offering you the chance to ask that question of Evo. If that question earned money for your employers, letting you come to that interview will be one of the greatest mistakes of my life. In any case, you lied to me, manipulated me.

So I want you to do a favor for me. Please *do not* respond to this note.

The fact is, we are both adults now, Gabo, and I'm sorry to say that this is too much for me. It's too much, not just as a mother, but as a person. I am truly sorry I can't see past this. Maybe that is a failing of mine. Probably! But it doesn't matter. Though I don't want to abandon you, it's clear you can take care of yourself. And I believe we need to be apart until you are through this phase. So I am telling you now that until you have quit this path, I will not answer your calls and I will not answer your e-mails.

I love you more than I love anyone else alive. I look ahead and I dream only of you returning to my life. Until that dream is true, my heart is more broken than you can possibly understand.

— Your mother

He read the e-mail twice more. By the end of the second time, his vision had been completely blurred by tears. He blinked them away and they skipped warmly off his cheeks. He wiped his eyes and sniffled. He swallowed the knot in his throat again and again, but it was no good. Then he got up and went to the business center's bathroom to blow his nose and wash his face. He considered calling her to try to convince her that he'd been doing it as an act of rebellion, that it was all about her. But he couldn't bring himself to lie to her any more.

He just logged out, closed the browser.

His flight left in three hours. He had an hour to kill, but he thought he might as well spend that hour at the airport, so he retrieved his luggage from behind the front desk.

The people at the desk seemed to want to talk to him, to see him off, but he was too upset to say much to them.

"Thank you," he said.

"Will you be back?" the female manager said. He'd seen her often as he'd come and gone, but he'd never talked to her, just dropped off his key or picked it up. She was petite, officious, of an indeterminate age. Her eyes were cold, circumspect, the color of gunpowder.

"I don't think I'll be back," he said. He was supposed to lie, of course. If ever there was a time, this was it. The lie was expected. He just couldn't bring himself to do it. "Thank you for everything."

As the taxi buzzed through La Paz, Gabriel asked the taxi driver a few questions about the country; the driver replied dutifully, but none of it was new to Gabriel.

Later, when they drove through El Alto, Gabriel inhaled deeply and could tell that the air was even thinner up there. The sky was clear, startlingly bright. He could see the flayed tips of a cirrus cloud above, a thin blotch of white splashed against an otherwise empty sky. There was no music in the car, only the sound of the blasting wind. Outside, El Alto was dusty, its streets patrolled by scrawny swine and mottled, hairless dogs. Chickens tiptoed around warily. Buildings abandoned halfway through construction, leaving only an empty collection of cin-

der-block walls, had become depositories for heaps of unidentifiable
urban detritus, garbage that ceased to retain the qualities of its discrete
ingredients. At the edges of each pile, scraps of this material flapped in
the wind. He rolled up his window and the air suctioned in. The subsequent stillness in the car felt peculiar to Gabriel after all those minutes
of steadily howling wind.

Approaching the airport, he could make out the squat control tower
off in the distance. The airport in El Alto—confusingly named John F.
Kennedy International Airport—was immense. Or, it was immense in
a way. Like everything in Bolivia, the scale was crazy. The terminal was
poky—only a handful of flights came and went a day—but the run-
way was twice the standard length. With the air so thin, planes needed
to achieve double the ground speed required at sea level to lift off. Out-
going flights typically had a number of empty seats because a full flight
would simply be too heavy to catch air at a sane speed. Incoming planes
needed special tires to land at those velocities.

The driver caught Gabriel's eyes in the rearview mirror and asked
how long he'd been in La Paz. Gabriel told him that he'd been there
since November. He'd been doing research, he said. There was a lull,
and then he added, "I went to a party hosted by Evo Morales last
night."

"Do you know him?"

"No. Well—sort of. I met him. I was close with his press liaison. I
was here on research."

"What do you think of him?"

Gabriel shrugged. "He seems honest. I think he means what he
says."

"We could use some honesty. So you found out what you came to
find out?"

"Yes."

The driver paused for a moment, seeming to consider something
that he wasn't sure he should say. Eventually, as they pulled onto the
half-mile-long driveway to the John F. Kennedy International Airport,

he met Gabriel's eyes in the rearview again and said, "This is your job? You come here, find out something, and go home?"

"I suppose so."

"That sounds nice."

Gabriel nodded. "I know."

Outside, the airport was nothing but a flat grassy field that went on for miles. Beyond that, El Alto—a slum with more than a million inhabitants—sprawled in every direction. The driver cruised at fifty miles an hour along the drive. There were few other cars. The parking lot, far ahead of them, was tiny, a minuscule patch of asphalt next to a squat whitewashed terminal and a functional little control tower. Gabriel rolled the window down a crack again, and the wind bellowed. It sounded like the static from a television on the wrong channel turned up all the way. Though he inhaled deeply, his lungs were still hungry for oxygen. He exhaled and inhaled again. The air smelled like nothing at all.

# A Room on the Tenth Floor

*Saturday, July 4, 2009*

THE CALLOWAY GROUP had booked the conference room for the whole day, but the meeting concluded in under an hour. It had been very simple. Gabriel had explained the offer, and the others had said they needed a week to consider it. That was it. They could have done it all on the phone. Gabriel called down to the front desk and canceled the catered lunch. He went to his room, put on gym clothes, and rode the elevator to the basement.

For forty-five minutes he jogged on the treadmill, perusing reports that his assistant had sent. He kept the speed low and the incline steep. He did two hundred crunches while listening to CNN International. After showering, he dressed in jeans and a long-sleeved T-shirt.

He stood at his window.

This was the second of two days in Lima. He had spent the last week in Santiago, negotiating the purchase of a minority stake in a mid-cap silver-mining operation, as well as much smaller stakes in an asphalt company and a glass manufacturer. Priya had been running, almost exclusively, options straddles and strangles since Lehman collapsed. It was pure mathematics now, so Gabriel had little connection to the bulk of

Calloway's capital. At the same time, Calloway had shifted a few hundred million dollars to a cluster of managed FDI projects in Latin America. This subsection would operate, essentially, as a private equity firm. And it was, for all intents and purposes, Gabriel's.

He had only the one meeting in Lima. Tomorrow, he'd fly to Buenos Aires for a few days, then Caracas for few more, and then briefly go to Mexico City before returning to New York. Bolivia was no longer on the books in any way. He gathered that, although Evo had not turned out to be a fraud, he had certainly been lively. The previous year, he had expelled the U.S. ambassador for "fomenting subversion and national division," according to a statement delivered by Evo's press secretary, Lenka Villarobles. The statement was now available on YouTube. In the past few months, Gabriel had watched Lenka read it dozens of times.

In Lima, Gabriel stayed at the Four Seasons. The hotel was on a ridge above the ocean. His room faced the dreary sea. He stood and took in the view, arms akimbo. Even ten stories up and with the sliding glass door closed, he could hear the mob below. That familiar roar; he barely noticed it anymore, except at moments like that, when there was nothing to do but listen.

The air in Lima was always damp but not hot; the Pacific Ocean kept it cool. The weather in Lima never changed. It was cool at night and humid always. It never rained. It hadn't rained in ten years. It averaged a fraction of an inch of precipitation per year, mostly in the form of a predawn mist. Lima was hostile to life. There were few native plants or animals. It was so arid that the streets had no gutters, no drains. Roofs were flat and not very water resistant. Were it actually to rain, the city would be in chaos: ceilings would collapse, streets would pool with water, and disease-carrying mosquitoes would flourish.

When he'd come to Lima with his mother nine years before, they'd enjoyed a day trip around the city on a tour bus. They'd stopped at the fireworks market, which would ignite on New Year's Day a few years later, killing scores of people. As they'd continued through Lima, the guide, holding a battered microphone and speaking in broken English, pointed at buildings and described them. This is Moorish architecture, he'd said, and that is Baroque. To young Gabriel, the city had looked merely brown, an enormous smudge. The guide was stocky, his skin oily. His resting expression looked pained. He pointed out the American ambassador's house, gleaming white, and said it was bigger than the Peruvian presidential palace. The tourists chuckled politely, all but Gabriel's mother, who cackled loudly for too long, drawing stares.

Their final stop of the tour was a sixteenth-century cathedral and its adjacent Franciscan monastery. According to Gabriel's mother, who whispered her own parallel lesson to him while the guide lectured, the Franciscans were the most scrupulous order of monks with their vow of poverty; they were also the most ruthless missionaries in the New World.

Gabriel could already smell the catacombs. Over centuries, the stench had mellowed into something musty. Down the narrow stone staircase, the odor grew stronger, sharper, and the air cooled. Their guide led them through a series of chambers, where Incan corpses had been disposed of with an efficiency that would have impressed the commanders at Buchenwald. There were twelve wells in a row. A souring cadaver would be dumped into a well and covered with lime and charcoal dust. The next body could then be dropped on top, covered with another layer of lime and charcoal, and so on. When a well could hold no more bodies, the monks would move along to the next. After a year, they would return to a full well and exhume its contents. Upstairs in the monastery's courtyard, under the relentless sun, they would sort through the mud and bones. Smaller bones were cast into the sea, but they stored the sturdiest bones in a series of pits throughout the catacombs. There were separate pits for femurs, for skulls, and for pelvises. The largest pit, at least twenty-five feet wide, contained a painstakingly arranged pile of femurs and skulls—the elegant detritus of centuries of their labor.

At the end of the tour, back aboveground, Gabriel and his mother wandered into the blinding square, where a barefoot and toothless old woman begged, groaning, her knotted gray hair askew. She smelled of hay and urine and looked like an exile from a previous century. Gabriel could see the structure of her skull under her skin. Her gums had receded so badly that he could see where her long narrow teeth, the color of molasses, entered her jawbone. He and his mother picked up the pace until they were practically jogging. The woman gave up. When he turned around, Gabriel watched her approach another tourist, her dirty hand outstretched and empty, shaking. Clusters of pigeons waddled around too, scavenging, all of them.

His mother looked at him. "What do you think?"

He shook his head, as if he didn't know. He was supposed to be outraged, of course.

On the far side of the square, a few paramilitaries were eating sandwiches by an armored vehicle mounted with a fifty-caliber machine gun. Alberto Fujimori, then president of Peru, wanted to discourage angry constituents from misbehaving, no doubt. The eight years of his presidency had, in fact, been a relatively prosperous and peaceful era, at least on the surface of things. In two years, he'd be chased out of the country amid accusations of corruption and human rights abuses. But, as they had with Pinochet, the people would remain conflicted about his reign and hesitant to prosecute him, pointing out that he had brought enduring economic stability after decades of chaos and turmoil. Gabriel's mother would never accept such a discordant perspective. While Gabriel admired the certainty of her viewpoint, he couldn't bring himself to the earnest embrace of her cause. The answers were just not that simple. Despite what his mother—and her fiercest opponents, for that matter—wanted to believe, this was not algebra. The numbers just didn't cooperate.

Back in their bus, its air conditioning hissing, they rode along a cliff beside the sea. It was twilight, and the sun melted into a ribbon of gray at the horizon. The Pacific Ocean was fetid and streaked with silt. It belched up clouds of brackish sewage.

Now, years later, back in Lima again, he stood at the window of his suite at the Four Seasons and gazed at that same stretch of sea. A bank of pink foam undulated on the tan water just past the breakers. A city of eight million, but there was not a single person on all those miles of tropical beach. He hadn't spoken to his mother since she'd sent him that e-mail in Bolivia. He hadn't even sent a reply to the e-mail.

That afternoon in Lima, he left the Four Seasons and wandered around the nearby open-air shopping mall. The mall had been built into the ridge of the cliff face. He found nothing of interest in the mall, so he walked south along a balustrade perched at the edge of the precipice. Seagulls hovered nearby in a steady southerly breeze. Hours passed, and when the sun slumped, he headed back to his hotel.

He stepped under the perfunctory awning, and a bellhop hurried to pull open one of the heavy, brightly polished doors. He continued to the swank bar, which was called poco. The self-consciously lowercase name was stamped, in a faux-modest Helvetica, on the door, the napkins, and a melon-colored sign embedded above a large fake fireplace.

Gabriel no longer drank alcohol. He had given it up a couple years ago, but he still liked to visit bars, particularly when traveling. He usually ordered a fragrant malt whiskey and just smelled it. At poco, he ordered sparkling water and a ten-year-old Laphroaig. He lifted the glass of whiskey and sniffed it. It reeked of saline, iodine. It smelled medicinal. He drank the water. The bar was quiet and unexpectedly had the atmosphere of an old church. Small groups of people huddled at mini tables at the edges of the room, whispering among themselves, but no one else sat at the bar. The place was swish in a vulgar way that reminded Gabriel of Miami. Everything was made of cold stone. Muted light emerged from improbable places: tabletops, large panels in the walls, beneath a thin sheet of polished sandstone on top of the bar.

From the background, Gabriel picked up a familiar voice. He turned to see who it was. There, he saw Fiona. Her hair was shorter, above her shoulders now. Otherwise, she looked much the same. He hadn't seen her since the night of Evo's party. She was in the lobby, talking on her mobile. She approached but still hadn't see him. He briefly considered trying to conceal his presence and sneak out, but he saw that it wouldn't be possible. Instead, he'd have to pretend that he was excited to see her.

She made it almost all the way to the bar before she noticed him and squealed with a mixture of undisguised horror and pleasure.

"Let me call you back," she said into her phone, and she hung up, dropped the phone into her handbag, stretched her arms out for a hug. He stood, hugged her. She was still using the same pricey shampoo, a scent that would be branded into his memory for life, no doubt.

They sat down. "It's great to see you," she said.

He smiled and said, "You too."

"Sorry, I can't linger. I'm meeting someone at the restaurant in ten minutes," she said. "What are you doing here?"

He shrugged.

"Oh," she said when it dawned on her that he probably couldn't explain. "Well..." She took a deep breath, staring at him and shaking her head, still surprised. "Wow."

"Wow, indeed." He could see that she was staring at his scars. She had sat down on his scarred side and had full view of his ear, which hadn't healed well. He turned his head to face her so she wouldn't be broadsided by it. "You still keeping an apartment here?" he said.

"I'm here full-time now. I bought a house last year. A mile south, in Buenaventura, a beautiful neighborhood."

"No more New York City?"

She shook her head. "I sold my place." She seemed pleased, even happy. She shrugged, and he noticed her very strong shoulders, not at all like Lenka's—too brawny, but nonetheless attractive. She was more relaxed than before. She wore an easy pleasure in her attitude. In fact, she was delighted in a way that reminded him of Grayson slightly, minus his sleaze. During the ensuing pause she stared at him eagerly, as if taking in a cherished and long-misplaced memento. When he still didn't say anything, she said, "So?"

"I heard that you quit the *Journal*?"

She nodded. "Two years ago."

"Murdoch?" Rupert Murdoch had bought the Dow Jones Company, which owned the *Wall Street Journal*, in the summer of 2007, and some *WSJ* reporters had resigned in protest.

"I just didn't want to participate," she said. She lit a cigarette. "Been with the *Times* bureau for the last year."

"Ah, sleeping with the enemy—"

She batted her eyes gamely. The gesture didn't quite carry anymore. She had no more enthusiasm for so much lunging and parrying. Gabriel sympathized. He didn't either. When he glanced at her fingers, he saw they were stained like new leather. And he wasn't sure if he'd noticed this before, but he now saw that her lips had thin cracks cutting directly perpendicular to her mouth from years of bunching up around narrow filters. He saw her complexion was grayish, as if, in exhaling all that pale smoke, she had somehow leached the color out of herself. Imagining her lungs, he visualized a chainlink fence he'd seen on the beaches of São Paulo a few months earlier, which had plastic bags embedded in it. The bags were blackened with sand and dirt, repositories for all manner of wind-borne garbage: plastic straws, cigarette butts, fragments of mystery items worn down to tiny nubs by the sand and the sea. Still, the burly fence stood there, sinking gradually, a vertical trash receptacle.

He'd given up cigarettes too when he'd quit drinking. He'd also quit coffee and all other drugs. But he knew he didn't look especially well either. Despite all the exercise and the mainly vegan diet, his complexion was sallow. His hair had thinned on top and was streaked with gray. He had lost even more weight. He had permanent dark bags under his eyes. All of this he blamed on a combination of circumstances, including perpetual jet lag, unpredictable diet, the fact that he could never get accustomed to a bed; also the wages of aging, chronic stress, watching too much hotel television at night, and relentless loneliness.

"How do you like the *Times?*" he said, for lack of anything else.

She shrugged, picked up his untouched whiskey and sniffed it, grimaced. She put it back down. "You offering me something better?"

"Like a job?"

"Yes."

Astonished, he furrowed his brow and shook his head. "But you can drink my whiskey."

"You don't think I'd be useful at Calloway?"

"No. I don't think you'd be useful. Or, I wouldn't want to be responsible. You have too much —" He wanted to say *heart*, but that wasn't accurate. "Maybe it's too little?" he wondered aloud. He thought about it. "Too little appetite, maybe? I don't really know."

She stared at him dubiously. Still, she seemed clearly lighter, more amused.

"Anyway, you're too old," he said. He'd said that just to test this placidity of hers, to see if she'd snap back and lavish him with abuse. But she didn't flinch.

After a pause, she said, "You have Oscar's job now?"

He nodded.

"He quit?"

He shook his head. "Fired. Now he's at Fortress. I run Calloway's direct-investment program."

"That sounds impressive."

He shook his head. It wasn't impressive — or anyway, not as impressive as it sounded. But he couldn't explain that. "Our portfolio has been radically redistributed."

"Calloway's been doing well though, right? I heard you've managed to not lose money."

"That's true."

"It's remarkable."

"Well," he said. In fact, it wasn't remarkable, but he couldn't explain that either. When the market cratered in 2007, Priya had simply stopped making directional bets (that is, betting on prices going up or down) and started using options strategies to bet on increased volatility. From then on, it didn't matter to her where the market went, just as long as it went there with uncommon violence. D. E. Shaw had done the same thing and had also profited every quarter of the downturn. It wasn't remarkable and it wasn't artful. It was just business.

He had a sip of the sparkling water and then, using his cotton coaster, mopped up the little ring of condensation on the glowing bar top. He put the bottle back down in the same spot. He said, "You know,

Priya kept trying to hire these forty- and fifty-year-olds as political ana-lysts—this is before my time—but they never lasted."

Her attention perked up. "Really?"

"Yes. It kept happening until she changed her applicant pool and started hiring younger people. Oscar was one of the first of that new batch, the late-twenties applicants."

Her expression hardened slightly and she said, "Okay, I get it."

She had misread his point, had thought he was making another dig at her age. He wanted to tell her that she didn't get it at all. He wanted to lash out, yell at her about how little she understood it, but he held back. He said, "I'm starting to get too old for it now too."

"Nah, you're still a kid," she said, but the lie didn't hold up. There was no getting around it: he was anything but a kid. Only three and a half years had passed since their adventure in Bolivia, but almost all trace of youth had been rubbed out of him.

Neither one of them said anything for a while.

She stubbed out her cigarette. "Whatever happened to your plan? Weren't you going to retire once you'd made a few million?"

"Did I say that?"

"Yes, you did."

Then he remembered it, the fantasy about wanting to be "done with the issue of money forever." He could have retired a couple years ago by that measure. But then what? It had been beyond naive. In hindsight, it was embarrassing. Specifically, it had been naive to think that life of-fered a broadening spectrum of possibilities when clearly the reverse was true. Life was funnel-shaped. There was only one way out. The breadth of possibility shrank every single day until there were no possi-bilities left, and then life was over.

She had a sip of the whiskey, kissed him on the forehead, and said, "I should get going."

He could feel the ghost of her lips on his skin and he knew the im-pression would last hours, maybe days. "I'll see you around."

She stood. "How long will you stay there?" she asked.

"At Calloway? I don't know. Maybe I'll replace Priya one day?"

She chuckled for a second and then said, "I'm sure you will."

She walked away. He watched her go. Once she was gone, he turned back and sniffed the glass. He could smell peat and kelp, the saline breeze. Seeing her lipstick imprint on the rim reminded him of that night near Christmas in 2005, when she showed up at his room with a bow around her waist. He couldn't quite believe that he'd been there that night. It didn't feel like a memory; it was as if he'd watched someone else be there with her. He felt no ownership of the experience. He looked at it and it looked absurd, fake.

Up in his room that night, he ordered a grilled vegetable sandwich from room service. Street vendors ten stories below hollered out the prices of their wares while he ate his sandwich in bed, watching the same shows he would have watched in his new condo in New York.

The condo was a two-bedroom on the Upper West Side. For many years, it had belonged to Roy Scheider, the star of *Jaws*. Gabriel had bought it in January. He had hired an interior decorator straightaway, and the place was repainted, the floors redone, and the light fixtures replaced. The decorator had purchased art, furniture, and identified the places those objects should reside. Gabriel had said he could take it from there, but he still hadn't managed to unpack any of it. The items all stood around, swaddled in huge sheets of plastic or bubble wrap, waiting to be put to use. Whenever he was there, he slept on his mattress on the living-room floor. To stop the pillow from slipping off at night, he pushed the mattress up against the wall. There were no curtains or blinds on the windows, and light streamed in at dawn, so he wore a sleep mask that he'd picked up on a flight. His kitchen supplies were still confined to their cartons as well, and the new stove hadn't even been attached to the gas line, so he ate carryout while sitting on the one armchair that he'd managed to unwrap. He got bored and went for long walks often. He watched DVDs on his laptop, either lying on the mattress or sitting in the armchair. He left his passport in the small pocket of his Tumi suitcase, which was always packed and stayed in the empty closet by the door.

That suitcase lay splayed open beneath the hotel window now.

Sitting upright on the bed in his room, he abandoned his sandwich and set the plate on his bedside table. The television played *Zoolander*. He read the subtitles and saw that very few of the jokes translated. He kept watching until, at last, he didn't even notice the subtitles anymore. Then, fading a little, he turned off the television, turned off the lights. He rolled onto his side, closed his eyes, and lay there, motionless, listening to the voices below.

# ACKNOWLEDGMENTS

FOR GENEROUS SUPPORT while I was working on this book, many thanks to Seattle Arts and Lectures, Bread Loaf, the Richard Hugo House, Yaddo, and the Elizabeth George Foundation.

For years of steady encouragement and cheerleading, the majestic Lilly Rubin. Too, I owe an incalculable debt to David Shields. I've had years of support from my siblings.

In the department of keen editorial advice: Sandy Mountford, Jennifer Mountford, and the inimitable Anne Connell. My HMH-appointed copyeditor, Dr. Tracy Roe (I'm not being funny, she's actually a physician), is a spectacularly astute reader. Also, lest she be forgotten, my very editor herself, Adrienne Brodeur, who is not only a marvelous and brilliant person in general, but, it should be noted, gave the most marvelous and useful editorial suggestions I've ever seen.

Much thanks to a killer agent named Henry Dunow. And, for always being there when I'm frantically in need of advice, Tina Pohlman.

And for guidance and advice some supremely generous Bolivians: Eduardo Arce Bastos, Juan Fernando, Luis Aranibar, Luz Maria, Alvaro, and Juan Carlos Calderon and Mercedes. Thank you all for helping me discover your magnificent country.